D1355390

Caroline Upcher has worked in film, publishing and journalism. She wrote two novels under the name of Carly McIntyre, *Next of Kin* and *Saskia*, as well as Naomi Campbell's *Swan*. She has also written three novels under her own name. Caroline Upcher lives in London.

By the same author

The Visitors' Book
Grace & Favour

Caroline Upcher

FALLING FOR
MR WRONG

ORION

An Orion Paperback
First published in Great Britain by Orion in 1996
This paperback edition published in 1997 by
Orion Books Ltd,
Orion House, 5 Upper St Martin's Lane,
London WC2H 9EA

Reissued 1999

A CIP catalogue record for this book is available
from the British Library

ISBN 0 75282 745 6

Typeset by Deltatype Ltd, Ellesmere Port, Cheshire
Printed in Great Britain by
Clays Ltd, St Ives plc

For Hanan al-Shaykh, in whose house at Cap d'Antibes I began this book, and for Deborah Rogers, in whose house in Notting Hill I finished it.

And in memory of John Creightmore.

Thanks as always to Annabel Davis-Goff, and to Celestia Fox, Amanda and Steve Lay, Lewis Esson and Jane Wood.

All over the world women search
for Mr Right. If, and when, they
find him it never occurs to them
that he might, in fact, be Mr Wrong.

PART ONE

Johnny left her in the middle of the night.

For years afterwards, every time she heard Paul Simon singing 'Fifty Ways to Leave Your Lover' on the radio, she would be reminded of it. It was the line 'Just slip out the back, Jack' that got her every time. That's how he must have left. He couldn't have gone out the front door. It had been stuck fast for a month. It had been his idea to have the front door painted. There had been a week of discussion about it. Well, not really discussion. He rarely discussed. He had merely announced one night at dinner that it was time to have something done about the front door and he would be putting Rachel on to it.

Rachel was his long-suffering assistant at the office although it was hard to imagine when she had time to carry out such conventional duties as dealing with correspondence and answering the telephone since she was permanently distracted by a multitude of errands relating to her employer's personal life.

The front door presented something of a challenge – most people expected an all-in job including the back door and the windows – but eventually Rachel came up with Arnold Pinner. Arnold was an odd-job man who used to work as a chippy on film sets. He regarded the front door as being decidedly beneath him and after barely half a morning's work, he shouted 'That should do you, missus,' up the front stairs and took off, leaving the hapless front door ajar. Twenty minutes later the wind blew it shut and it jammed. It hadn't been opened since.

A man who decides to have his front door painted is not perhaps the most likely person to desert his wife but when he went, she wasn't really surprised. In fact she had been half expecting it.

She woke up about 8.45 and opened an eye. His side of the bed was empty. He'd gone. To the office, she assumed, until an hour later when he telephoned. This wasn't unusual. He often called throughout the day. He was a great checker-in.

'Just checking in to see what's happening about the Andersons coming to stay. You haven't forgotten? They're arriving in the morning. From Los Angeles. They'll be dog tired. Will their room be ready?'

'Just checking in. Did you take my jacket to the cleaner's because if not I can bring it in tomorrow and have Rachel take care of it . . .'

'Just checking in . . . are you OK? You were a bit quiet last night.'

This time there was silence on the other end of the line. She knew it was him since he'd had the faithful Rachel call first and put him through to her.

'What do you want for supper tonight? I thought I'd make a meatloaf and a salad. That all right with you?' She waited. He loved her meatloaf, loved the way she slipped in thick slices of chicken amongst the beef and flavoured it with sesame oil.

'Did you look in my cupboards?' he asked quietly.

'No, why? Do you want me to take something to the dry—?'

'Did you look in the bathroom cabinets?'

'Are we out of mouthwash?'

'No. I've left you.'

'Oh.' She said it flatly, almost uninterested.

'I packed last night while you were out with your author. How was dinner, by the way? Did she like Cibo's? Did you have the fruit in zabaglione?'

'Yes,' she confirmed.

'I emptied all the cupboards in my dressing room and took all my things out of the bathroom cabinet and put them in a couple of bags. I put the bags in the broom cupboard under the stairs. You never noticed anything.'

'But . . .'

'No, you weren't meant to. I crept out around 4 a.m. You'd just taken my second pillow away from me in your sleep like you always do and pulled it over your head. You never heard a thing. I didn't want to discuss it. I just wanted to leave. I suppose I could have left a note. Hello? Hello, are you still there?'

'Only just. Jesus, Johnny, what do you want me to say? Should you have left a note? You make it sound like you were committing suicide. Much better to call, shows you're still alive at least.'

'You think so? That's what I felt.' He sounded pleased with himself. 'I didn't know how you'd take it. I wanted to hear your reaction.'

But you didn't want to see it. What was her reaction anyway? Shock, yes, but also a curious sense of relief. Should she tell him this?

3

'It's lucky I did it last night,' he continued chattily. 'As it happens, I'm having lunch with Luana today. I can explain it all to her.'

Luana was her stepdaughter. How about explaining it to your wife, she thought. Poor Luana. She would be more confused than ever. Although she never actually said as much, Luana went around sending out the message 'Please, please love me. My mother's a complete nutcase but that doesn't mean I am and even though my father still thinks I'm five years old, I'm actually a grown-up', as if it were emblazoned across her chest on a T-shirt. Of course she wasn't grown-up. Probably never would be, not with a mother like the demented Edith hovering in the background.

'What shall I tell her if she calls before you've seen her?'

'Tell her to phone the office. They'll know where I'll be.'

'What about tonight? Do you have a place to go?'

'Oh, I'll be fine. Don't worry.'

'Just one thing . . .'

'Yes? I've got a ten-o'clock. Is it a quickie?'

'I just wondered. Is this permanent?'

'Oh Lord! I can't get into discussing anything now. I just can't. You do understand?' And he rang off.

That's my trouble, thought Polly, I always bloody understand.

So Johnny was gone. Coward! Polly thought as she lay in her bath. What a pathetic coward he was not to have had the guts to tell her to her face. Whoever heard of anyone creeping out of their own house in the middle of the night like a cat burglar? Typical childish Johnny behaviour. Of course she'd seen it coming. She could have done something about it but then she'd never taken it seriously. In many ways she'd never taken Johnny himself seriously. In any case, how long would he last out there on his own? He'd be back.

Polly finished dressing. No lunch today, mercifully, no meetings all day. Nothing to dress up for so she selected a pair of cotton leggings patterned with tiny black flowers and a sleeveless black top long enough to hide the bulging reminders of last night's sinning at Cibo's.

In the kitchen she opened the fridge and pressed two ice-cold oranges to her eyes for twenty-five seconds before cutting them in half and juicing them. She told herself it tightened the skin under her eyes and reduced the bags, and of course it was particularly soothing after she'd been crying. For after the bathtub accusations and the reassurances to herself that he would come running back by the end of the day had come the tears. She told herself it was the shock and maybe it was, but whichever way she looked at it, that Johnny had gone so far as to actually move out of the house made her feel terribly sad.

She made herself a pot of coffee and took it through to the office on a tray, balancing it precariously with one hand as she stooped to pick up the mail in the hall. Her secretary did not arrive until eleven bringing the parcels delivered to Polly's PO Box with her. Polly liked an hour of relative peace at her desk, opening her mail, preparing the day's work.

She worked in a conservatory, what had once been an open red brick terrace on the end of the house. She had extended by adding another 14 feet of glass. Her visitors entered through a gate from the street half-way down the garden and came up a path to the glass end. Polly entered from the house through a door beside the kitchen. In summer the tiled floor rendered it cool and the long narrow blinds, pulled across the glass roof and down the windowpanes to various lengths, kept out the sun on the rare occasions when it became too hot. In the winter heat emerged from a Norwegian stove jutting out of the kitchen wall and connected to it by a fat snaked pipe. Into this Polly threw bundles of wood, often opening the door and hurling them into the blaze when she felt a meeting was going on too long and she wanted to get rid of whoever it was. The sight of the roaring flames invariably made visitors extremely nervous as they sat on Polly's striped sofas arranged in a semicircle around the stove. Once, when faced with someone who was particularly entrenched, Polly began to toy with the edge of the wooden coffee table. 'I've never really liked this,' she said casually, 'do you think it would fit?' She eyed the stove. Five minutes later she was saying goodbye.

The glass door at the end of the conservatory opened straight out on to the garden and Polly had a rather disconcerting habit of suddenly rushing out in the middle of a boring telephone conversation to grab some chives for lunch, or check on her lettuces leaving Mrs Flowers, her secretary, to reach for the phone and explain that Polly would be right with whoever it was, could they just hang on a second, something had just come up on the other line.

Polly worked from two long refectory tables standing side by side running the entire length of one side of the conservatory, beginning at the brick end and finishing at the glass end looking out over the garden. The tables were littered with cordless phones, calculators, staplers, overflowing wooden filing trays, long yellow legal pads and square transparent Perspex containers crammed with pens, pencils, paperclips, bulldog clips. Where the two tables met there was always a tall vase of beautifully arranged flowers. Several chairs were scattered along the tables, some of them on castors, on which Polly swivelled about, grabbing phones, dragging her keyboard with her as she went.

Down the other side of the conservatory was a line of bright red filing cabinets broken by a gap in the middle over which had been placed a block of wood. This was Mrs Flowers' desk and the gap was for her arthritic knees. Mrs Flowers did not swivel. She stayed – decidedly – put. She had her screen placed firmly in front of her and she knelt before it on a kind of designer prayer stool Polly had bought her from the Back Shop. There was support for her knees and she was tilted slightly forward all the time. 'Architects use them,' she told Polly's authors seriously, defying them to giggle or to point out that she was not an architect.

Mrs Flowers had been with her ever since Polly had left her job at an established firm and branched out to start her own literary agency. Mrs Flowers had been the temp she'd been sent around the time of her decision to break away.

'Oh, take me with you,' begged Mrs Flowers.

'Well, of course I'd love to but to begin with I simply couldn't afford to.'

'I'm sure you could. Lucy Richards will come with you and the others will soon follow.'

'That's rather wishful thinking.'

'Not at all. I'm certain of it.' Mrs Flowers nodded emphatically.

'Why, exactly?' Polly was curious.

'I was holding on in the middle of a telephone call to her while she took a call on her other line. She didn't quite cover the mouthpiece and I heard her say, "I'm on the phone to my agent's office." And the other person must have been someone in the know who mentioned something about you leaving and I heard Lucy Richards say, "Yes, I know, I've heard the rumours about that too but I'll tell you one thing, if Polly goes anywhere, I'm going with her. If she'll have me, that is." '

'If she'll have me. Did she really say that?'

Lucy Richards' first novel had sold 15,000 copies in hardcover and there was a 200,000 first printing set for the paperback. Secretly Polly had thought the book to be in rather poor taste when she had first read it but she had been forced to admit that since she couldn't put it down, she was almost bound to be able to sell it. It was about the daughter of a prominent member of the cabinet and the artistocracy who, while on holiday in the South of France, falls in love with a St Tropez beach bum, becomes pregnant, has the baby and then discovers, rather late in the day, that the beach bum is gay, is HIV positive, and her baby has AIDS. When her father rather ill-advisedly washes his hands of her, she promptly sells her story to the tabloids finding true love (yet again) in the arms of the first journalist sent to interview her who stays with her while the baby withers and dies. LOVE STORY FOR THE NINETIES screamed the strapline on the paperback cover proof. A movie option had been sold to someone who had once worked for David Puttnam, and Madonna was said to be tempted.

'A likely story!' said Mrs Flowers, who knew a thing or two. 'Shouldn't think she's even read it. Be that Sinead O'Connor more likely. I mean, she'd be perfect as an English aristocrat's daughter.' Nevertheless the Madonna rumour had been circulating at exactly the right moment and it had secured an advance of $40,000 from the Americans and Lucy Richards – and several other lucrative authors – had indeed followed Polly when she left.

So did Mrs Flowers. At the time she had in fact been Miss Flowers but Polly couldn't help noticing that whenever her new secretary answered the telephone she always said: 'This is Mrs Flowers.'

'What does Mr Flowers do?' enquired Polly, feeling nosy one morning.

'My father is dead. He was a porter. At Liverpool Street,' she added after a beat lest Polly think he had worked at Billingsgate fish market or at an hotel.

Polly left it at that yet she had a feeling she did not know Mrs Flowers' whole story, that behind the bustling, efficient exterior with all the trappings of late middle age – the tightly permed hair, the old-fashioned Mrs Thatcher handbag, the silk scarf tied round the neck and the sensible flat brown shoes – lurked a more sensitive, romantic soul, someone who still dared to hope . . .

Polly still had a little time before Mrs Flowers arrived. Should she telephone a dozen friends and tell them what had happened? She thought about it for a second. It would be so horribly predictable. To begin with they'd shriek. To them it was, after all, the ultimate disaster. They'd be embarrassed by what they would imagine would be her humiliation. Then, after about seven minutes, they'd start getting restless, anxious to get off the phone and call someone else with the gossip.

No, thought Polly, I won't call a soul. It's my marriage and it looks like it might be over. I'll just sit back and see how long it takes them to find out.

That did not include Joan.

Joan Brock had been a habit in Polly's life since they were thirteen and new girls at boarding school. Joan had been – and indeed still was – small and dark with a sleek black bob framing her pointed face while Polly had been large and cumbersome. Joan darted every-where and Polly galumphed and Joan always made sure Polly felt like an awkward lump by comparison. Yet in the way that outsiders are often thrown together, Polly and Joan became Best Friends. Except that Polly wasn't really an outsider. She just felt sorry for 'the Jewish girl', as Joan was called behind her back. No one knew for sure if in fact Joan was Jewish but her father was apparently a refugee who had changed his name. He was also a self-made millionaire who doted on his sons and ignored his only daughter, a fact that made Joan strive constantly to seek his attention. Polly was by far the cleverer of the two but Joan was quick-witted and sharp and survived by getting away with the proverbial murder.

After school – neither went to university – they had arrived in London at more or less the same time when Joan had thrown herself at every available man while Polly watched shyly from the sidelines. Joan had succeeded in landing an eligible young Old Etonian antique dealer. They were married at Chelsea Register Office – all crushed velvet suits and floppy hats over flowers in the hair and absolutely no sign of Mummy and Daddy. Polly was a bridesmaid. In the wedding photos she stood predictably huge and galumphing, towering over the tiny bride.

The marriage lasted five years, by which time Joan had discovered she couldn't have children and the Old Etonian had decided he wanted an heir and divorced her. But by then Joan had wormed her way into a job on *Vogue* and was too busy clawing her way up the Condé Nast ladder and being smart and chic and fashionable to remember Polly's existence except for a frantic 'catch-up' lunch once or twice a year.

Then Joan was fired from Condé Nast, ousted from Vogue House and thrown out into the wilderness of freelance journalism. Since then she had telephoned Polly at least four times a week, generally first thing in the morning. Just as Polly had been there to support Joan the outsider at school, Joan had known Polly would also be there to pick up the pieces later on in life.

'Any sex? Any cheques?' Joan's life now revolved around getting work (her main aim was to get herself a column but it appeared to be the main aim of all newspaper and magazine editors to deny her one), and looking for a man. At one point she announced she was going to write THE NOVEL which, she told Polly, would outraunch Julie Burchill. She gave up after four paragraphs.

'Not exactly. Johnny's gone.'

'Well, that's great if he's going to be out of the way because I want to come over for lunch today instead of tomorrow. Something's come up.'

Joan rescheduled everything. She had no consideration whatsoever for anyone else's timetable. She was one of those people who found the thought of being left to her own devices for half a second so daunting that she crammed as much as she could into every day with the result that she frequently found herself overbooked. Polly was used to it. She knew better than to write a date with Joan in ink and kept a pencil with a rubber on the end inside her diary for the express purpose of rescheduling Joan. Her stepdaughter Luana disapproved strongly and called her Polly Pushover for being so obliging.

'No, Joan, listen for a second. He's gone. He's no longer living here. He's –'

'You mean *he's left you*? That's completely and utterly wonderful. The best news. Who is she?'

'What do you mean?'

'Who's he left you for?'

'No one as far as I know.'

'Oh, bound to be someone. Some little floozie in his office, much younger than you. When did you last have sex? Months ago, I bet. So can I come over for lunch today?'

'No, Joan, I don't think so. Not today. Do you mind?'

'But what am I going to do? I haven't got a lunch. I'll go mad. Anyway, I want to hear all about why he's left you. He was a mega-loser, called himself a bloody film producer but what's he ever produced? Polly, you're well rid of him. You do know that, don't you?'

Was this what everyone was going to tell her? That she was well rid of him? It wasn't, Polly realised, what she wanted to hear. Joan had never liked Johnny but that was no reason to go slagging him off at the first opportunity.

'Joan, I have to go. Mrs Flowers will be here at any minute.'

'I do not understand why you employ that menopausal old bat. It's bad for your image.'

'I rather think Mrs Flowers is well past the menopause. I, on the other hand, in the not too distant future . . .'

'Your husband leaves you and you immediately blame it on the menopause. You're too negative for words, darling. Call me when you've got a grip. Don't sit there feeling sorry for yourself. He's done you a favour. Now we'll find you someone sensational. After we've found me someone sensational. I must get off this phone and find someone to have lunch with. Bye.'

Polly finished her coffee, relieved at the welcome distraction of Mrs Flowers coming in through the garden door bearing parcels of manuscripts. Mrs Flowers flapped her *Daily Mail* at Polly.

'Nice piece about your Mr de Soto in Nigel Dempster's column. Something about him and his "constant companion", that Lady Whyte, having a quiet dinner together to talk about the new film . . . and look, that Hector O'Neill's been in the news again. Broken up with his girlfriend right in the middle of shooting his new film. Says it's the last time he's going to play Conway so I suppose they'll have to replace him like they did Sean Connery in James Bond. It was never the same though, was it, Mrs de Soto? Look at Hector O'Neill! Irish, is he? Something like that. Dreamboat like that, make some girl a wonderful husband if only he'd settle down. Pity you've already found your Mr Right, Mrs de Soto.'

Polly realised she wasn't going to get away with it. She would have to tell Mrs Flowers about Johnny going. She would have to tell everyone. That night Luana called her and Polly was surprised at her stepdaughter's reaction: 'What a jerk my father is!'

Yes, Polly told herself firmly, what a jerk! Every morning she would wake up and shout *what a jerk*!

But she wouldn't really mean it.

Hector O'Neill raised his glass of champagne to toast the supermodel – he couldn't for the life of him remember her name – sitting in the seat beside him. He figured she must be a supermodel if she was flying First-Class. He wondered if he could be bothered to chat her up all the way to London in return for a quick fuck when they got there. Then he'd want to get rid of her and she probably wouldn't take the hint. They never did. He decided to give it a whirl and then feign sleep if she proved too stupid.

'Saw you on the cover of *Vogue* last month. What were you up to in LA?' What the fuck was her name? She couldn't be that super or he'd remember.

She giggled predictably. 'American *Vogue*? That wasn't me. That was Cindy Crawford. I look a bit like her. Everyone says so.'

'No, no, I meant British *Vogue*.'

'Well, I wouldn't be on that either. I'm not a model. Far from it. I'm an actress.'

No, you're not, darling, you're an MTA if you're

15

anything at all. Model-turned-actress and a wannabe at that. Why was he wasting his time?

'Course you are. Been filming in LA?'

'Just seeing a few people. You know. You?'

'Meetings about my new Conway film. I start shooting next week.'

'Fully cast, is it?'

Oh, God, she'd never let him go. Then it hit him. Had he been set up? Had her agent fixed it so she'd be sitting next to him? Was she poised to make a play for him to try and get a part in the film? Stranger things had happened. He'd wait a little while so as not to offend her and then move seats.

'Not my department, darling, but I think it is, yes. It's the last Conway I'm doing, that's all I know. Yes, you do look a bit like Cindy. Talking about *Vogue*, they want me for a fashion shoot, model a few old rags with one of the girls.'

'Oh, that's nice.'

'Might be.'

'Will they do an interview too? What do they call it? In-depth. Get to the real you?' She giggled again. She was beginning to irritate him. Seriously.

'Not *Vogue*'s style, darling.'

Thank God!

No one in his new life was ever going to get him to do an in-depth interview. No one was ever going to find out the truth about his background. What a relief to be going home to England. Funny to think of it as home when he'd been born in America. How he hated going back to the States. It always reminded him of the past he wanted to forget.

The Kennedys had put the Irish on the map in

America when Hector was growing up. He was only four when President Kennedy was assassinated but he was nine when Bobby was killed, old enough to recognise a hero when he saw one on television. That was when Hector decided he too would become an Irish hero – and here he was flying First-Class, an international movie star, the perfect Irish hero and, for all anybody knew, Boston born and bred just like the Kennedys.

Except that he wasn't. He was poor shanty Irish, born John Hector Maguire, in a small town near Pittsburgh, Pennsylvania, descended, if he chose to believe his grandfather's blarney, from Celtic stock from Co. Mayo who had come to America in the 1870s to seek their fortune and wound up in the mines. He would probably fly right over the miserable dump he'd grown up in. His prevailing memory of the place was always of smoke rising into a grey sky peppered with jagged pylons and tall chimneys. The smoke came not only from the chimneys but also from the steam engines roaring through on the railroad raised high above the ground and from the trucks, the oil tanker rigs, the semis charging past belching smoke.

His father worked at the steel mill. He had another picture from his childhood: that of his father and his buddies coming home from work, a line of them appearing on the crest of a hill, lunchboxes and helmets tucked under their arms, silhouetted against the horizon, smoke rising behind them. They all dressed much the same: wool hats, fur hats, baseball caps; sleeveless quilted jackets over plaid shirts, hands plunged deep in jeans pockets, shoulders hunched against the cold. And they never made it home before midnight. Every day John Hector watched them stumble into the saloon with the red neon Budweiser sign winking at them in the window. Once, sent by his mother to find his father, he had gone into the bar and found his father lying fast asleep in the middle of the pool table, his white vest riding up over his belly, jeans loosened for comfort, boots sticking straight up in the air. All around him on the green baize were overturned beer cans.

Throughout his boyhood John Hector never saw his father hold a conversation with a woman. Jimmy Maguire was uncomfortable around women, a great brute of a man who only lost his shyness when drunk and he only drank with men, men who could be counted on to say little more to him than 'Hey buddy', 'Hey man', ask him how they were hangin?, tell him he was full of shit, let him tell them they were, too.

John Hector didn't blame him for never coming home when home was a trailer without wheels. The boys who went to school with him, steelworkers' kids like himself, lived in rows of wooden houses originally painted white, now grey with the smoke, with front porches where people sat out at night, but the Maguires were too poor even for this humble accommodation. John Hector often looked at his mother and wondered how it felt to be so poor when she had been born rich. He was eight when his mother first took him to Philadelphia and showed him his grandparents' house on Henry Avenue. It was a four-storey mansion, standing in its own grounds. Fourteen rooms minimum, and he had to share a bed with his mother in the trailer.

'I went to stay with my Auntie Kitty in Pittsburgh and I met your father in a store,' Mary Maguire told him. 'I fell in love with him and I married him. Your grandfather hasn't spoken to me since. Your father wasn't the wreck of a man he is now. The drink did that to him. If I'd known I was going to wind up living in a broken-down mobile home with a steelworker who never came home for a husband, I'd have listened to my father, of course.'

'Does he know about me?'

'He does. I wrote him. Told him I'd named you for him. Those are your grandfather's names: John Hector. Only he's John Hector Kennedy.'

And that was when it had begun: his dreams of being related somehow to those other Kennedys. He'd seen where his mother was raised and it gave him a new-found sense of pride in himself to know that he came from good lace curtain Irish stock. He might be the son of a bum but he was also the child of a Philadelphia princess.

Only he wasn't.

He brooded over the Philadelphia mansion day after day. Why didn't his mother take him and run away, go back there, go back to her roots, where she belonged, where he belonged? Each time he saw his father jostling with his buddies, coming over the horizon and down the hill to the saloon to drink himself into oblivion, John Hector wanted to taunt him with the truth but Mary Maguire had made him swear never to tell his father what she'd shown him. So he hugged his secret to himself as a way of keeping out the cold and the smoke, and he dreamed.

He was nine when he wrote the first letter to his grandfather. Cheap paper, bad spelling, devoid of grammar – but the message was there. He was the old man's grandson. His mother was Mary Maguire. They lived in hell. Please would Mr Kennedy save them?

No reply.

He wrote again. Five times, before someone

answered. It wasn't John Hector Kennedy. It was his wife. John Hector couldn't read his grandmother's spidery hand. He took the letter to the parish priest, Father Dominic. Father Dominic read the letter.

'Who is this lady, Nora Kennedy?'

'My grandmother,' said John Hector.

'No, son, I don't think so.'

The priest was kind. He broke the news gently. Nora Kennedy was confused about the boy who had been writing to her husband. They had no daughter called Mary Maguire. The only person she knew called Mary Maguire was the little daughter of a maid they had employed several years ago.

The truth was simple. John Hector's grandfather had not lived on Henry Avenue. He had been an out-of-work builder in the poor East Falls immigrant area of Philadelphia. His wife Annie had worked in the scullery at Henry Avenue to support her family. Little Mary Maguire had been one of eight children and as soon as she could had escaped to Pittsburgh where she had met Jimmy Maguire – and here was the only reality in her story – in a store. She was not even able to change her name when she married and the only reason her father never spoke to her again was because he was too blind East Falls drunk to notice she had gone.

But little Mary Maguire had witnessed something her father never had. She had seen the way the rich lived even if she had never lived that way herself, and in memory of that brief glimpse into another world she had named her son after a wealthy Henry Avenue socialite and concocted a childhood fantasy for him as a way of holding at bay the hell into which she had descended.

Once John Hector had discovered her deception, his

mother gave up on him. She couldn't play the game with him any more, couldn't pretend it was all going to end some day when she would whisk him away to the life where they really belonged. She was just a poor Irish girl who'd married a poor Irish bum and between them they'd produced John Hector. Now she realised she was stuck in the smoke for ever, her child became a burden to her, holding her back. She could have taken to the bottle like her husband but she had discovered something better. It was 1968, pretty late on in the decade, when Mary Maguire had began to smoke dope.

She was turned on to grass by a dropout student from Philadelphia who picked her up outside the supermarket and told her she looked like Joan Baez. Mary Maguire had barely heard of Joan Baez. Patsy Cline was more her style. Yet within weeks she was out every night with a crowd of hippies who gathered round a camp fire on the outskirts of town and sang half-hearted protest songs while someone strummed on a guitar and the joint was passed from hand to hand.

John Hector didn't mind. He had the trailer to himself. He lived off cans of cold beans and watched TV every night until he fell asleep in front of it. The irony was that when the draft call for Vietnam in January 1968 rose to 33,000, John Hector probably knew more about the growing futility and escalation of the war from all that he had seen on TV than either his father, drunk in the bar every night and about to be part of the draft, or his mother, stoned by the camp fire and playing at being an opponent of the war.

In the summer of 1969, with Jimmy Maguire safely out of the way in the Mekong Delta, Mary Maguire left John Hector with a neighbour and took off with her hippie gang to the music festival at Woodstock. When she returned she had a young Englishman in tow with blond hair down to his shoulders and an accent John Hector couldn't understand.

'John Hector,' she said casually, 'this is Tony. He's going to get us out of here. He's going to take us to England.'

'Coo-ee!' twinkled the model-turned-actress, wiggling her fingers at him, 'wakey-wakey. Shall we have something to drink and get to know each other better?'

Hector placed a hand on the inside of her bare thigh. I didn't go to sleep, you silly cow, I just closed my eyes to make you think I had. He squeezed the soft pink flesh a little.

'Listen, love, the Conway movie's cast. There's nothing I can do for you in that department. In fact I'll be totally straight, there's nothing I can do for you in any department other than where my hand is right now. How about it?'

'I'm not like that,' she said, model-turned-actress-turned-prim-and-proper all of a sudden.

Like hell! 'Suit yourself. I'm going back to sleep.'

olly met her husband at a party. She had just begun work as an assistant at the literary agents Patrick Fisher & Dunbar with the promise of promotion to baby agent status after an initial trial period. Before that she had been a secretary to an American film producer for whom she still read scripts and it was at his Christmas party, held in a cavernous film studio just off the Fulham Road used to shoot commercials, that she first encountered Johnny de Soto.

She still acted as a kind of scout for the producer, scouring publishers' lists for potential properties – books he might want to make into films. Once she had read the book she then had to 'cover' it which meant writing a five-line idiot's description of the plot (most of the money men in the film industry were barely capable of taking in even that much), followed by a longer, more detailed synopsis which could run from three pages to fifty-three. Each time a major character was introduced his or her name had to be typed in capital letters. Finally she had to write a short comment with helpful suggestions like 'suitable vehicle for Dustin Hoffman' or 'perfect for Greta Scacchi if the main character had surgery and the picture was reset in England.'

Polly was aware that the American never took the slightest bit of notice of anything she said yet she always took her coverages seriously. Long, multi-generational sagas were particularly demanding and it was because she had been tackling a synopsis of one of these that she was late for the party. She had become so absorbed in the task of chronicling every twist and turn of the baroque story that she had forgotten the time. When she arrived at 8.45 with her streaked hair still wet from the shower, the drinks were almost over.

The American's wife pounced on her the minute she stepped inside the door.

'Polly! There you are. Now, may I introduce Johnny de Soto?'

If you absolutely have to, thought Polly; what a seriously dreadful name. She eyed the rather grizzled-looking character being propelled towards her. He was on the stocky side, dark hair cut short, almost in a crew cut, and already greying at the temples. His face was square and smiling with rather a pugnacious nose and wide-apart dark brown eyes – the kind Polly described as 'melting' in her coverages. His mouth was twitchy, ready to break into a grin. He wore jeans, loafers, a beige crew-neck sweater underneath a black light wool jacket. He looked relaxed.

'It is, isn't it?' he said, taking her hand.

'What is?'

'A terrible name. It was written all over your face, as they say. Don't worry. I'm sure everyone has the same reaction. It's actually Gianni de Soto but I've sort of changed it to Johnny.'

'You're Italian?' He didn't sound it.

'Yes, but I was born here. My father came over from Naples and opened an ice-cream shop in Soho. It's still there. I'll take you there one day.'

Polly was startled. 'Will you? You don't even know my name.'

'Well?'

'Oh. I'm Polly Atwell.'

Someone slapped him on the back.

'Johnny, you old devil, how are you? Good to see you. This is . . .'

And he was gone, turning back to her with a rueful grin and a shrug before he was moved on.

To her intense irritation, Polly found herself thinking about him over Christmas with her parents in Norfolk. On her return to London in the New Year she rummaged through her cupboards till she found the Rolodex she had used when working for the film producer. She found his card under 'S'.

> Johnny de Soto
> 25 Roberts Gardens
> London SW7

Funny, she'd never noticed it before. Her predecessor had made a tiny note on the back:

> Wife's name: Edith
> Daughter: Luana

Wife's name: Edith. Damn! Forget it, Polly told herself firmly, just don't even think about it any more.

He turned up at Patrick Fisher & Dunbar four days later. He'd obviously done a bit of homework.

'Is he in?' He nodded towards Patrick Fisher's office.

'Do you have an appointment?' Wife's name: Edith. Be cold, Polly, be snotty.

'Don't give me that. I only want to ask him if I can take you out to lunch.'

'Well, why don't you ask me?' said Polly, falling straight into the trap.

He took her to Langan's and said 'Hello Michael' to Michael Caine as they passed his table. Michael Caine nodded vaguely. Polly wondered if he had the slightest idea who Johnny de Soto was.

She had the spinach soufflé with anchovy sauce because Johnny said she absolutely had to although she noticed he chose the *salade frisée aux lardons* for himself. He didn't say much as they ate their first course, just kept looking at her. Suddenly he said:

'You have the most perfect ears.'

'Have I?' said Polly, puzzled and a little thrown. 'How?'

'Flat against the side of your head, small, tiny lobes. Why don't you have them pierced?'

'I'm scared. I expect it hurts like hell.'

'Rubbish! Have them done.'

He lapsed into silence again until Polly's steak arrived. He made her have French fries with it although she pleaded that she was trying to lose weight. He ate a couple of mouthfuls of yet another salad, pushed it to one side of his plate and began to ply her with questions as she chewed her way through her steak.

'Tell me about yourself? How long have you been working in our business?'

It was worse than going to the dentist, thought Polly. They waited until they'd filled your mouth with the drill, clamps and cotton wool swabs and then they began making small talk. Besides, moonlighting as a part-time reader for a producer who didn't take her seriously hardly constituted working in the movies.

'Oh . . .' she shrugged as she dispatched the last mouthful, 'I'm in the book world now. What about you?'

'Me? Oh, I'm just getting going. I've got this property and –'

'You're a producer?'

'Yes, well, I am, I mean I want to be. No, skip that, I am a producer.'

'What films have you produced? Have I seen any of them?'

'Well, that's just it. I haven't actually made anything yet but I've got this property and I'm in the process of developing it. It's called *The End* and it's going to be *Jaws 2* and –'

'Didn't they make *Jaws 2*?'

'No, I mean it's as horrific as *Jaws*. It's about this couple who buy their dream house and they're set to retire there and live happily ever after and their grandkids come and stay – or maybe it's a young married couple starting out, we haven't really decided yet. Anyway they have acres and acres of land or a big garden or whatever and every day they get closer to exploring the perimeter. One day they're going to go down to the end of the garden and when they get there they're going to find the evil that lurks there.'

'What evil?'

'Haven't quite finalised the evil yet but, believe me, it'll be scarier than sharks.'

'Sharks at the end of the garden?'

'Oh, shut up. You're not taking me seriously. The whole point is that we, the audience, will know about the evil, the alien, or whatever it is because we'll see it intermittently throughout the movie. The suspense will be a killer.'

'But why do you want to make *Son of Jaws* when we've already had *Jaws*? Why not try and make something new and different?'

'You try telling the money men you want to make something completely different from something that's just been one of the biggest grossing pictures of all time. They'd laugh in your face. It will be different. I know that. But I have to pretend it's going to be something they're familiar with. So I've got this guy writing the script down in a basement in Chelsea somewhere . . .'

'And you're paying him peanuts . . . '

'How'd you know?'

'I just did.'

'Well, it'll be his big break. He'll make his name with *The End* and I'll be the guy who made it all possible. He owes me.'

'So do you have a treatment to be going on with?'

He looked at her in admiration.

'It really does make a change to talk to someone in our business. I tell most girls I take out I've got a treatment and they think I'm talking about a course of penicillin. Yes, I've got a treatment and I'm talking to financiers, you know, venture capitalists and so on.'

'Yes, of course.' Polly nodded seriously. He was ridiculous but at the same time there was something enormously appealing about his enthusiasm, his optimism.

He glanced at his watch.

'Christ! Eh, do you want coffee?'

She did but since she would clearly be drinking it on her own, she declined.

'I'd run you back but I have to be in Wardour Street by three.'

'It's OK.'

They parted outside the restaurant. He didn't kiss her, didn't even take her hand, just jumped in a passing cab and waved goodbye through the rear window.

It was raining. Polly set off back to the office. What had been the point of that lunch? She should have asked him about his family. Wife's name: Edith. Daughter: Luana. Why did a man take a girl to lunch – and from the sound of it she wasn't the only one – when he had that written on the back of his address card?

He called a week later.

'Well, have you had them done?'

'What?'

'Your ears. Have you had them pierced like I said?'

'No.'

'So when are you going to get around to it?'

He booked her for dinner in a week's time on condition that she arrived at the restaurant with pierced ears.

She had them done at Harrods and treated herself to a new black skirt from Agnès B in the Fulham Road. It was a size 12 and normally she took a size 14 but she managed to squeeze into it. Polly was a big girl. Not fat, just big. Johnny de Soto was not a tall man. Nevertheless Polly put on a pair of three-inch heels when she went to meet him at La Poule au Pot in Ebury Street. She liked La Poule au Pot. They brought you huge bottles of wine and you only paid for what you drank. It had a warm, comforting French nursery atmosphere, the perfect restaurant for the misery of winter. She already knew what she would have to eat: the gigot of lamb with lentils.

'Had them done?' He stood up to greet her, pulled back her chair and then brushed his hand through her hair, drawing it away from her ear. 'Good girl' he said when he saw the tiny gold studs and leaned forward to kiss her cheek.

'It really hurt,' said Polly, sitting down.

'Well, of course it did. What did you expect?'

'But you said –'

'Never mind what I said. Here's your reward.'

The little black box had the name Argenta written on it. Polly had seen Argenta, passed it many times. It was a jeweller's on the Fulham Road. She opened the box and parted the tissue paper.

To her horror her initial reaction was one of disappointment. But then what had she expected from someone on a second date, someone she barely knew, someone who had a wife named Edith? Diamonds? The earrings were tiny. Black dots circled with gold. Exquisitely tasteful.

'They'll look great when you've had your hair cut,' he told her.

Two weeks later, shaven and shorn at Molton Brown and wearing her new earrings, Polly allowed herself to be taken to bed by Johnny de Soto. At Johnny's insistence they watched a video of *The Boys from Brazil* and ate a Chinese takeaway.

'Trash!' complained Johnny, 'utter trash. How could Olivier allow himself to appear in such trash?'

'I thought he was brilliant. His character was based on that man, what's his name? The one who . . .'

'Simon Wiesenthal, the Nazi hunter. I'm not saying Olivier was bad. It's just the whole story was so unbelievable: Gregory Peck rushing round the world assassinating fathers and these identical boys all over the place. Ludicrous.'

Polly couldn't help wondering what exactly would make *The End* so credible when Johnny came to make it but she decided now was not the moment to ask him. Instead she said:

'He's a terrific storyteller, Ira Levin.'

'Who's Ira Levin, for heaven's sake? There was no one called Ira Levin in that movie.'

'He's the author of the book on which it was based,' said Polly patiently. 'He was only twenty-five when he wrote his first book, *A Kiss before Dying*. Now there's something you could have made a film of. It's full of suspense.'

'I know *A Kiss before Dying*. It's the one about the guy who goes after an heiress but he gets her pregnant which means she'll be disinherited so he stops and goes after her sister. They made it already, Robert Wagner and Joanne Woodward, I forget who directed . . .'

'Recently?'

'No, back in the Fifties. You're right. Great story.'

'Well, why don't you do a remake?'

'To tell you the truth I heard there's one in the pipeline. Anyway, where's the excitement in doing a remake?'

'Where's the excitement in doing another *Jaws*-type movie when it's already been done?'

'I told you. I'm going to make it different. Have you seen *Return to Peyton Place*?'

'Have I seen what?'

'I knew it. Greatest soap film ever made and it's on TV late tonight. We'll watch it in bed.'

His apartment was right at the top of the building and there was no lift. He hadn't turned on the light when they'd arrived but had taken her by the hand and led her up the staircase in the darkness to the fifth floor, pausing on the landings to draw her into his arms and nuzzle her neck.

She was surprised by the humble size of the flat: just one room under the eaves with a small kitchen leading off it, a box-like bedroom with only room for a king-size bed and built-in closets and a bathroom in which she could barely turn around. A bachelor apartment. No sign of the family.

As she had somehow expected he was an attentive lover, full of affection. First he ran her a bath and poured something sweet-smelling from a Floris bottle into it.

'Undress in the bedroom. Leave your things in there. No room in here, as you can see.'

He helped her into the bath and squatted down fully clothed beside her.

'Don't be shy. You have a sensational body.' He leaned back on his haunches to admire her. 'Now which soap shall I wash you with?'

He built up a lather in his hands and began to smooth it all over her, bringing the soapsuds to little points on her nipples. As she stepped out of the tub he wrapped her in a big towel and hugged her dry.

'Come on. Into bed now. Movie's about to start.'

He must have spent at least half an hour stroking her, kissing her, massaging her until she floated into a warm liquid sensation and heard herself begging him to make love to her.

As they watched the movie she nestled against him and he stroked her hair continuously. She could hear his heart hammering in his chest beneath her head and found she could barely concentrate on the film.

Suddenly a line with the word 'wife' penetrated her drowsiness.

Wife's name: Edith.

'Johnny?'

'Hmmm?'

'Are you married?'

'No.'

'Divorced?'

'No.'

'What?' Polly sat up in bed. He tried to pull her back down but she resisted.

'What's this all about?'

'You've never been married?'

'Not exactly.'

'Well, who's Edith?'

'Ah, someone's told you about Edith.'

'No . . .'

'Then how –'

Polly explained about the Rolodex.

He laughed. 'Come here, you.' He clasped her to him and her head bumped up and down on his chest as he continued to laugh. He kissed her fiercely on the forehead several times. 'I like hearing you did that. You looked for my card because you were interested in me. I like that.'

'And Edith?'

'Edith was . . . is . . . the mother of my child.'

'Luana?'

'Hah! Her name was there too?'

She was silent. Waiting.

'All right. I'll tell you about Edith. She was my . . . we were together for four years. We had a child but we never married.'

'Why not?'

'She didn't want to. I confess I asked her several times but she wouldn't. Then, in the end, she left me.'

'Where is she now?'

'Battersea. South of the river.'

'And Luana?'

'Mostly with her. Sometimes with me in the house I have in Notting Hill Gate.'

'So what's this place?'

'This is just . . .'

'Where you bring scrubbers?'

'You said it . . .'

She punched him. He bit her – gently. She began to tickle him.

'What happened in the end?' she whispered after they had made love and were about to fall asleep.

'With me and Edith?'

'No, the movie . . .'

'Oh, she stays there in Peyton Place, she tells Jeff Chandler goodbye.'

'Like Edith told you . . .'

In the morning as they bumped into each other trying to make breakfast together in the tiny kitchenette, Johnny told her:

'We won't be coming back here. This place was Edith's old flat before we had a baby. We never got around to selling it. She probably doesn't even know I still have a key. So when are you going to meet Luana? You'd better make it soon if you're going to move in with me.'

As she walked up the aisle, Polly had time to catch her breath for the first time in two months.

'Polly and Johnny were lovers. . .' she sang in her mind to the tune of 'Frankie and Johnny'.

Would he do her wrong like the Johnny in the song? How could she tell? She'd barely had a chance to get to know him. Did all brides feel like this? A moment of sheer panic, the question 'what have I done?' better left unanswered.

'Where's the blighter got to?' muttered her father, fractionally tightening his hold on her elbow to restrain her. They were half-way up the aisle and Johnny, whose back view clad in morning suit had presented a disturbingly unfamiliar picture when she had first seen it on entering the chuch, had now disappeared.

Well, that's that, she concluded. It was never meant to happen. Then she saw him pacing nervously up and down to the right of the altar. He caught sight of her standing transfixed in the middle of the aisle glaring at him and gave her a broad wink. For one ghastly moment Polly thought he was going to vault over the pews and come running to her.

The rest of the service passed without a hitch. Johnny, a lapsed Catholic whose memories of the Catholic Church receded so far into his past he couldn't remember when he last went to confession, had agreed to be confirmed into the Church of England so he could make Polly happy by marrying her in church. Polly knew her parents were sad that the little Norman flint church in their Norfolk village had been rejected in favour of a London wedding but she just couldn't see Johnny in Norfolk.

She sensed the electricity in the congregation behind her when the vicar said:

'Do you Gianni Mauro Ludovico de Soto take this woman . . . ?'

OK, so he was a wop and she was going to take him to be her lawful wedded husband whether they liked it or not.

'Engaging fellow, your Johnny,' chuckled her Uncle Matthew to her during the reception. That was the trouble, thought Polly. So engaging she had been unable to resist him.

Luana was not at the wedding. Polly had only met her once. She almost met her the day after she and Johnny had first spent the night together. Johnny had invited her to have dinner with him and his daughter at his house. Polly's friends didn't live in houses. They lived in flats and shared them if they couldn't afford the rental on their own. The only people she knew who lived in houses in London were friends of her parents.

As she climbed the stone steps to the front door she

noticed it was open. She was about to knock when she heard a girl's voice from within.

'She's, like, moving in? Dad, are you crazy? How can she move in?'

'She's moving in because I'm going to marry her.'

This was news to Polly, who stood rooted to the doormat, trembling all over. Very slowly and very quietly she edged backwards down the steps till she reached the pavement whereupon she rushed into the street and flagged down a cab.

Every now and again Polly went into emotional shock. She protected her inner core with what appeared to be an efficient no-nonsense exterior but occasionally something shot straight through to the heart and dislodged her. Hearing that Johnny actually planned to marry her completely knocked her for six. For two days she simply could not function. She didn't go to the office and later she realised Patrick Fisher must have given Johnny her address since he turned up and rang her doorbell for eleven minutes until she answered.

'I've saved you your job. You can't do this sort of thing, you know. He was about to fire you by mail but I stopped him.'

Polly burst into tears.

'Oh, Polly, Polly, Polly! Come here.'

He held her, standing in the middle of the hall, patting her on the back as if she were a baby with wind. 'What's this all about? What's wrong? Don't tell me you were a virgin. You weren't, you know, even if you think you were. No use trying that one on. I've had 'em before. I can tell.'

'Not funny,' blubbed Polly into his shoulder, 'I'm far too old.'

'Yeah, well, getting on a bit, that's for sure. Feel like an old maid, do you?'

She hit him. And giggled.

'That's better. Now, I came to ask you to marry me. God knows why, your nose is all red but I want you. I really do. I want a Polly with a red nose and tiny pierced earlobes and great long legs to wrap around me when I'm cold and lonely. So what do you say? Will you marry me?'

He asked her every day for two weeks until she said yes. She wasn't especially confident with men and she hadn't had many lovers. She had no idea what Johnny de Soto saw in her but she knew she was not likely to encounter anyone like him again. If she turned him down she was destined to marry a nice young English gentleman who might inherit a bit of land somewhere (probably Norfolk, since most of the nice young men she knew came from there), where he would expect her to be chatelaine of his manor and raise a well-brought-up brood.

Johnny de Soto was totally different and she fell deeply in love with him without ever daring to ask if he was in love with her.

His mother, Carla de Soto, was five feet if she put on a pair of high heels.

'She's not a Catholic. She's taller than you are. Whatever would your father have said?' she gabbled in Italian when Johnny took Polly to the flat above his father's ice-cream shop in Soho where his mother still lived. Polly looked at Johnny helplessly and he translated.

'Do you mind?' Polly asked him.

'That you're not a Catholic? Are you kidding?'

'No – that I'm taller than – '

'I love it!' Johnny wrapped his arms around her and bent his knees, pretending his head only came as far as her navel.

'Gianni, *basta.*' Carla pushed him out of the way with surprising strength for one so small. She took Polly's hand and looked up at her seriously.

'You love my Gianni?'

Polly nodded.

'For ever and ever?'

Polly nodded again.

Then Carla wrapped her chubby little arms around her future daughter-in-law and her head only did come as high as Polly's breasts. 'So,' she said, 'I give him to you.'

'Mamma!' Johnny rolled his eyes.

'But first I want to tell you about him. Gianni, go away. Go to the store and fetch us some pastries for tea.'

To Polly's amazement he went without a word.

'Gianni is not like his father,' she explained in the privacy of her kitchen, 'my Mauro, for him, the shop, selling ice-cream, it was enough. All day he sell *gelati* then he come upstairs and I cook pasta for him and he is content. Gianni is different. I think I knew when he was in here – she patted her shapeless black dress in the region of her stomach – 'in my womb. Our life is not enough for him. He is Italian but he is also English. He wants the excitement of London. I knew he would marry English girl.'

'Was Edith English?'

'Edith is not important.'

Polly was shocked. 'But she's the mother of his child.'

'Now you will be the mother and you will have bambinos of your own.'

40

'But this daughter, your granddaughter, lives with Edith.'

Suddenly the tiny woman exploded. 'Edith! Edith. All I hear is Edith. She was wrong for my Gianni. She take too much from him. She demand this, she demand that. Edith is no mother for his children. She's just a child herself. He need someone stronger. Someone like you. Edith couldn't keep up with him.' She clutched Polly's wrist. 'Don't let him get away. Don't hold him back like Edith did. Let him go fast and keep up with him.'

As she came down the aisle on Johnny's arm Carla's words haunted her. What did she mean – keep up with him? Maybe she should have listened to Joan Brock, who had been totally against the marriage.

'He hasn't a bean as far as I can make out. No one who's anyone has heard of him. He's not even particularly attractive. I just don't know what you see in him, darling. And why you have to get married two days before Paris fashion week starts, I just don't know. It's hugely inconvenient but I suppose I'll have to come otherwise you'll never speak to me again.'

Polly had refrained from pointing out that she never spoke to Joan anyway because Joan was far too busy playing at *Vogue* or wherever it was. She also omitted to mention that Johnny claimed to be allergic to Joan. 'She's a midget, she's got bad breath, she's a snob and she's seriously unintelligent. How you two ever became friends is a mystery.'

Why was all this going through her mind on her wedding day? Polly smiled in what she hoped was a suitably radiant fashion at the rows of guests and family on her side of the church – there was Joan Brock in the row behind her parents decked out in a little number she had undoubtedly swiped from the fashion cupboard at whatever magazine currently employed her – and the pathetic gathering of film people scattered about the pews on the other side. Surreptitiously Polly moved a little faster beside her husband. If only Luana had come then he would have had a family on his side of the church instead of just a little old lady standing there crossing herself.

Polly's one meeting with Luana had been a near disaster. At least as far as she was concerned; Johnny seemed to think everything had gone fine.

Polly had decided she wanted to meet her future stepdaughter on her own territory. Armed with Carla's recipes, she spent an entire day preparing a veritable Italian feast. Johnny ushered in Luana a little after 7.30, gave Polly a quick hug, thrust a bottle of Chianti into her arms and said proudly:

'Polly, this is my daughter.'

From then on he was utterly useless. He slumped in an armchair and turned on the television.

'Hello Luana. Come in.' Polly winced at how stilted she sounded in her embarrassment.

'Do you actually live here?' was Luana's opening gambit as she surveyed Polly's studio flat. Polly looked around in surprise. She'd given the place a thorough cleaning. Her futon was rolled up neatly. A vase of fresh flowers dominated the low Japanese table beside it. Impressive-looking books were stacked in piles. The floorboards were polished. The cushions were plumped on the sofa and on the two armchairs either side of it. All the usual debris on the trestle table she used as a desk had beeen cleared away. A fire was burning in her little Victorian grate and the octagonal Italian dining table was laid for three with the tomato and mozzarella salad already in place. Maybe it was a little too Habitat for some people's taste, but it was warm and welcoming.

Wasn't it?

'I certainly do. Why wouldn't I?'

Luana just shrugged. It was a nervous tic, Polly realised after a while, something Luana did when she didn't have an answer, couldn't care less. She was a skeletal creature, stick thin with olive skin, Italian-looking like her father but her face had a precociously elegant bone structure which made Polly think immediately that her mother must be something of a beauty. Bones like that didn't come from Johnny. She was nervy, forever fiddling with her fingers. In a few years' time those fingers would be occupied with cigarettes. Maybe they already were when her father wasn't around. How old was Luana? Polly realised Johnny had never said. She looked about twelve but she must be older.

'Are you hungry?' Polly asked her. Luana certainly needed fattening up. She shrugged predictably. Polly had a sudden panic that she might be anorexic.

'What's for dinner?' asked Johnny, barely looking up from the television.

'Tomato, basil and mozzarella salad and lasagne.'

'Where'd you get the mozzarella and the lasagne?' asked Johnny.

'Camisa,' said Polly, omitting to add that she had spent half her salary on the meal at Camisa as well as half the day in the kitchen.

'Of course. So, my little peachy girl, Polly went to Camisa for you. Maybe she even went across the street and got some of Grandpa's ice-cream too?'

Polly looked stricken. And she noticed Luana glared at the 'little peachy girl'.

'Well, if she did she can keep it because we bought some for her . . . Give her the ice-cream, Luana, there's a good girl.'

Luana handed Polly a plastic bag, scowling. Polly didn't blame her. Johnny treated her as if she was still about six.

'Come and sit down and have your salad, Luana. Are you still at school?'

Luana nodded.

'Exams this year?' Did they still have 'O' levels? Polly couldn't remember.

'Next.'

'Do you like school?'

Luana looked at her as if she was mad. Which I am, thought Polly, I used to hate it when people asked me these kinds of questions when I was a kid. But what kind of conversation should she make with Luana? She hadn't a clue. She tried a different tack.

'I'm an agent.'

Luana brightened visibly.

'Who do you look after?'

'Well, I'm just starting but we represent Lucy Richards.'

'What's she been in?'

'Nothing. She's a writer.'

'So you don't look after actors or rock stars or any famous people?'

'Nothing like that, no.'

Luana lapsed back into silence. She barely touched her lasagne. Johnny watched *Match of the Day* with a plate on his knee, which Polly thought didn't set a very good example but she didn't say anything.

'Good food,' he said vaguely with his eyes fixed on

the screen, 'no, no more, thanks. I'll have some of my ice-cream.'

Polly carried the lasagne into her tiny kitchen and felt the tears pricking. She'd worked so hard to make the food a success. She'd thrown away her first attempt and spent half the afternoon on the second. Johnny and Luana had only eaten a quarter of it between them. Polly herself had been too nervous to swallow a thing and now it looked like she'd be living off it for days.

'Polly's crying.' Luana was standing in the doorway watching her.

'Crying again!' Johnny came in and put his arm around her. 'How about some coffee?'

Johnny made desultory conversation while he drank his coffee. Luana sat looking miserable. At one point her eyes fixed on Polly's nails which were an unfortunate bright pink, a disastrous experiment with a new varnish that Polly had forgotten to remove.

'My mum uses that colour,' Luana informed her.

'Does she?'

'I think it's really disgusting.'

'Tell you the truth, I do too,' confessed Polly.

Once again Luana looked at her as if she was mad. If she didn't like it, why was she wearing it?

Why indeed, thought Polly.

'Come on, little one,' Johnny stood up. 'Time to go home. Say thank you to Polly, there's a good girl.'

'Don't keep saying that to her,' Polly turned on him without thinking, 'she's not a little kid.'

Luana didn't say thank you but she did reward Polly with a look of real respect and the first smile of the evening. Her big brown eyes lit up like shiny buttons. She's beautiful, thought Polly suddenly, and resisted the

45

urge to grab hold of the wiry black hair and plant a kiss on Luana's forehead.

'Come and see me again soon,' she called down the stairs after them, wondering if she dared ask Luana to be a bridesmaid.

Two days later Johnny called and said Edith had decided to go and live in Cornwall and take Luana with her.

For their honeymoon they went to Tuscany, to a farmhouse buried in the countryside outside Siena. It was built into the slope of a hill on several levels so that you could walk out of the bedroom on to the hillside and then down the slope and enter the kitchen or the living room below. It had belonged to Johnny's aunt, as had his London house.

'My father's little sister,' he explained, 'she married a rich man. A rich English businessman who wanted to spend his holidays in Tuscany so they bought this house. My father thought it was crazy. "You're from Napoli," he used to tell his sister, "why do you buy a house in the north?" He hated that she married an Englishman. He refused ever to go to her house – my house now – in Notting Hill. She couldn't have children so she left it to me. My father would've been furious to see me living there. Fortunately he died before she did.'

'And this house is yours too?' Polly envisaged family holidays in the future, imagined herself extending gracious invitations: 'What are your plans for the summer? Johnny and I will be in Tuscany as usual. How about coming down for a week or two? Bring the children . . .'

'No, it isn't mine,' said Johnny.

'Whose is it, then?'

'My aunt's rich English husband's.'

'But he's dead, isn't he?'

'Yeah.'

'So who did he leave it to?'

'Dunno.'

'What do you mean, you don't know? How did you get hold of it? How did we get in?'

'I've always had a key.'

'So we're here illegally? Someone – the rightful owner – might walk in at any moment?'

'Nobody knows we're here, if that's what you mean, except for the old woman in the village who looks after it and she won't say anything. I hope.'

Polly felt a lurch in the pit of her stomach. There it was again, the question she kept asking herself: what had she done? Who was this man she'd married?

They stayed in bed for four days and when they got up to pee or to fetch food from the kitchen, he insisted she remain naked. It was as if there was a magnet floating between them at all times. Some part of their bodies was always touching. In the kitchen it took them an hour to make a salad as they constantly interrupted each other with their fondling and kissing. When she went outside to search, naked, for herbs he pressed himself to her until she sank to the earth and pulled him into her, squashing the basil plants beneath them. He would not let her bathe that night because she smelt of basil and he lay alongside her, sniffing her skin.

'There's some lavender bushes round the other side of the house . . .' Polly suggested.

'Tomorrow, maybe.'

On the fifth night he took her to dinner in Siena. They sat outside at one of the restaurants in the Piazza del Campo and Johnny told her about the violent horse

47

race that was run in July called the Palio when the square was packed to capacity. Polly didn't much like the sound of it and she was pleased that they had come at a time when the square was relatively empty and she could gaze at the tall clock tower. But they couldn't finish their meal. Johnny's hands were stroking her shoulders, slipping down inside her top while she tried to eat her risotto.

'Come on, eat up, we'd better leave before I get arrested.'

She lay across the gear shift with her head in his lap as he drove home in the rented car. They left the car doors open in their urgent need to get to the bedroom.

'Lavender . . .' murmured Polly, 'we forgot.'

'Don't talk!' he silenced her and she smiled in the darkness. However much he might joke and tease her out of bed, for Johnny lovemaking was a serious business. It almost frightened her how much he seemed to immerse himself in the glorification of her body. If there was any talking it was his questions as to what she liked – This? Here? Higher? Lower? Only at the very last moment did he allow himself to lose control and then again she found the intensity of his release terrifying as well as exhilarating.

Afterwards he liked to talk.

I'm going to call my production company Polly Productions. You're going to bring me luck, Pol, I know it. I'm going to finally get something off the ground. Lord knows, I've been trying for long enough but from now on it's going to be different.' Once he started there was no stopping him. By day seven of their honeymoon he was the saviour of the British film industry. Polly was content to lie beside him in the darkness and listen to his excitement. 'I'm going to make want-to-see pictures.

Word-of-mouth pictures. The sort of pictures the press will latch on to early, create a buzz, and everyone will have to go and see them to find out what all the fuss is about. They'll be critical successes too but totally accessible. I'm going to develop scripts every major studio in Hollywood is going to want to make.'

'Where are you going to find them?' asked Polly, ever practical.

'Well, isn't it obvious?' He gathered her up in his arms and held her tight. 'That's where you come in. You'll quit that job you have and come and read scripts for me. You'll go out looking for properties, see the publishers, see the agents, working alongside me at Polly Productions.'

Polly couldn't help giggling.

'You can*not* call it Polly Productions. You just can't. It's silly.'

'Well, what do you suggest then?'

'You really want to call it after me?'

'I really do.' He gave her a squeeze.

'Well since I have to face up to the fact that I'm now Polly de Soto and no longer Polly Atwell, why don't you call it PDS Productions. It sounds more heavyweight somehow.'

'You know you're right. PDS. I like it. PDS. Looking forward to your new job as story editor at PDS?'

'Actually, no.'

She felt him tense.

'You don't want to work for me?' She couldn't make out the hurt little boy look in the darkness but she knew it was there.

'The thing is, Johnny – and I was going to discuss it with you, of course, but you have to admit we've sort of had other things on our minds – I've been offered a promotion at Patrick Fisher & Dunbar. They're willing to make me a kind of baby agent, a few minor clients of my own to look after, no one important but it's a start.'

'Baby agent. Oh, well if that's what you want.'

'Johnny, don't be like that. It's an opening for me. I'll learn about the agency business.'

He was silent for a while.

'Johnny?'

'OK, Pol. I think you should take it. They're big, you'll have access to a lot of material at an early stage. That could be very useful to me.'

'Of course, and I could always read stuff for you on the side,' said Polly, bending over backwards to please him as usual in her relief. Why did she always do this? She'd all but accepted the job before the wedding but somehow only Johnny's approval would make it a reality.

'I'm going to make it big, Pol, and I want you there with me. Don't you ever forget that. When I go up for my Oscar I want you by my side.'

'Johnny, what about Edith? Did she help you in your work?'

He didn't answer, just shifted over on to his side, away from her.

'Johnny?'

He rolled back and pinned her down.

'Just don't ask me about Edith, OK? There's only three things you need to know about her. One: I'm no longer with her, I'm married to you. She's the past, you're the present. Two: she's a very sad lady but it's nothing to do with you so stay out of it. Three: any mention of her name is always going to put me in a very bad mood, so don't say I didn't warn you.'

'But if we're going to see Luana won't I have to speak to her?'

'What have I just said? Drop it, Polly. If anyone has to speak to her about Luana, I will. I'm her father. End of story.'

He fell into a deep sleep after he had made love to her again but Polly lay awake. Although he was always saying what a wonderful father he was going to be, so far there had been no mention of children during their honeymoon, no mention of that side of their future and she was beginning to realise why. What was the point of contemplating children with Johnny when she was going to have her work cut out dealing with the fact that, despite his determination and his ambition, Johnny was in many ways still a kid himself.

To her immense surprise Polly found herself adapting to life as Mrs Johnny de Soto with ease once they arrived back in London. Having never had to cope with more than a studio apartment she was suddenly confronted with the running of a house. True, it was not exactly palatial but barely a week went by when Polly did not stop to give thanks to Johnny's childless aunt for leaving him a place to live. What they would have done otherwise she dreaded to think. Her salary at the literary agency was not exactly impressive and although Johnny appeared to have a little money of his own (which was just as well since he didn't seem to be earning any) Polly had never quite discovered where it came from. Her father had quizzed her on the subject before her wedding and while she had managed to fob him off with vague explanations, Polly was still a little uneasy. Meanwhile, another thing she was grateful for was the existence of a cleaner – Donnatella, an Italian who spoke no English, supplied by Johnny's mother – since there were four bedrooms, two bathrooms, a living room and a dining room running the full length of the ground floor, connected by dividing doors, and a large kitchen. The vast master bedroom on the first floor ran from the front of the house to the back above the living room/dining room. A guest bedroom lay across the landing and Polly turned this into a little sitting room she and Johnny used in the evening for TV suppers.

Johnny, true to his word, started PDS Productions. What Polly hadn't bargained for was the fact that he would start it at their dining-room table. His first step was to kill the script for *The End*. Someone had apparently told him it sounded too like another film. Polly wondered sadly about the fate of the struggling scriptwriter in the Chelsea basement who presumably now wouldn't even get his peanuts.

She needn't have worried. In the ensuing months the young man, a willowy youth by the name of Lawrence Bedford, was forever in their dining room. Polly would arrive home from work to find the ground floor a hive of activity. PDS was up and running and Polly was beginning to see why. It wasn't only her Uncle Matthew who found Johnny 'an engaging fellow'. He clearly had no trouble getting people's attention. No end of young writers and directors appeared to want to work with him (despite the fact that he had not yet produced a film), often after what appeared to be their first meeting with him. Polly didn't know any of them but she was content to rush in and out of the kitchen with plates of sandwiches and beer and then sit quietly in a corner while Johnny and his team talked 'development'.

They tried having a few of the young men from Norfolk and Polly's unmarried girlfriends (except for Joan, whom Johnny had banned from his house) over for dinner but Johnny never opened his mouth so they didn't repeat the exercise. The place was filled with Johnny's movie crowd daily and Polly didn't get much of a chance to open her mouth but somehow she didn't mind. She felt needed even if no one spoke to her. It didn't seem to matter, since she had the progress she was making at Patrick Fisher & Dunbar to be proud of. Very soon now she would be starting to look out for some authors of her own to represent at the agency.

One night Polly went home around 6.30 to find the living room and the dining room deserted for the first time since she had moved in. She started upstairs to have a bath but stopped on the landing when she heard voices. Polly was angry. She had created what they called 'the little sitting room' for her and Johnny to use in the evenings, a private cosy retreat for just the two of them. She was outraged that Johnny should take someone in there. She was about to stride into the room but she stopped on the threshold when she heard Lawrence Bedford say:

'It's a natural, Johnny. Women are obsessed with finding Mr Right. Subconsciously they're looking for him everywhere in all areas of their lives. So here's this guy and he's a playboy, glamorous as hell, right? They all fall for him, rich women, poor women alike. But the reality is he's *Mr Wrong*! He's a serial killer. Not always women, but mostly. Then there's this detective. He knows Mr Wrong is his guy. At least, he suspects it but he can't prove it. So he sets a woman cop to trap him and this is a woman cop he loves, right? But there's this one big problem.'

'What's that?' asked Polly, coming into the room and seeing Lawrence by the fireplace. 'Hi Lawrence, haven't seen you in a while. How are you?'

'I'm fine, Polly. How about you? I've just had this

great idea for a picture so of course I had to come right over and tell Johnny about it.' He spilled some of his drink and dabbed vaguely at himself. Polly smiled. Once he stopped pitching his idea Lawrence reverted to his usual awkward gangly self.

'Of course you did. Now, you've got Mr Wrong the serial killer and the detective who puts his girlfriend, the woman he loves, on the case to snare him. You were about to tell us the problem.'

'She's not his girlfriend. At least not yet,' corrected Lawrence. 'He wants her to be but he hasn't done anything about it yet.'

'Get on with it, Lawrence,' growled Johnny, who was slouched in front of the television with the sound turned down. 'What's the problem? It's clearly the hook.'

'She – the cop – falls for Mr Wrong too.'

'So what happens?' demanded Polly and Johnny almost in unison.

'Well, I suppose the detective saves her just in time and right at the last minute she realises that he is the man she really loves. He's Mr Right,' Lawrence finished lamely.

Johnny mimed playing a violin. 'Television!' was all he said.

'Johnny, it's not, it's wonderful. Think about it: romance, murder, woman in jeopardy, cop hero . . .' Polly clapped her hands in excitement. She stared admiringly at Lawrence. He was absolutely correct about women looking for Mr Right. Her girlfriends – with the exception of Joan – never stopped telling her how lucky she was to have found Johnny. Sometimes she thought about what she would have done if he hadn't come along when he did. It bothered her that she always arrived at the same conclusion: she'd be on her own. Mr Right had never been part of her plan for her future. Dream heroes existed in books and movies just like the one Lawrence had just described. She might have married eventually, but Polly had grown up thinking that marriage was something that would happen to other women, not to her. How wrong she had been. She had found Mr Right right away, ha ha!

'What are you smirking at?' asked Johnny.

She looked at him sitting there with a morose look on his face.

'I'm not interested,' he snapped. 'TV cop movies, that's all it is. Sorry, Lawrence, nice try and all that. Look, let me fill your glass. There is something I want to talk to you about while you're here. Polly, what's for supper? Enough for Lawrence?'

'Always,' smiled Polly, feeling sorry for Lawrence, 'and you're wrong about his idea.'

'Wrong about Mr Wrong. Oh Yeah? Well, wait till you hear about my idea.' Johnny was up on his feet, slapping Lawrence on the back, kissing Polly on the nose. 'Wait till you hear about my idea, pretty Pol.'

Polly served the casserole into the big wide soup plates and handed them round the table. She gave Lawrence an extra large helping because she thought he looked like he needed building up. Johnny was now in fine form, shovelling his meal into his mouth and wagging his finger at them.

'Wait till you hear,' he kept saying, 'I'll tell you over dessert. You'll love it. Love it.'

Polly delved in the freezer for some ice-cream. She hadn't planned on pudding but since Johnny clearly wasn't about to divulge his great idea until she produced one, she had to come up with something.

'So here it is: werewolves and bikers.' Johnny waved

his napkin in the air triumphantly. They stared at him with blank faces. 'Kid came to see me this afternoon with a proposal,' he continued. 'He wants to direct it and he's looking for someone to package it for him.'

'Werewolves and bikers,' repeated Lawrence dumbly.

'That's it. You write it. I develop it. The kid directs. Youth market. Up and coming.'

'Johnny, could you maybe tell us a little more?' Polly gave him another scoop of ice-cream to encourage him.

'Where'd you get this stuff, Pol?'

'Sainsbury's.'

'Don't touch it, Lawrence. It's poison. My old man makes ice-cream for thirty years and she has to go to Sainsbury's.'

'Johnny . . .' Polly warned.

'It's dead simple. There's this biker and he's part of a gang and he's trying to date a girl who is sort of dating a guy from another rival gang but he has this problem . . .'

'Him too . .'

'Every time his bike reaches a certain speed he turns into a werewolf so when he finally makes it with the chick and she's riding away with him, pursued by the other gang, he can only go so far – '

'Johnny, you can't be serious?' Polly's mouth had dropped open. She had never heard anything so stupid.

'I'm perfectly serious. It's *The Wild One* meets *West Side Story* crossed with Michael Jackson's *Thriller*. The kids'll love it.'

'It's pure popcorn,' argued Polly. 'Lawrence's idea had such a ring of truth to it. Women all over the world will identify with it. Have you any idea how many women fall for disastrous men? To have him be a serial killer makes it perfect. You have to see that.'

'Polly, you're over-reacting in a typically emotionally feminine way. You have to look ahead. "The Wild Wolf" – or maybe we should call it "The Wolf One", what do you think? – incorporates everything the kids go for these days. We'll add a strong rock soundtrack. It's a natural. The video sale will be huge. I tried it out on Luana, she thought it sounded great.'

'When did you see Luana? You never told me you'd seen her.' Polly was quite agitated. For some reason Johnny kept quiet about his meetings with his daughter. She only came to London sporadically and he never brought her to the house. Polly tortured herself with the thought that whenever he saw Luana, he also saw the mysterious Edith.

'I talked to her in Cornwall, for God's sake. On the phone, OK? I only heard about this project today. Now, Lawrence, how about it? Shall I give you the treatment, see what you think? I'd love you to write it.'

Neither of them noticed Lawrence quietly getting to his feet, pushing his chair into place and creeping out of the dining room. He paused at the entrance to the hall.

'If it's OK, I think I'll be on my way. Great meal, Polly. Thanks. See you.'

And he was gone.

Polly called him the next day.

'Lawrence, I don't know what to say. Johnny seems to have taken leave of his senses. There's only one suggestion I can make and it's the only area where I might be able to be of help. Have you ever thought of writing fiction? I can't get 'Mr Wrong' out of my mind. It's such a great story. Why don't you write it as a novel first?'

Polly was very aware that since the wedding they had seen very little of Carla de Soto, Johnny's mother. Johnny didn't seem to care.

'Don't worry about her Pol. She has a life, believe me. Loads of little ladies just like her, all dressed in black, all banging on about Italia, endless widows' get-togethers in tiny kitchens all over Soho. If she wanted to come over here we'd know about it. She's probably just waiting for you to produce bambinos and then we'll never see the back of her.'

'What about . . . ?'

'All in good time, all in good time. I can't think about having children while I'm in the middle of getting PDS Productions off the ground, now can I?'

And I'm not ready to have a baby until I've become a fully-fledged agent, thought Polly, but that wouldn't come into Johnny's equation.

'Actually I was going to say what about if I ask her if I can go over and see her in Soho?'

'You can ask. Why you'd want to is beyond me, but

go ahead, ask, go and learn how to be a little old Italian widow. After all, you'll be one yourself one day.'

But Carla – when Polly went to see her – had other ideas. She welcomed Polly into her apartment on the top two floors of the house in Old Compton Street above the old De Soto ice-cream shop which had now been expanded into a delicatessen. Polly was fascinated by the evidence of real style in the choice of décor. Heavy old Tuscan farmhouse furniture blended in with lighter Conran pieces and here and there she spotted some beautiful antiques. Carla served lunch in the kitchen, and the round table was laid with crisp white linen and colourful hand-painted pottery. Carla produced a simple but delicious lunch of *prosciutto crudo* and thin slices of *soprassata* sausage followed by pasta with her own *sugo di pomodoro*, a tomato sauce the recipe for which she wrote down for Polly.

'I am so pleased you came to see me.' Polly noticed the old lady's English was much better when she was alone, without her son to ridicule her. She also noticed how elegant Carla was. She might be small and dumpy and dressed in black but when Polly looked closely she realised it wasn't just any old black dress but something with a solid Italian label and her white hair was soft and silky and gathered up in an expert chignon. She wore tiny pearl earrings and her make-up was immaculate. On a visit to the bathroom Polly saw the little white Clarins jars and realised her mother-in-law was a woman who took care of herself.

'I always knew Johnny would marry a proper English girl.'

'Were you secretly hoping he would marry a nice Italian Catholic girl?'

'His father, yes. Me, no. There was no point in

60

hoping. Johnny was not Italian. I told you this when we first met. You are an English couple, an unusual English couple maybe, but you and he are not Italian. Johnny has Italian blood. He plays at being Italian when it suits him. You will see. But he is not like his father.'

'Tell me about his father. I'm sorry I never knew him.'

Carla uncrossed her tiny feet. Polly noticed a pair of smart shoes in soft Italian leather. Carla caught her glance and laughed.

'Yes, I buy nice things. I am a rich woman. My Mauro was very successful even if it was in a boring way. At least, I found it boring. Maybe you don't know De Soto ice-cream like you know Walls or Häagen-Dazs but you go into an Italian restaurant and they give you ice-cream and nine times out of ten it will be my Mauro's. Italians know it. Italian delicatessens, everywhere – here, Manchester, Glasgow. Johnny's cousin took over the business because Johnny was not interested. He only want to make films. But he is happy to live off his share in the company. But you asked about his father. He was successful in his own way but he was also very sad. In the beginning he thought he come to England for a very short time to help his older brother with the business. But his older brother die and we have to stay here.' Carla had begun to mix her tenses, a sign, Polly realised, that she was uncomfortable. That meant her own son must make this proud little woman uncomfortable. Carla continued. 'My husband always missed Italy. He always looked forward to the day he would go back. He was always waiting for Johnny to take over his business then he could leave London.'

Polly was horrified. 'You mean he waited in vain?

Surely it must have been obvious that Johnny wanted to do something else. Why didn't his father go back?'

'There was no one to take over. Johnny's cousin was still in Italy, still too young. I knew how Johnny was but his father didn't understand. His father was a quiet man with no ambition beyond carrying out family business. Sadly he carried it out until he die. But Johnny is different. Johnny want more. Johnny want the world.' She smiled at Polly.

'Johnny is like me. I love my Mauro but in many ways for me he was too slow. Always sitting here wanting to go back to Italy. Never wanting to go forward, maybe to America. Everyone wonder why, now Mauro is dead, I don't go back but I love it here in London. I have lots of friends. Johnny thinks I just sit and have coffee with other Italian widows but he's wrong. I have other friends, but don't tell him. It's our secret – between women.' And the old lady actually winked. Can she be taking such good care of herself, Polly wondered, because she's on the lookout for Mr Right Number 2? 'Here, have some *biscotti*. I make espresso. So I tell you, Polly, Johnny is a bit crazy, I know, but he is not slow like his father, he is fast, he's ambitious and he always hope for the best.'

'He's an optimist.' Just as well, thought Polly wryly. He hasn't exactly got very far. He might as well have hope to keep him going, not to mention a little family money.

'Just like me,' Carla was becoming positively giggly now, 'I have one dream and I know it will come true. I want to stand up there beside Johnny when he receive his Oscar.'

'You and me both,' said Polly. 'Will there be room for me on his other side?'

'Only if you keep up with him.' The smile on Carla's face evaporated. 'It will take the two of you. Johnny cannot do it on his own. I told you, there is a little money for him from the business but soon he is going to have to provide for himself.'

'Does he realise this?'

'You know Johnny. I tell him but he only listens to what he wants to hear so I mean it, Polly, everything will be fine for you both but only if you look after him and keep up with him. Not like Edith.'

Polly pounced. 'Tell me about Edith. What is she like?'

But it was no good.

'Johnny call me when he know you are coming to see me. He ask me not to talk about Edith. She in his history now.'

Poor Carla looked very uncomfortable indeed.

I might have known, thought Polly, and wondered just how long it would be before Johnny's family income ran out. Would she find herself supporting them both all on her own?

Johnny went into action. He raised $50,000 development money for *The Wolf One*, split between ten people investing $5,000 each. The deal was that they would get 10 per cent of the net profits of the film split between them.

He was never off the phone. At night while Polly was trying to get to sleep beside him he would talk to potential investors way into the small hours. If this was how he went about getting the relatively small development money, Polly dreaded to think what it would be like when he set about raising the production money.

He found another writer and commissioned a first-draft screenplay. When it was finished he showed it to Cruise, the lead singer with Cruise Missile. Cruise's real name was Billy Powers. He was a degenerate Liverpool heavy metal star with a notorious cocaine habit. Cruise had his girlfriend, Belle – who was really Lady Annabel Creightmore, educated at St Paul's with a first in English from Girton, and Cruise's supplier – read the script to him and then explained it to him scene by scene. When he had finally grasped the plot he called his manager and conveyed his desire to star in it. No one had ever approached him to be in a film before for the simple reason that it was widely believed that he had little brain power left, assuming he had had a brain in the first place. To play the Wolf One, he didn't need one, just the ability to ride a motorbike – preferably a Harley Davidson Fat Boy, something for which, luckily, he had a remarkable gift.

After a few well-placed phone calls by Johnny, the press went to work.

CRUISE TO STAR IN MAJOR MOTION PICTURE

Heavy Metal idol Cruise of Cruise Missile says he won't need stunt man for his role as the Wolf One. The 22-year-old Liverpool star says he will perform his own stunts for the picture. 'I'm going to give them music, I'm going to give them action,' promises Cruise.

Polly sat at her desk at Patrick Fisher & Dunbar and waded through the tabloids, telling herself that if this was what Johnny wanted then it was what she wanted too. But then the phone rang and the switchboard informed her that a very disturbed Rebecca Price was on the line and Polly knew the tabloid stories were only just the beginning of what looked like turning out to be one of those days.

Patrick Dunbar was away in America. Rebecca Price was one of his biggest clients. Up to now she had written megasellers, long detailed historical sagas set in Cornwall. They had each sold well over half a million copies in paperback. The problem, if it could be viewed as such, was that Rebecca Price had tired of writing this kind of book and was demanding to be taken more seriously. Polly felt she had every right. Although she had been categorised as a historical writer, Rebecca Price's prose was definitely a cut above that of other writers in the same genre. Her publishers, however, were decidedly nervous. Change terrified them as it did many large publishing houses led by their marketing departments. Marketing and sales directors thought retrospectively. The idea of a bestselling author delivering something new and different was enough to send them into instant panic. When they told the world that their flagship title on the Spring list would be 'the new Rebecca Price' what they really meant was, 'Here's more of the same, everyone knows what they're getting. Go out and flog it like you did the last one. Piece of cake!' The notion that they might have to use their non-existent creative powers and market Rebecca as a new kind of author altogether was just not on.

'The old bag's going through the menopause, must be,' Rebecca's publisher had told Patrick before he left for New York. 'Maybe we'll just have to bite the bullet and accept we won't have a new Rebecca Price next year and wait until her wretched hormones calm down.'

Polly was outraged. Rebecca Price was forty-nine years old and it was possible that she was in the throes of the menopause but to make it an excuse for her perfectly rational decision to write a different type of novel was ludicrous.

Still, it wouldn't do to upset either Rebecca or her publisher and with five hours to go before she could call Patrick in New York for guidance, Polly took Rebecca's call with apprehension.

'Rebecca?'

'Polly hello how are you is Patrick there?' Despite her proficiency with the written word, Rebecca Price invariably ran all her spoken sentences into one.

'No, I'm sorry, he's not. He left for New York yesterday. He won't be back for two or three weeks.'

'Of course I'd forgotten, Aahhh ...' Rebecca's sigh blew down the line in desperation, 'have we had a reaction yet do you know Polly?'

Polly knew she ought to let it wait until Patrick came back, that he should be the one to break the news to Rebecca that her publishers were holding out for 'more of the same', yet she knew that Patrick would never tell Rebecca the whole story and Polly felt that Rebecca deserved to hear it. And then, as she was trying to think how to phrase it, Rebecca beat her to it.

'They want another *Dark Shores of Tregarra* or another *Penhaligon*, don't they?' she said, referring to two of her earlier successes. 'Don't they understand that I want to break out of that type of thing? I want people to realise that I have something to say about the world we live in now rather than Cornwall in the last century. I want to be reviewed.'

'It might mean less money,' Polly warned.

'I'm rolling in it. It wouldn't matter a damn.'

'And it might mean changing publishers.'

'Well for goodness sake of course it will if all they want is more of the same. I'll have to find someone who's prepared to gamble with the new. Do you think it will be hard Polly?'

'Not in the slightest. Rebecca, have you any idea how many requests a year we receive from publishers asking if there's a chance you'll move? Now, I shall have to give them one last chance to change their minds about their attitude to your new plans and if they still say no I think you should come up to London for lunch with Patrick so we can draw up a list of publishers to whom we can submit the new outline.'

'Well you must be there for lunch too Polly.'

'Yes, well, maybe.' Polly was suddenly beginning to wonder what Patrick would make of her suggestion. Maybe he would have been able to talk Rebecca into yet another Cornish saga and a hefty advance to go with it. But once again Rebecca Price second-guessed her.

'I shall want you to be at the lunch Polly because I trust you and I want you to handle me from now on. I'll let you into a secret. I know Patrick would have tried to make me write another saga and I'll tell you something – if he had I'd have left Fisher & Dunbar in spite of all they've done for me. You say there are publishers after me. Well has it ever occurred to dear Patrick bless his balding head that there are plenty of other agents after me too? But I'll stay put Polly on one condition. You take care of me from now on.'

'But I'm only just starting to take on clients of my own. I've been Patrick's assistant up till very recently,' blurted Polly.

'Rubbish. He ought to be yours. Bye dear.'

Polly sailed home that night on the top of a 31 bus, desperate to tell Johnny her news. Rebecca Price was hers. She'd saved the day for Patrick Fisher & Dunbar. She was about to become a fully-fledged agent. She walked up Westbourne Park Road, swinging her book bag in her excitement, but when she finally arrived home and turned the key in the front door she was greeted by a heavy silence in the hall. There wasn't even a light on downstairs. She found a note propped up against the toaster in the kitchen.

Darling Pol,
Tried to call you this morning but you were on a long call to Rebecca someone and they said you couldn't be disturbed, not even for me! Have had to

go to Los Angeles. V. last minute. Chance of raising money for Wolf One. Staying at Chateau Marmont on Sunset. Will call on arrival. Don't be lonesome.

All my love. J.

Polly climbed into bed at nine o'clock and tried to watch television. Extraordinary though it seemed to her this was the first time in their marriage that she had been separated from Johnny and the worst thing was that she had had no time to prepare herself for it. She was amazed at how quickly her euphoria over Rebecca Price evaporated when there was no Johnny waiting for her to share it with. She could imagine the conversation. He would be lying in the bath, she would be crouched on the floor beside him, reaching out to pass him his whisky, the soap, the ashtray, whatever he wanted.

'So who is this Rebecca Price woman?'

'Johnny, you must have heard of her. She's been a number one bestseller for years. Don't you remember *Penhaligon*?'

'The LWT series? A thirteen parter, three or four years back? It was huge.'

'Yes, they did make a TV series of it. Rebecca hated it.'

'You should get her to do something contemporary. No call for costume drama. Too expensive. No one could afford the budget. I'd never get it set up.'

'Johnny, you haven't been listening. That's exactly what she's going to do and I'm going to be her agent . . .'

'Will you get the commission? Personally?'

'Well, no . . .'

'Make sure they give you a whopping great rise and show me an outline as soon as you've got a first draft.'

No 'Well done, Pol' or 'I'm so pleased for you, Pol!'

but even so she missed him. She could almost hear her mother's voice: 'We mustn't boast about our achievements, Polly. We must let other people congratulate us and even then we must pretend it's nothing.' The trouble was, Polly had always thought to herself, if you didn't tell people what you'd achieved, how on earth could they congratulate you? And in the end no one ever seemed to congratulate her anyway. Looking back, the only thing her friends had ever congratulated her on was Johnny.

She wished he was with her now and arranged his pillows down the middle of the bed, hugging them to her as a poor substitute. He might view everything she did in terms of how it affected him but at least he was interested, at least he encouraged her. Keep up with him, his mother had said. Well, she would but in her own way. He'd be a successful producer and she'd be an equally successful literary agent right along with him.

It was only when she woke up the next morning that she realised Johnny hadn't rung her on arrival in LA as he'd promised.

Johnny was away for nearly a month during which time Polly received two or three telephone calls a week and in each one his mood was more euphoric than the last. To begin with, Polly was mystified.

'He says they've put him in a bungalow at the Chateau,' she told Patrick at the office, 'he sounds deliriously happy about it. A bungalow in a castle. What on earth is he on about?'

'He means exactly what he says, Polly. They're self-contained bungalows away from the hotel itself – which is called the Chateau Marmont – and they're right by the pool. Of course, he really ought to be at the Beverly

Hills Hotel or the Beverly Wilshire if he wants them to take him seriously.' Patrick was rather proud of his knowledge of America, not that he'd ever been further than New York. Another part of the agency took care of the film deals.

'Why aren't you staying at the Beverly Wilshire or the Beverly Hills Hotel?' Polly couldn't resist asking after getting an earful of Johnny's lunch at the MGM commissary with Jane Fonda.

'Much cooler at the Chateau, more of a funky crowd around here, more into *The Wolf One*, saw Leonard Cohen at the pool yesterday . . .'

'I had no idea he was still with us.'

'Oh he is, Pol, he certainly is. He thinks Cruise is really amazing.'

'Was she wearing a leotard?'

'Who? Oh, Jane. Don't be silly, Pol, it was lunchtime but it is incredible, she looks as young as you.'

'Thanks,' said Polly drily.

By the second week he was into the lifestyle.

'It's all so outdoors, I can't believe it. Everyone's got two cars, at least four bedrooms, a garden, a maid, a pool – '

'And a psychiatrist, so I've heard,' said Polly.

'They call them analysts. They kind of become your friend. Everyone's so friendly and hospitable. I'm going to people's houses all the time, Pol. When does that happen to us in London?'

'Well, never, because you're always inviting them to ours.'

'Imagine it, Pol, when I'm really off and running. We'll move out here and have this great lifestyle.'

'It sounds like a great place for kids.'

'You're right. You're absolutely right! Luana would love it.'

'No, I meant our kids.'

'Yeah. 'Course. They'd love it too. Not trying to tell me you're pregnant, by any chance, Pol?'

'No.'

'Phew! Would have been very bad timing. I've thought it all out. We ought to do a movie then a baby, a movie then a baby. Soon as *The Wolf One*'s in the can we'll start a family. What do you say?'

What could she say?

While Johnny was safely out of the way in California, Polly rang Joan and invited her to lunch one weekend.

'I'll cook us something sinful and delicious and we can kick off our shoes and have a good old gossip.'

But Joan would have none of it.

'Darling, you know I can't bear home cooking. Much too fattening. Let's doll ourselves up to the nines and go out and be seen. Tell you what, I'll do you a huge favour and come up to Notting Hill Gate then we can go 192 and you won't have to move an inch.

Polly understood the subtext. 192 Kensington Park Road was a fashionable media restaurant and Joan could bounce up and down from the table and go hopping all over the room, networking frantically. As usual Polly gave in.

Polly ordered a starter followed by risotto. Joan ordered a salad. Polly was wearing a long T-shirt and jeans. Joan was wearing a Sonia Rykiel jacket and a pair of baggy linen Italian trousers. Joan had a tan even though she hadn't been anywhere as far as Polly knew.

'Sunbeds! Polly, don't you use them? What do you do about looking pale in the winter months?'

'Nothing.'

'Doesn't Johnny complain?'

'He hasn't yet.'

'Does he ever see you starkers?'

'He's my husband. Of course he – '

'Oh, never mind. What's he doing in California anyway?'

'I'm not really sure. Seeing people about getting money for his film, I think.'

'Typical, Polly. You're so unclued up. And why aren't you out there with him, swanning around LA, getting a bit of sun while he's in meetings, doing the producer's wife number?'

'Well, he never asked me to go with him.'

'That's exactly what I mean, Polly. You're such a pushover. Why didn't you ask? In fact what you should have done was just announce you were going with him, got his secretary to book your flight and everything.'

'But he doesn't have a secretary. He works from home, from our dining-room table.'

'Talk about Mickey Mouse productions!'

'But in a way it's just as well I didn't go because I would have missed Rebecca Price.'

'Miss who?'

'Rebecca Price. She's a wonderful saga writer who wants to move up a notch . . .'

'Is she good looking? Who's she married to? Do they live in a beautiful home? Does she collect art? Whose clothes does she wear?'

'Oh, Rebecca's beautiful. She must be over fifty but she's still got this wonderful rosy skin. She's married to a retired vet and they live in this rambling old place on the Welsh coast with dogs and cats and sheep and ponies wandering all over the place. She collects brass rubbings, I think, and she once confided to Patrick Fisher that she wears her husband's old clothes because they're the only ones she can get into these days.'

'Polly, what on earth made you think this woman might be the subject of a *Vogue* feature?'

'Oh, she'd be quite wrong for *Vogue*. She'd hate it. She's terribly shy in many ways.'

'Then why are we talking about her?'

'Because I'm going to be her agent. It's a wonderful break for me.'

'Rubbish! How do you think it's going to sound, Polly? People ask you what you do. You say I'm a literary agent. They ask who are your clients and you come out with this old bat who collects brass rubbings and lives in the back of beyond with a lot of smelly animals and wears her husband's old clothes. Why can't you represent the new Martin Amis?'

'I'd have to find him first. It takes time but now I'm starting to take on my own clients I'll be on the lookout everywhere. I'm going to write to – '

'Darling, of course you are. I'll alert the media, as they say. Oh, there's Duncan. I must just go and say hello. Now he's a real agent. He looks after Hector O'Neill and we're doing a feature on him in the autumn.'

By the time Joan came back – rather quickly Polly noticed, Duncan-the-real-agent didn't seem to have much time to spare for her – Polly had been joined by a publishing editor who had been lunching at the next table. He stood up to let Joan sit down.

'Forgive the interruption but I couldn't help eavesdropping. When I heard that Polly here is to represent

Rebecca Price I had to try and persuade her to give me first look at the new book. It's a real coup for you, Polly. Congratulations! Sorry, you are . . . ?'

'Oh, this is my friend Joan Brock. She works on *Vogue*. She's the features . . .'

'I'm features assistant,' said Joan quickly. Polly never read *Vogue* so she'd always spun her a line, told her she was features editor. But this bloke looked like he might check her out.

'But I expect she'll be features editor very soon,' said Polly cheerfully, totally unaware that for once she'd actually managed to put Joan down.

Johnny came back on a major high and walked through the door on a particularly hot July morning before Polly had left for work.

'We gotta get AC,' he said, dumping his bags in the hall, shrugging off his jacket and loosening his tie. He had stripped off his shirt before Polly had rushed downstairs and into his arms.

'What's that?' Polly had only ever heard of AC/DC, an expression she believed was used to describe someone who swung both ways sexually. What had Johnny got into while he had been away?

'Air conditioning,' he murmured into her ear before he bit it, 'everyone's got it in LA.'

'Did you really have lunch with Jane Fonda?' she asked as he started upstairs, unzipping his trousers as he went.

'You bet! Well, she was at the next table.' He sat down at the top of the stairs and grinned at her, holding out his hand. 'Come on, Pol, time for a quick one. Just to show you how much I've missed you.'

It was a very quick one. He came almost as soon as

he entered her but Polly didn't mind. His excitement was infectious and she understood it because she was excited about something herself. Today was the day she was to have lunch with Patrick and Rebecca Price to talk about which publishers should be shown Rebecca's new book. Much to Polly's relief, Patrick had been wholly supportive of the way she had handled Rebecca.

'The most important thing is that she stays with the agency and from where I'm sitting it looks as if that's all down to you. You deserve her, Polly. She'll be your first proper client.' Polly knew she had really lucked out. Her first submission of a Polly de Soto book would be by a megaselling author.

Johnny had launched into a long monologue from the shower:

'So I took it to Tri-Star, I took it to Paramount, I took it to Orion. I was talking about a budget of $8–9 million. I told them I could get half of that in foreign pre-sales. Cruise has got a European tour coming up, should be a sell-out. His American tour last year was dynamite. Dy-na-mite!

Anyway, Orion really went for it. They love Cruise. They love Jason, that's the kid who'll direct. Of course they only know his commercials but they love the idea of him . . . so anyway, it looks like it's a go, pending one small thing.'

'What's that?' asked Polly, trying to sound interested.

'We still have to cast the female lead. Cruise's love interest. She's got to be American and she's got to be bankable. As soon as the rewrites are done the script is going out to Demi Moore, Rosanna Arquette, Susan Sarandon (she can age down), Alley Sheedy, Debra Winger, Carrie Fisher, Kathleen Turner . . .'

'To play the teenage girlfriend of a werewolf?' asked Polly incredulously, 'but then, what do I know?'

They all said no. Johnny threatened suicide.

'Why don't you get Cherry Fox to play her?' suggested Luana who was staying with them for a couple of days. She was having braces fitted on her teeth by the London dentist she had always gone to. Apparently she refused to go to a Cornish dentist.

'Who on earth is Cherry Fox?' asked Polly.

'Oh *Polly*!' Luana and Johnny accused her in unison.

'Well, sorry, I know I'm just a fuddy-duddy old books person but you're just going to have to tell me.'

'She's a model. Only about nineteen years old but a smash hit both here and in New York. The kids are crazy about her. Luana, you're a genius. You ought to go and work with Annie Martin. She doesn't appear to have an original idea in her head.'

'Who's she?' asked Luana.

'Oh *Luana*! Don't you know who Annie Martin is?' teased Polly.

'She's the casting director on *The Wolf One*,' Johnny explained.

'Casting director,' repeated Luana thoughtfully. 'If you get Cherry Fox can I come up again and meet her?'

'Johnny, get a move on,' Polly told him. 'They called from the production office. You were due there an hour ago.'

Johnny had finally vacated the dining room now *The Wolf One* was in pre-production and had rented offices in Soho. He had also hired himself an assistant called Rachel who had appeared the previous day to escort Luana to the dentist.

'Hardly the sort of work she was expecting,' commented Polly. 'Treat her like a skivvy and you'll lose her.'

'No I won't,' Johnny assured her. 'I laid it on the line when I hired her. She gets to take care of all my personal shit – dry cleaning, appointments to get my hair cut, getting the car serviced, stuff like that. You should be pleased, means I won't ask you to do it although in fact I do need her today so if you wouldn't mind taking Luana back to the dentist. . . She's so terrified of having her teeth done if she doesn't have a minder she'll never get there.'

What if I'd had an important meeting, thought Polly, who would take care of Luana then? As it happened she'd deliberately taken the day off in order to be able to spend time with Luana. She had not exactly got off to a good start with her stepdaughter at their only meeting before the wedding and she hadn't even spoken to Luana on the phone since. This visit to London was a golden opportunity for her to establish a bond for the future.

The visit to the dentist was pretty hair-raising and Polly felt unbearably sorry for Luana. No girl should still have to wear braces when she was bound to have started thinking about boys. Besides, Luana appeared to be using the braces as an excuse to maintain an uncomfortable silence no matter how hard Polly tried to draw her out of it. Then, as they were going down the Haymarket, she suddenly came to life.

'McDonalds!' she breathed with more respect than Polly had seen her show for anything, 'please, Polly?'

'Those braces you've just had put in, will they be able to stand the strain of a Big Mac?'

Luana nodded. Polly relented. 'Here,' she handed

Luana her purse, 'you can get me some chips while you're at it but don't tell your father.'

'And you won't tell Mum either, will you?'

Polly refrained from pointing out that she never spoke to Luana's mum. 'Edith? Tell her what?'

'That I've had a Big Mac.'

'Doesn't she approve?'

'She'd die!'

'Well, in that case . . .'

'Polly, I adore you . . .'

Polly was amazed at the endearment. She's so scrawny, she thought, watching Luana running up to the counter.

'Want another?' she asked when Luana had demolished her burger in seconds like a dog wolfing its dinner and was rewarded with a look of utter devotion in Luana's eyes.

'Why doesn't Edith let you have them?'

'She says they're poison. They're not organic.'

'No, I don't suppose they are,' mused Polly. 'Tell me, darling, what does Edith do with herself all day in Cornwall?'

If neither Johnny nor Carla would tell her about Edith, Polly was forced to turn to Luana.

'She cries.'

'She what?'

'She cries,' said Luana beginning to look rather uncomfortable.

'Why? What about? Does she miss your father?'

'Oh, probably. But she was miserable long before that. She can always find something to make her unhappy. She's always telling us that if we eat the right food, you know, organic stuff, it'll bring us inner peace but I think if she'd only have a Big Mac every once in a while she'd feel a whole lot better. Any chance of a strawberry milkshake?'

And that was as far as it went. No more information about Edith was forthcoming. No matter how hard Polly tried to engineer the conversation back to the subject of Edith, either Luana wasn't about to be drawn or she simply wasn't interested.

'I don't suppose we could go to a movie?' She eyed Polly hopefully: 'one with lots of actors. I have this competition with Susie at school. We write down all the actors in all the films we see on telly or in the cinema during the holidays and when term starts again we see who has the most. And actors in cinema films count double, d'you see?'

Polly took her to see *Working Girl* even though she'd already seen it herself. She was touched by the sight of Luana tearing down the aisle in her duffel coat, the hood flapping behind her, to sit in the front row and furiously scribble down the cast list by the light of the screen.

'Who's your favourite film star?' Polly asked her on the way home.

'Daniel Day-Lewis.' The reply was instant.

'I don't think I know him.'

'Oh, you will, you will. You can see him soon in *My Left Foot*. I tore his picture out of *Spotlight* and put it up on my wall. He's special.'

'I see,' said Polly, 'and how come you have a copy of *Spotlight*?'

'Mum's got a set.'

'Oh really? Is she an actress?'

'She says she was once. Probably a hundred years ago before I was born. I heard her fighting with Dad about it. She said it was because of me she never made it. He said how could she have made it when she never even went to drama school and was never offered any parts? Then she started crying again . . .'

The next day, as she put Luana on the train back to Cornwall, Polly kissed Luana for the first time and even though Luana didn't really return the embrace, Polly felt she was beginning to make a little headway.

'Bad luck always comes in threes.' Polly recalled her superstitious grandmother's dark warning, repeated at every opportunity, and towards the end of the following year Polly began to see what Granny Atwell had been on about. Later she would look back and realise that the three deaths, which seemed to happen one after the other with frightening symmetry, marked the turning point of her marriage.

Johnny was hardly ever there. *The Wolf One* was almost a month into shooting, mostly on location. He left the house at 5.30 every morning and arrived home dead on his feet every evening rarely before ten. Polly was well aware that the producer didn't actually need to be on the set the whole time but she appreciated that as it was his first film he wanted to make sure everything was running smoothly.

In fact everything was swimming along for both of them. Cherry Fox had indeed been cast as the love interest and the publicity this had generated had been phenomenal.

Whatever the quality of the outcome, Johnny's first

film was already fixed firmly in the public's mind. Polly too was deriving enormous satisfaction from her work. She had negotiated a successful two-book deal for Rebecca Price with a shrewd and sympathetic young publishing director to whom Rebecca was already devoted, and other authors were beginning to come her way. Even though they barely spent any conscious time together except on the occasional Sunday, Polly and Johnny were each making exhausting but happy progress and the news they brought each other from the front was always cheerful.

Until one evening Polly came home from work and for several seconds was transported back to the days when Johnny had run PDS Productions from their dining-room table. The place was in chaos. Empty beer bottles and overflowing ashtrays covered every available surface. Grimy leather jackets had been thrown on the floor. Polly's seventeeth-century French mirror (a present from her superstitious grandmother: 'my dear child, whatever you do, don't break it, you'll have seven years' bad luck'), had been removed from the wall and placed on the dining-room table. Razor blades and jagged lines of cocaine lay on the glass.

Assorted members of Cruise Missile lay sprawled about the room while Cruise crouched in a corner, his head in his hands, his whole body heaving as he emitted loud, disgusting sobs. To Polly he looked like a caveman with his shoulder-length mane, freed from its habitual pony tail, springing matted and wild from his head.

'Johnny?' she appealed.

Johnny was standing over Cruise, ineffectually patting him on the back. He looked up, put a finger to his lips and gestured to Polly to go upstairs. He joined her a few minutes later.

'It's Belle. She's OD'd. Someone found her in the bath at lunchtime. Looks like it was an accident. She was on smack. I mean, I didn't know, thought they both did coke and that was it. I closed down the set and brought Cruise straight home. He can't handle it. As you see.'

They kept Cruise with them for two days – Polly insisted the rest of the band went home – and then his mother came down from Liverpool to fetch him.

'Come on, Billy lad, come home to me and yer dad. Look at the state of you! We'll get him sorted in no time,' she assured Johnny, 'always was a bad influence on him, that woman.'

Polly watched in fascination as the huge leather-jacketed oaf allowed himself to be helped into a taxi by his tiny white-haired mother and marvelled that Mrs Powers could still have such control over her son. Lady Annabel's family closed ranks and barred Cruise from the funeral. Johnny frantically rearranged the film's schedule to shoot around Cruise but if he was away for longer than a week they would be in trouble. But little Mrs Powers delivered him back on the set three days later. There was only one problem. She'd cut off all his hair and the continuity girl nearly had a heart attack until Hair and Make-up came up with a wild and matted wig within hours and filming resumed the next day.

The second death occurred on a balmy September afternoon. Patrick Fisher had just taken delivery of a manuscript he had been awaiting with unusual anticipation. He was rather proud of the fact that he represented a handful of eminent politicians and the fact that one of these had decided to write his surprisingly scurrilous memoirs pleased Patrick enormously.

'Don't disturb me, Jennifer, there's a dear,' he told his secretary. 'I'm going to spend the afternoon reading Sir Godfrey. Bring me some tea around 4.30, otherwise no calls please.'

It seemed Patrick had taken advantage of the clement weather to lift a chair through the French windows on to his balcony. There he had placed the manuscript on the parapet, where it lay precariously poised, and settled down to read, reaching out for handfuls of pages as he went. A witness saw it all. A sudden gust of wind had swept a hundred pages into the air and Patrick had instinctively leapt after them. The parapet was low, Patrick large and clumsy. He had lost his balance and plunged head first from the fourth floor to the pavement below, narrowly missing the basement railings on which he might have been impaled.

The ambulance men said there was nothing they could do.

Patrick's partnership with Jules Dunbar had been a jocular and affectionate one. Patrick had always referred to Jules as the Old Codger. Polly looked at Jules now as she sat across the table from him in the window of Hilaire in the Old Brompton Road, Patrick's favourite watering hole, resplendent in his red braces and habitual bow tie. Later they would go back to the office and spend the afternoon planning Patrick's memorial service at St Martin-in-the-Fields.

'Come on, old girl, you must have a drink. What's your poison?' Polly nearly giggled. She hadn't realised people actually said things like 'What's your poison?'

but if anyone did it was bound to be Jules. 'Well, I'm going to have a Martini. Join me?'

Polly nodded. She'd never had a Martini before but Jules was a notorious drunk and Polly had long since resigned herself to the fact that this lunch was going to be a question of if you can't beat 'em, join 'em.

'It's awful to think of such a thing when it's barely a fortnight since the funeral but will you be looking around for a new partner, Jules?' Polly reckoned she'd better get down to basics before Jules became too pissed.

'He was only fifty-two,' remarked Jules, neatly evading the question. 'I remember when my father took him on as an office boy. He was only just down from Balliol . . .'

'Trinity, Cambridge,' corrected Polly.

'Well, who was at Balliol?'

'No idea, Jules. Maybe you were?'

'No, don't think so. Anyway Patrick was only a kid and keen as mustard. Made me feel quite exhausted just to look at him. Just as well, since I've never had the energy to bring in the blasted authors. I think the old man knew it, that's why he took on Patrick. He's devastated, by the by, never thought Patrick would pop off before he did. Talking of the blasted authors, what are we going to do about them, Polly? Patrick's, I mean.'

'Well, I brought along a list –' Polly proffered a sheet of paper.

'Good girl. Any on here you fancy?'

'Jules, are you serious?'

'Never more so. I don't want to look after anyone under thirty-five. How many of these scribblers are under thirty-five?'

Polly leaned over and glanced down the list.

'Only four I think.'

'Oh Christ, Patrick always did go in for pompous farts. Boring politicians, diplomats, lady horticulturists, no, worse, botanists. Who was that fearful old bat who produced that lengthy tome on fleas, Hortensia someone? Before your time, probably. I suppose I shall have to look after them all for the time being. Do you know what that prize fart, Godfrey Moore, said on the telephone the day after Patrick's accident? I rang to tell him what had happened and the first thing he said was, 'Did anyone retrieve my manuscript?'

Polly groaned. Johnny's reaction had been almost as bad when she'd told him about Patrick: 'Well, look on the bright side, Pol. It's bound to mean a step up for you. They'll probably give you all his clients.'

'Rebecca Price. She's yours now, isn't she? And you've got a few more of your own. Sure you feel up to handling Patrick's leftovers as well?' asked Jules. 'I'll have the gigot and bring me the wine list, would you please? Oh, it's here. So it is.'

Polly knew that once Jules' attention switched from the client list to the wine list, she would lose him.

'Yes, Rebecca's mine,' she said hastily. 'So, I'll take over these four, shall I? Oh, and what about Lucy Richards? Have you read what there is of her manuscript? I don't think it's quite your thing, Jules. Better leave it to me. I'll write to them all this afternoon and you'll deal with the rest. Would you like me to write a preliminary letter to them all for you, Jules, explain the situation, say you'll be in touch in due course?'

Jules looked at her through his bifocals. 'Would you, my dear? Most kind. Do me a little memo thing about who's due to deliver what and when and perhaps you'd have a go at getting Sir Godfrey to deliver us another copy of his manuscript now he's calmed down a bit. S'pose I'd better read the bloody thing. In the meantime perhaps you could hold the fart . . .'

'Jules!'

'Oh, you know what I mean.'

Polly did know exactly what he meant. Poor old Jules, he really was a bit of a disgrace. She felt rather sorry for his clients, inherited from his father who had founded the agency and none of them under sixty, but somehow, she had observed, they and Jules seemed to rub along. It was a style of gentlemanly, rather lazy agenting that was rapidly going out of style. She doubted if Jules had ever auctioned a book. He merely relied on the relevant editor being in the same place when an author had a new book to be sold. The book was delivered to the editor, who duly read it, lunch was then consumed and at the appropriate moment the subject of money was hurriedly discussed, after which Jules forgot all about the book until he was invited to the publication party.

He's going to be lost for a while without Patrick, thought Polly. Patrick had always shielded Jules from the more cut-throat side of their business while quietly bringing it further and further into the latter part of the twentieth century. The least she could do was hold the fort until he had recovered enough to administer to Patrick's clients, although quite what Jules would administer Polly was at a loss to say. All she knew was that she intended to be a very different kind of agent – she would really care for her authors, for their work and their well-being. Like Patrick – indeed, in his memory– she would be, what had Jules called it, keen as mustard?

Cruise came off his Fat Boy at 180 m.p.h. He had never

made any pretence of recovering from Lady Annabel's death and it was as if with each new stunt he performed in the film he was entertaining some kind of personal death wish.

'My friends were always putting him down, down down,' sang Polly under her breath, wondering why she had this particular song on the brain, 'they said he came from the wrong side of town. . .'

'Why did he have to go and be the bloody Leader of the Pack?' sighed Johnny on his return from the hospital, giving her her answer. 'He's getting worse every day.'

There it is, thought Polly, bad luck always comes in threes. This is the third death.

But she was wrong.

CRUISE LIVES screamed the headlines, omitting to mention that he might never walk again.

'I'm ruined,' moaned Johnny, choosing to ignore that it was entirely his own fault. First, Cruise was on Pay or Play which meant that even though he would never return to the film, he would be paid for it. Second, Johnny had been foolish enough to overlook the necessity of a completion guarantee in the budget. Like an insurance premium, a guarantor is paid a fee in exchange for which he agrees to pay all costs above the agreed budget in order to guarantee completion and delivery of the picture. The fact that Cruise had insisted on doing his own stunts had resulted in his insurance being so ludicrously high it was out of the question, but Johnny should have put in a completion guarantee. Now with no Cruise and no money with which to hire a replacement star to finish the film, even if he had wanted to at such a late stage, Johnny had no choice but to announce that *The Wolf One* had 'bitten the dust'.

His film has died, thought Polly. That's the third death.

Again she was wrong.

Prudence Atwell telephoned at eight o'clock on a Friday evening in late October.

'Polly darling, your father's gone into the Norfolk and Norwich. The thing is – ' there was a catch in Polly's mother's voice – 'this time I don't think he's going to come out.'

'Why on earth haven't you told me? Christ, Mummy, cancer!' Polly's agitation made her uncharacteristically aggressive with her mother when Prudence picked her up at Norwich station the next morning.

'Don't get in. Wait!' Prudence threw a rug over the passenger seat before Polly's black Agnès B jacket and trousers became covered in dog hairs. 'There. I didn't tell you for the simple reason that your father asked me not to. He didn't want you to know he was dying.'

'I see,' said Polly abruptly. Until that moment she had not in fact acknowledged that her father was dying. They drove in silence to the hospital and Prudence drew to a halt in the car park.

Polly shuddered. 'Horrible place. Why's he in here, Mummy?'

'And not in some private nursing home, you mean? Oh, you know your father, Polly. He's always supported the National Health. Never one to spend when he could save,' she added drily. It was an old family joke that Polly's father had installed central heating in their home in only those rooms open to the public, leaving the family to freeze over antiquated electric fires in the rest of the house.

They'd put him in a room on his own instead of in a

ward, which told Polly they didn't hold out much hope at the hospital. He was in a coma. Her mother hadn't told her that either. It put paid to the heart-to-heart with her father Polly had rehearsed in her mind on the train journey up from London. She was horrified by his breathing: the long silences followed by an agonising rasp. It seemed to Polly, as she sat in the sparse hospital room at her father's bedside, that the gaps grew longer and longer between rasps. The suspense, waiting to hear if he would breathe again, was almost more than she could bear. She waited for her mother to leave the room then clasped his hand and spoke to him.

'I'm all right, Daddy. I know you thought I wouldn't be but I am. I love Johnny. We have had an odd life together. I don't imagine you've been able to make much sense of it. Not exactly what you expected for me but we both have to work very hard otherwise it wouldn't work, the marriage I mean. I'm sorry we didn't have grandchildren for you, sorry we haven't yet anyway. I want them, Dad, but there's time. I like my work. I know I'm going to be a good agent. I only wish I knew Johnny was going to be a good producer.'

A nurse came into the room and caught the last sentence. 'No use talking to him, love, he can't hear you. All right, is he?'

'Fine,' said Polly. He's just dying, and how do you know he can't hear me?

She was rather shaken by what she had just told her father. She had, she realised, been talking to herself whether or not her father could hear her, using him as an excuse to face up to a few things she had been trying to keep buried inside her. Did she really think Johnny wouldn't make it?

'I may be totally wrong, Daddy. He'll probably come

marching home one day with Oscars under both arms. Doesn't matter whether he does or not, I still love him. He knows who I am, Daddy, like you did. Like you do,' she corrected herself quickly, glancing up at him. 'Mummy hasn't a clue who I am. I've given up expecting her to see the light. She sees me as she wants me to be, a nice country girl, grown up and married, living in London and waiting to have her grandchildren. I think she prefers to think I don't go out to work. . .' She stopped guiltily as the door opened again, expecting Prudence, but it was only another nurse.

'That's it, dear. You talk to him. I'm sure it helps. Looks like he can't hear you but how do we know for sure? Most likely he can. You his daughter, then?'

Polly nodded gratefully. She could have sworn her father's hand, clasped in hers, gave an almost inperceptible squeeze.

The next morning as they walked through the swing doors of the ward next to his room, three nurses came flying round the corner to head them off at the pass. Cups of tea materialised out of nowhere. Polly's father had died twenty minutes before they arrived.

'Can't we see him?' begged Polly.

'Best not, dear,' said the nurse who had thought he could hear her. 'They're not a pleasant sight when they've gone like he did. He was in pain at the end but he's at peace now. You had a nice chat yesterday, said your goodbyes then though you probably didn't realise it. He wouldn't want you to see him. Here, drink your tea.'

Bet she says that to all the girls, thought Polly miserably and put her arm round her mother who had begun to cry quietly.

To Polly's amazement, Johnny drove up for the funeral.

It was four days after her father had died and she had gone for a long walk towards the end of the afternoon having spent most of the day on the telephone, telling people all over the country of the funeral arrangements, speaking to the vicar and the undertaker, putting announcements in the newspapers, while Prudence entertained a stream of visitors to what she called 'condolence tea'. She's loving it, thought Polly, she hasn't had so much attention in years.

Polly put on her wellingtons, picked her way across a cattle grid and stomped off across the field. As a girl she had imagined herself walking across these same fields one day in her wedding dress to be married in the little flint church that stood on the edge of their land. She had always planned a harvest wedding so she and her bridesmaids could form a procession between the bales of hay. As it had turned out, she had married in London and the only procession here in Norfolk would be that of the pallbearers carrying her father's coffin through the mud in two days' time.

She squelched through the slimy red earth and suddenly broke away to walk towards the woods. The gloom of the narrow brambled paths, cut off from the weak sunlight by overhanging branches, was somehow comforting. She was really getting into her stride, approaching a clearing where she intended to lean against the vast trunk of an oak and rest, when she heard rustling from the thicket to her left. A deer, probably. She stopped and kept absolutely still. If it leapt out and saw her it would be very startled. The rustling grew nearer, twigs snapping underfoot. Then a dog crashed through the path, dripping wet.

'Ashby!' The retriever shook itself, sending a shower

of muddy water all over her and padded up to her, wagging its tail. Ashby was her mother's dog. 'Ashby, clever dog. How did you find me?'

As if in answer a figure appeared in the clearing at the end of the path and began running towards her. He held out his arms and beckoned to her to come and meet him. She ran with outstretched arms feeling as if she was in the final frame of a weepie movie. Then, just as she was about to rush into Johnny's embrace, he stepped to the left and she missed him, continuing on down the path, arms still flapping.

'Oh, Johnny!' She couldn't help laughing. He clowned around for a while, pretending to look for her, and when she reached him she punched him on the arm. 'You idiot! What are you doing here?'

'I arrived in time for what I hoped would be a terrific tea, buns and things, only to find you'd gone out. Your mother gave that – what's it called? – retriever a pair of your knickers and told it to find you. I followed. Here we are.'

'My knickers? Oh, no, he's probably dropped them somewhere in the woods for everyone to see.'

'No, wait, here he comes, he's got something in his mouth. Bit grey, Pol.'

'Ashby, come here. Good dog! Now, drop! Go on, drop.'

Ashby dropped a dead squirrel at Polly's feet. She screamed hysterically and then she lost control. She hadn't let go since her father died, hadn't cried, had been proud of her composure. Johnny wrapped his arms around her and began to lead her slowly back to the house.

'Blubbing again, Pol, what are we going to do about

you? There, there, go on, spit it out. I never knew you could look so disgusting.'

She hit him again half-heartedly.

'You know, my father died once,' he said conversationally.

'Anything I can do you can do better,' grumbled Polly into his chest.

'What's that? Accusing me of being competitive, are you? Typical! Poor old Poppa. He would have liked to go back to Italy to die but he never made it. Oh no, don't go blubbing again just when we've dried you out. Your mother will think I've been beating you up. Shall we have a practice funeral here in the woods? Ashby's got something over there he wants us to bury so he can dig it up again on his next walk.'

'Oh, shut up, Johnny. Were you close to your father, did you love him?'

'No. Yes. I loved him, he was my poppa, he was warm and Italian and I recognised myself in him, but I didn't respect him.'

'Why not?'

'He never made anything of himself. Not in a way that impressed me in any way. He was just an ice-cream maker all his life. OK, so he made money but. . .'

'So? Did he enjoy being an ice-cream maker?'

'Dunno. 'Spect so.'

'Well, what's wrong with that?'

'Oh, Pol, you just don't understand.'

'No, I don't. Do you think Luana respects you?'

'Oh, she sends her love, even wrote you a letter. Here, I've got it somewhere . . .'

Edith, thought Polly immediately, he's seen Luana so maybe he's seen her.

Why couldn't they just bury Edith?

'Have you seen *Beverly Hills Cop*?' Johnny asked Great-Aunt Molly over dinner. 'D'you know, it was originally conceived as a vehicle for Sylvester Stallone. Great idea having a black cop, great moment when Eddie Murphy arrives in LA and his girlfriend from Detroit calls his car "a crappy blue Chevy Nova", real put-down.'

Great-Aunt Molly beamed happily at him. She was almost completely deaf but stubbornly refused to wear her hearing-aid.

Polly toyed with her food. Johnny was busy doing what he called 'making an effort' with her relatives and in return they all thought he was a lunatic. At lunch the next day he excelled himself. The dining room was at the front of the house with a clear view of the flat countryside dotted with gnarled trees bent into slanting positions by the Norfolk wind like arthritic old women. Conversation had already totally dried up and everyone was trying hard not to slurp their soup in the ensuing silence. Suddenly a group of ramblers sauntered past, the adults looking studiously ahead while the children stared blatantly through the windows at them.

'Want me to see 'em off?' asked Johnny, getting to his feet, 'trespassing etc.'

'That won't be necessary. They're not trespassing,' Prudence said calmly, tipping her soup plate away from her and dipping her spoon to catch the last drop, 'it's a public footpath. They're perfectly entitled to walk past the house.'

'But they're on your land.'

'It really doesn't matter, my dear Johnny, do sit down. We're quite used to them.'

'But that's a bit frigging much!' Johnny wasn't about to sit down. He rushed over to the window and watched as the last of the walkers climbed over the five-bar gate at the edge of the fields. 'What's the point of living in a posh place like this' – Prudence winced at the 'posh' – 'if you've got people traipsing past while you're eating your lunch, going Coo-ee...'

'Johnny!' warned Polly.

'I mean it's hilarious ...' Before she could stop him he had run outside and was walking past the window like Charlie Chaplin, pretending to swing his walking stick and grinning in at them.

'Coo-ee, coo-ee!' he called. Great-Aunt Molly waved back. Everyone else ignored him for the rest of the day.

Polly had to admit to herself that she couldn't have done without him at the funeral. Although she had grown up amongst these excruciatingly polite relations who surrounded her now, she still felt they patronised her, that she was an oddball amongst her numerous cousins in their uniform Alice bands, pearls and pie-frill collars, braying at their husbands-who-did-something (probably nothing)-in-the-City. Johnny held her hand as they walked across the fields to the church and continued to clasp it throughout the service, stage-whispering 'No blubbing, Pol, good girl, keep it up' at intervals.

At the drinks afterwards she saw him deep in conversation with her Uncle Matthew. Uncle Matthew had always been something of an embarrassment to the family and if it wasn't for the fact that he was loaded (and enormously generous, a reliable soft touch in times of need) he would have been dropped from family gatherings years ago. He had once had a reputation as a bit of a bounder. This wouldn't have been too bad in itself except that Uncle Matthew himself was extremely proud of his reputation and bored everybody who came near him to death with much-embellished stories of his flings with 'poppets' and 'floozies' in the past.

As Polly wandered by, Uncle Matthew hailed her:

'Fellow works in the films. You never told me, Polly. I've been telling him all about my little adventures in the film business.'

'With Rank starlets, Uncle Matthew?'

'Those were the days. We've been having a good laugh. He's been telling me about his misfortune with this wolf business. Terrible shame. I've offered to help but he won't hear of it. I've told him any time, any time. I'd like to get back to the films, meet a few popsies.'

'He's eighty-two,' Polly whispered in Johnny's ear, 'it'll be pop-off time before he meets a few popsies.'

Prudence appeared at Polly's side.

'Polly, I'm a little worried about Joan. So sweet of her to make the effort to come and so well turned out as always. That's a Chanel suit, I'm sure of it.' Prudence looked rather disdainfully at Polly's eternal Agnès B.

'What's the matter with her?'

'How can you ask such a thing? She's desperately upset about your poor father. I found her in absolute floods in the pantry and sent her up to my bedroom. Do pop up and see if she's all right.'

Polly found Joan crumpled in a heap – having first removed the jacket of her Chanel suit which was hanging over a chair – in the middle of her mother's bed.

'Polly, it's the cruellest cruellest thing that ever happened. I don't know how I'm going to show my face in London again. I've been fired by Condé Nast!'

'What's your mother going to do with that great pile?' asked Johnny on the drive back to London, 'Sell it?

Carve it up into flats? Old man leave you quite a bit, did he?'

Polly had known for some time that her father had left her £25,000 with a good deal more to come to her on her mother's death. She hadn't told Johnny and she wasn't going to just yet. She didn't know why. She had never kept anything from him before. It was her money and at the back of her mind she was beginning to plan what she could do with it.

'Is that why you came up for the funeral, Johnny? Lured by the smell of filthy lucre?' She had no idea what made her say such a thing and when she saw the hurt look on his face, she wished she hadn't, especially when he began to steer the car with one hand so as to be able to reach out with the other to push her hair away from her face and stroke the back of her head with infinite tenderness. And she felt even worse when he said: 'Poor old Pol, you really loved your dad, didn't you? I never reckoned you'd be so upset when he popped his clogs. But you have got me, you know. Pretty crappy substitute but I do love you and I will take care of you. You're lumbered with me, Pol, an embarrassing Italian who worships you even when you've got a red nose and piggy little eyes from blubbing all the time. Here, I'll even lend you my best silk handkerchief. . .'

She laughed as she always did when he said that and then handed her a filthy screwed-up bit of Kleenex. He was so corny but he always touched her and she loved him.

Yet she still didn't tell him about the £25,000.

Now that she was out of work and at a loose end, Joan was never off the phone to Polly, demanding that she be free to lunch at least three times a week. Joan always behaved as if Polly's job was nothing more than that of a glorified secretary. She would ring Polly every morning around eleven.

'Hi, darling, it's me. Can you talk or are you taking dictation or something?'

If Polly said she had an author on the other line, Joan would merely come back with: 'OK, I'll hold on till you've put him through to whoever it is.'

'Joan, they're ringing *me*.'

'Are they? Why? Oh, never mind. Call me back.'

One of her first questions was always: 'Where shall we go?'

'Go?' Polly was invariably distracted, wishing Joan would get off the line but sensitive to how she must be feeling, banned from the centre of her universe, Vogue House.

'To lunch. Where shall we go today?'

'Joan, I told you, I have a lunch today with a client.'

'Oh, well, we'll have to natter on the phone then.'

Polly would try to get on with her work with the phone crooked to her ear while Joan prattled away.

'There's a perfectly wonderful picture of Hector O'Neill in Dempster today. Have you seen it, Polly? He's finished shooting the last Conway film. Did I ever tell you how sweet he was to me when we did that shoot with him for *Vogue* last year? He's so utterly classy. Boston Irish, you know, like the Kennedys.'

'He's American? I never realised. The Kennedys were hardly classy. Old Joe Kennedy came from the East Boston slums, he was a bootlegger.'

'Oh Polly, you're such a pedant. So what if he was a bootlegger originally? Rather romantic. He became Ambassador to the Court of St James later on. That's what matters.'

'And Hector O'Neill grew up with the family?'

'Something like that. One didn't like to pry too closely. Dempster says he's here in London for a while. I wonder where he's staying. Maybe he has a house here. Someone will know. Now listen, Polly darling, I can't sit on the phone gossiping with you all morning. I've got to rustle up some freelance work. Can you do lunch tomorrow?'

Polly couldn't but she said yes just to get Joan off the phone. She felt very guilty. It wasn't as if she could even invite her round in the evening, because Johnny still wouldn't have her in the house. In any case since *The Wolf One* had collapsed he needed Polly's undivided attention at night which was a bit of a problem given the amount of manuscripts she had to read.

And there was one in particular which just couldn't wait.

In the summer of 1989 Lawrence delivered the final draft of *Mr Wrong*. When Polly read it she knew without a doubt that she had a star author on her hands. Lawrence might look like a prize wimp, all goofy and gangling with stringy black hair and glasses so thick you could hardly see his eyes, but his books showed that he certainly had a better understanding of women than most men. Polly was entranced. She sat up in bed reading into the night while Johnny grumbled away under the duvet beside her.

'What the bloody hell's that? For God's sake, Pol, turn the light out, let's get some sleep.'

'Nothing that would interest you,' she told him tartly.

After all, Johnny had sent poor Lawrence away with a flea in his ear. Why should he care what had happened to *Mr Wrong*?

Polly couldn't wait to sell *Mr Wrong* but she forced herself to take everything one step at a time. First she had to get a buzz going. Then, when she had enough people begging to see it, she would auction it to the highest bidder. She duly lunched several prospective editors and hyped *Mr Wrong* as much as she dared.

Polly picked her restaurants carefully. It would never do to take one particular young power editor in her thirties to a place where she wouldn't be seen and be able to wave at people. Ally Keppel was an editor without talent but who had been given a fair amount of financial clout at a hungry house with a large chequebook. She'd expect nothing less than the Groucho or Le Caprice or else she'd assume Polly – and worse, Lawrence – weren't worth her attention.

Similarly, Rosemary Perkins, an enormously experienced, rather dowdy lady editor in her late fifties whose unerring judgement and care with authors had earned her an excellent reputation, hated noisy fashionable restaurants and liked to sit quietly in the corner of a run-down Greek taverna and talk about gardening. Yet Polly knew her endorsement of a book often encouraged her employers to dig deep into their coffers.

As it turned out, the *Mr Wrong* auction was not without its complications. By the second day there were only three bidders left in the auction out of the nine to whom the book had been submitted. In the first round, one of them, Pat Walsh of the Lambert Group, had come in with a staggering £50,000 opening bid.

'That should see off the competition, babe,' Pat boomed down the phone to Polly. 'Barely worth you going any further, I shouldn't think.'

Polly couldn't abide Pat Walsh's bossy, jolly hockey sticks manner and her curious predilection for calling absolutely everyone 'babe'.

She was also rather worried when four people promptly dropped out. She listened to the standard excuses:

'Too rich for my blood, I'm afraid, Polly. Wonderful book but in the current climate, fifty thou for a first novel, a bit steep . . .' Scaredy cat!

'I'd like to offer more, Polly, but I'm being sat on by my editorial board . . .'

Wimp!

'If I thought it'd stay at 50K I'd hang in there, Polly, you know I would, but you've got a high roller there or you don't know what you're doing . . .' Oh, thanks!

In round three Pat Walsh was at £95,000, Rosemary Perkins was at £97,000 (her endorsement the best news so far: that meant everyone would know the book was good when it came to post-mortems), and the third contender, Arthur Allen-Jones, had pushed it over the £100,000 mark to £105,000. Arthur and his high offer was the complication. Eighteen months ago Arthur had been Pat Walsh's assistant (secretary, to be precise) but his general pushiness and obsessive ambition had secured him, at twenty-seven, the job of editorial director at the brand new publishers Hollywood House (so called because of their offices in Hollywood Road off the Fulham Road rather than any affiliation with the film industry). Arthur, who insisted on being called Art, or Artie, was fiercely competitive and desperate for books to fill his first list. But Pat Walsh had absolutely no intention of losing out to her erstwhile minion. She would be the laughing stock of the industry. She was overheard slagging off Arthur in the Groucho: 'I tell you, babe, he never read more than fifty pages of a manuscript. He just went by the reader's report depending on which reader he was sleeping with.'

Arthur retaliated from 2 Brydges Place, a smaller, more exclusive club in a tiny alleyway next to the Coliseum.

'Talk about paranoid!' he told a table of rising young Turks from *GQ*, *The Face* and Channel 4. 'She even arranged for the conception of her children so that the births should not coincide with the ABA or Frankfurt.' Annual jaunts to the American Booksellers' Association and the Frankfurt Book Fair were standard fixtures on publishers' calendars.

In the end Polly decided to go for a sudden death. Let them all make their final bids and whoever came in the highest would acquire the book.

They all bid £124,000 (the previous bid had been £120,000 from Pat). There were slight variations in the frills over and above the basic offer. Pat offered a £5,000 escalator if the book stayed in the top ten on the *Sunday Times* bestseller list for a minimum of six weeks. Top ten wasn't good enough, thought Polly, it had to be top five. Rosemary Perkins guaranteed a £25,000 promotional spend (not excessive but a smart gesture), and Artie Allen-Jones remained true to Hollywood by throwing in a movie escalator of an extra £7,500 if a 'major motion picture' of *Mr Wrong* was released in the UK.

Polly was about to go back to each of them and ask them all for their final package, with everyone including promotion budgets plus film and bestseller escalators, when Lawrence threw a spanner in the works by revealing, rather late in the day, his dependency on astrology.

'Polly, when is Pat Walsh's birthday?'

'Lawrence, I have no idea. It's not an event I celebrate. Besides, she hasn't actually won the auction yet so you don't have to start thinking about her birthday.'

'Oh, but I do. I must know what sign my editor is before I sign with them, and the other thing is I've had the book's chart done by a mundane astrologer. *Mr Wrong* is a Scorpio and he has to be published on either November 28th or the following April 2nd. I want it written into the contract.'

Polly silently counted to ten very slowly. This was the most important step of her career so far. She must not lose her cool.

'Lawrence, I have £124,000 sitting on the table. I simply cannot go back to people and ask them when their birthday is.'

'I knew the book should never had been submitted when Mercury was in retrograde. I meant to tell you that. Call me when you get their sun signs and try and go for their moon and their ascendant as well. You'll need to know the exact time they were born.'

Polly allotted each of the bidders a star sign without even asking them, waited twenty-four hours and then called Lawrence back.

Lawrence said he was personally allergic to Geminis (Pat Walsh) but that Artie Allen-Jones' sun in Pisces and moon in Cancer were perfect with his own Cancer star sign and *Mr Wrong*'s Scorpio.

'So we're all set then?' Polly was weak with relief. 'The book goes to Hollywood House for £124,000 with a £35,000 guaranteed promotion spend plus a further £10,000 movie bonus and an extra £5,000 if it stays in the *Sunday Times* bestseller list for longer than six weeks.'

'One more thing.'

Polly couldn't trust herself to speak.

'What sign are you, Polly?'

'I'm Cancer, Lawrence, just like you but I am beginning to think that is the only thing we have in common. I'm going to hang up now, Lawrence, before you ask me what sign this telephone is.'

When Polly proudly showed Johnny the report of her *Mr Wrong* auction in the publishing trade magazine the *Bookseller*, he was more interested in hearing about the rivalry between Pat Walsh and Artie Allen-Jones.

'I like it, I like it. Very *All about Eve*. There might be something in doing a remake with a new twist, a Bette Davis character and an ambitious young boy instead of a girl. Call him Eddie instead of Eve. All about Eddie. Great! Thanks, Pol.'

'Don't mention it.' All About Eddie! Polly shuddered. 'So you aren't impressed then?'

'By what? Your little sale? I suppose it's OK for this pathetic country but you've got to understand that the agents I'm around, the agents in my business, I mean, we're talking millions.'

'In your business.'

'Yeah.'

'Johnny, what exactly is your business right now?'

Polly knew it was below the belt but she was smarting from his condescending attitude to what was for her a tremendous achievement.

'That just about sums it up,' he snarled at her. 'You're so uninterested in what I do, so wrapped up in your own life, that you actually have to ask me what I do.'

'I didn't ask you what you do. I asked you what you were doing right now. It's almost a year since *The Wolf One* fell apart.'

'Go on, rub it in. How am I supposed to option anything without any bloody money?'

'Banks?'

'There's a better way, something where we could work together.'

'Johnny, I am not giving you my father's money.'

'It's not his money. It's yours to do with as you want.'

'Precisely.'

Conversations along these lines had become a regular occurrence between them ever since Polly's mother had told Johnny about the £25,000. Prudence hadn't known she was revealing a secret. In fact she'd assumed Johnny knew about it. She was, she told Johnny, merely enquiring as to what he planned to do with it. Presumably he looked after Polly's investments, didn't he?

No, he didn't, but not for want of trying.

'I simply can't understand it,' said Prudence. 'Her father always looked after my money.'

One night, when he was especially low, Johnny even accused Polly of having fallen out of love with him.

'You mean I can't love you because I won't give you my money. Johnny, my money and my love are not one and the same. You can't expect to receive one and think the other goes with it automatically.'

'But do you, I mean are you still in love with me?'

'Much much more than I was when we were married.'

That shook him.

'Really, Pol? He sat up in bed, reached for the remote and jabbed it in the direction of the television. 'Well, that is a turn-up. Much much more, you said. How much much more? Come on, show me.' He was reaching for her under the bedclothes.

'Turn that bloody thing off. I've got to make an early start.'

'You're such a boring old woman these days. No late nights. Always sitting there with your glasses on, reading through those blasted boxes of paper. How do you ever expect to get pregnant if you sit up reading all night?'

'Pregnant?'

'Right. Pregnant. My movie went down the tube and I can't even console myself with being a father.'

'Johnny, we're going to start a family but there's something I've been planning and I feel I ought to discuss it with you first. I feel nearly ready to break away from Patrick Fisher & Dunbar. I want to start my own agency and I want to do it here, in this house.'

'Fine by me. Perfect timing. You'll be right here at home to look after the baby.'

Polly had never liked his approach to motherhood. As his mother had warned Polly, Johnny played the all-Italian male only when it suited him, and it suited him now to turn her big career step into an excuse for motherhood.

'That's just it. If I decide to go ahead with my own agency I shall need to devote all my time to it. I'd want to wait and have a baby once the agency's up and running.'

'You're not getting any younger, Pol. Thirty-six? Thirty-seven?'

'I saw my gynaecologist a couple of weeks ago and she

says I'm in tip-top condition. No problem waiting a year or two.'

'Well, I'm not going to wait a year or two to do another movie. Whereabouts in the house are you planning to have this agency anyway? Going to do deals in the kitchen or what?'

'Well, that's precisely what I wanted to talk to you about. I want to use my father's money to build a conservatory.'

'You what?'

'On the back of the house. It'd be beautiful and it could be heated and I could have my office out there. People could come and go through the garden gate.'

'Got it all worked out, haven't you? Just as well I already have a child. Doesn't look like I'm going to have much chance of fatherhood while you're pottering around in the conservatory, talking to your bloody plants.'

Polly sighed. 'Johnny, why did you marry me?'

'You thought I wanted to marry you to have children? Just for that? I married you because you were so warm and loving and natural and bright and I knew if I had you with me I'd be all right. I know it sounds corny but I wanted you to share my dreams.'

'Didn't it ever occur to you that I might have dreams of my own and I'd want you to share them with me as well?' asked Polly.

She had him there. Johnny was generous by nature but he didn't exactly lie awake at night worrying about anybody else but himself.

'I thought you were, you know, just a kid. I thought I'd teach you everything and you'd sort of be here beside me . . . not like Edith . . . she was so. . .'

'What?' Polly grabbed his arm. 'Edith was so what?'

'It doesn't matter.'

'No go on, Johnny. Tell me about Edith.'

'Well, it was just that she was so terrified of life itself I couldn't tell her anything in case it set her off on one of her . . .'

'One of her what?'

'Nothing. Leave it alone, Pol. All in the past. Anyway, she left me and I found you. Except now you're trying to run the world and don't have time for me.'

Johnny was looking very sorry for himself, sitting hunched up on the pillows in his pyjamas, his arms around his knees.

His hair, very pepper and salt by now, was dishevelled and the stubble on his chin made him look decidedly swarthy.

But Polly loved him like this. He was so far removed from the type of man she had been programmed to love. He was vulnerable. And any second now he would probably make her collapse with laughter in a way that no one else could, and no matter how badly he behaved he always managed to make up for it in some way.

She crawled into the space between his knees and slipped her arms around his neck. She pretended to bite his stubble, taking nips here and there. She licked the inside of his ear. Then very slowly let her tongue slide down over his cheek and into his mouth. They kissed for five minutes, ten minutes, on and on and all the time Polly thought: this is what it's all about. He's got no work. We've got no children. But this is all I want. The fusion of their bodies never failed to reassure her. She loved this man and one reason for this, amongst many many others, was that she hadn't a shred of doubt in her mind that he loved her too.

When she was here at home in bed with him, she never needed to ask him if he loved her. She *felt* it.

In the morning she retrieved the *Bookseller* from under his side of the bed. He looked up at her sheepishly.

'Well done, Pol. That *Mr Wrong* thing, don't know much about your business but it looks like you did good.'

But as she was going out of the front door he called down the stairs:

'It'd make a crappy movie though. Poor old Lawrence. He hasn't got a clue.'

A week later she had made up her mind once and for all, told Jules Dunbar what she was going to do and there was no going back. That night, lying in bed next to Johnny, she knew she had to try one more time to make him understand.

Johnny was watching *Sweet Smell of Success*, one of his favourite films, occasionally reaching out to pat her and murmur mechanically: 'You all right, Pol? Bit quiet tonight.' He was watching the bit where Sidney Falco, the opportunistic publicist played by Tony Curtis, pretends to call J.J. Hunsecker, a powerful columnist played by Burt Lancaster, and get him to place an item about a comedian in his column. The comedian is standing right beside Tony Curtis, hears every word and is suitably impressed without realising that in fact it is only Curtis' bewildered secretary on the other end of the line.

Johnny knew the film so well he picked up the telephone in the bedroom almost on cue and began to mouth the lines:

'J.J., Hi, how are you sweetheart, I know it's late but is it too late to add something to the column?'

Polly watched him. She had to admit he did look rather like Tony Curtis and it was weird seeing him sitting there talking into the phone and then looking at the screen and seeing Tony Curtis saying the same words.

Johnny went on and on playing Sidney Falco so when Polly said in a small voice, 'Johnny, I told you about my plan to use Daddy's money to build myself an office at home. Well, I'm definitely going to do it. Is it OK with you? It is your house, after all. What do you think?' he never heard a word.

That year Polly and Johnny spent a quiet Christmas at home. It wasn't a good one and later Polly dubbed it the 'Love you too' Christmas.

Prudence rang up on the dot of 3.16 for her annual post-mortem of the Queen's speech on television.

'I do wish there wasn't so much of her going blah, blah, blah. I do so like it when they have those jolly films of them on holiday and having picnics and things with all those little cartoon doggies trotting around her.'

'I think they're called corgis, Mummy. Well, anyway, Happy Christmas. Thank you for my apron and my set of tea towels and Johnny was thrilled with his trowel. Here, he wants to say Happy Christmas ... what?' Johnny was signalling frantically. 'Oh, you loved your bedjacket? Well, we know how draughty it gets at home.'

'Has he done anything about your money?' hissed Prudence.

'No, Mummy, not a thing.'

'Why not, for heaven's sake?'

'Because (a) I won't let him and (b) I'm planning on doing something with it myself. Very soon, actually.'

As soon as she had put the phone down, it rang again. Luana for Johnny. Polly chattered happily to Luana who appeared to be ecstatic about her present, a VCR machine. Who wouldn't be, thought Polly. It was a ludicrously precocious present for a sixteen-year-old but Johnny had insisted.

'I've taped four movies already,' she told Polly proudly.

'Well, in that case you cheated and opened it early. Come and see me again soon. Here's your father.'

'Hi, my little sweetie-pie, taping away are you? No, Luana, we discussed this already. You are too young to see *My Beautiful Laundrette* and you have to understand that Daniel Day-Lewis will still be there when you're old enough to see it. That's a promise.'

It was only some time later that Polly realised that Johnny was no longer talking to Luana. She tried to pretend she wasn't listening. She had never actually been in the same room before when he spoke to Edith. He had lowered his voice but Polly could still make out the odd sentence.

'I thought you didn't let it get to you any more. You've got to put it all behind you. You're doing fine now. You've got to believe in yourself. Come on now, promise me you won't fret.'

That's what he says to me, thought Polly. That's his way of comforting me when I go over the top about something. How dare he say it to her. Yet, of course, she reasoned, he had probably said it to Edith long before he'd ever said it to her. Did he still see Edith? Did she come up to London? Did they meet? He sounded incredibly close to her still. Polly strained to hear his next words . . . and wished she hadn't.

'Yeah, yeah, all right. I know. Sure, sure. Look, I've got to go now. Yeah. Love you too.'

Love you too!

Love *you* too.

Love you *too*.

Whichever way she played it back in her mind, Polly knew that Edith had said the words 'I love you' to Johnny and Johnny had responded with 'Love you too.' But Edith was supposed to have left him. She wasn't supposed to love him any more.

That night as Johnny snuggled up to her and suggested that he engage her in some energetic festive sex, she went through the motions until the tip of his penis was about to penetrate her and then the words 'Love you too' began to scream silently in her head. For the first time ever her vagina clenched as he entered her and the pain made her cry out. Johnny withdrew immediately.

'What's up? Why did I hurt you?'

Polly rolled over on her side and began to heave noiselessly.

'Pol?' said Johnny a little nervously. 'Tired?'

Polly nodded her head up and down on the pillow.

'Well, you'd better get some sleep. Go on. Good girl. You go to sleep,' he told her and turned on the television full blast so that Polly wondered if anyone anywhere in Notting Hill Gate would get any sleep that Christmas.

When *Mr Wrong* was published it went straight to Number 7 on the bestseller list. On Wednesday of the next week they heard it would be Number 1 in the

Sunday Times the following Sunday and Lawrence decided to throw a party. Johnny refused to go and Polly arrived making excuses, saying he had a stomach upset and fooling no one.

Polly was amused to see the transformation in Lawrence. Among his other guests he had invited all the top literary editors and their partners, various columnists and a number of influential actors' agents she was quite sure he did not count among his closest friends. Lawrence was going to make it big but he wasn't about to leave it to chance.

On the way home, Polly decided there could not be a more auspicious time to make the break from Patrick Fisher & Dunbar, always assuming the likes of Lawrence, Lucy Richards and Rebecca Price would follow her. She rushed into the house anxious to tell Johnny but it turned out he had made an important decision of his own while she'd been gone.

He was watching Crufts on television, perched on the edge of his seat, yelling at the judge.

'Pick the Irish setter, you bloody wally, the Irish setter, can't you hear me? Best in Show, Pol,' he explained, seeing her come in, 'if she doesn't pick the Irish setter, she should be shot.'

'Incredibly stupid dogs, most of them. Very highly strung.'

'Who asked you? Go on, you stupid woman, get it over with.'

The judge walked past the Irish setter and picked another dog. Johnny slumped back in his armchair, totally dejected.

'Nobody bloody listens to me any more,' he said gloomily, 'that's why I'm going to get one. It'll listen to me. It'll have to.'

'What will?'

'A dog. Polly, I am going to get myself a dog. Why do you think I've been watching Crufts? I wanted to get a look at all the different breeds before I decided.'

He only ever said Polly instead of Pol when he was in seriously bad shape. Polly delayed yet another conversation about starting the agency to give him her full attention.

Together they studied the *Observer Book of Dogs* and together they finally decided on a springer spaniel on the grounds that it wouldn't be too 'poncy' (Johnny's words) but neither would it be too big to keep in London (Polly's stipulation).

The next day Johnny went out and came back with what looked to Polly like an overgrown chihuahua.

'What,' she demanded 'is that?'

'A Papillon. Don't look like that, Pol. It's a very special breed. When its ears stand up they look like butterfly wings. *Papillon* is French for butterfly.'

'I know that, Johnny. What happened to the springer spaniel?'

'They didn't have any.'

'Who didn't have any?'

'Harrods.'

'Well, why didn't you try the springer spaniel club of Great Britain and find a breeder, why didn't you ring the Kennel Club?'

'Because Zutty looked so sad when I walked away.'

'That's the oldest trick in the book. It looks pretty miserable now. What did you call it?'

'Zutty. His real name is Zut Alors! which means Damn and Blast in French but I suppose you know that. But we'll call him Zutty for short after the drummer, you know, Zutty Singleton, on my Fats Waller records.'

Zutty dined with them. He watched television with them. He tried to shower with them and he came to bed with them. Polly marvelled at the irony of Zutty's arrival. He was the baby they had never had yet instead of her maternal instinct being showered upon him, Zutty was basking in non-stop attention from an ever-anxious Johnny.

'Zutty slept through the night for the first time,' he told Polly as she was preparing to leave for work.

'Wonderful,' said Polly, 'he'll be on solids next. Better add dog food to the weekly Sainsbury's list.'

Yet she was happy that Johnny had something to occupy his time. If he didn't get a picture soon she didn't know what they were going to do. She had already called around for advice about builders for her new office on the back of the house but she didn't want Johnny hanging around doing nothing when she started working in it.

In the event the construction of the conservatory over the next few months didn't bother Johnny in the slightest. By then he had a new interest in his life in the form of Lady Whyte.

Every morning Johnny lay in the bath and belted out 'Sixteen Tons', a hit record from his childhood, while Polly fished her tights out from under the bed and applied what she called 'whirlwind make-up', protesting: 'Oh, Johnny, please!' in between gulps of coffee.

'It's all right, Pol,' he said one morning, 'one day I'll be another Gordy Whyte and you'll be Lady de Soto. Sounds good. What d'you think?'

Sir Gordon Whyte had been knighted for his services to the British film industry. After producing a string of highly successful romantic comedies dubbed the Ealing

Valentines, he went on to mount lavish costume dramas followed by an action adventure film series featuring a daredevil Special Branch operative called Conway. The violence was extreme, the sex explicit, but Conway's dialogue in the scripts was that of a sophisticated stand-up comic and the character made a star out of Hector O'Neill, who had now played the role at least half a dozen times. But the future of the Conway films was in abeyance following the sudden death of Gordy Whyte from a coronary.

'Maybe I should offer my services to produce Conway,' suggested Johnny, surveying his naked body in the mirror while he rubbed his back with his bath towel.

'Christ!' said Polly suddenly, 'that reminds me. Jules gave me tickets for his charity thing.'

'Whose charity thing? Gordy Whyte's? Jesus, Pol, nothing like keeping a secret from your old man.'

'His widow – what's her name? – Juanita's running it now. Whyte Knight it's called. In aid of MS. Jules is on the committee, God knows why, the only thing he can raise is a glass. But he can't go to the charity première of the latest Conway film and he gave me the tickets.'

'When is it? Whoopee, Pol. This might be my big break.'

'Johnny, you do not go prancing up to people touting for jobs at charity premières.' Polly was scrabbling in her handbag: 'Here they are. Oh, it's tonight. Black tie. That means a trip to the same-day cleaner's for my old Valentino. I suppose you want me to take your monkey suit while I'm at it . . . ?'

Johnny insisted on hiring a limousine to drop them at the Odeon Leicester Square and was furious when they were deposited round the corner in Charing Cross Road and had to walk conspicuously through the cordoned-off area to the cinema entrance. He brightened up when they took their £100 seats in the front circle upstairs.

'This is more like it. Where's Princess Diana?'

'It's Princess Michael.'

'She'll do. This is great, Pol.' He leaned over the balcony. 'Blimey! Place is stiff with clapper loaders and gaffers. Hey, Steve, up here, hey!'

'Johnny, shut up. Anybody'd think you'd never been to a royal première before.'

'There she is, there's Juanita.'

'Lady Whyte to you, Johnny. You don't know her.' Polly shifted in her seat, curious to see Gordy Whyte's exotic widow, reputed to be Nicaraguan.

'Goggles!' she said loudly and clearly and completely involuntarily. Juanita Whyte stiffened and sat down without looking at Polly, although everyone else did.

'I was at school with her. I can't believe it. Goggles Grant. She had specs thicker than Lawrence's, poor thing. Couple of years ahead of me. What on earth has she done to herself? Who would have thought ... Goggles Grant becoming a society beauty. But I'll tell you one thing, Johnny, her name was never, ever Juanita. It was something like Sandra. Sandra Grant. I know it's her. Nicaraguan, my foot! Bournemouth, more like.'

At the party afterwards Johnny insisted on Polly introducing him to 'your old school chum'.

'She's not my old school chum. I was a little squirt to her. She won't remember me.'

But Johnny wasn't about to pass up a golden opportunity.

'Lady Whyte – ' he planted himself squarely in front of her – 'you may remember my wife, Polly. She says you were at school together.'

Juanita Whyte took in Polly's five-year-old sale-bought Valentino, her insignificant single strand of pearls, her hastily Carmen-rollered bob, her 'whirlwind' make-up and her rather down-at-heel Charles Jourdain pumps with their clip-on grosgrain bows. She patted her own immaculately highlighted hair, obviously cut and coiffed that very afternoon, fingered her stark jet choker and stood triumphantly in her hot-off-the-collection Karl Lagerfeld.

'Polly?' she looked blank.

'Polly Atwell,' murmured Polly.

'Of course!' Juanita extended her arms, moved forward and without actually ever touching Polly, kissed the air beside her left cheek.

As she felt the cool hiss of air Polly looked over Juanita's shoulder straight into the eyes of the most gorgeous man she had ever seen. Tall, dark and handsome – TDH, as they'd called them at school – and then some. This creature was the perfect specimen, the dreamy Celt with the melting blue eyes, good strong nose and cruel, sardonic mouth. She'd never seen Hector O'Neill in the flesh before and having him standing so close right after she'd drooled over him as Conway in the film for the past two hours somewhat unnerved her. As Juanita turned to Johnny, Hector slipped past her, ducked and whispered quickly in her ear:

'If I ever kissed you I'd make sure I didn't miss.'

'So good of you to come,' Juanita was telling Johnny. 'Gordy would have been so pleased to see you.'

Artificial bitch, thought Polly, watching as Juanita

allowed her hand to be clasped in Johnny's. She hasn't a clue who I am but one look at my clothes tells her she doesn't want to know.

A week later she dragged Johnny, moaning all the way, to dinner at Jules Dunbar's.

'I know it would have been good for your career, Pol, dinner with the boss and all that, if you still worked for him but you don't any more and besides, what's in it for me? Can't I stay home with Zutty and watch the fight on the box?'

'No,' Polly insisted, and in so doing unwittingly signed the death sentence on her marriage.

Juanita Whyte was the guest of honour and Jules placed her next to Johnny.

'You can talk shop until the fish,' he told them genially.

'Can we really?' Juanita leaned towards Johnny. 'What is it that you do exactly?'

Johnny told her. And he didn't stop at the fish. Polly caught the fatal words 'in our business' over and over again but as far as she could see, Juanita Whyte was riveted.

Eventually Jules had to prise Johnny away with the offer of an Armagnac.

It's like he used to be, thought Polly, watching him. He's his old self, engaging as hell. She's loaded. He knows it. She hasn't got a prayer.

Indeed, Polly decided Juanita was the best thing that could have happened to them when she agreed to provide the funding for whatever property Johnny wanted to option – if not buy outright.

'And she's not even after my body,' Johnny winked at Polly.

'Well at least she learned something at that dreadful

school we went to. Do me a favour, Johnny, get her to rent you an office and hire Rachel for you if you can find her. I don't want you cluttering up the dining room all over again.'

Polly couldn't wait to tell Joan about 'Goggles' Grant.

'You must remember her, Joan,' she said when, true to form, Joan telephoned at eleven the next morning, 'she wore specs as thick as pebbles. She was seriously stupid.'

'Sandra Grant. Yes, I remember her. Well, good for her. She's really come up in the world if she's become Lady Whyte. Why are you being so down on her, Polly? Bit jealous, are you? She's done really well for herself.'

'She's married someone successful, that's all,' protested Polly, 'it's not as if she's done anything herself.'

That was Joan all over. It was who you were married to, where you stood on the social ladder, that's what counted with Joan. When Polly had told her about *Mr Wrong* going to Number 1 on the bestseller lists and that she was now breaking away from Patrick Fisher & Dunbar to start her own agency, Joan had gone strangely quiet and just stared at her for a while before going 'Hmm, well I suppose you know what you're doing.' She hadn't seemed pleased for Polly, hadn't congratulated her.

'Anyway she's taken a real shine to Johnny and she's going to back his next production.'

'What do you mean, his next production? He hasn't made a film unless you mean that Wolf fiasco. You're right, Polly, she must be a bit stupid if she's taking up with a loser like Johnny. Sorry to be so brutal about your precious husband but I've never made any secret

125

of the fact that I think he's hopeless. You'd better keep an eye on him, Polly, hadn't you?'

'Why? He'll be fine now.'

'She's after him. You don't seriously imagine she wants him professionally, do you? Polly, why are you always so naive? What's that wonderful nickname Luana has for you?'

'What nickname?' said Polly. But she knew perfectly well.

Polly Pushover.

Johnny moved out to his new office the week the builders finished Polly's conservatory. Polly was delighted to be rid of him. When he was at home it was non-stop 'Juanita this' or 'Juanita that' so that Polly became so sick of the sound of Juanita's name that she stopped asking about how he was progressing in his search for a film property. As far as she could make out, Juanita had found him some offices in Shawfield Street in Chelsea and he had installed himself and Rachel, who had been discovered earning a small fortune as an advertising copywriter. One lunch with Johnny and she chucked it all in for what Polly knew was a ludicrously hollow promise that she would be associate producer on whatever film Johnny eventually made.

Polly had the number at Johnny office's should she wish to call him but she found, rather to her surprise, that as the weeks – and then the months – went by, she didn't particularly wish to do so.

As for Johnny, he rarely bothered to look outside the back door and see how her new office was coming along.

'Beats me why you want to work in the bloody garden,' was his only comment. 'I would have thought the way your career was taking off you would jump up and down a bit till you got snapped up by ICM or the Morris office, became a real player. Now, Pol, I've been thinking, why don't you call Juanita? You girls could have lunch at San Lorenzo one of these days. Old school chums' reunion. Be nice, wouldn't it?'

Polly registered from this first snippet of dialogue Johnny had thrown her way in some time that he obviously wasn't up to any hanky-panky with Juanita, not that she'd ever really suspected it. The way he still snuggled up to her every night and murmured idiotic things, almost in his sleep, reassured her that however much he might be trying to toughen up his image in the outside world, affection was still his middle name.

Polly wasn't a lady who lunched – unless it was for work – and told him so. Nor would she trot round London every night to whatever chic soirées were being hosted by the ladies who did. She went to book launches – for her authors only – and when she came home she was usually so tired she put her feet up and watched television while eating her supper before invariably returning to her desk in the upstairs sitting room for an hour or so.

Polly and her new assistant, Mrs Flowers, moved into the conservatory. To stop herself from going mad while she waited for the builders to finish her new office, Polly had begun to garden furiously and now, able to view the fruits of her labours from her desk, she thought she had never been so happy. Her new cordless phone enabled her to wander outside and weed while she negotiated. She wondered what the ambitious Pat Walsh would say if she knew she had just offered an advance of £43,000 to someone whose knees were buried in moist soil instead of sitting in a corner office at a black desk with a hi-tech Italian lamp.

Polly threw a party to launch the new office. She called it the Atwell Agency since Johnny already had PDS – Polly de Soto Productions. *Le tout* publishing turned up and as they wandered happily around her garden, champagne glasses clinking and Mrs Flowers' home-made bite-size vol-au-vents and sausage rolls disappearing rapidly, Polly knew she'd made it. There were people here who wouldn't even take her calls two years ago. She hadn't asked them but the news of her hit authors – Lawrence, Lucy Richards, Rebecca Price *et al.* – had made them curious and they'd come along and crashed her party. A sure sign of success.

There was one person who didn't enjoy the party at all: Joan. The problem was that she was out of work so when Polly introduced her and people asked her where she was working, she didn't have an answer. No one was interested in her, Polly was the centre of attention for once and Joan wasn't used to it. She left after an hour pleading an entirely phoney dinner date.

Polly could see Johnny was proud of her. He didn't know who any of the people were either but unlike Joan he didn't let it bother him and he was enjoying his role as the successful agent's other half. Before long his notebook was being extracted from inside his jacket and he was busily scribbling numbers and, Polly realised, plots of books from various gushing editors who would declare at their editorial meeting that 'the film rights have just been sold in this book or that . . .', such was the naivety of the publishing world that a producer had only so much as to say they were interested and the editor thought the film was as good as made.

A hard core of twenty or so were still scoffing vol-au-vents and sausage rolls at ten o'clock. Polly heard the doorbell in the distance, and groaned.

'I'll go,' said Johnny. When he didn't return Polly extricated herself from one of her more inebriated authors and went looking for him. As she started down the long passage to the hall, she heard Luana's voice.

'But I had to come, Poppa. Where else could I go?'

'You shouldn't have gone anywhere. Edith will be worried stiff,' Polly heard Johnny reply.

'She won't, Dad. That's the whole point. I just can't take it any more. She's crazy. She keeps threatening to –'

Polly stepped forward and Luana ran to her.

'Polly, I'm sorry to arrive without any warning. Please let me stay.'

'Of course you can stay. Your room's always waiting for you but why didn't you let us know you were coming?'

'She's done a runner.'

'She's what?'

'Run away from home.'

'Why?'

Luana looked at Johnny. Johnny slipped his arm around Luana's shoulders and took her upstairs.

'Bed for you, sweet peach. We'll decide what to do with you in the morning. Polly's got a party to take care of, haven't you, Pol?'

Johnny wouldn't even discuss it. Amidst the remains of the party he poured himself a whisky and refused to be drawn. He had gone very calm and still as he always did just before he lost his temper. Acidly polite. Answering all Polly's questions – what had happened? Had Edith gone away? What couldn't Luana take any more? Why had she run away from home?' – but never giving her a proper answer.

Finally he stood up.

'Polly.' Polly. Not Pol. A danger signal. 'I've said this before and I'll say it again. Please don't ask me questions about Edith and I don't want you quizzing Luana either. Edith is my past life. You are my present. That should be enough for you.'

'Why should it be enough for me? Why is there this mystery surrounding Edith?'

'There's this mystery because she wants to be left in peace and I respect that. I do not want her disturbed. Is that understood?'

He was livid now. He had gone perfectly still. Polly could feel his anger charged towards her. She left the room and went back to her party.

'Po-leee!' called Luana from her bedroom window, 'are you still down there? Come and tell me what Hector O'Neill was like? You must have met him at the Conway première. He's so scrummy! Polly . . .'

Luana had obviously been briefed. She became nervous whenever Polly mentioned Edith.

'I promised Dad. Mum's ill. No, actually, she's better now but you just have to be careful. Please let's not talk about her, Polly, please?'

And Luana was so appealing – like Johnny in a way – that Polly could never refuse her anything. She was growing to love her stepdaughter. Luana was sent back to Cornwall two days after Polly's party, but two weeks after that she was back. For good. No explanation. No message from Edith. Nothing.

Nor was Luana forthcoming.

'It's what I've always wanted to do, you know that,

Polly. Dad's been trying to persuade Mum for yonks. Every time he comes down he talks about it. Now he's finally got her to agree.'

Every time he comes down.

Polly couldn't believe it. Going down to Cornwall from London took a good five or six hours. He must have been lying to her when he said he was going to Paris or wherever it was he went. But she knew better than to raise it with him.

Mr Wrong went to the top of the American bestseller list and Juanita Whyte read it because *Vanity Fair* told her to. In actual fact she was reading one of the interminable serial killer profiles in *Vanity Fair* which mentioned *Mr Wrong* en passant.

Juanita told Johnny that they absolutely had to make the film. Johnny told Juanita to talk to his wife.

Suddenly it was 'Polly, darling, we simply must see more of each other. What about lunch next week at the Caprice?'

Fuck the Caprice, thought Polly with the phone cradled to her ear; if she wants to negotiate for the film rights in *Mr Wrong* what's wrong with here and now? Sitting in a wicker chair beside the Norwegian stove in her conservatory and marvelling at the stark beauty of her snow-covered garden, Polly played her tough agent role to the hilt and took Juanita to the cleaner's. If only you could have heard that, Joan, she thought. Johnny didn't speak to her for a week.

'All that sodding money to that scrawny little bastard!' she heard him mutter in his sleep.

Still, now he was back at work for real. He had to find a writer. Polly knew better than to suggest Lawrence immediately. She bided her time and sure enough Johnny shelled out Juanita's money for one dud script after another until Juanita came on the phone again.

'That boy you represent, darling. Johnny seems to think he couldn't possibly write his own screenplay. What do you think?'

'Of course he could – for the right price . . .' said Polly and promptly took Juanita back to the cleaner's.

'You'll take her money but you won't be friends with her!' complained Johnny.

'Oh, and what do you think you've been doing? Taking her money and supping with her. That makes your behaviour OK, does it?'

'I just wish you could be around a bit more for me, give dinner parties, that sort of thing.'

'I thought Juanita gave her little dinners for you. You spend enough time at them.'

'Well, why won't you come?'

'Because they bore me. It's like reading *Harpers & Queen* out loud all night. I've got better things to do. I'm sorry, Johnny.'

'But Pol, people are beginning to ask about you. I mean I was at Sophie Warner's party last week – Juanita took me so we could network –'

'I hate that word – network! There you are, Johnny, that's the difference between us. You go out and network and I stay in and tune in to the networks in the comfort of my own living room.'

Johnny wouldn't give up.

'People know who you are, you know. They say to me: "You're married to Polly Atwell, aren't you?" By the way, when did you change your name back, Pol? Anyway, they want you there, they want to see who you are.'

'Oh, I'm somebody now, am I?'

'Yeah, that's it. We could become a real London couple. I want everyone to know about you. We'll be invited everywhere.'

'That's just it, Johnny. I don't want to be invited everywhere just for the sake of being seen. I want to get on with my work, take care of my authors and Luana and see people who really mean something to me.'

'Mean something to you? Where do I fit in?'

'Wherever you want, Johnny. What you have to understand is that I don't fit in out there with all that crowd and I never will.'

'But I need you, Polly.'

'In what way, exactly?'

'I need someone to share everything with. I don't understand you. Here we are on the brink of making it all happen and you want to stay in every night.'

'Not every night.'

'Well, most nights. You go off and sit on your own and I never know what you're doing.'

'I'm reading manuscripts, I'm working. You know I have to read in the evenings. And as for not knowing what I'm doing, are you always where you say you are?'

'What's that supposed to mean?'

'Made any more trips to Cornwall lately?'

He acted as if she had never said it, just moved right on.

'I don't know how else to explain, Polly. I'm no good on my own. Some people just aren't. I want you out with me, that's all, by my side.'

'Johnny, I don't think it really matters who it is by your side. You just need someone. Anyone. What's wrong with Juanita? She seems to be prepared to hang on your every word. Why doesn't it ever occur to you that I need someone here at home with me in the evenings every now and again? Oh, God, now where are you going, Johnny? Come back. Don't rush off like that. Hold on . . .' As the front door slammed behind him she suddenly remembered his mother's words: 'Keep up with him, Polly. Don't let him get away. Don't hold him back. Let him go fast and keep up with him.'

As she lay in bed, surrounded by manuscripts she could no longer concentrate on, Polly found herself looking at the telephone, waiting for it to ring, waiting to hear Johnny's voice with the noise of a restaurant in the background begging her to join him.

Had he gone too far ahead of her and she'd been left behind? Or was it – could it be that it was the other way round? Had she gone too far ahead and he didn't like it?

She had her answer soon enough. The very next week he left her in the middle of the night.

PART TWO

Hector O'Neill was scared. He kidded himself he was excited at the prospect of looking for a new role to play now Conway had come to an end but in fact he was terrified. The world knew him as Conway. The world loved him as Conway. Worst of all, there was now a chance the world would discover that he couldn't act. Playing Conway he hadn't had to. He just had to look good and leave the rest to the special effects. Now his agent was proposing that he do something completely different. He picked up the script that had just arrived by messenger. That was another thing. He didn't really know how to read a script. For Conway he had just read the pages given him by the script girl every night, learned his lines for the following day's shooting, and then delivered them in the Irish brogue familiar to audiences all over the world. That had been enough. Lucky for him he had a good memory. His only preparation for his roles had been daily workouts in the gym and nightly workouts with available women.

That was something he had developed to a fine art:

the art of seduction. Before the sex he wined and dined the women and over the years he had honed his patter to perfection. He had learned that what women liked most of all was a man who listened to them.

He opened the script and saw the title.

Mr Wrong.

'All over the world women search for Mr Right. If, and when, they find him it never occurs to them that he might, in fact, be Mr Wrong.'

Too true! Take his mother, for example. She had picked Mr Wrong twice – his father and then Tony. If anyone had turned out to be Mr Wrong it was Tony.

He could have been Mr Right if it hadn't been for his parents. The universal hippie uniform worn by everyone attending Woodstock – jeans, T-shirts, waistcoats over bare chests, beads, flowers, long flowing dresses and shawls, sometimes nothing at all – had done away with any kind of class distinction. Somewhere in the back of her mind Mary Maguire must have known Tony had some kind of money, otherwise how could he afford to whisk her and her son away to a new life, organising their passports, and then their air tickets with the flash of a credit card. It was the first time John Hector had ever seen a credit card and he thought Tony must be some kind of magician to be able to wave a piece of plastic in the air instead of money and acquire things immediately.

Mary Maguire was so ecstatic at the thought of leaving behind her miserable existence in the shadow of the steelworks that she never stopped to wonder what kind of life awaited her in England. When the taxi made its way up a drive bordered by tall pines and drew up outside a Tudor mansion, Mary thought they had arrived at a castle. It would be some time before she understood the reality of her situation. It was a mock-Tudor house in Surrey and Tony's father was an ex-army stockbroker. After a stifling suburban childhood Tony had escaped to London where he had embraced all aspects of Sixties permissiveness, culminating, after the obligatory trips to India and Morocco, in the journey to Woodstock.

Nothing could have prepared Tony's parents for the arrival on their doorstep of an almost illiterate American steelworker's wife and her ten-year-old son. When he had told them he had met 'someone special' in America, his mother had implored him to forget whatever differences they might have had in the past and bring her home to meet them. Tony, who had not taken into account that his Chelsea pad would be too small to house his new family, welcomed it as an invitation to move Mary and John Hector into the Surrey mansion.

Tony's mother was appalled. After a week under her roof Mary Maguire traded her flower-power glad rags for polyester and cheap perfume. She left dirty coffee cups in every room. She roamed around the house in her underwear, rarely dressing before dark. She played loud music in Tony's room and she let her child stay up until all hours of the night.

'How long do they plan on staying, Tony? Do they have nowhere to go?'

'They're here for ever. They're with me,' Tony told his mother.

'Well, where is the child's father?'

'Killed in Vietnam.'

This was a myth that had been created by Mary. She hadn't exactly lied to Tony and told him her husband had been killed. She just hadn't bothered to correct him in his assumption that that was what had happened. John Hector was left in a similar hazy state as to the whereabouts of his father.

'Tony, they can't stay here. I can't have people to the house while they're here. It's embarrassing. You'll have to take them to London.'

By this time Tony had realised what he'd done. In a drug-crazed field in upstate New York with Ten Years After blasting out 'I'm Going Home', from the stage, Mary Maguire, her skin damp and glowing, clawing at his body and telling him he was blowing her mind, had seemed exactly what he wanted. So what if she had a kid. They could start a commune. But nobody started communes in Surrey, not even in Chelsea for that matter. Suddenly Mary and her kid had become a liability, a bore. Tony wanted out so he did what he always did when things became too heavy. He left.

His mother would have thrown Mary and John Hector out after him if it hadn't been for the intervention of Tony's father. He was, after all, a military man and the fact that the child's father had served his country in Vietnam and died for it made him a hero and they couldn't turn a hero's family out into the streets. As usual he would clean up after his son's mess.

But how?

Mary Maguire flatly refused to go back to Pennsylvania. She had been in Surrey for nearly two months and she liked it.

'John Hector has to go to school,' Tony's mother told her. 'You will have to find a job. It is our responsibility to support you until you have found one.'

Unfortunately Mary was unskilled and virtually unemployable. In the end it was the cleaner at the

Surrey mansion who came to her rescue. She had been making good use of Mary's idle hands and had shown her the delights of domestic work. To everyone's amazement, given the slut she had been when she arrived, Mary proved to be a natural cleaner and she asked Tony's mother for a job. This was acceptable. Providing the girl knew her place she could stay in the house. A live-in cleaner was an unheard-of luxury. She could be described as 'my new maid'. In the end Mary Maguire had come full circle from below stairs at Henry Avenue, Philadelphia to the kitchen wing of a mock-Tudor mansion in the stockbroker green belt of Surrey. She had always told John Hector that one day she would return to the life from whence she came and now, as she piled laundry into the washing machine and vacuumed the bedrooms, she felt she had fulfilled her promise.

On arrival in England John Hector retreated into himself as a kind of self-defence. He didn't understand where they were, he barely had time to get to know Tony before Tony upped and left, and he couldn't make out whether they were there to stay. With a child's simplistic intuition he could sense that he and his mother were not welcome in Surrey and he lived in constant fear that they would depart as suddenly as they had arrived and return to the Pennsylvania mobile home. Yet at the same time he became accustomed to the new-found luxury surrounding him. He slept in Tony's boyhood bedroom and played with Tony's abandoned toys. So when suddenly Mary moved him downstairs to a bleak little room behind the kitchen he didn't like it. He observed that they no longer had their meals with Tony's parents and he was relieved that he no longer had to listen to the old man's endless stories about the war – what war? – and the constant reminders that he must be so proud to have a father who had died for his country.

John Hector didn't have a photograph of his father. The only picture he had he carried in his mind: that of Jimmy Maguire coming up over the horizon in the haze of smoke and mist with the steelworks behind him, joshing with his buddies and disappearing into the saloon. Yet when he went to school, he found that Jimmy Maguire's alleged heroic death in Vietnam was one of the ways to put an end to the merciless teasing of his new English schoolmates in the playground. That and his American accent. These kids, he realised, had never met a real live American before. To them he was the nearest thing to the movies they'd ever seen. When they all sneaked in to see *Kelly's Heroes* one afternoon, suddenly John Hector sounded just like Clint Eastwood to them. They invited themselves to tea just so they could sit at the kitchen table and stare up at Mary Maguire, imagining she was a star from Hollywood.

Mary Maguire barely noticed them. She had her own problems. There was a man she'd met down the bingo who wanted to marry her but how could she marry him when as far as she knew she already had a husband? She didn't know how to find out what had happened to Jimmy Maguire without revealing her whereabouts to those she had deserted back in Pennsylvania. She was beginning to tire of being a cleaner. It was demoralising when Tony came home for the odd weekend with his parents and found she'd become the maid. But what could she do? For the second time in her life she felt trapped.

As for John Hector, it was one thing having the boys

forever getting him to do his Clint Eastwood impersonation. It was quite another to discover the effect his American roots had on the girls. He hadn't been aware that he was good looking. When he had arrived at the school he had been too young for the girls to notice him but when his voice changed and his legs grew longer and longer, he found himself surrounded. And confused. He had begun to lose his accent. There were traces of it here and there – he always said 'plenny' instead of plenty – but he was actually making a determined effort to become English in every way. Then the girls began to feature in his life and they wanted him American again. Yet while he could *sound* American, he now felt English. England was his home. So he had to pretend to be American. He had to act American.

He didn't have to act horny. He wanted all the girls he could get his hands on but just as he was poised to fall in love for the first time something happened to shake his faith in the female sex. From that point on, without even being fully aware of it, he distrusted women.

Mary Maguire left him.

She ran off for the second time – with the man from the bingo – only this time she left her son behind. OK, so he wasn't a small boy any more but he was an impressionable sixteen-year-old.

John Hector crumbled. By way of consolation he demanded sex of every girl who presented herself to him, ignoring them if they refused, dumping them the next day even if they consented. He smoked dope, he started drinking and Tony's father threw him out.

'You're a disgrace to your dead father's name,' he told him. 'Go and find your mother.'

It wasn't as if Mary Maguire had made a secret of her whereabouts. She had just made it clear that her new man did not want John Hector around, so the last thing John Hector was going to do was go looking for his mother.

He went to London and for two years he eked out a living as a labourer, an Irish brickie, whistling at the girls from the scaffolding and developing the powerful muscles that were to become part of the devastating overall Hector O'Neill package. Gracie Delaney's first sight of him was a pair of long jean-clad legs and a rippling bare torso. She responded to his 'I'd give you one any time, darling' not because she wanted him but because she was scouting for a male hunk to feature in a television commercial.

The product, predictably, was aftershave. John Hector, once persuaded down from the scaffolding, attended a casting and landed the part. He had to shave, naked from the waist up, looking at himself in the mirror and stroking his chin. Footsteps could be heard approaching throughout the commercial. As they reached John Hector he had to whip round and point what the audience assumed would be a gun at the intruder but which was of course the product, a product which was totally upstaged by John Hector's brilliant blue eyes.

John Hector received a sad little note from Tony's parents, who traced him through the advertising agency, informing him that his mother had died suddenly. When he called them for further details it became clear that she had been pregnant – at forty-four – with the bingo man's child and had tried to abort it dangerously late. They told him where she had been buried but John Hector was surprised to find that he had no desire to visit her grave. Thinking about her depressed him. Mary Ellen Maguire, dead at forty-four. What a pathetic, useless life. Thank God it was over. Now he could get on with his own.

He was living off the repeats from the commercial, waiting for something else to happen and trying to get into Gracie Delaney's knickers without success when he had the call for the Conway role.

Gracie was not a beauty. She was large and plain with a big nose but she had glossy chestnut hair and the most beautiful white skin John Hector had ever seen. He longed to touch it, to see more of it, but Gracie evaded any attempts he made to steer the conversation towards sex and went right on talking about his work.

'You'll go for the audition, of course?' Gracie was making him lunch at her flat. She was Irish American just like him and – the beauty of it – she was also from Pennsylvania. But she was a good Catholic girl and she wouldn't sleep with him just like that.

'But why not, Gracie? Where's the harm? You like me, don't you?'

If he only knew it, Gracie was dangerously close to falling in love with him but her time in London was up. She was due to return to Philadelphia the following month and she didn't want to complicate her life.

'I like you fine but I've a sweetheart waiting for me back home and I can't let you distract me, now can I?'

'Why not?' said John Hector, grinning at her and maddening her and thoroughly enjoying it. 'Tell me about him. How long have you known him?'

'Four years.'

'But you've been in London for two years. He's waited for you all this time? Is he good looking?'

'Not especially.'

'So what's so wonderful about him? Is he gentle with you? Does he understand you? You're an unusual person, Gracie.'

'Am I? How so?'

'You're sensitive. You need someone who can see beyond that stupid tough-girl "I can take care of meself" image you're always promoting. I bet you cry a lot when you're on your own, at music, at sentimental movies with happy endings. Am I right?'

'How does a brickie know what makes me tick? But yes, you're not far wrong. Frank is the "what-you-see-is-what-you-get" type. It'd never occur to him there's anything more to me than good old reliable Gracie Delaney, always there when you want her. My parents like him. He's from the neighbourhood. He's Catholic. They know where he's coming from. His brother's a priest. Frank's a teacher. Don't look like that, John Hector. Some of us want stability in our lives. Anyway, what about your parents? I bet they want you to marry a nice Catholic girl too. Oh, God, why does it always come down to what my parents want? Why can't I grow up and break away from them? I thought coming to London and landing a job in the glamorous world of casting would place me beyond their reach. But here I am going right back to them.'

'And to Frank.'

'Damn Frank! I don't want Frank. He's so . . .'

'Boring?'

'Unadventurous. He wouldn't come to England with me. He's not interested in anything that happens outside of his precious little world. How can he teach anybody anything when he hasn't even got an enquiring mind? Oh, why am I telling you all this?'

'Because I'm listening.' John Hector said it without

thinking but he also realised that because he had remained silent without distracting her, she had let it all spill out. Now, typically, she felt guilty. 'And because there's a part of you that is terrified at the thought of settling down in Pennsylvania for the rest of your life. Believe me, I'd be pretty confused if I were you. But you'll be OK once you're back there.'

'All this talking about myself when it's you we should be thinking of. And you never answered my question. What about your own parents? Are they not after you to bring home a nice Catholic girl?'

'They're dead. I think.'

'They're not? How altogether terrible. What do you mean, you think? Don't you know?'

She was the first – and only – person John Hector told about his background, probably because of the coincidence that she too came from Pennsylvania. As he talked about his father and the fact that he didn't know whether he was dead or alive, he choked on his words. Gracie put her arms around him. She held him close and kissed his temple, stroked his hair and soothed him. Within minutes she was letting him make love to her and afterwards John Hector reflected on how he had learned another valuable lesson. Open up to a woman, tell her a sob story, make yourself vulnerable, engage her sympathy and the chances are you'll hit a home run.

Gracie was angry with herself. She should have seen that coming. To hide her embarrassment she became super-practical.

'I've been thinking about this Conway audition. You need to have something to make them remember you. A whole new image. How Irish can you be?'

'As Irish as you want.'

'Then we'll work on the accent. Use the American angle. OK, so you don't want to say you were raised in a mobile home and you're a steelworker's kid but you can still be Irish. Why don't we change your name? With a new name you can psych yourself into a whole new persona. How about O'Neill? The O'Neills from Beacon Hill, Boston. You grew up on Newbury Street. Your mother shopped at Bonwit Teller, no Filene's bargain basement for the O'Neills. And you should lose the John. Just Hector from now on. Hector O'Neill.'

It was a game they played until she left, a diversion to distract her from what had happened, to stop her thinking about life with Frank as a schoolteacher's wife. On her last morning she approached him shyly and told him she had an idea.

'Why don't I go back to your home town and find out what happened to your father? I could make the trip, easy, and you have to know one day. I'll be discreet, find out all I can, then I'll write you.'

He knew it was in part a way for her to keep in touch with him but he agreed. Again he was surprised that while he had been ready to bury his mother for good, he remained curious about his father. The picture of him coming over the hill with his lunchbox was as vivid as it had always been.

Her letter arrived the day his newly acquired agent confirmed that he had been cast as Conway. The press were on their way to interview him. It was a great story: young Irish American heart-throb catapulted from nowhere to instant stardom. They had the brand name all ready: Kennedy/Conway.

Hector read the letter as his agent's voice rose in excitement on the other end of the phone.

Dear John Hector,

I am going to give you the truth because that's what I promised you I would do.

Your father, Jimmy Maguire, is alive. He came back from the war and found you and your mother gone and apparently it hit him very hard. He started drinking heavily and he hasn't stopped. He's on welfare. I had someone point him out to me and I'm sorry, John Hector, but I had to go and speak to him. He is a mess. He has only one set of clothes and they stink. He sleeps rough most nights. He was wounded in 'Nam and he has difficulty walking. John Hector, you have to do something. I can't pretend your father is a hero. He's a vile smelling drunken bum but he needs your help. Send him money care of me as soon as you can. I'll see he gets it.

The letter went on for two more pages. She was going to marry Frank, she missed John Hector, she prayed for his success, but always she returned to the subject of his father.

In a flash Hector saw how it would look to the press. With a washed-up Vietnam vet for a father, his story would take a very different turn. It'd have to be dirt poor Pennsylvania instead of Boston. Everything would have to come out. He was on the brink of entering the kind of world his wretched mother had fantasised about in vain. What was the point in jeopardising such a chance?

He threw away Gracie Delaney's letter without answering it.

Yet he never forgot her. She had discovered him. She had changed his name for him, she had reinvented him. As he read *Mr Wrong*, he found himself wondering what

151

she would have made of it. When he finished it he knew he had to do it. His agent had been right. It was a logical step to take. Suave playboy murderer seducing women in every frame. He dialled his agent.

'It says Whyte/De Soto Productions. Who the hell's De Soto?'

'Some wop Juanita's got into bed with, metaphorically speaking I hope,' said his agent.

'You mean it was Juanita Whyte who thought of me for this role? She's got more brains that I've given her credit for.'

'No, Hec, it was the other guy, Johnny de Soto. Matter of fact it wasn't even him. It was his daughter. Kid called Luana. Works in a casting agency.'

Just like Gracie Delaney, mused Hector. He wondered what she was like, this Luana de Soto.

Luana had never met the man placed beside her at dinner. She hadn't even been introduced to him before they sat down and so far he had spent the entire meal deep in conversation with the girl on his left.

So it was all the more exciting when she felt his hand move under her skirt, his fingers firmly kneading the flesh on the inside of her thigh beneath her stockings. She almost choked on her apricot soufflé as he unpopped a suspender.

She moved her chair further under the table to enable him to continue his exploration unwitnessed by their fellow diners, but to her intense disappointment he removed his hand. She was about to turn and silently implore him to go on when the man on her right began to talk to her again. She tried to concentrate on the earnest young publisher's description of the biography he was bringing out next month, was about to ask him if he knew her stepmother, the literary agent Polly de Soto – or did she call herself Polly Atwell since Johnny took off, Luana never could remember, probably not, it wasn't as if they were divorced – when she felt the hand return. Higher this time. To her horror she sensed the button at the side of her waist being undone, the zip of her skirt sliding down and the hand reaching in, moving across her stomach, skin on skin, and down to her cunt. It squeezed. An index finger probed, found her clitoris, stroked.

Luana plunged a spoonful of apricot soufflé into her mouth and sucked on her spoon.

The hand withdrew.

Luana discreetly did up her skirt and murmured to the publisher: 'I'm so sorry, I have to go to the loo. Would you excuse me?'

'Of course.' He half rose to his feet as she escaped. Outside the dining room she realised she didn't know where it was. She went into the hall and sat on an ottoman at the bottom of the stairs, wishing she could masturbate, staring at the black and white tiles on the floor, wondering how long she would have to wait.

She had noticed him the minute she'd arrived with Frederick, the young actor who had brought her. Frederick had introduced her to her host and hostess, friends of his parents, and the stranger had watched her from across the room, never looking at her face, staring at first one part of her body and then another till she obliged him by deliberately dropping her bag on the floor and bending over to pick it up so that he could see right down the front of her low-cut dress to her tits, and probably as far as her navel.

He came into the hall and grabbed her by the hand, pulling her up the stairs. Half-way up, before the stairs doubled back to the first floor, there was a door. He drew her into the bathroom behind it, closed the door and pushed her up against it. A pair of towelling robes fell to the floor. Without even taking off his jacket, he undid his flies and took out his erect penis, thick, uncircumcised with a large smooth cap. He fished a condom out of his pocket.

'Want to suck first?'

Luana opened her mouth automatically. She did want to suck but she didn't have time. She flicked her tongue in and out of her mouth at him and he sucked on that a few times, squeezed her breasts through her dress and turned away to ease the condom on to himself. Luana took hold of him and guided him back to her, hoisting her dress up with the other hand. In one quick movement he was right inside her. He began to move fast, taking her by the shoulders. Behind him she could see them reflected in the mirror above the basin, his trousers down to his ankles and just below his jacket his bare buttocks thrusting into her, banging against the door making a hard rhythmic sound that increased in momentum. She wouldn't climax. She never did. Her mind began to wander. She recalled what their position reminded her of: the scene in *The Godfather* where James Caan screws a guest in an upstairs room at his sister's wedding.

Her moans increased as she pretended to come and he clasped a hand over her mouth although the sound of her body being hurled against the door had been just as loud. She was trembling all over as he withdrew from her. He pulled up his trousers, tucked himself away and left without looking at her once.

When she went back down they had left the dining room and were having coffee next door. He was sitting on the arm of a chair, stroking the blonde hair of the woman sitting in it. He was the hostess's brother, she learned, the blonde woman his wife. She would never see him again. How did they always manage to pick her out, she wondered. How did they always know about her?

Frederick drove her home, or rather back to his flat in Earls Court. It never occurred to Luana that she had already fucked one man that night. She let an eager Frederick undress her and attempt clumsy foreplay before entering her. It took him over a quarter of an hour to come. His skinny penis inside her rendered a pleasurable tickle but there was no way he was going to satisfy her. No one could, especially not Frederick. She licked his face absentmindedly and as she began to feel sleepy, she began to tweak his nipples to hurry him up a bit. It usually worked.

Poor Frederick.

As soon as she arrived at the Hendersons', Polly saw that they'd asked Edward Holland again. Christ, Grania Henderson was persistent. Polly's only Mills & Boon author, Grania clearly thought that her career as a romantic novelist gave her an automatic licence to be the perfect matchmaker. Ever since the news about Johnny's leaving had begun to travel, Grania had been on the telephone once a month with unfailing regularity, issuing invitations. Polly had managed to be busy for all except two and on each occasion Edward Holland had been there. Now here he was for the third time. Polly had not really said more than a few words to him at the drinks party and the buffet supper to which they'd both been invited before but this was a sit-down dinner and, feeling somewhat trapped, Polly realised she was being placed beside him.

'Did you get a chance to chat to Edward Holland?' Grania had asked after the buffet supper, trying to sound innocent. 'You know, you met him once before at our Christmas drinks, remember? No? What a shame. He's been divorced for just two years. She was a complete cow. I hated her. Dear Edward, we do so love him . . . never mind. I'll make sure you meet again.'

And here they were. He was attractive enough, Polly conceded. Fiftyish. Not much hair on top but what there was of it was surprisingly thick without much grey. Nice grey eyes. Rather florid cheeks. Not very tall. Square frame. Expressive hands with carefully manicured fingernails. Polly hastily took her elbows off the table and placed her unvarnished nails in her lap out of sight.

'We've met before, haven't we?' He offered her the bread basket. 'I'm Edward Holland. I'm in advertising. You're Polly, aren't you?'

'Well remembered. Polly Atwell.'

'Remind me what it is you do.'

'I'm a literary agent.'

'Of course. You're Grania's agent. How's business?'

'Pretty good. How's advertising?'

'Better than ever. I worked with Peter Mayle, you know?'

'Really?'

'Oh yes, me and Peter. Like that, we were.'

'Heavens.'

'Long time ago, of course.'

'Of course.'

'I wonder if I've got a bestseller in me?'

'I don't know. Have you?'

'Well, I am an ad man. Like Peter.'

'I'm not sure it follows. Can you write? Have you spent a year anywhere? Like Provence?'

'Eh, no, not really. Been stuck in Camberwell for years. Ever since my wife left.'

Polly ignored it.

'So did you enjoy your old friend Peter's book?'

'*A Year in Provence*? Truth is, I never read it.'

'Truth is,' said Polly laughing, 'nor have I – at least not that one. But I did read – or rather look at – *Wicked Willie*.'

'So what on earth is that?'

'Huge hit. Cartoon book about a talking dick.'

Edward Holland went bright pink. Oh God, I've embarrassed him, thought Polly, he really is rather sweet.

At the end of the evening she asked Grania for the number of the local minicab firm and Edward leapt to his feet.

'I won't hear of it. I'll drop you home.'

'Edward, we're in Clapham. You live in Camberwell. Polly's in completely the opposite direction. She lives in Notting Hill Gate.' Even Grania was amazed. 'The Simpsons are going right past her door.'

'I insist,' said Edward gravely and Polly tried hard not to giggle.

'That *Wicked Willie* book,' he said as he drew up outside the house, 'sounds fun. I shall buy a copy.'

'Then you can get your friend to sign it for you.'

'Well, he's not really my friend,' Edward confessed. 'I was just showing off a bit.'

'Well, thank you so much for the lift. I fear I've taken you terribly out of your way. May I offer you one for the road by way of compensation?' Polly was half out of the car, assuming he'd say no.

He leapt out with her.

'That'd be wonderful.'

As they walked up the steps a ferocious yapping broke out from inside. Polly tentatively unlocked the front door and was assaulted by Zutty, flying up at her, feathery tail uncurling and wagging. She picked up a note from Johnny on the hall table.

> Dear Pol, where are you? I rang and rang but just got the answering machine. No answer when I came round so I let myself in. Hope you don't mind but I've left Zutty. Got to go to Paris till day after tomorrow. His food is in box under hall table. Ditto his new basket. I'm trying to train him not to sleep on my bed. Bit late now but still. Say BARKEY! to him, point at the basket and he's supposed to jump in it and go to sleep. I'll pick him up in 48 hours. He eats once a day in the evening. I've fed him tonight so don't give him anything whatever fuss he makes.
>
> J.

Zutty didn't like Edward Holland and went for his shoelaces, growling.

'Barkey!' said Polly firmly. Edward looked very startled. 'Not you, Edward. That. *Barkey*!' Polly picked up Zutty by the scruff of the neck and shoved him in his basket. 'Now, stay! Bloody dog. What'll you drink, Edward?'

'Whisky please. With water. Right up to the top.'

'So how long have you known the Hendersons?' she asked him.

'Oh, years. My wife was at school with Grania. Grania adores her. She was devastated when we broke up.'

Polly heard Grania's voice saying distinctly: 'She was an absolute cow!'

'You're divorced too, aren't you?' said Edward, edging crab-like along the sofa towards her.

Zutty saved her by going berserk, charging out of his basket and sniffing the bottom of the front door, tail going wag, wag, wag.

'Zutty! Barkey! This minute!' began Polly, then there was the sound of the key in the lock and Johnny came in wearing a baseball cap and a long black coat over jeans and sneakers.

'Hi, Pol.'

'What happened to Paris?'

'Missed the bloody plane. Pile-up on the M4. Cab couldn't get round it. How's my *Baby*?' Zutty had flown into his arms.

What an utterly ridiculous sight, thought Polly fondly. 'Johnny, this is Edward Holland.'

Johnny came forward, still carrying Zutty.

'Edward, this is Johnny de Soto.'

'Your husband?' Edward looked utterly bewildered.

'Yes, and the film producer,' said Polly. 'Edward's in advertising. He was a friend of Peter Mayle's.'

'How is Peter?' Polly raised her eyes to heaven. She knew perfectly well Johnny had never met Peter Mayle in his life. 'Pol, did I tell you I was going to Paris to get the final go-ahead for *Mr Wrong*? Any day now. After all this time.'

Johnny had set up *Mr Wrong* as a French co-production on the understanding that half the picture was relocated in France.

'I'd better be getting back to Camberwell.' Edward put down his drink.

'Couldn't drop me and Zutty off on the way, could you? Roland Gardens.' Polly turned away. Johnny sometimes used Edith's old flat where he had first seduced Polly and the reminder of it still made her nostalgic. As she showed Johnny out, Edward whispered nervously: 'May I call you? Could you give me your number?'

'I'll give it to you in the car,' yelled Johnny over his shoulder. 'Night, Pol.'

Polly kicked the door shut behind them.

She opened it again a few seconds later.

'Johnny,' she yelled into the night, 'you forgot Barkey!'

And she flung it after him.

Polly went out early the next morning before Mrs Flowers arrived. She wanted to shop for food in Portobello Road. Luana was coming to supper that night and Polly had been looking forward to it all week. Her stepdaughter had moved out of the house to share a flat with a friend and Polly missed her. Worse, she worried about her. Luana was so thin. Polly was convinced she never ate anything unless someone else fed her so she insisted Luana come to eat with her at least once a month when Polly would cook a veritable feast and always ensure that Luana left clutching the leftovers in little silver foil takeaway containers.

Polly bought a couple of sirloin steaks from Lidgates, some new potatoes, some tomatoes to grill and some mangetouts. She had left a bowl of chick peas to soak and planned to cook them and mix them in a salad as a starter with lemon, walnut oil, garlic, salt and pepper, and fresh coriander and flat leaf parsley. For pudding there was tiramisu for which she had made a special trip to Soho the day before. Luana adored tiramisu and Polly had bought enough for the takeaway containers as well. There would be some of the chick pea salad left over but it would be hard to eat cold leftover steak the next day. Polly returned to the butcher's and exchanged the steak for a fillet of beef to roast. They could have it hot and then Luana could take away a pile of cold slices to pick at from her refrigerator.

As she walked back down Ladbroke Grove to the house, Polly thought about Johnny's surprise appearance the night before. Not that it was a rare occurrence. In the time since he had left she realised she still saw him every couple of weeks. The problem was that wherever he lived there was never enough space for all his clothes. The basic plan was that he took his summer wardrobe and left his winter one and then returned to exchange it when it grew colder. But being Johnny, he never seemed to have the right things. There was always something he needed just as he was going away on a trip.

Then there was Zutty to be looked after. In the beginning Polly tried to explain in vain about the existence of kennels but Johnny wasn't having any.

'Zutty doesn't like kennels.'

'How do you know? You've never sent him to one.'

'We discuss it. He tells me. I say, Zutty, old fruit, want to go to kennels or Polly? He says Polly every time. He loves being with you, Pol. You should be flattered. He doesn't like everybody.'

It wasn't just when he went away. Johnny arrived on the doorstep at seven o'clock one morning holding his dog at arm's length.

'Zutty's got fleas!' he told Polly accusingly as if it were her fault, and nipped into the hall before she could shut them out.

'Well, what do you expect me to do about it?'

'You know about dogs, Pol.'

'I don't know how to deal with fleas. Take him to the vet. Get some powder or something.'

'I don't know a vet.'

'Yellow Pages.'

'I haven't got a Yellow Pages.'

'Is Rachel still on this planet?'

'Rachel hates dogs.'

'She didn't until you got one. Does she hate Yellow Pages too?' But he looked so genuinely crestfallen that as usual she relented and dealt with Zutty's fleas. In her mind she heard Luana's voice: 'Polly, you shouldn't be such a pushover with Dad. You spoil him rotten!'

But now that Luana had left and Johnny no longer picked her up from the house, Zutty, Polly realised with a lurch, was their only bond. Yet she loved her freedom – manuscripts spread out all over the bed and no need to clear them up to make way for him. She could eat whenever she wanted. No more hours wasted in the kitchen preparing his meals according to his 'just checking what's for dinner' requests issued down the telephone only to receive a further call at nine o'clock to say he was at Le Caprice, the Ivy or wherever.

No more videos blaring in the bedroom till three in the morning. Now she could bank up her favourite soaps and watch them in peace. But the most infuriating thing about Johnny had been his constant need to know exactly what she was doing every second they were in the house together – and even when they weren't.

'What are you doing, Pol?'   'I'm on the loo.'

'What are you doing, Pol?'

'I'm dicing carrots for the casserole.'

Five minutes later. 'What are you doing now?'

'I'm putting them in the pan.'

Or: 'Johnny, where are you?'

'I'm in a phone booth at Charles de Gaulle. What are you doing?'

'I'm standing here answering the phone.'

'But what were you doing?'

'I just walked through the door.'

'Well, what are you going to do now?'

It was always the trivial everyday things that interested him, never her big deals or her excitement when she read a wonderful manuscript by a new author but where she had been for lunch that day, what she had eaten, who with, what had they said?

Grand dramas left him cold. 'There was a security alert on the Underground. They found a bomb. They defused it but think, Johnny, if I'd been there five minutes earlier I'd have been killed' was greeted with 'Why didn't you take a bus? I like buses. Did you buy me my toothpaste?'

Well, he was gone now. She no longer thought about him every day.

Now she only thought about him every other day.

M rs Flowers was in the midst of opening parcels
when Polly arrived back with the meat.
'Mrs Brock called. She wanted to know if
you were free for lunch.'

'Call her back and say yes, fine. Ask her to meet me
in First Floor at 1.15.'

Polly disappeared into the kitchen to put away the
meat. She could hear Mrs Flowers on the phone in the
conservatory.

'Well, she did say First Floor. Just a minute, I'll ask
her. Mrs de Soto, Mrs Brock was wondering if you
would meet her at a new Lebanese restaurant she's
discovered in Knightsbridge?'

'No!' shouted Polly, 'I've got far too much to do. If I
have to go all the way to Knightsbridge I won't be back
here till three. She's not working, ask her if she'll . . .'

'She's rung off, Mrs de Soto.' Mrs Flowers always
insisted on absolute formality. 'Just as well I wrote down
the name of the restaurant.'

It was an old trick of Joan's. If Polly rang her back
she would already have left – or at least she wouldn't

pick up the phone so it would look as if she had. That way Polly was forced to go to wherever Joan had chosen.

'Cup of coffee, Mrs Flowers?'

'Decaf?' Mrs Flowers was on a health kick. She brought in a container of lentil soup every day which she proceeded to heat up for her lunch.

'Decaf beans, no less,' called Polly. 'I went to the Monmouth Coffee House yesterday.'

Mrs Flowers took her cup and looked at Polly gravely.

'Don't think I don't appreciate what you do for me, Mrs de Soto.'

'It's just a cup of coffee . . .'

'Maybe, but if I was working at Patrick Fisher & Dunbar or any of those other big offices nobody would be making me a cup of coffee, it'd be the other way round. And after all you've been through . . .'

Polly began to look through her mail. The words 'And after all you've been through' always heralded a recitation of the ills Mrs Flowers imagined Polly had suffered as an abandoned wife. Mrs Flowers had taken Johnny's leaving far worse than Polly had and there were times when Polly wondered whether the mythical Mr Flowers had indeed existed and done a similar bunk.

Polly found she had been sent four special book proofs – early promotional paperbacks of hardcover books printed to garner publicity and support for the book from the trade. She looked at the covers. Each one had a dashing young man in uniform clasping a beautiful fragile heroine in his arms. 'An epic story of a love that triumphed,' said one. 'An epic tale of a love that triumphed,' said another. Story, tale, what was the difference? thought Polly. 'They braved everything for each other in World War I,' said the third, and 'Their love conquered all in World War II,' said the fourth. Turning them over she was informed in more or less the same words that the books would all paint a passionate picture of love and loss, sweep the reader along on a tide of emotion, depict a cast of unforgettable characters, brilliantly capture the intensity of the period, and last but not least, they were all 'Fiction on a Grand Scale'.

The nationwide promotion for each one would include:
HUGE MEDIA COVERAGE, SPECTACULAR WINDOW DISPLAY MATERIAL, 12 COPY DUMPBIN AND HEADER, FULL COLOUR POSTER, TRADE MAGAZINE INSERT, COLOUR ADVERTISING IN 'COSMOPOLITAN', 'SHE', 'GOOD HOUSEKEEPING' AND 'WOMAN'S JOURNAL'. They were all being published in the same month, two in the same week.

Polly stared at them. If she hadn't been able to see the authors' names she knew she would not have been able to tell them apart. Yet as they were all written by her clients she knew they were all very different books. It looked as if the same book was being published by four different publishers. How would the public know which story of tumultuous passion to choose? If Polly had a problem recognising their books how would the authors themselves feel? She knew she ought to be jumping up and down because her authors' books were getting such a big push from their publishers but there was one book that caused her particular concern: the new Rebecca Price.

There had been a takeover by one of the big conglomerates of the publishing house to which Polly had sold Rebecca's novel when she had changed direction prior to Patrick Fisher's death. Rebecca's editor was still there but hanging on to her job for dear life. She no longer had any clout whatsoever. The marketing department ruled and had decreed that Rebecca Price should get a new look. This, it would appear, was it. No matter that Rebecca had in fact written a sensitive and delicate exploration of the feelings of a young novice in love with a reckless Fenian, a piece of writing worthy of entry for a literary prize. Here it was, tarted up like a Mills & Boon (why was there a man in a British soldier's uniform on the cover and why did the woman look like Vivien Leigh in *Gone With The Wind* when even Audrey Hepburn in *The Nun's Story* would have been a step in the right direction?), with the words 'They braved everything for each other in WWI'. World War I hadn't even started by the end of the book – and what had happened to the marvellous quote from William Trevor?

'Mrs de Soto, there's someone called Zoë Nichols on line two. Shall I ask her what it's in connection with?'

Polly shoved the book proofs aside and reached for the phone in relief. She knew she would have to wade in and sort out the marketing of Rebecca's book but she just couldn't face it right now.

'Presumably it's in connection with me,' said Polly who hated it when Mrs Flowers asked her that question. She knew Mrs Flowers was only trying to protect her but she thought it sounded so offputting, as if Polly Atwell was just too grand to talk to most people. That simply wasn't the case. Polly needed access to any potential client who might come her way. The name Zoë Nichols rang a bell somewhere but she couldn't quite place it. 'Put her through.'

'Hi, my name's Zoë Nichols. You probably won't

have heard of me. I've written a couple of Mills & Boons and the odd piece of journalism. The reason I'm ringing you is that I've been meaning to get myself an agent for some time as I'm in the middle of writing a novel. Now something a little more pressing has come up and I feel I need some advice. I've been approached to ghost a novel for a supermodel.'

'Well done, you. Which one?' Polly remembered now. She'd read a piece on casting directors Zoë Nichols had written for one of the colour magazines. It was warm and funny and Polly had enjoyed it.

'Aroma Ross.'

'Good Lord!' Aroma Ross was trouble, or so the tabloids would have everyone believe. On Sunday afternoons, Polly sometimes took a break from the pile of manuscripts to watch *The Clothes Show* and they featured her as much as they could because, despite her exotic heritage, Aroma Ross was a British citizen and alongside Naomi Campbell and Kate Moss, one of the few British supermodels. Polly was fascinated by her. She was half Italian/half Thai and the mix resulted in a smouldering Latin look with long black hair, a strong jaw, a beautiful long straight nose, high cheekbones and a slightly slanting Oriental cast to her huge doe eyes. 'Why does she want to write a novel? She can't be more than twenty.'

'I'm not even sure she does. I've just been approached by the publishers. It's probably their idea, or her agent's.'

'Well, look, I can't talk now. I'm due somewhere for lunch. To tell you the truth I'm more interested in the fact that you, Zoë Nichols, are writing a novel than I am in you writing Aroma Ross's great work. How are you fixed tomorrow?'

Polly jumped in a cab feeling rather excited as she always did at the prospect of a new client. When she arrived at the restaurant Joan was sitting there fuming, literally, puffing furiously at a cigarette. Patience had never been one of her virtues.

'Darling!' she blew smoke into each of Polly's ears by way of greeting, 'any sex, any cheques?' she asked as usual. 'Any men ring you this week? Waiter, ashtray, waiter!' The word 'please' was not part of Joan's restaurant vocabulary.

'No,' said Polly truthfully. 'You?'

'Only Victor.' Victor was a crime reporter from Nottingham who had a face like a bloodhound and had been in love with Joan for twenty years. Or so Joan claimed. Polly knew the entire lunch would focus on the subject of men or rather the lack of them. If Polly ever said something like 'I went to see *The Commitments* last night', Joan's first question was always 'Who with?', never 'What was it like?'

'So how was it at the Hendersons'?'

'How did you know about the Hendersons?'

'You told me you were going ages ago. Who was there?'

Polly realised she couldn't remember anybody besides Grania, her husband and Edward Holland.

'Oh, there were about eight of us.'

'Yes, but who? Who did you sit next to?'

'Edward Holland.'

'Who's he?'

'Friend of the Hendersons.'

'Well, obviously. Now, Polly, what are you going to have to eat? I don't suppose you know anything about Lebanese food. I'll order for you. We'll have some *kibbeh*, some *tabbouleh*, some *fattoush*, some *falafel*, some . . .'

Polly tried to convey that she adored Lebanese food and knew exactly what she wanted but Joan rattled on.

'Polly, see that bloke sitting behind us, big, thickset, heavy man having lunch on his own. Don't look at him for heaven's sake. Well, he's a bodyguard. Bound to be. Those two women sitting in the corner with the veils and whatsits, one's a Saudi princess and this man sitting here is her bodyguard. She sent him out to get her something while I was waiting for you. So what was he like?'

'What was who like?' Polly looked round again at the bodyguard.

'Edward thing. The man you met at the Hendersons'. What was he like?'

'What do you mean?'

'Is he married?'

'Oh. No. Divorced.'

A rare species. Joan's eyes widened with interest. 'Really? So what happened?'

'We had coffee in the drawing room after dinner and – '

'Poll-ee, did you sleep with him for heaven's sake?'

Polly sighed. All over London, she assumed, available women went out to dinner and leapt straight into bed with the man they sat next to. Everyone, it seemed, except her.

'No.'

'Why not? Why didn't you go home with him?'

'I did. Or rather he came home with me.'

'So what went wrong?'

'Johnny came in.' Polly felt rather pleased with herself. It had never entered her head that Edward

172

Holland wanted to sleep with her but now she could pretend to Joan that he wanted to and Johnny had ruined it.

'So did you sleep with Johnny?'

'I didn't sleep with anybody. I read twenty pages of a manuscript and fell asleep.'

'Have you slept with Johnny since he left you?'

'You know I haven't. Have you?' she added wickedly. Just for a second Joan looked quite taken aback.

'He's your husband. You know I wouldn't. In fact I find him quite repellent as you very well know and you're well rid of him but we won't go into all that again. Just to put your mind at rest, he's never even asked me out. Fact is, no one has for over two months.'

'What happened to that guy on *Newsweek?*'

'He went back to Washington. It was a week of bliss, just enough to really whet my appetite then nothing, not even a phone call.'

'Maybe he'll be back.'

'Maybe he will but meanwhile I need someone now. I gatecrash drinks parties every single night but it just doesn't seem to work like it used to. These days they all seem to have dinners arranged before they arrive. They're all work parties. No one comes to drinks parties any more looking for a dinner date, especially not someone with lines all over her face and varicose veins all over her legs. May God be eternally thanked for opaque tights but what will happen if I ever get as far as the bedroom again? Do I clamber 'tween the sheets in my opaques in case he catches a glimpse of my unsightly calves? So, Edward Holland. Attractive?'

'I suppose so.'

'Rich?

'Advertising.'

'Any money of his own? Oh, don't look so horrified, Polly. I'm sure you didn't ask him outright but there are ways of finding out these things. Where does he live?'

'Camberwell.'

'Camberwell? Oh, dear.' Joan made it sound like the Outer Hebrides. 'Well, maybe he's got a house in one of those nice Georgian squares one hears about. So when are you seeing him again?'

'I'm not as far as I know.'

'You mean you let a divorced man disappear into the night without getting a date out of him?'

Polly nodded glumly. Here she was, becoming a highly successful literary agent, yet Joan always managed to make her feel as if she wasn't trying hard enough.

The truth was that since Johnny had left, Polly's life had settled into an ordered calm that was really rather comforting. To exist without a man in her life brought a certain serenity she had never before experienced. Not having to pander to Johnny's whims and whirlwind tours in and out of the house meant Polly could give far more attention to the areas in her own life that were important to her. Her work flourished; she felt less tired at the end of the day and the abundance of early nights she was getting was doing wonders for her skin. Trying not to feel smug, she observed the wide fan of lines etched out over Joan's cheeks away from her eyes.

'Well, Polly, there's just no hope for you. I must tell you though, I do have a treat in store later this week. You know I've been doing some freelance work. Well, I've hit the jackpot. I've been commissioned to do a profile of Hector O'Neill.'

'Conway!'

'Exactly, except he says this is the last Conway he's going to do.'

'Bet they all say that. I met him once.'

'Polly, you dark horse! Did you sleep with him?'

Polly frowned in exasperation. Why couldn't anyone mention a man without Joan wanting to know if you'd been to bed with him?

'I met him for twenty seconds at a première I went to with Johnny. We weren't even introduced. He just whispered something in my ear.'

Joan looked incredulous. 'Was it filthy?'

'I honestly can't remember. How many words do they want on him?'

'Three and a half thousand.'

'Long. Actually, I've got a treat tonight too.'

Joan looked up from her onion soup.

'Luana's coming to supper.'

Joan raised her eyes to heaven.

'Your stepdaughter? Why do you still see her? Trying to keep tabs on Johnny?'

'Not at all. I adore Luana. You know that.'

'I suppose I do although I just don't get it. There's something creepy about that girl. What does she look like now that she's grown up?'

'Frighteningly thin. She darts everywhere. Never still for a second. She sort of flashes at you like a streak of lightning . . .'

'How exhausting.' Joan yawned.

'No, she's beautiful. Honestly!'

'Polly, you're too kind for your own good.' Joan rested her chin in her hand and smiled at Polly. 'That kid always did take advantage of you.'

'Nonsense. I genuinely adore her. I'm so looking forward to seeing her.'

'What about her mother?'

'No idea. Luana never mentions her. She lives in Cornwall.

'Yes, of course she does. Did I tell you that I was lunching at Kensington Place last week and Johnny was at the next table. Come to think of it, he said he'd just come back from Cornwall. Is he making a film there?'

'Not as far as I know.' Did Joan do it on purpose? Surely not.

The waiter appeared at their table.

'The two gentlemen sitting over there would like to buy you lunch.'

'Oh no,' said Polly, 'we couldn't possibly – '

'Thank them very much.' Joan looked in their direction and flashed a phoney smile.

'Joan, we can't. They'll come and sit with us.'

'No, they won't. They're Arabs, for heaven's sake. In their world they don't like to see two women eating on their own. The man should pay. If they were half-way decent looking I'd invite them over, if only to do my bit for your predicament.'

'My predicament?'

'Husband left you. No man. Got to find you another one because you obviously aren't trying hard enough yourself.'

Polly decided it was time she got Joan off the subject of men.

'Did you ever come across Aroma Ross when you worked on *Vogue*?'

'Of course. She was darling. She was always asking me over, wanted me to be one of the girls.'

'Weren't you a bit old?'

'Ooh, bitchy Polly. Thank you very much!'

'Sorry. What I meant was, if you were a friend of hers, tell me, what was she like?'

'I told you. Darling.'

'So you wouldn't mind if a client of mine came to talk to you about her?'

'Who's that?'

'Zoë Nichols.'

'Two-bit writer who does the odd piece for the colour mags? Why would I want to talk to her?'

'So you've heard of her. She's been approached to ghost Aroma Ross's novel.'

'Oh, I don't think I could help her there. In fact I don't think I'd have anything to do with her if I was you, Polly.'

'Zoë Nichols or Aroma?'

'Zoë Nichols. Bit of a loser, frankly.'

'We'll see,' said Polly, feeling suddenly disheartened. She'd rather liked the sound of Zoë Nichols on the phone. 'You will keep quiet about this, won't you, Joan?'

'Who on earth would be interested? Anyway I didn't know Aroma that well.'

You mean you probably didn't know her at all, thought Polly. By now she was becoming wise to Joan's desperate need to be known to be on first-name terms with celebrities. Once she'd interviewed Hector O'Neill, it would be Hector this and Hector that for months.

It was as if Joan had read her mind.

'It's probably about time for a biography on Hector, wouldn't you say, Polly? Who do you think you could sell it to?'

'Who said I had a biography of Hector O'Neill to sell?'

'Well, I'm just speculating here but if the interview

goes well, I could cultivate my association with him, develop it into a book, you know . . .'

And she automatically assumes I'll be her agent just like that. For some reason she couldn't quite fathom, the idea made Polly furious. When it suited her Joan was perfectly capable of remembering Polly was not just a secretary. Polly called for the bill, ignored Joan's frantic flutterings about the two Arabs who wanted to pay for them, slapped down her Access card and didn't say a word till they were out on the pavement.

Polly didn't go back to the office. She was rather surprised at the extent to which the news about Johnny having been in Cornwall had shaken her. She didn't even know if he had been anywhere near Edith. It was ridiculous to give it a moment's thought. She decided to take the afternoon off. She rang Mrs Flowers from a call box and was instantly reassured.

'Very quiet it is. Very quiet indeed. You go off for a couple of hours. Do you good. After all you've been through . . .'

'Yes, thank you, Mrs Flowers. See you later.'

Polly went to the gym and worked off her rage at Joan, at Edith, at Johnny, and most of all at herself, on the stairmaster for half an hour. Dripping with sweat, she showered and flopped naked on a towel in the sauna.

Conversations between other naked women and girls of varying shapes and sizes were going on all around her. As Polly lay and listened, willing the toxins to ooze out of her, she realised they were all variations of the same theme.

'Has he called you yet?'

'Have you heard from him yet?'

'So he finally called last Saturday and I told him . . .'

'So when are you seeing him again?'

It was the way the world worked, thought Polly. You were nobody unless you had a man to talk about. Why was it that she didn't want to be one of these silly chitter-chattering women, why didn't she have Joan's desperate longing for a man, any man? What was wrong with her?

She picked up a lemon tart for Luana's supper and only remembered afterwards that she'd already bought tiramisu. Never mind. She'd slip the tart into Luana's takeaway bag. The phone was ringing as she walked into the hall. She had no idea what made her pick it up and say 'Johnny?'

'No,' said a puzzled voice. 'Edward.'

'Edward.' repeated Polly in a flat tone of voice.

'Edward Holland. You remember? Last night . . . ?'

'Oh yes, of course, how are you?' asked Polly as if she hadn't seen him for months.

'Fine. You?' He didn't wait for her to answer. He sounded nervous. 'Polly, I was wondering if you would be free to have dinner with me tonight?'

'Oh, I can't possibly,' said Polly trying to keep the relief out of her voice. 'I've got my stepdaughter coming to supper.' She could almost hear Joan's groan: 'Don't tell him it's your stepdaughter. Pretend it's another admirer. Honestly, Polly!'

'Ah, well, another time.' Edward Holland seemed disappointed but determined. 'What about tomorrow. Bit short notice I know but . . . ?'

'Oh, no, you see – ' began Polly automatically then stopped. She knew that she was in fact utterly, blissfully free for night after night as far as she could see. She recalled Joan's face drenched in misery because there was no man on the horizon. She thought of the endless happy hours of speculating enjoyed by the girls in the sauna. Edward Holland was giving her a chance to join in. 'Has he called you yet?' Yes, he has and I shouldn't be churlish about it, thought Polly.

'Actually, Edward, that would be very nice. Tomorrow night.'

'I'll pick you up about eight.'

'Make it 7.30 and come and have a drink first,' Polly heard herself say before they hung up.

She went into the kitchen to begin preparing Luana's supper. She turned on Jazz FM and sang along to the radio, far happier at the thought that she had half an hour's pottering about the kitchen ahead of her than at the notion of a date the following night. She'd better get a move on. Luana was due in less than forty-five minutes.

Polly hoped she would be hungry.

Luana was starving – but not for food. She wanted sex – with Chris Perrick.

She'd had a nightmare day and Chris Perrick, a twenty-year-old James Dean lookalike, had been the only good thing about it.

Luana worked as assistant to Clovis Redmond, a casting director. Luana's obsession with films and actors had not gone away and eventually Johnny had decided there was no point in keeping her at college if all she wanted to do was learn about casting. She might as well learn on the job.

Clovis was larger than life, literally. She weighed in at fourteen stone. Her dress sense was non-existent. She tended to act upon advice from others, often disastrously, and then leave the suggested style change in place for the next twenty years. Thus a purple-black punk haircut from the Seventies, an Armani jacket (actually a man's but Clovis had never noticed) from the Eighties and a pair of eternal Gap tracksuit trousers became her standard daily wardrobe. She hailed originally from Dublin and had never lost her accent.

'We'll not be wanting him,' she had a habit of yelling down the phone at actors' agents, 'he's much too young.' She pronounced it Jung and behind her back actors cheerfully told each other, 'You're much too Freud for that part, darling.'

Clovis was tactlessness itself when it came to actors. She would walk in and interrupt a reading she'd set up between an actor and a director and shout over the poor actor's head to the director: 'Wrap it up right now, if I were you. Wastin' yer time. The pairfect pairson's just become available.'

Yet Clovis Redmond was the undisputed queen of London casting. She had an eye for talent that was unparalleled. The minute a young *ingénue* walked on stage in rep Clovis filed him away in her mind. She knew all five volumes of *Spotlight* backwards and rarely even referred to them, and while she was curiously insensitive with actors, she was beloved by producers and directors alike for her ability to deliver the perfect cast well within the budget. Other casting directors, jealous of her success – she was said to earn £250,000 a year – were overheard muttering about how she took kickbacks from the producer whenever she brought in the casting under budget. But the real secret of Clovis' success was simple: she was a complete whore. She didn't care who she cast for. Unlike other casting directors who would only cast feature films for a big-name director and the occasional prestigious theatre production, Clovis would cast commercials, training films, Europuddings, short films, TV series, feature films, anything as long as she was paid top whack. And she was.

All week she had been casting an American mini-series. The story was ludicrous. Someone had had the bright idea of taking the basic theme of the musical *Seven Brides for Seven Brothers* and updating it to the Nineties with seven American Rhodes scholars seeking seven brides at Oxford. The leads were now in place but there was one outstanding part that was proving extremely difficult to cast.

One of the English brides in the script had a brother who categorically refused to let her go off and marry an American and who further complicated matters by falling in love himself with another of the seven brides and trying to stop her going off too. The role called for a handsome, headstrong, truculent-looking young actor and the part was that of support lead and a vital element in the overall casting.

It didn't bother Clovis in the slightest that the loud American director wanted to see the actors every five minutes. Keep 'em coming, was his attitude, let's get it over with as quickly as possible, never mind whether they can act or not. But then it was all right for Clovis; she was closeted with the director in the drawing room of his suite at the Dorchester. Outside, in the little entrance hall, Luana was trying her best to inject some sort of order into the proceedings. If only the director could have had a casting session at Clovis' office, Luana could have made the actors cups of tea to keep them happy. It had taken her a day and a half to call virtually every agent in town and check the availability of the actors on the list Clovis had drawn up and then fix a time for them to attend the casting. Ordinarily Luana would make sure actors up for the same part never bumped into each other at a casting. Now they were arriving in quick succession, Clovis was calling 'Next!' through the door with embarrassing speed, the actors were backing up and running into each other and there was nothing Luana could do except hand out pages of the script for them to read and apologise again and again for the discomfort.

They were not exactly a silent bunch.

'Can I ring my girlfriend?'

'Who's he then, ducky?'

'How much longer?'

'Can I call my agent?'

'Give us a read through, Luana, there's a love.'

'So who did old Clovis cast in that part I was up for last week?'

'Don't know why I'm here. American telly? Me? Not on your life.'

'Why can't we use the phone?'

'Darling, you were wonderful in that thing on Sunday night. They wanted me but I turned it down, you know?'

'Cheer up.'

Luana jumped. The man was talking to her. It was Chris Perrick. She hadn't realised he'd been watching her.

'It's such a nightmare and Clovis just doesn't care,' she told him, feeling guilty at her disloyalty.

'Well, it's nice that you do.'

'Not much I can do about it except open the door to let them in and out. I can't even give you a place to sit down.'

'No problem.' He slouched against the wall in his

183

white T-shirt, jeans and loafers. Was he coming on to her?

'*Next!*' shrieked Clovis.

Chris Perrick winked at Luana and slipped through the door.

On the way home on the bus to the tiny flat she rented in Shepherd's Bush Luana wondered if he'd get the part. If he did it meant there was a chance she'd see him again. He fancied himself but then, didn't they all?

Her phone rang twenty minutes after she got home. 'It's Chris.'

'How'd you get my number?'

'Simple. I asked Clovis.'

'And she gave it to you? Just like that?'

'Just like that. Actually, she's called me back for another read-through with that girl they've cast as the second sister but in the meantime I thought I'd get a little practice in with you. Here's my address. Can you make it in, say, an hour? And don't forget the script.'

He opened the door to his flat naked and took her straight to bed. He's not fucking me to get the part, Luana told herself as she did every time she screwed an actor from a casting session, it's Clovis he'd have to fuck for that.

Still, she'd put in a good word for him the next day. If Clovis asked.

And even if she didn't.

Polly sat quietly at the kitchen table laid for two until ten o'clock. Then she slowly put away the unused plates, the knives, the forks, the spoons and the glasses. She scooped a small amount of the carefully prepared chick pea salad into a soup bowl and stood at the kitchen window silently spooning it into her mouth. She had called, of course, but there had been no answer from Luana's number.

She must have forgotten, thought Polly.

It wasn't the first time.

'Deirdre, love are yer there? If y'are please pick up, there's a good girl. Hello? OK, so yer not there. Now listen, soon as you get this give me a call. They want you for a Screen 2, y'know, those high falutin' fillums that go out Sunday nights. They're talkin' to Alan Bates so they say. The script's in the mail. So give us a call. Bye.'

Clovis turned to Luana.

'If they give her the part they're mad. She's an old slag, so she is, and her looks went years ago. Don't know why I called her at all. Oh, sweet Jesus, have I done it again?'

She grinned as Luana leaned over and settled the receiver back on its hook. Clovis had a disturbing habit of not replacing her receiver properly and when she had been speaking into an answering machine this could be dangerous. Everything she'd just said both to – and about – Deirdre McShane had been recorded for Deirdre to listen to on her return.

The phone rang again immediately.

'Oh my God, she was there all the time and listening to me. I'm not in. Tell her I had to rush out. Emergency.'

Clovis disappeared into the kitchen.

'Any casting?' The usual bleat Luana heard twenty times a day from desperate agents touting for non-existent work for their clients.

'Sorry. Nothing at the moment.' Luana's stock reply.

'Want some, then?' The voice at the other end of the line had dropped several octaves.

185

'Dad! How are you?'

'I'm fine. Couldn't be better and there's a reason. I've finally got the go-ahead on *Mr Wrong*. The script's approved and the Frogs and the Americans have come up with $16 million between them. Now I've got a star interested I'll start pre-sales and get even more cash.'

'Who do you have in mind to play Mr Wrong?' asked Luana, who had read the script.

'Oh, it's gone to all the usual suspects. Pacino, De Niro ... but it was your idea to send it to Hector O'Neill. His agent's called and says he really loves it. Of course he's not in the same league as De Niro etc. but I'm going to go with him. So thanks, little peachy one, you've done me a big favour.'

'And he's available. But Dad, there's something you have to promise me. Don't tell Clovis I thought of Hector O'Neill otherwise my life won't be worth living. We have to make her think the idea came from her, you know what she's like.'

'Whatever you say. I'll get Juanita on to it right away. She's good at planting suggestions in people's heads and then letting them think they suggested it in the first place. But I did tell O'Neill's agent you were the one who thought of him. Credit where credit's due, and I was so proud of you. So, seen Polly lately? You two were due to have dinner this week, weren't you?'

Polly! She'd forgotten all about Polly. She hadn't even rung her. She'd spent a long and sweaty night in Chris Perrick's bed without paying Polly a moment's thought.

Furthermore, it had all been in vain. Clovis had come in that morning announcing that she had spoken to the director last thing the night before and he had gone and changed his mind and decided Chris Perrick's legs were too short or his neck was too thick. Whatever his deficiency – and as usual it had nothing whatsoever to do with his acting skills – he wasn't going to be offered the part. Luana knew this meant she might well not see him again. She had not delivered and while it was not in any way her fault, she was under no illusion that Chris Perrick would invite her into his bed until he was up for another plum part in something Clovis was casting. Pity. He had shown the potential to become the first man to give her an orgasm.

'Luana? You still there?'

'Sorry, Dad. I was miles away. No, I didn't see Polly after all.'

'Well, I saw her the other night. She had a man there.'

'Probably an author.'

'At nearly midnight?'

'Dad! You were the one who left, remember?'

'OK, OK. No prying. It's just that Zutty didn't like him. He told me. So, is herself there? I'd better get on and see if she'll condescend to do my picture.'

'Hello, Johnny, how are yer?' Clovis was all charm. 'What can I do fer you? What? 'Course I am. Fer you I'm always free. Who's the director? Well, who's he when he's at home? A friggin' Froggy? Does he speak English? No, I don't speak bloody French, Johnny, don't be daft. Can't you give him English lessons? I don't care if you've got Japanese money, you're not telling me you'd get a Japanese director if you had. All right, all right, send over the script. I'll have a read. Have you anyone in place? You're thinkin' of Hector? Well don't be tellin' me he speaks French. What? You simply can't ask the likes of Hector O'Neill to read for a friggin' Froggy. He's too big a star already, that's why.

I'll tell you what. I'll take a look at the script and if I like it I'll meet with your Froggy. Meet, I said! Don't be committing me just yet. I don't know. Your father . . .' she said, turning to Luana, 'if this fillum goes it'll be me summer holiday out the window. Script's coming over this afternoon. *Mr Wrong*. Sounds like he's got Mr Wrong Director for a kick-off.'

But Luana wasn't listening. She rang Polly and listened while Mrs Flowers told her her stepmother was in a meeting, was there any message? No message. Luana hung up and the phone rang again instantly.

'Sorry, nothing at the moment,' she said automatically. 'No, wait, call back in a couple of days. There might be something then.'

'Come on *Mr Wrong*,' she said to herself, 'make my day!'

Polly wasn't in a meeting. She was riding the elevators in Harvey Nichols staring at the name Thyssen on each step. She reached the first floor in a daze and wandered through the halls, stopping occasionally to rifle through some dresses. The trouble was she had no idea what she was looking for. All she knew was that for some idiotic reason she had woken up that morning strangely excited at the thought of her impending date with Edward Holland.

The anticipation of it had sustained her through a particularly trying morning. A young and pretty author with considerable potential had proved to be totally irresponsible by calling to say she was going off on someone's yacht and wanted to extend the delivery date of her manuscript by a further six months. Since Polly had sweated blood to get her the commission in the first place, she was not about to let her get away with it and for the first time in her career as an agent she heard herself say, 'If you go ahead and do that then I no longer wish to represent you.'

Then an irate, self-important editor had rung demanding to know why he had not been included in Polly's recent multiple submission of a book. Polly refrained from telling him that it had been because she thought he was utterly hopeless at his job and there was no way she would allow an author of hers to be published by him. Instead she told him tactfully: 'I'm sure when you come to read it, Peter, you'll find it just wouldn't have been for you.'

'I'd have liked to have seen for myself,' he had whined. 'Everyone's talking about it.'

Then the photocopier went on the blink and a fax had come through from one of Polly's more controversial authors saying a politician was suing him for libel and what should he do? Four New York agents had faxed asking when she was going to decide who would sell her clients' books in America and Mrs Flowers had brought in something for her lunch that was so foul smelling in its health-giving properties that it stank throughout the conservatory. At this point Polly had simply upped and walked away from it all to wallow in her dreams of Edward Holland.

It was ludicrous. The night before last he had just been a friend of the Hendersons who had given her a lift home. Lunch with Joan and being stood up by Luana had made her vulnerable. Edward Holland wanted her, he was a man, growing more eligible and attractive in her mind by the minute. Where would he take her for dinner? More important, where would he take her *after* dinner? Would she even recognise a pass, it had been so long since she'd been out with anyone?

In the end she didn't buy herself anything new. She knew from experience that it was fatal to go out and look for something for a special occasion on the day. She always wound up buying something far too expensive and regretted it for ever more. On top of which she never wore it.

Her futile shopping expedition made her run late. She had only half an hour to wash her hair. She was kneeling on the floor with her head over the bath, rinsing out the shampoo, when she heard footsteps coming up the stairs.

Johnny had come into the bathroom and moved up behind her. This had been one of their marital rituals. Whenever she washed her hair Johnny would always rinse and towel it dry. He had what she called 'magic hands', like a really good masseur's. When he massaged her head she had invariably wanted to have sex, so sensous was his touch, and as she felt his fingertips on her scalp now an involuntary shudder went through her. At least, with a T-shirt over her bra and pants, she wasn't naked.

'There. Now I'll dry it for you.' He pulled open a drawer. 'Where's the drier? You've moved the drier!' he said accusingly as if he had only been gone a day.

'Doesn't it ever occur to you that things just might have changed a fraction since you left?' snapped Polly, using irritation to cover her surge of desire for him. 'I mean you walk in here without so much as a quick ring first to see if you might be disturbing me . . .'

She'd sworn she'd never act like this, never give him the injured party number, never show any sign of bitterness. She need not have worried. Johnny, true to form, was barely dented by her tirade.

'All right, keep your hair on, especially when I'm

about to dry it for you. What's up? The old PMT strikes again? Juanita swears by B6. Ever tried it, Pol? Juanita says . . .'

'Johnny,' warned Polly, 'shut up about Juanita. I don't want to know what Juanita uses. I don't want to know what you use. I know it's still your house but I just think you might use your key with more discretion.'

She sat at her dressing table in the bedroom where she now kept the hairdrier and proceeded to blow-dry her hair herself, waving Johnny away when he tried to do it for her. He sat gloomily on the edge of the bed they had once shared and watched her reflection in the mirror. Finally, above the noise of the drier, he mouthed the words:

'I came to talk to you about something.'

She pointed to the drier and mouthed back: 'Nearly finished.'

As she put in the Carmen rollers, wincing and knowing they were too hot and would ruin her hair, Johnny came and sat beside her on the long stool in front of the dressing table, something he had always done when he wanted to be sure of her full attention.

Polly found herself holding her breath. Just when he'd given her a sexual jolt, just when she was about to go out on her first proper date since he'd left – was he going to ask if he could come back?

'It's Luana,' he began, and Polly didn't know whether to be relieved or disappointed.

'Tell me about it!' she said with feeling. 'What is the matter with that girl? I waited three hours for her to turn up and have supper with me last night. Three hours! I'm going out tonight and all the food I've cooked is going to go to waste.'

'What did you make?' Johnny looked hopeful.

Polly glared at him although she had to admit she'd rather he took it than throw it in the bin.

'As long as you don't give it to Zutty. So what's your problem with Luana?'

'Word's got back to me. She's beginning to get herself something of a reputation.'

'In what way?'

'A nympho.'

'A what?'

'A nymphomaniac.'

'Oh, don't be ridiculous. You don't even know the meaning of the word, Johnny.'

'Is that a slur on my wop heritage? No, I'm serious. It's common knowledge apparently. You go for a part in a casting session with Clovis Redmond and you have a pretty fair chance of getting laid by her assistant, if you're a bloke that is. I've heard actors talking about it. They obviously don't know she's my daughter.'

'Does Clovis know? Have you spoken to her?'

'Of course not. And yes, I expect she does and turns a blind eye. There used to be plenty of stories about Clovis asking actors to come and pick up the script at eleven o'clock at night at her home.'

'Well, I don't know, maybe that's what happens. The casting couch, maybe it still exists.'

'Not with my daughter, it doesn't. Not if I have anything to do with it.'

Polly looked at him in the mirror. She could see he was agitated.

'It's probably nothing,' she tried to reassure him, 'it's probably all talk. Actors bragging to each other. Maybe they do try it on with her. Who wouldn't? She's such an attractive girl. But why rush to believe everything you hear? Have you talked to her?'

'Oh, Pol please! How would I begin? I'm her father, for Christ's sake. It needs a woman. I did ring her today to sort of try and sound her out but I chickened out and started telling her about getting the go-ahead for *Mr Wrong* instead. Hey, Polly, did I tell you? I've had this brainwave about who should play the lead. Hector O'Neill.'

'Oh, Johnny, that's a brilliant idea. How clever of you.'

Johnny kept quiet about whose brilliant idea it actually was.

'Well, I always wanted Clovis to cast it so I would have been ringing there in any case but this other matter I know I just haven't got the bottle. That's why I came over and barged in like this. I was wondering, Polly, would you talk to her for me? Find out what's going on?'

'Johnny, I'm not her mother.'

'Jesus, Pol. Edith's the last person I'd want to let loose on Luana, not in the state she's in now . . .'

'What state?'

The doorbell rang very loudly.

Edward Holland.

Polly extracted the hot rollers from her hair and dived back into her jeans. She'd give him a drink then make her excuses and come back up to change. Somehow she had to get rid of Johnny. How on earth was it going to look to Edward when they walked downstairs together?

As it happened Johnny's untimely arrival had saved Polly considerable embarrassment. Edward Holland was dressed very casually in jeans and a sweater.

'I thought we'd go somewhere informal and relax,' he told her on the doorstep. 'I don't know about you but

I've had a hell of a week. Oh, hello.' He had been leaning forward and Polly assumed he'd been about to give her a peck on the cheek until he saw Johnny coming down the stairs behind her.

'Just leaving, just leaving. Eh, Pol, what about that food that's going to . . .?'

Polly stood firm, holding the door wide open until he slipped out and down the steps, turning to point at Edward and make a face behind Edward's back and a thumbs-down sign, grinning at Polly. Polly slammed the front door.

Bugger Johnny! Although if he hadn't arrived when he had she'd have had time to put on a chic little black dress and high heels and be looking a right overdressed tart beside Edward in his jeans.

Edward took her to Lou Pescadou in the Old Brompton Road where you couldn't book and had to stand outside ringing the bell until you were let in. Luckily they had a table and Polly followed Edward past the long bar to the more secluded raised area in the back. She liked this restaurant. It was a downmarket version of La Croisette or Le Suquet, fancy fish restaurants Johnny used to take her to because he'd seen Mick Jagger in one of them once and always hoped he would again. At Lou Pescadou you could have oysters when in season, *fruits de mer*, pizzas, pasta or an omelette, wash it down with a pichet of *rosé* and, if you got sufficiently drunk, pretend you were on the Côte d'Azur.

Edward got around to talking about his marriage rather sooner than Polly had anticipated. She had hoped they would steer clear of their respective ex's as a topic of conversation but Edward clearly saw it as the most important thing they had in common. Which it probably was.

'The thing is, Barbara was never really my type. I like tall girls like you, Polly, and she was only five-foot-four.'

Polly looked away. So he liked the way she looked and he wasn't afraid to tell her before she'd even finished her *soupe de poissons*.

'So what attracted you to her?'

'She wanted me. It was as simple as that. She was a very pretty little thing – still is, I suppose – and she gravitated towards me at a party and sort of latched on. Before I knew it everyone was saying what a wonderful couple we made and everything just seemed to follow on from there.'

'Are you saying you didn't actually love her?' Polly was rather appalled by her question but she was curious. He seemed to want to talk about it and besides, these sort of details would be lapped up by the insatiable Joan.

'Quite the contrary. I fell head over heels in love with her. I'm a romantic, Polly, like you.' (Bloody nerve, thought Polly, how would he know if I'm a romantic or not?)

'She was exactly the kind of pretty girl a chap fell in love with.'

'But?'

'I didn't really fancy her. I mean in the beginning I thought I did but after a couple of years I found I just wasn't interested in her in that way any more. She used to wear these little girly gingham nighties and she put her hair in bunches when she went to bed. Bunches! She looked about twelve years old. I know that's a real turn-on for some men but I'm not one of them.'

The waiter was hovering to take away the first course.

He grinned at Polly. Could he understand? Polly had always thought Lou Pescadou waiters were so super-French they didn't even understand a word of English. They always spoke French – 'Et pour Madame? Voulez-vous des legumes? Et comme dessert?' – and if you asked a question in English they immediately summoned *le patron* in panic. Perhaps it was just an act.

Polly didn't really want to hear any more. It looked as if Edward might start revealing what had happened, or rather hadn't happened, when he unbunched Barbara's hair and pulled up her girly nighties. She hoped to God Johnny wasn't running around London regaling people with stories of her bedroom eccentricities, although once she thought about it she was hard put to recall a time in the last year of their marriage when Johnny had taken his eyes off the television long enough to notice her in the bedroom.

Edward was talking again. 'The children took her mind off it for a while once they came along. When they were babies she was too tired for anything anyway. But then she got her energy back and started coming out of the bathroom in her birthday suit, drenched in Joy. She'd come marching round to my side of the bed and I'm afraid somehow her stretch marks were always at eye level.'

Polly winced at the 'stretch marks'. Barbara sounded a bit of a nightmare but Polly couldn't help feeling sorry for her.

'Didn't you ... couldn't you talk to each other? I can't believe she walked out because of sex alone. There must be thousands of couples who've stopped making love but they don't automatically get up and go.'

'Yes, we did talk,' said Edward, 'but the trouble was, all we talked about was our sex problem. She went on and on until she got me to admit it. She got me to look her in the eye and say, "I don't fancy you." What she kept saying was, "If we're completely honest with each other, completely honest, Edward, then it'll be all right." Well, the minute I was completely honest with her, then it was all over bar the shouting. She walked out a week later. Bloody hell, Polly. I've never told this to anyone. I don't know why I'm wittering on to you like this.'

I don't know why you are either, thought Polly. But she said: 'It's good that you are. Do you miss her?'

'Do you know, I'm not sure that I miss her but I miss being part of a family. I miss the kids. I'm rattling around in Camberwell on my own while she and the kids are crammed into a tiny flat but she would insist on being the one to move out. Now I can't sell Camberwell. Ah, what a mess, and the worst thing is there's loads of miserable blokes just like me.'

'Really?' said Polly, 'I thought it was the other way round, that there were loads of lonely divorced women all desperate to find a man and there weren't enough of you to go around.'

'Well, that doesn't make sense. For every divorced woman there's got to be a divorced man out there looking for an available woman. Women never look at it like that.'

'I have to admit you've got a point.' Polly smiled at him. 'You make it sound like it ought to be one big musical chairs.'

'Well, it would be except you women are much more picky the second time around. You found Mr Right and he didn't work out so now you're all so paranoid you go around with this ideal man in your heads which, of course, you're never going to find. It's not enough for us to be kind and courteous and gentlemanly. I'm not sure even rich works any more. You take a woman out and before you know it she's quizzing you like you're there for a job interview which, as far as she's concerned, you are: as her potential significant other. Running through her mind is not, "Should I let him take me to bed? Does he make me laugh?" but, "There's no way it would work out because he wears a cravat but then of course he does have a house in the country which would be nice for the children (hers, not mine), he's a Leo and I'm a Capricorn but he does have moon in Gemini same as me, he contributes nothing to the conversation when he's with my work friends because he's not in television, he lives in Camberwell and I couldn't possibly move south of the river, he's away so much on business trips he wouldn't be able to come to dinner parties with me but on the other hand he does go to some rather dishy places and could take me with him . . ." Meanwhile, us poor bastards are pretty bloody hopeless on our own, lonely and desperate for someone to look after us, but we haven't got a prayer unless we become a New Man overnight. What is a New Man, that's what I want to know? Maybe you can enlighten me, Polly?'

Polly was warming to Edward Holland by the minute. It had never occurred to her that on her first real date since Johnny's departure she would be given such an insight into the male point of view even if Edward's was rather woolly.

'So you've had lots of affairs since Barbara left?' How could she be asking such questions when she barely knew the man; yet he seemed to be inviting them, and beside it was much more fun than talking about what they'd read in the paper or watched on television.

'I wish! Women are so blatant now. Whatever

happened to good old-fashioned subtlety? Unless they're in the cradle-snatching category which, frankly, isn't my scene at all, they make it crystal clear from the outset that what they're looking for is a relationship. Capital R. Some even mention the M word. Jesus! Every breath you take they're assessing whether or not you're husband material. I mean, as I've said, I'm lonely, I want someone but I rather fancy a bit of a courtship before I take the plunge. To tell you the truth, that's what I liked about you, Polly. I meet you three times and you barely even notice me. And marriage is out for you because of course, you are still married, aren't you?'

Polly looked at him, speechless. He was absolutely right. She was still married. There had been no talk of divorce between her and Johnny. Edward had seen him at the house twice. Poor Edward. He must think he had found himself in a highly awkward situation. Did he think she was planning to commit adultery? But then he'd given Johnny a lift home the other night so he knew he wasn't living with Polly and surely Grania Henderson must have been forthcoming with the details at some point.

'He left you, I understand, your husband?' prompted Edward on cue. 'Turned out to be Mr Wrong?'

'Oh, no, not a bit of it.'

'So he's come back? Listen, Polly, are you married or aren't you? I wouldn't have asked you out except that . . .'

'We're separated.'

'But he comes back from time to time?'

'Not in that way.' She wasn't gong to elaborate. She was damned if she was going to give Edward the same details about Johnny as he had imparted about Barbara.

'Was he Mr Wrong in every department?'

'He wasn't Mr Wrong in any department,' said Polly, aware that she was being over-defensive but Edward was overstepping the mark. 'He was funny, he was affectionate, he was terrific in bed . . .' And I loved him! She didn't say it out loud.

'So why?'

'Why did he leave me? He left, you know. Of course, you know. Everyone knows. I'm not like Barbara. I didn't up and leave. I waited until I was left. And you want to know why I was left? Well, I'll tell you. It's quite simple. I wasn't keeping up. His mother did warn me. She knew her boy. She knew he would always be running, like some scalded chicken. Johnny never stops. He marks time at a hundred miles an hour. If anybody nailed him down he'd probably peck himself to death. Well, I'm not like that. I wanted to progress more slowly, to grow gradually into who I was and where I wanted to go. He was moving farther and farther away from me until eventually he just moved out of the house. The funny thing is, I see him and speak to him now about as much as I did during the last year of our marriage. So am I still married to him? Yes, I suppose in a way I am.'

Their main course had grown cold in front of them. She might not have gone into the same kind of detail, Polly realised, but in her own way she had opened up to Edward Holland as much, if not more, than he had to her.

'The tortoise and the hare,' said Edward quietly, taking her hand across the table. Polly let it rest there. 'But you'll get there just the same.'

'Get where?' asked Polly, 'that's what I don't understand.'

'Terminé?' The waiter appeared and looked disapprovingly at their untouched plates. Edward let go of her hand abruptly.

'Let's pig out on puddings instead,' he suggested, 'and then I'll take you home. If I may?'

'I've got a better idea.' Polly looked him straight in the eye. She'd made up her mind about Edward Holland.

Johnny was the only man she'd slept with since her wedding day. It was time for the tortoise to progress to the next stage: sex after Johnny.

'You may take me home but why don't we have pudding there?'

She laid out Luana's tiramisu, the lemon tart and a giant tub of De Soto ice-cream on the coffee table. Furtive glances through the kitchen door showed her that Edward had kicked off his shoes, piled his plate high and made himself comfortable on the sofa. The only trouble was that he was stretched out full length and there was no room for her unless she lay alongside him. Was this a deliberate move on Edward's part? But there were two empty armchairs staring at her. Polly's nerve failed her and she sat down in one of them.

He finished his pudding. She poured coffee. They drank in silence. Polly didn't know what to do next and Edward kept glancing at her as if he expected her to make the next move. But that wasn't her style. Not that she'd exactly had much style lately. She had forgotten how to be seduced. It was years since Johnny had led her up the staircase to what had turned out to be Edith's flat and taken her into his arms in the darkness. She'd known exactly what was going to happen then. Right now she hadn't a clue. Did Edward fancy her? Was he sitting there wondering if she fancied him? Were they going to sit like this all night?

Polly got up to pour herself another cup of coffee and it was while she was bending over the tray on the coffee table that she felt Edward's hand on her leg. It took her by surprise to the extent that she sat down rather abruptly and found herself in Edward's lap. Her instinctive reaction was to say, 'Oh, how clumsy of me, I'm so sorry', and begin to get up again before Edward put both arms around her waist and held her down.

'Where do you think you're going?'

Her face was now inches from his. Several things immediately popped into her head.

Was she still wafting the garlic from the *soupe de poissons*?

Was her forty-something-year-old body up to being scrutinised by a first-time lover, even if it didn't have any stretch marks?

Then she nearly blacked out with the shock of Edward's unfamiliar lips meeting hers. They were so different from Johnny's. Johnny had been a long, slow kisser. Edward proved to be a quick aggressive stabber, his tongue prising her mouth open with sharp piercing movements.

He moved fast, too fast for Polly who began to panic as she felt his hand on her knee, moving up along her thigh to pull down her tights. She felt awkward and clumsy lying across him. She realised she ought to be participating in some way so she fumbled with the buttons on his shirt. To her amazement they opened to reveal a hairless freckled chest – quite a shock after Johnny's swarthy growth which, even though she hadn't seen it for a year, she recalled instantly – but there, right in the middle, Edward had a mole which looked exactly like a third nipple. Polly laid her head on top of it to suppress a giggle. Edward promptly began to stroke the top of her head, moving his fingers through her hair. At the same time his other hand had reached inside her panties to touch her there.

There was something familiar about him and after a while she realised it was the smell of his aftershave: the same as Johnny's. Polly closed her eyes and it was as if Johnny was still there, washing her hair. She began to move dreamily against Edward and it was only when she felt him grow hard through his jeans that she remembered.

This wasn't Johnny, someone she'd slept with for years. This was Edward, someone about whom she knew very little other than what he had told her at dinner. If he hadn't fancied his wife then presumably he'd had other women, however much he might pretend he hadn't. So wasn't there something they should discuss before going any further? Polly simply did not know at what point you brought it up. Pre-Johnny, before her marriage, the subject had never arisen. Nobody had even heard of it then.

Now she had been off the open market for so long, she had never had a chance to learn the language.

She sat up abruptly and moved away to the armchair, leaving Edward lying in an ungainly heap on the sofa.

'AIDS,' said Polly helplessly, 'I forgot. Aren't we supposed to . . . ?'

'Polly, what *are* you talking about?'

'Shouldn't you be wearing something? Safe sex?'

Edward stared at her and shook his head in apparent amazement.

'A johnny? Is that what you mean? We're lying here necking on the sofa and you want me to wear a johnny?

Christ almighty, Polly, I think I've had enough. I haven't got a johnny, as it happens. You're the one who has if you bother to think about it. He was here the other night, he was here when I arrived and to all intents and purposes he's still here in this room with us and you're still bloody married to him. You want a johnny, Polly?' By this time he was almost dressed.

'Go whistle for your husband and stop wasting my time. Goodnight, Polly.'

Casting on *Mr Wrong* began a month later.

'I'm only doing it because he's your father,' Clovis told Luana twenty times a day. 'Fuckin' Froggy director! He may have won the Director's Festival prize at Cannes but, shite, it was only for some crappy little film with subtitles and the only people who saw it in the Yoo-Nited States were two men and a dog which isn't going to make my life any easier.'

Clovis had agreed to cast the film because (a) she cast anything if the money was half-way right, and (b) Johnny had promised her she would deal only with him and not have to spend time with Froggy. Because Luana's father was the producer and because, as Clovis had inevitably discovered, she had been the one to come up with the idea of Hector O'Neill, it was agreed at the outset that Luana would be very much involved in the casting.

'Fine by me,' said Clovis cheerfully. 'Your father's coming in this afternoon so we can talk through what we want. You'd better sit in.'

Johnny climbed the narrow stairs to Clovis' Soho

office an hour later than he had said he would, which did not exactly put Clovis in a good mood. He was followed by Zutty who flew into the room and jumped straight into Clovis' lap, wagging his tail in her face. Clovis had such a shock her fag fell out of her mouth.

'You've set fire to my dog,' Johnny accused her, grabbing Zutty.

'I've done no such thing. Now, what'll youse all have to drink?'

'Bit quiet, angel one,' Johnny bent over and kissed Luana. 'Too many late nights? Boyfriend keeping you at it?'

'What a thing to say to your own daughter.' Clovis poured three glasses of whisky.

'I haven't got a boyfriend.'

'Is that true, Clovis?'

'You're askin' me?'

'Don't any of these hunks who come and audition take any notice of you?'

Luana pretended she hadn't heard him and picked up Zutty for a cuddle. Why was her father being so beady? He couldn't know about Chris Perrick (not that there was anything more to know) – or any of the others before him – could he?

Clovis saved her further interrogation. Whisky in hand, she was ready for action.

'So, you've got Hector O'Neill. He signed yesterday. As Conway I suppose you can say he's an international star but only just. So you've got to find the detective and the detective's girlfriend. Now, you badly need an American because of this Froggy director. You want to hook a US distributor for this fuckin' fillum, you'll need an up and coming US name for the girlfriend, the lady cop, the one who falls for Hector.'

'Why up and coming?' Johnny wished there was a bit more 'we need' instead of 'you' to Clovis' approach. She was making it clear he was more or less on his own on this one on account of the Froggy director. Really rubbing it in, she was, but what else was he supposed to do when half the money was coming from France?

'Look, Johnny, this is *Mr Wrong* we're casting, not Indiana fuckin' Jones. We're not talkin' major first-grade stars like Julia Roberts or Michelle Pfeiffer.'

'They weren't in *Indiana Jones*,' Johnny pointed out, 'so who are we talking then?' He had descended into a dejected slump, still in his overcoat and baseball cap.

'Well, Winona's too jung, Geena Davis is too hot and too busy. Could she be black, d'you think?'

'What? Could who be black?'

'The fuckin' part we're trying to cast, that's who.'

'But the script – '

'Oh, she's not black in the script. What I'm askin' is could you rewrite her black? Then we'd be talkin' Whitney Houston, Robin Givens . . .'

'Lisa Bonnet?'

'She hasn't really cracked it in movies. People think *The Cosby Show*. She's much more a TV name. Think, Johnny!'

'Sorry.'

'What age are we talkin' here? Hector's thirty-three or thereabouts. This girl's presumably younger? Twenty-seven, eight?'

'What about Naomi Campbell?' said Johnny, suddenly brightening, 'I could do for her what I did for Cruise in *The Wolf One*.'

'Break every bone in her body, you mean. What else did you do for Cruise in whatever it was? What happened to it anyway? Oh, this is too hard. Let's go back to white.'

'Demi Moore?' said Johnny hopefully.

'CAA would give youse such a hard time it's not even worth thinking about her. There's Ellen Barkin but she's already played a cop. Besides, her husband's Gabriel Byrne, he'd be pissed off altogether that you'd cast his Irish rival, Hector, as the lead. Jodie's a possibility, I suppose, but is she glamorous enough? Now what about Andie MacDowell?'

'And what about the detective?' asked Johnny.

'I suppose he'll have to be French to get you quota money, one of those bilingual American actors who has a French passport and works under the quota ...'

'Christopher Lambert,' suggested Luana. Hardly worth saying, he was such an obvious candidate. She wondered what he would be like in bed. There she went again. Movie stars, gas station attendants, politicians on TV, it didn't make any difference who they were. Of course some she discounted straight away. She had never fancied redheads, so Mick Hucknall was quite safe. Simply yucky as far as she was concerned. All those freckles and that pale skin.

Luana's friends teased her and called her 'a slave to sex' and she reckoned they were probably right but she just couldn't help herself. She'd never had what other people called a 'relationship'. In fact when she stopped to think about it there were precious few men she had slept with twice. So she tried not to think about it. She was nineteen years old and having fun. Who needed to get emotional? Tina Turner had got it right – What's love got to do with it? She'd always been wild about Tina. All that bump and grind. Luana wouldn't dream of mentioning Tina to Mum, though. She hated noise of any kind.

Ever since she had been a very small child Luana had been aware that her mother was different. She was never the same from day to day. Luana knew that whatever else happened, she must not upset her. She learned to tiptoe around Edith and not disturb her in any way. Where other mothers bashed and clanged around in their kitchens, preparing their family's meals, Edith cooked her organic messes while everyone was out and left them in the fridge to be eaten – or thrown away in Luana and Johnny's case. The rest of the time she spent alone in a room with the door closed and Luana knew an enquiring knock would not be welcomed.

When Edith left Johnny and moved them to a sprawling, dark mansion flat across the river in Battersea, Luana had missed her father. 'He was too fidgety. I need peace and serenity,' was Edith's only explanation. Luana had cried herself to sleep every night, silently of course. She missed the way her father took the mickey out of Edith, creeping round the room with his finger to his lips in exaggerated compliance with Edith's rule of silence, winking at Luana while Edith said grace then leaping up when she'd finished and running out of the room calling back, 'I forgot to wash Mr de Soto's grubbby paws!' But at least Luana still saw Johnny fairly frequently and when Edith suddenly went round the world to find herself, Luana spent months with her father in Notting Hill. Johnny sent out for pizza virtually every night, ignoring Edith's nutritional instructions, and he clasped Luana to him and asked her a dozen times a week: 'Who's my beautiful peachy girl?' And when her father introduced her to Polly, his new girlfriend, who seemed to be genuinely interested in her, Luana thought she was in heaven although she made sure she didn't let on for quite a while.

Heaven collapsed when Edith swooped down like a maniacal Mother Goose and took her off to live in Cornwall. She tried to pretend it had nothing to do with Polly's arrival on the scene but Luana knew that the unthinkable had happened. Edith's fragile world had been disrupted and she was taking flight.

Edith sold the Battersea flat and retreated to a desolate Cornish farmhouse, square and gloomy with a stone façade covered in ivy and standing behind a wall encrusted with lichen. At the end of a narrow dirt road, the house stood in an exposed position at the top of the cliff and in winter the rooms were literally freezing, with the exception of the kitchen which had been unimaginatively modernised at some point in the Fifties. Later, when she came to read Daphne du Maurier's novels, Luana dubbed the place Formica Inn on account of the kitchen's incongruous plastic feel.

In Cornwall Edith promptly took to the bottle. Luana had watched her mother's gradual disintegration through precocious child's eyes, hitting the vodka, disguising it in tumblers of juice squeezed from organic oranges.

From the moment they moved to Cornwall Luana had started to feel she no longer existed as far as Edith was concerned. Edith barely left her room for the first six months. Trips to London to visit her father and Polly became the high points in Luana's life. Eventually everything Luana did was calculated to get Edith's attention even if it meant destroying the precious silence and playing Van Morrison and Them blasting 'G-L-O-R-I-A! GLORIA!' Still nothing. She wore her Flip baseball cap twenty-four hours a day. Edith never noticed. Luana turned it back to front, went to school in ripped jeans and DMs instead of her school uniform and told Edith she wanted to be a rock guitarist and play with Springsteen or Prince. Edith responded by saying she was starting to write a book and would Luana please not disturb her for six months. The only time she vaguely took an interest was during the Summer of Love revival when she started talking about becoming a New Age traveller. She wanted Luana to accompany her to love-ins and sit around cross-legged in damp fields waiting for the dawn. Luana went along with it in the hope that her mother might want her. Luana could not make anybody understand that she had so much to give: to her mother, to her father, to anybody, but nobody, it seemed, wanted her.

Until she met Roger Mainwaring. It was the summer of 1988. She had just turned fifteen and she had spent so much time outside, roaming the cliffs, away from the misery of Formica Inn, away from her mother, that her skin was nut brown and she looked like a wild Sicilian bandit with the bandanna tied around her black hair. She lived in a pair of tight black Lycra pedal-pushers and a big floppy white T-shirt which she knotted on her hip. She never bothered to exchange them for a swimsuit when she went swimming in the sea with the result that the drenched cotton clung to her sharp little triangular breasts, leaving nothing to the imagination when she climbed the narrow cliff path, cautiously edging her bare legs past the brambles, and bumped into Roger.

He was on holiday with his mother. They lived in Hemel Hempstead. He worked in a bank. He accompanied her up the cliff path and asked if she swam there every day at that time? They arranged to meet the next day. Luana was in a state of bliss about the fact that at last someone seemed to enjoy her company and she never noticed that he did all the talking and never asked her anything about herself. On the third day when he mentioned how pretty she was she received such a mammoth jolt of adrenalin, it was better than any rock'n'roll high. He kissed her mouth on the fourth day, her breasts on the fifth and her pussy on the sixth. And on the seventh day he didn't allow her a moment's rest. He went home a week later but he was followed by plenty of other summer Rogers. Suddenly she wasn't lonely any more. In exchange for her body men were prepared, it seemed, to take an interest in her and having been ignored for the first fifteen years of her life that was all Luana required of anybody. Interest was interest and sexual interest was as good as any other.

Two years later, she couldn't take Edith any longer and ran away to live with Johnny and Polly and it was then that Johnny sat her down and told her the truth about her mother, the reason why she had left him, the explanation for her erratic behaviour and why they must all take special care not to upset her.

'Oh Dad, for goodness' sake, I've known about Mum all along.'

'Well, whatever you do, don't tell Polly.'

When her father left Polly, Luana went into a state of panic that she would be sent back to Cornwall. She never rang her mother unless prompted to do so by her father or Polly. Polly, she noticed, always hovered in the background obviously hoping to pick up some clues but Luana was careful to keep her conversations with Edith on an even keel. If her mother embarked upon one of her hysterical fits, Luana would hang up. Once she tried to whisper, 'He won't come back to you, Mum. Just because he's left Polly it doesn't mean he's coming back to you. You left him, remember?'

Polly could not control her curiosity.

'Is she sitting down there in Cornwall waiting for him to come back now he's left me?' she asked Luana.

'Well, are you sitting here in Notting Hill waiting for him to come back?' Luana fired back, more brutally than she had intended. 'Polly, you know I promised Dad I wouldn't discuss Mum with you. It's Dad's problem. Don't get involved. Believe me, you're better off this way. If I had my way I'd tell you all about Mum. Don't you think I want to talk about her to someone? I feel like I'm piggy in the middle, caught between the two of you. When I was down in Cornwall she wanted to know about you. Now you want to know about her. Why can't we just drop it. Please, Polly!'

Apart from the ghost of Edith hovering between them, Polly and Luana muddled along very well together. For the first few months Luana had worked hard at acquiring an Attitude. Polly, it transpired, was a complete pushover, seemingly happy to produce a key to the front door and mouthwatering meals on tap. Polly had never heard of raves or Acid House. She did not know of the existence of Steve Strange, as Luana discovered when she tried to establish some kind of common ground with Polly by asking her if she used to go to Blitz. It was when Polly confessed to being an Old Romantic rather than a New one that Luana abandoned all hope. Still, the fact that her stepmother never asked what she did outside college hours endeared her to Luana and in return she consented to accompany Polly to the movies every once in a while although vast concessions on both sides had to be made when it came to the choice of film. Luana wanted action, the more violent the better. Polly sat through *Lethal Weapon 2*, *Rambo III* and *Black Rain* with her hands over her eyes. On those occasions she allowed Polly to drag her to *Accidental Tourist*, Merchant Ivory's *Maurice* or one of those slow, soft-focus sloppy French films her stepmother liked to cry her way through, Polly couldn't help noticing that Luana spent rather a lot of time in the Ladies and prayed she wasn't doing drugs. Then Luana chucked in college to go and work for Clovis and, tired of sex in a different bed every night, she moved out to a rented flat.

Luana observed her father as he flicked through his script and held up a protesting hand to halt Clovis, who by now was thoroughly carried away with the idea of casting *Mr Wrong*. Luana tried to imagine Polly in bed with Johnny. As far as she could make out Polly had embraced celibacy with open arms ever since Johnny had left. This was completely beyond Luana's understanding and she kept a lookout for signs that her stepmother was about to shrivel up and wither before her eyes as a result of such deprivation. Poor old Polly. Luana knew she really ought to call and apologise for not showing up the other night.

'Call your mother, don't forget,' said Johnny.

'I will. I promise. I just clean forgot, I swear, Dad. I'll take her to see one of those slushy French movies she likes, the ones that make her blub.'

'Everything makes Polly blub,' said Johnny, smiling rather wistfully. 'No, I meant call your mother. Call Edith.'

214

When Luana saw Hector O'Neill for the first time she was on the telephone to the girl-friend who was her current favourite. Luana had a mild problem with her friends – she tended to drop those who told her things about herself she didn't want to hear.

'You really shouldn't drink so much. You're a nightmare when you're drunk.'

'Luana, are you one hundred per cent sure you're in love with him? Last week you were in love with Harry. You can't fall in love with every man you meet.'

'Why don't you wait at least for the second date until you go to bed with them? How do you expect them to respect you if you don't respect yourself?'

'Jesus, Luana, you can't afford that jacket. Why do you have to shop at Joseph? You still haven't paid off your overdraft. Why make it worse?'

In other words, anybody who criticised her or challenged her about her lifestyle was out. Luana got out of bed every morning, pushed everything under the carpet and started a brand new day. It was only a matter of time before a prince would come along and carry her off.

Ironically, the only thing her friends were wrong about was the reason she was working for Clovis. They thought she worked in casting in order to have a constant supply of men to screw in her role as a 'slave to sex'. Nobody realised that she had been fascinated by the world of casting since she was a child. Except perhaps Polly. To Polly, who could remember the girl in the duffel coat running down to the front of the cinema at the end of *Working Girl* and frantically scribbling down the cast, Luana's chosen career made perfect sense. For to Luana it was a career. Working for Clovis was just the beginning. Eventually she would move on and start up on her own, just like Polly had done.

The man who walked through the door was drop-dead gorgeous. Six foot two inches tall. Black hair with a lock falling over his forehead. Huge wraparound sunglasses. Long arrogant nose. High cheekbones. A wide slash of a mouth, very mobile. Broad shoulders and chest, incredible muscles on the arms. White Gap T-shirt with a pack of Marlboro Lites in the breast pocket. Jeans. Very long legs. Loafers.

Luana had stood up without realising it and now found herself peering right over the desk. She ran her eyes quickly back up to his face. He'd taken off his shades to reveal dark blue eyes.

'You're . . . you're . . .'

'Yes. Got it in one. I'm Hector O'Neill. Got any twenties?'

'Any what?'

'20ps? For the meter? I've only got half an hour's worth.'

'Oh, sure, wait a sec.' Luana emptied Clovis' meter piggy bank on to the desk and gave him the contents. He pocketed them, winked and left.

Five minutes later the phone rang. It was him.

'Luana, do me a favour. Tell Clovis and Johnny I'm at the Groucho, upstairs in the Soho Room, waiting for them, would you?'

'Yes, of course.'

'And is it OK if I pay you back another day?'

'Oh, no, please, be my guest.'

'Beautiful and generous.' He laughed and was gone.

Half-way through lunch at the Pizza Express with the man she had draped herself over the night before, Luana suddenly wondered how Hector O'Neill had known her name.

To Luana's immense relief he came back four days later. She had washed her long black hair every morning and dragged herself out of bed half an hour earlier than usual in order to put together several different looks before finally setting off for the office satisfied that she was as alluring as possible in case he dropped in.

She had nearly been fired when Clovis had come flying in after a long lunch in a panic because the wardens were lurking only to find her meter money piggy bank was empty. She was furious. There was a lot of sniping along the lines of 'if yer sainted father weren't the producer of this shite and onions film I'd . . .'

'Yer supposed to keep that full at all times, yer dozy mare,' she told Luana. 'Turn out yer purse! Give us all yer 20ps.'

'Can I be a knight in dirty basketball boots?' said a voice behind Clovis, and Hector O'Neill walked in dangling a polythene bag full of 20ps. 'It's not her fault, Clovis. Don't give her a hard time. I made her raid the little piggy for me earlier in the week.'

'Well, she should have said,' grumbled Clovis, only slightly mollified, and marched out.

'So, Luana, how's things?'

'Fine.' Luana smiled at him to cover the fact that she suddenly felt very gauche and awkward.

'My agent tells me that it was your idea to approach me for the lead in *Mr Wrong*.'

Luana nodded.

'What made you think of me for the role?'

'Oh, you know . . .'

'No, seriously, I'd like to hear. It's a fantastic part and it's come up just at the right time. It's got me out of doing another Conway. I have a lot to thank you for. In fact, why don't I buy you lunch? Are you free tomorrow?'

'Yes, of course.' Shit! thought Luana. I was too quick, too available.

Clovis came huffing-stuffing-puffing back upstairs.

'Fuckin' clampers'll not be getting me. Come on in, Hector. Luana, if you can make a cup of daycent coffee in under an hour you've got a taker.'

Hector winked at Luana and followed Clovis into her office.

'Will I be sitting in on this meeting?' called Luana.

'You will not,' Clovis called back.

Well, shite and onions to you too, whispered Luana under her breath, I'll have him to myself tomorrow.

'You still haven't told me why you cast me.' Hector squinted at the menu on the blackboard at Joe Allen's. 'What are you going to have to eat?'

He was oblivious to the surreptitious glances he was receiving from half the restaurant, or at least he was pretending to be, whereas Luana had been positively basking in the attention ever since they walked in together.

'I'll have a caesar salad and I didn't cast you. Clovis does the actual casting. I'm her assistant. I just suggested you to my dad.'

'Yes, but why me?'

'Dad had French co-production money. I thought he'd be more popular if he produced an actor who could pass for Latin if necessary but was still an international star. I mean, part of the film is going to be set in France. Your role in the script looks flexible to me. You could be a French womanising serial killer if necessary. And besides, you'd come cheaper than the big American names that immediately spring to mind.'

She'd said it without thinking. She felt herself going red. How could she have said that?

'But then, of course you're younger than most of them and better looking and . . .' she floundered.

'The quality of my acting was never part of the equation, I suppose?'

'Well, you never really had to act as Conway. All you ever had to do was look good and . . .'

She'd done it again!

'You're absolutely right. That's exactly why I was looking around for something else. Why are you looking so miserable? You've only spoken the truth, which is more than an actor hears from most people who work in casting.'

'Have you taken a big cut financially?'

'Up front, yes. But I've got points. So, OK, you didn't think of me because of my acting but your reasons were good ones, shrewd ones, and I'll repay your faith in me. I'll surprise you. Do you want to be a producer like your father? You seem to have the right instincts.'

'Producer?' Luana was genuinely baffled. 'I haven't even cast a film on my own yet and I won't for years. I haven't thought any further than that.'

'Don't worry, you will and probably sooner than you think. Those are beautiful earrings you're wearing. And that's a great jacket. You've got sensational taste.'

Luana blushed again. What was wrong with her? Normally she'd be acting cool and laid back but for some reason today she seemed to have totally abandoned her act. The insecure bundle of nerves beneath the flirt was coming out and taking over. She reached for her cigarettes.

'You don't need those.' Hector had his lighter out instantly.

'Well you do.'

'True.' He laughed and turned his head sideways as he exhaled so the smoke wouldn't blow in her face, looking back at her with half-closed eyes. 'So tell me about yourself.'

'What do you want to know?'

'Don't be so defensive. I just want to get to know you.'

'Why?'

'Why are you so suspicious? Relax. Have another glass of wine and tell me – I don't know – whether you have any brothers or sisters?'

She shook her head.

'You're the only one and the apple of your father's eye.'

'I don't know what my dad thinks and I don't care. I'm just his little peachy girl.'

'Well, what's wrong with that?'

'Nothing. Ten years ago. But I'm grown up now. He ought to take me more seriously. I mean, who thought of you for *Mr Wrong*?'

'So, boyfriends?'

'Why do you want to know? Oh, sorry, mustn't be defensive. My stepmother once said I rebuild the Berlin Wall the minute someone asks me a personal question.'

'I don't know your stepmother.'

'Don't know Polly?'

'Well, at last here's someone who brings a smile to your face.'

'She's so funny. I mean, like, she's sweet. I love Polly. I really do. She's always been terrific to me but she's so sort of, you know, out of it. Of course, she's middle-aged . . .'

'How old is she?'

'Forty-something, I think.'

'Ancient!'

'She's not bad looking when she remembers to get her hair highlighted. She's got great legs but her breasts are sort of wobbly and her tummy comes and goes. It's just so sad. Ever since Dad left her she never goes out. She works flat out all day then makes herself this huge supper on a tray and takes it up to bed to eat it watching telly. She says it's what she wants.'

'Then maybe it is.'

'It can't be. I think she's chicken. It's easier for her not to face the world so she hides from it. She hides from the truth. She hides from men in case they reject her. She spends too much time putting herself out for other people. I call her Polly Pushover. She's a literary agent. She's good at that, but she lets Dad walk all over her.'

'And do you walk all over her too?'

Luana looked up in surprise. 'Yes, I suppose I do but she asks for it.'

'Luana, what is it that makes you so angry with Polly?'

'How do you know I'm angry with her? All right, I admit I am but it's because she's so bloody happy. No, that's going a bit far. She's contented. She seems to actually enjoy a life without men. She has no problems being on her own.'

'And you resent that? You don't like people who are comfortable with their lot because you're miserable yourself.'

'Who said I was miserable?'

'No one. I'm asking, that's all. Are you?'

'What's Clovis been saying? What did my dad tell you?'

'Nothing. Nothing at all. Clovis said you were great at your job.'

'Did she? Did she really?'

'And your dad said you were his little peachy girl.'

Luana frowned automatically then saw he was laughing at her.

'You've got to lighten up,' he told her, 'you're so pretty but there's an air of "Hey, what about me?" about you as if you think people don't care about you. You've got to give them a chance. You've got to learn to trust people when they take an interest in you. Now, I'm going to take these cigarettes away for the time being and order you some pecan pie with whipped cream. You're too thin.'

'I'm not anorexic.'

'I never said you were. There you go again, assuming I'm thinking the worst of you. You're too thin and nervy but you're still very pretty. You're dark like your father but you don't have his pugnacious bone structure, thank God. You must take after your mother.'

Luana said nothing.

'Well, do you? What about your mother? She's the one person you haven't mentioned.'

'Nothing to tell.'

'Please yourself,' said Hector with a shrug.

For the rest of the meal they discussed the film and who was up for the other roles, yet discussion was hardly the right word since afterwards Luana realised all he had done was coax out her suggestions as to who should play what role. He offered no opinion of his own nor, she reflected, had he said one word about his own family or indeed about himself. He'd provoked her into talking about herself for almost the entire meal. It was a first. No one had ever bothered to listen to her before, not properly. Sure, men had taken an interest in her but it had always been in her outer casing, never in what went on inside her head.

He walked her back to the office and there was something odd about it. It was only as they turned into Old Compton Street that she realised what it was: each time they crossed a street or turned a corner and he wound up on the inside, he quickly ran around her so that he was walking on the outside between her and the street.

Working in a casting director's office Luana had come across plenty of well-known actors before, but Hector O'Neill was her first exposure to a gentleman.

Hector would have laughed out loud if he had known Luana thought of him as a gentleman. He was anything but. He found he couldn't stop thinking about her

223

throughout the afternoon and comparing her youthfulness with the brittle sophistication of the journalist who had come to interview him.

Inviting Luana to lunch had been a spur of the moment thing although if he thought about it, it made sense to charm his producer's daughter. Yet if anything it had been the other way round. Hector had been surprised at how captivated he had been by Luana, how her vulnerability had touched a nerve in him making him want to draw her out and protect her. He knew what she was going through, he'd been there.

At least she made a refreshing change to the kind of hard-nosed middle-aged bitch sitting here with him in his hotel suite, crossing and uncrossing her scrawny little legs, flashing her panties at him whenever she got the chance. The trouble was, he knew once the interview was over he'd probably find himself giving her exactly what she wanted, more out of habit than anything else.

'Luana, will you come down out of the clouds, for goodness' sake, and photocopy the scene in the script where Hector kisses the lady cop for the first time right after he's taken her to dinner.'

'Hector . . . kissed . . . who?' Luana tried to keep the misery out of her voice. It had been a week since her lunch with Hector and the one time he'd called, all he'd said was 'Hello darlin', that was a wonderful lunch the other day. Is herself there?' and she'd had to put him straight through to Clovis. Now here was Clovis talking about him kissing someone else.

'Will you just listen. For all I care he can kiss the blarney stone for a publicity photo opportunity and be done with it but what we're trying to do here is cast the fuckin' fillum. In case you've forgotten, perhaps I can remind you that there's a cracking good part for a woman. The cop's girlfriend. Well, sweetheart, we've got all these tarts they call actresses coming in tomorrow to read with himself. You made all the appointments with their agents but I suppose you've forgotten that too. Now, I reckon they should read the scene where they get to kiss Hector for the first time so we can see which one clicks best with the old ham since they're going to have to act the ro-mantic couple. No point casting a girl he's allergic to. Or vice versa, come to think of it.'

'How could anyone be allergic to Hector?'

'Oh, you'd be surprised. To my way of thinking there's something not quite right about him. They say he's Irish American from Boston but he hasn't got a Boston accent. No trace of it. Then he's supposed to be Irish but he never talks about Ireland to me. Never even asked me where I'm from. OK, since you've come back to life you can photocopy the scene. We've got eleven girls coming in. They can do the dialogue from the end of dinner right up to the kiss.'

Luana knew she had to come to terms with the fact that she was going to have to watch Hector kissing eleven girls. He arrived the next day with the director. Luana had had no warning that the director was coming to the casting. Nor, apparently, had Clovis, who went into a major snit. Hector introduced him to Luana.

'Luana, this is Henri La Plante, our director. Henri, this is Luana de Soto, Johnny's daughter. It was her idea to cast me.'

'Bravo!' Henri was a good ten years younger than Luana had imagined. He didn't look much more than thirty. He had a tousled mop of curly brown hair, eyes crinkled from smiling and a warm, friendly manner. Not at all the pseudo-smooth charming Frenchman.

'Clovis darling,' called Hector, 'you don't mind Henri being here, do you? I thought he ought to see me with the girls.'

'I'd have brought him in for the short list,' muttered

Clovis. 'How do, Henry, we've met before. Luana, get yer father on the line and ask him why he's not here.'

'Because we never asked him,' explained Luana.

'Well, we never fuckin' asked the Froggy but he's turned up so we might as well have Johnny in on the act as well,' hissed Clovis so loudly Luana was convinced Henri must be able to hear.

The first girl arrived and Luana sent her straight in, handing her the pages. The other girls began to arrive at intervals and Luana kept herself busy in the outer office, unable to resist glancing through the half-open door every now and then. She need not have worried. Henri was in the process of putting Clovis' nose severely out of joint. Two hours went by. Hector still hadn't kissed anyone. Henri never let it go that far. He clearly knew exactly what he was looking for and as the actresses came and went, he wasn't finding it. He let them read with Hector for a few minutes then he politely interrupted, chatted with them in halting English before sending them on their way.

'So what was wrong with her if it's not too much to ask?' By the eighth girl Clovis was seething. 'I'll have you know I've hand-picked those girls. They're pairfect – at least three of them anyway – pairfect!' Clovis had broken her golden rule of never arguing with the director. 'One thing you have to learn in this business,' she was fond of telling Luana, 'is you always have to let the director think it's his idea, not yours. Even if you find someone who turns out to be the new Emma Thompson or the new Julia Roberts, it's the director's discovery, not yours.'

Henri wasn't thrown. 'Is no good,' he explained, crinkling his eyes at her, 'is too preety-preety. I need woman who is strong but who also cry.'

'He only wants the shite and the bleeding onions!' Clovis told Hector, smiling sweetly at Henri all the while.

'He wants vulnerability. I can understand that. Frankly, I'm getting a bit frustrated myself at not being able to play the whole scene. What time's the next girl due, Luana?'

'She'll be here in fifteen – twenty minutes.'

'Fine. We've got time. Come in here and read the scene with me all the way through.'

'I can do that – ' began Clovis.

'No. Is good. Luana young. Is better,' said Henri.

'Well thank you very much!' Henri had made an enemy for life.

Although she was quaking inside, Luana calmly read through the scene with Hector, feeding him his lines, already aware that there was no trace of Conway left in him. Henri was watching him with a bemused look on his face.

'You are killer, 'Ector. Never forget you are killer' – he pronounced it 'keeler' – 'even when you make love,' he murmured as they neared the end of the scene. 'Now you are walking down the street, you stop, she say "Bonsoir" and you kiss her . . .'

Luana felt Hector's arms go around her and draw her to him. She felt him grasp the back of her head and propel her face towards his. She felt his mouth on hers forcing open her lips. She felt his tongue dart quickly into her mouth before he pulled away abruptly.

'Henri, should I kiss her as she's actually saying good night or let her turn away and then grab hold of her?'

Luana's eyes were pricking. Here she was about to swoon, literally, yet to Hector it was all part of the job. In the background she could hear Henri asking them to run through it again and yes, this time could Luana please turn away so Hector could grab her. Fighting back her tears, Luana stumbled through her lines wondering if she would be able to contain herself when Hector kissed her again.

On cue she turned away, felt Hector reach out and roughly pull her to him, felt her heart hammering. Any moment now . . .

'Excuse me. Sorry to interrupt. Am I in the right place? There was no one outside.'

Hector released Luana a fraction of a second before his lips met hers. They all turned to see an unbelievably attractive woman standing in the doorway. She was tall, five foot nine at least, with a small head on a long neck. Her dark red hair was cropped in a gamine feathery cut but her face had an undeniable strength: wide apart green eyes, a long straight nose and a big mouth with a full lower lip. Her skin was white with freckles and even though she was wearing a beat-up denim jacket, pale grey T-shirt and frayed jeans, she exuded elegance.

'Hello, Julianne, good to see you.' Clovis seized her opportunity to regain command of the proceedings while Luana retreated, both literally and metaphorically, into the background.

Julianne Reynard, twenty-nine years old, daughter of a French father and an American mother, born in France, educated in America, bilingual, dual nationality, able to work both in Europe and America and already known in both countries following her hit film, *Violette*, in which she played a young French woman who becomes engaged to an American living in New York in order to obtain her Green Card only to discover he's a murderer. If she turns him in will she jeopardise her chances of US nationality?

Luana watched as Henri, who obviously knew Julianne, kissed her warmly on both cheeks and introduced her to Hector, who was watching her with blatant appreciation. Luana wanted to run, to get as far away from Clovis' office as she could, but some masochistic force compelled her to watch Hector and Julianne read through the scene. She even leaned closer to get a better view as Hector's mouth fastened on Julianne's. Was it Luana's imagination or did the kiss seem to go on for twice as long as hers had?

A noise in the outer office alerted Luana to the fact that the next girl had arrived. Aware that Hector and Julianne were preparing to run through the scene again, Luana fled. Eventually Julianne emerged with Hector's arm around her shoulders. They went out on to the landing together and Luana could hear a quick muted exchange. On his way back Hector barely acknowledged Luana. The last three girls were called in and out with indecent haste and by the end of the afternoon it was clear Julianne would be offered the part.

'Shouldn't someone call my father?' asked Luana. 'She's not going to come cheap, not after *Violette*.'

'It's his fault for not bothering to show up for the casting in the first place,' said Clovis.

'Besides, he's in Paris,' volunteered Hector. 'I spoke to him earlier in the day. That's why I brought Henri along in his absence.'

'But he can't be,' protested Luana, 'we were supposed to be having dinner tonight.'

'In that case I shall have to stand in for him *ce soir* as Henri did this afternoon,' announced Hector.

'That's fuckin' gallant, O'Neill.' Clovis looked at him sharply. 'I don't ever recall you askin' meself to dinner.'

'Well would you like to join us?' asked Hector as Luana held her breath.

'I would not. But I do not want you keeping her out half the night, Hector. We've got a load of little Froggy boys dragging their non-existent bollocks in here tomorrow for the next casting and I want herself fresh as a daisy to cope with them. She'll have to read with them and all unless we can sign young Julianne overnight.'

'I'll just have one course,' said Luana, studying the menu as she sat with Hector at the corner table by the stairs in the Ivy. She'd been to the Ivy once before and she'd seen Al Pacino sitting at this very table. In fact she was sitting where Al had sat and a flush of warmth ran through her at the thought.

'Now why is that? Aren't you hungry after all that work today?'

'Oh, yes, I'm starving, I could eat a . . .'

'Then why?'

'Well, I know you only asked me out because Dad stood me up. You're probably dying to get home and rest or something.'

'Luana, I rarely have to do anything I don't want to any more. I enjoyed our talk at lunch the other day. I really wanted to spend some time with you again.'

'Why?'

'Why not? You're a very pretty girl – I mean woman – and you're very bright. Apart from the fact that you have a warped and deeply suspicious mind, I enjoy your company and if you ask why again I shall get up and leave you here.'

Luana wanted to ask him if he had enjoyed kissing her that afternoon. She wanted to know how she had compared with Julianne Reynard. But instead she sat quietly as several luminaries passed their table and greeted Hector.

'This is Luana,' he told them each time and she smiled, pleased by the fact that he didn't explain her connection with him via work so they assumed she was his date.

Well, she *was* his date. Relax, she told herself, for God's sake relax.

'So what's Dad up to in Paris?'

'Haven't a clue. I called him about something, said I'd look forward to seeing him at the casting and he said he had to go to Paris at the last minute. Maybe he's got a lover over there.'

'Dad?!'

'Well, it's been a while since he left – Polly, is it? Surely he must have seen a few other women since then even if he is your ancient father.'

'I suppose you're right. It's just what with Polly appearing to have taken some vow of celibacy, I sort of lumped Dad in there with her. Of course, there is Juanita.'

'Juanita Whyte? Think there's something happening there?'

'Not if there really is a God.'

'Bad as that, is she? What about your mother? Might they ever get back together?'

'No way. Can I have the smoked salmon and scrambled eggs?'

She looked straight at Hector for a second and her gaze said: I do not talk about my mother.

'Tell me, do you like Clovis?'

This was so out of left field it threw her, as it was meant to do.

'She's a very good casting director.'

'That's not what I asked.'

'It's my way of answering what you asked. I want to learn the business. She's good. I'm learning. It's not important whether or not I like her.'

'Ambitious little thing, aren't you? But you don't like her.'

'No,' replied Luana without looking up at him. 'Do you like her?'

'Not much. She's so brash.' And they both laughed.

'Do you live on your own?' he asked, another unexpected question.

'Yes.'

'Like it?'

'Yes.'

'Don't get lonely?'

'Sometimes.'

'What do you think about marriage?'

'Well I don't think about it. I'm too young.'

'But you're not against it?'

'Why on earth should I be?'

'Child of divorced parents.'

'No I'm not. Dad and Mum were never married. Dad's married to Polly even though they're separated.'

'So who do you think of as your mother?'

'Well I call Mum, Mum and Polly, Polly so I suppose . . .'

'But you don't like her: your real mother, I mean . . .'

'My biological mother is what they say now, isn't it?'

'Why don't you like her?'

'Maybe I do. She doesn't like me.'

'How do you know?'

Luana realised suddenly that he'd done it again, slipped in underneath her guard and started her talking about herself – and not only about herself but about her

233

mother. But, dammit, she wanted to tell someone about Edith. She'd always longed to talk to Polly about her mother but her father had made it quite clear that was out of the question. Now she was nineteen, an adult, able to make decisions about her own life. Hector seemed genuinely interested in her, which was more than she could say about anyone else.

'Mum ignored me. She was always wrapped up in her own world, shut away from us. She'd always been sick, I knew that, but I never realised just how bad she was until Dad and I talked about it recently. Poor Dad. When he met her she was only seventeen and he can't have been much older. From what I can make out he was heavily into his Italian father role, wanted to start a family. He gets like that sometimes and it's completely stupid. He's a perfectly ordinary English bloke but sometimes he comes on like he's the original Italian Catholic poppa, all hugs and kisses and don't you dare let a boy so much as look at you. Anyway, Mum was young and very pretty and she got pregnant with me so he must have done more than just look at her! He wanted to marry her, so he told me, but she wouldn't let him. He should have suspected something then but he's dead thick sometimes. He's a born optimist. He just kept hoping she'd say yes if he kept asking her enough times. Then I was born and apparently it was after she'd had me that she really began to go crazy. Post-natal depression or whatever it's called. They reckon she must have always been pretty fragile. Then one day I came home from school and found her unconscious. I was too young to understand but I remember there was a hell of a fuss, people running and carrying her off.'

Hector leaned forward. 'You mean she took an overdose?'

'I suppose. After that, well I suppose she needed Dad too much and he just couldn't take it. He's pretty needy himself.'

'So he left her?'

'No. She left him. That's what did his head in. She said she knew what she was doing to him and she knew she couldn't be the woman he wanted, so she left. You can just imagine it, all his Catholic guilt came rushing to the surface. That's why he won't let any of us upset her. He's terrified she'll do herself in and he'll be to blame. Poor old Polly, she can't understand why there's this mystery surrounding Mum. I've tried to drop as many hints as I can but Dad has forbidden me to discuss Mum with Polly. Polly's pretty smart though. She must have sussed out Dad's guilt complex by now.'

'Is your mother still having any kind of treatment?'

'That's just it. While she was still in London she was going to this shrink of hers once or twice a week but once she moved to Cornwall she never found anyone down there. Hence Dad's paranoia. He holds himself responsible. You see, the thing is, if he hadn't met Polly and married her he might have gone back to Mum out of sheer guilt.'

'Do you really believe that?'

'Sometimes I do, sometimes I don't, but I'm sure it's what Mum thinks.'

'But she left him.'

'I know. Ironic, isn't it?'

'Would you have wanted them to get back together?'

'Well, that's where my lapsed Catholic guilt comes in. The answer is no. I respect Polly. She's good for Dad. Oh, here's my scrambled eggs.' Suddenly Luana felt uncomfortable. Had she said too much?

Hector was rather quiet for the rest of the meal. This

made Luana even more nervous and she chattered frantically to make up for it. Now and then he took her hand and smiled and once he leaned over and kissed her on the cheek.

By the end of the meal Luana was in a state of elation. She wondered if he could possibly understand the relief she felt at having been able to talk to someone about her mother. He had come into her life at exactly the right moment and he was meant to be the one she talked to. It was destiny, she told herself dramatically. She felt closer to Hector O'Neill than to any other person she had ever encountered.

As they walked to the car, Hector slipped his arm around her as if it was the most natural thing in the world. She was oblivious to the fact that she had drunk so much that if he had not supported her she would have fallen in the gutter.

That night she fell in love for the first time. She realised that everything that had come before had been infatuation. This was the real thing and the reason she knew was that she climaxed for the first time.

It didn't happen until nearly dawn. They made love as soon as they were in Hector's suite but unlike the other men Luana had slept with, he knew she hadn't come. He asked her in the darkness, holding her close to him:

'Why did you fake it?'

Luana made no effort to pretend.

'I always do.'

'But why?'

'I always want to please . . . the man.'

'And it doesn't matter if you're not satisfied?'

'I'm always afraid he won't want me any more if I don't pretend that it was great for me too.'

'So have you always pretended you're happy – with your mother, for example? Does she have any idea of the effect her illness has had on you?'

He rocked Luana to sleep as she cried into his chest. Later he woke her and began gently to arouse her, stroking her all over, forbidding her to touch him, forcing her to submit to his caresses. He did this for a long time, and when he finally entered her he was quite rough, deliberately, and it worked. It excited her. She came noisily, surprising herself with her first ever genuine cries of pleasure.

He left her to sleep again and went to the window, stretching. He wandered into the sitting room where he had had an answering machine installed and listened to his messages. Joan Brock had called four times. He plucked a piece of hotel writing paper from the folder on the desk and scrawled a note.

> Dear Joan,
> Can we call it a day? I'm off to France
> to begin filming in a month or so. It
> was fun but it was really only a fling.
> Let's be adults and put it behind us as a
> terrific memory.
>
> Hector

He'd get the hotel to fax it in the morning as soon as he'd sent little Luana on her way.

Polly was furious with Joan. It had been weeks since they'd lunched and Joan hadn't returned a single one of her calls despite the many messages she'd left on Joan's answering machine.

Joan might be an aggressive, competitive friend who often made Polly feel inadequate but she was also a good listener and Polly wanted to tell her about her night out with Edward Holland. She wanted to inform Joan that she, Polly, was now through with men for ever. She was even looking forward to Joan's look of horror and the subsequent lecture on how she'd better get a grip on herself and stop uttering such crap, they were neither of them getting any younger.

In the end she decided to drive over to Joan's house off the Fulham Road and bang on the door late at night. Joan would be livid if she had miraculously managed to lure somebody into her bed but Polly didn't care.

There was no answer.

Joan hadn't managed to lure anybody into her bed but she had managed to worm her way into someone else's. The previous week she had interviewed Hector O'Neill for the profile she was writing, after which she had enjoyed three successive nights of carnal lust with him in his suite at the Berkeley. Only now she had received his fax and was indulging in some very un-Joan like behaviour: crying her eyes out. When her doorbell went she rushed to the window in relief only to glimpse Polly standing at her front door. Joan returned to bed and pulled the pillow over her head. Polly was the last person she wanted to see.

In the end Polly asked Zoë Nichols to come for a drink at the end of the day. It would be easier to talk without Mrs Flowers fussing around. It turned out to be a particularly frantic day and when Zoë arrived, Polly was in the midst of some delicate negotiating on the phone.

'Take her into the drawing room and give her a drink, would you, Mrs Flowers?' Polly mouthed. 'Stay and chat with her if you have the time until I get there.'

When Polly finally went through she could hear Mrs Flowers in full flow but she couldn't make out what she was saying and then when Polly arrived in the room Mrs Flowers suddenly stopped as if she had been talking about Polly herself.

Zoë Nichols was attractive with expressive brown eyes set very wide apart and a mass of curly blonde hair. She was small with big breasts and a curvaceous figure. She reminded Polly of an upmarket Dolly Parton. She was older than Polly had expected. Polly realised they must be about the same age.

'Goodnight, Mrs Flowers. Thank you so much,' said Polly, knowing she ought to invite Mrs Flowers to join them for a quick drink.

'Yes, goodnight, it's been fun to talk to you. Good luck,'

added Zoë and Mrs Flowers reluctantly took the hint and left.

Good luck with what, wondered Polly. With me? Am I that bad a boss? Has she been having a moan?

'What a character!' said Zoë. 'What's it like having an author for a secretary?'

'I don't,' said Polly. 'What will you have to drink?'

'You mean you don't know?'

'Know what?'

'Your secretary is Mabel Lucy Flowers.'

'Are those her names? I had no idea. How clever of you to worm them out of her. She's always insisted on being just Mrs Flowers to me.'

'I'll have a whisky if I may. Mabel Lucy Flowers. She's a Mills & Boon author. Haven't you seen her books at the supermarket? I think she's one of the successful ones.'

'I don't believe it.' Polly had stopped pouring whisky in amazement. 'You come in and get more out of her in twenty minutes than I have in all the time she's been working for me. Why is she working for me, as a matter of mild interest, if she's so successful in her own right?'

'Oh, she's got it all worked out.' Zoë was obviously highly amused. 'She's given up writing Mills & Boons and she's working on something much bigger. She went to work as a temp at, where was it, Patrick Fisher & Dunbar in order to learn more about the requirements in the marketplace for that kind of novel and that's where she met you.'

'But she never breathed a word to me about the fact that she wrote herself. She sits here all day working for me and – '

'Then she goes home and works on her own block-buster at her kitchen table. It's coming along rather well, so she says. It's going to have a very happy ending, a real weepie. She's very keen on happy endings, thinks we all need to be uplifted more. She nearly had a fit when your husband left because I gather the timing coincided with her hero behaving rather badly, had a bit on the side and all that and was thinking of leaving her heroine.'

Damn Mrs Flowers. How dare she be so indiscreet about Polly's private life with a total stranger.

'And did he?'

'Yes, but as she keeps saying, her book will have a happy ending although personally, from the sound of her characters, I think it'd probably be happiest all round if her hero and her heroine walked off into two different sunsets and stayed there.'

'Did she indicate what she was planning to do with this masterpiece once she's finished it?'

'I'll give you three guesses. You happened to walk in just as I was asking exactly the same question.'

'I wondered why she went so quiet. You're not married then, Zoë?'

'I'm not, actually. Never have been. I'm thirty-eight and somehow it just hasn't happened and I can't say I'm in any way unhappy about it. I'm more worried about what I'll do if I ever meet anyone who wants me to move in with him. I've got so used to being on my own and doing exactly what I want when I want, I don't think I could accommodate anyone else very easily. Do you have children to keep you company since your husband left?'

'I had his daughter but now she's got a flat of her own and I'm all on my own but the terrible thing is, I'm getting to be just like you. Johnny used to watch TV till the middle of the night. He couldn't be on his own for a second, spent the whole time following me about asking me what I was doing. He didn't like me doing anything that didn't include him: as a result I wound up doing very little of what I actually wanted to do and rather a lot of what he wanted. Now I'm making up for a great deal of lost time, and it's bliss.'

Zoë laughed. 'Don't you miss him just a bit?'

'Sometimes I miss him desperately, sometimes not at all.'

'Do you want him to do a Mabel Lucy Flowers and come back to you? Oh, I'm sorry, that's a pretty personal question.'

Polly put down her drink. 'No, it's OK. It's a perfectly reasonable question and one I happened to have avoided asking myself so I can't give you an answer right this minute.'

'I'll stop being so nosy. Forgive me, it goes with the job. Listen, it's very good of you to see me. I've done a bit of homework and your client list is really amazing, considering how short a time you've been going. I absolutely loved *Mr Wrong*, lapped it up and begged for more. Is he writing another? I gather it was your idea to get him to write the book in the first place. And Rebecca Price, now her books are a real treat. That's who Mrs Flowers ought to be looking to for guidance. A superior writer in her genre, as they say. The reviewers are so snobby about her. It seems the more successful a writer is financially the worse the reviews, and even if they are good, they're always so removed. I mean, you never get someone writing something as straightforward as, "If, like me, you like Jackie Collins, Sidney Sheldon and Barbara Taylor Bradford you'll absolutely love this new novel by X." It's always, "The writing is execrable, the grammer non-existent, the characters half-dimensional but no doubt fans of the genre will be fooled yet again" sort of thing. Obviously written by some former Booker prize judge who collapses if he has to read anything that hasn't recently been translated from the Latin or Greek or even Serbo-Croat. Of course, if it has a good story it's damned for ever.'

'How enormously refreshing to hear a member of the so-called Mass Market speak out. I wish you'd do it in print. Irwin Shaw said when he was reviewing one of Mario Puzo's books, I forget which one, "For some literary critics, writing a book that is popular and commercially successful rates very high on the list of white collar crime." I agree with you, Zoë. It's hard enough for anyone to write anything without people being put off at the first fence by mean-spirited critics. It never seems to work both ways. The elitist reviewers can dump on popular fiction but the plebs who enjoy a good story, bless 'em, are never allowed to review William Gaddis and say they don't understand a word, now are they? So, what's happened with Aroma Ross?'

'Well, I was right. It was her agent's idea, her model agent. Seize the moment and all that, supermodels are the world's new icons, they've replaced film stars in the eyes of the young; more teenagers in the United States can name a supermodel than their own president and so on and so forth. I've had a giggly girly meeting with her and a couple of the bookers at her London agency. She kept me waiting for an hour but what the hell, she's not the first and I've waited worse places than Claridge's lobby. She's rather sweet and quite shrewd in a childlike way. No one's got any idea what the book should be about, least of all the publishers. All they'll say is that it should be "like Ivana Trump's book". How *passé* can you get? At least Aroma knows exactly what she doesn't want the book to be about: her. Nothing about her boyfriends or her private life. She's pretty paranoid about that, but fair enough. We discussed the market and she figures it's kids, twelve to twenty. I felt a bit mean: in order to get her OK on doing the book I let her think it was going to be some kind of Sweet Valley High romance but in fact it'll have to be more than that to justify the publisher's advance, which is £100,000 by the way. She says she's going to dictate stuff into a tape recorder but to be honest I suspect I'm going to have to conceive and write the whole thing from start to finish and frankly, it's easier that way. I can just get on with it.'

'But you don't have a deal with her yet?'

'I won't have a deal with her at all. She and I will have separate contracts with the publishers and never the twain shall meet.'

'So you'd like me to negotiate your deal for you?'

'If you think it's worth your while.'

'It could sell very well. We'll have to get you a royalty, not one of those flat fee deals. Who's the publisher?'

'Artie Allen-Jones at Hollywood House. Do you know him?'

'I know Artie. Younger than springtime but keen with it. It'd fit his profile perfectly doing a supermodel's novel. Leave it to me. Now, another whisky? Where are you from, Zoë? London?'

'Born and raised, but my mother's French. Poor woman met my father during the war and came over and married him. He's south London working class, a costermonger. I was bilingual thanks to my mum. I started writing for the music press when I left school, just bulldozed my way in and took it from there. I wasn't proud. I wrote for anyone who'd let me – the *Mirror*, the *Sun*, *Woman's Own*, and now it's the *Guardian* and the *Sunday Times* and *Tatler*. Get that – a costermonger's daughter writing for *Tatler*. But it's not a patch on what you've done, Polly, starting up your own agency and everything.'

'My father left me £25,000,' Polly confessed. 'I used it to build the conservatory, my office through there, and since then I've just been lucky.'

'Money isn't everything. You've been shrewd and smart and you've clearly got excellent judgement. Don't run yourself down. You're a budding success story. Be proud of it. I would.'

After she'd gone Polly made herself a snack and watched television but she didn't really take anything in because her mind kept on going back to Zoë Nichols and how good she'd felt at the end of their meeting. She kept on comparing Zoë with Joan and wondered why. They were both journalists but they could not be more different: Zoë with her get-out-and-do-it attitude and Joan with her elitist Vogue House airs and graces. Well, it was not hard to see who was going to go further in the end. But the more she thought about it the more Polly realised that it was not their work that made her lump Joan and Zoë together. It was their approach to her. Joan was competitive and always succeeded in putting Polly down whereas Zoë had made her feel wonderful with her generous praise, and Polly was sure it had been genuine, that she wasn't just saying it to make Polly feel more inclined to get her a better deal. Polly went to bed having decided that she wanted to see more of Zoë Nichols whether she became her agent or not. While she'd been talking to Zoë, Joan had left a message on Polly's machine, the first in over two weeks. It sounded suspiciously like Joan was in tears.

To her own surprise, Polly didn't ring Joan back that evening or the following morning. She rang Zoë Nichols instead and suggested they go and see a movie.

'**M**y goodness, you look smashing,' commented Mrs Flowers, looking at Polly admiringly as she came back into the conservatory having been upstairs to have a quick bath and change before going out. 'Must be someone really special. Someone new?' she asked coyly.

Polly had rung her Mills & Boon author Grania Henderson and asked her about Mabel Lucy Flowers. Grania was riddled with guilt.

'Of course I've known who she was and I knew you'd find out sooner or later but she made me swear not to talk about it. I think she thought she was quite safe. I'm your only Mills & Boon author, after all, and although you pretend to be a champion of popular fiction, you never come to any of the Romantic Novelists' Association lunches. If you had you would have seen Mrs Flowers hiding in a corner.'

'Well, she always says she'll go as my representative. Now I know why. She's there as an author. Oh, Grania, what a mess. Why do you think she blurted it all out to

Zoë Nichols? She must have known Zoë would mention it. Do you think I should tackle her about it?'

'Polly, I'm going to be fearfully indiscreet here and don't jump down my throat when you hear what I've got to say. Mrs Flowers has shown me this saga thing she's writing and it's simply awful. She hasn't got a clue. Don't be upset that she hasn't shown you. She's terrified of what your reaction will be. I've headed her off at the pass and suggested some more work she might do on it before she shows it to you. I don't think you need say anything for the time being. You don't want to lose a good secretary, do you?'

Mrs Flowers might well ask if she was on her way to meet someone special. Polly knew she looked good in her grey silk top, long silk-knit black cardigan, which clung seductively to her hips while hiding their bulges and her black Italian trousers with the little slit just above the ankle. The two-inch heels on her mules showed off her legs to perfection. The overall effect was chic but casual. But why was she all dolled up like this? She was only going to have supper with Johnny in his new flat. Was it pride? She wanted Johnny to see she looked good with or without him. Or did she really want Johnny to take notice of her again?

As she drove to Mayfair, she wondered why Johnny wanted to see her. The words 'happy ending' flashed into her mind but she banished them immediately, cursing Mrs Flowers. Johnny had called at the beginning of the week.

'Pol? How are you? Fancy a bite at my new place? Love you to see it. I'll cook. You will be astounded.'

Polly arrived to find he had an antiseptic flat on the first floor above a shop in Mount Street. Johnny didn't belong in Mayfair. However much he might think he had acquired a sophisticated veneer, he was wrong, and in Mayfair his rough-and-readiness stood out even more. The flat was like a hotel suite. It was as if Johnny had rented it for the night, not for the next three years or whatever it was. Polly found herself looking at the ashtrays to see if there were matchbooks with his name on them. She pressed the brand new wood panelling to see if it would open to reveal a minibar. It had never occurred to her that someone was actually commissioned to paint the usually dreadful paintings hanging on the walls in hotel rooms until she read Dirk Bogarde's novel *Jericho* where a character did just that. Looking at the motley collection on Johnny's walls, she deduced it must be a job lot from a defunct hotel.

She had been met by the most extraordinary sight when she walked through the front door. Johnny was arranging flowers, hopping about in his jeans and sneakers, trying to tuck stray stems into a tall rectangular glass vase standing on the hall table. The result looked decidedly unprofessional. Broken lilies and squashed foliage lay on the floor in a puddle of water. Polly gently pushed him aside and began again. She was oddly touched by the sight of him attempting such a task.

'I've got a Mrs Thing,' he explained, 'and she orders these flowers for me once a week to cheer the bloody place up and then she leaves them for me to deal with.'

'Well, I'm glad you've got someone to look after you.'

'Yeah. Me too. Ivana.'

'Ivana?'

'It's not her real name. That's something quite unpronounceable. She's Czech so I call her Ivana.'

'Does she mind?'

'Never asked her. She makes me dinner too and leaves it in the fridge. Come and look, Pol. Same thing every

248

day. Two pork chops and boiled potatoes. I never touch it.' He opened the fridge in the tiled and chrome kitchen and pointed to a row of Pyrex ovenproof dishes, 'See: Monday, Tuesday, Wednesday . . .'

'Is this what we're having for dinner?'

'Of course not. I'm cooking, I told you,' he said proudly.

'But it's such a waste! Can't you tell her not to do it?'

'Oh, it all goes to good use, you'll see. Besides, I like the notion that someone cares about me.'

Polly refrained from pointing out that he hadn't even kissed her hello or said how nice she looked and if he wanted someone to feel sorry for him he was going the wrong way about it. Yet strangely that's exactly what she felt. She yearned to go home and return with fridge-loads of nourishing home-made food for him. But she couldn't resist commenting on the décor.

'What's wrong with it?' Johnny was immediately defensive. 'Don't blame me. Juanita handled everything. Found the place, did it up, hired Ivana, and Bob was my uncle. All I had to do was move in – and here I am. Now, food! Go and sit down and relax with your drink while I rustle up a little something in the kitchen.'

'A little something' turned out to be Marks and Spencer's Chicken Kiev followed by De Soto ice-cream.

'Do you know about M&S, Pol? Amazing place for food.'

Polly smiled. Trust Johnny to go for megabucks microwave cooking. It really was rather sweet – the thought of him pottering round Marks & Sparks and tottering back to nuke his salmon *en croute* or his fish pie every night before he curled up in front of the telly with endless tubs of the family *gelati*. She wondered what his mother would say if she knew he was living off frozen meals.

She poured herself a glass of wine and started idly flicking through *Hello!* She stopped at a massive spread on Juanita Whyte and goggled. It was just as well Johnny hadn't actually fed her yet otherwise she might have thrown up.

'FIVE YEARS AFTER HIS TRAGIC DEATH, SIR GORDON WHYTE'S BEAUTIFUL WIDOW INVITES US INTO HER LOVELY HOME . . . and tells us how she is gradually beginning to enjoy life again.'

Polly studied the pastel décor of Juanita's Chelsea mansion and saw immediately how her bland taste had extended to Johnny's flat. The last few pages showed Juanita in Paris posing under the Arc de Triomphe, outside Chanel, in the rue de Rivoli, on the banks of the Seine and, to Polly's horror, having dinner with Johnny who was described as 'a new companion who has brought a sparkle back to Lady Whyte's eyes'. Hardly a new companion, thought Polly, and besides it was more likely to be a new facelift that had brought about that sparkle.

'Johnny de Soto, co-producer with Lady Whyte of the forthcoming film *Mr Wrong* starring Hector "Conway" O'Neill,' read the caption. 'Mr de Soto has been a firm fixture in Lady Whyte's calendar ever since he offered his kind and sympathetic support at the time of her husband's death.'

'My arse,' said Polly.

'What's that, Pol? Now, I've just got to feed Zutty then we'll have ours. *Zutty*! Where are you hiding? Din-dins!'

There was a frantic scrabbling underneath one of the sofas and Zutty shot out, a tornado of red and white fur, skedaddling across the parquet floors, paws splayed in all directions in his desperate haste to get to his food. Polly hadn't even realised he was there.

'Say hello to Pol,' said Johnny firmly, holding the plastic dog bowl high in the air. 'After all, you're going to have to be very nice to her, aren't you?'

'Just why is he going to have to be very nice to me? Johnny, give him his dinner, for Christ's sake. He'll do himself an injury.'

Zutty was prancing about on his hind legs, pirouetting, leaping in the air, losing his balance on landing and falling over.

'Here you are then. See, Pol, Zutty gets Ivana's pork chops and spuds. They don't go to waste. Now, you do like Zutty, don't you?'

'I suppose so, yes.'

'Well, that's terrific because he really likes you.'

'Well how come he didn't utter a sound when I arrived?' Polly was beginning to smell a very large rat.

'You're looking great tonight, Pol.'

'Johnny!' warned Polly. If only he'd said that when she walked in.

'OK, OK. I'll come to the point. We start filming in France in about three weeks.'

'I know.'

'Well, I can't take Zutty.'

'Oh, Christ, Johnny!'

'He does adore you.'

'Bullshit! He adores anyone who feeds him, just like any other dog. How long will you be away?'

'About a month, maybe six weeks.'

'Why can't Luana look after him?'

'Luana? Luana doesn't know how to look after a dog.'

'What on earth makes you say that? She takes care of actors, doesn't she?'

'Oh, I get it. What's the difference? Ha, ha! Have you seen her lately, by the way? She's looking terrific.'

'Well, tell her that and she'll probably agree to look after Zutty.'

'Oh, shut up, Pol. Seriously. I popped into the office and there she was, my little peachy girl again.'

'Well, for heaven's sake don't let her hear you calling her that. She hates it. So that other problem has blown over?'

'What other problem?'

'The constant nymph of Central London.'

'Haven't heard any more about it.'

'Because, you know, I think she does have a man.'

'Really? Who?'

'I don't know but she keeps hinting she's seeing someone. Johnny, what's this?'

'Salad. I thought you liked it. You lived off the stuff when we were living together.'

'You're meant to take it out of the packet. In fact, you're not meant to buy it in a packet in the first place. You're supposed to buy lettuces and rocket and endive and wash them and chop them up and serve them with a good dressing.'

'No shit? Well, I'll chop open the packet if you make the dressing. So what's she said about this bloke?'

'Nothing specific. In fact she seems to be quite secretive about him but I saw her the other day and she showed me this present she'd bought him. Johnny, it was a gold propelling pencil. It wasn't exactly cheap. She'd obviously gone to a lot of trouble choosing it and she wanted my approval. My guess is the man has to be considerably older, otherwise why would she ask what I thought and why would she get a gold pencil as opposed to the latest R.E.M. CD? The other thing that intrigued me was when

I asked her if it was his birthday, she said, oh, no, it was just that he'd lost his old one and she wanted to replace it.'

'Sounds serious. Do you suppose we'll get to meet him soon?'

Polly warmed to the 'we'. It made it sound as if they were still a couple. Zutty's nose pressed its way into her lap.

'See, he adores you.'

'Johnny, he wants the rest of my Chicken Kiev.'

'Oh, you're so cynical. I want you to have him, Pol, because you're there all day. He's used to coming with me to the office and being with me all the time. I dread to think what Clovis would say if Luana turned up with him there and he'd go mad if Luana left him in her poky little flat all day. Probably chew his tail off or something.'

Polly knew she was going to have to give in.

'Mrs Flowers likes dogs,' she began by way of capitulation.

'Does she? That's perfect. She can look after him when you're away.'

'Now what do you mean? I'm not planning on going away.'

'No. I'm planning on you going away. Thought you might like a little holiday, Pol. We're shooting down in the South of France. Cap d'Antibes. That bit where Mr Wrong is seducing all those rich women at the Hôtel du Cap and bumping them off. The opening sequence of the film. The cop hasn't even sussed him yet. Why don't you come down for a few days, long weekend, something like that? Do you good. My way of saying thank you for finding *Mr Wrong*. After all, if you hadn't made Lawrence do the book I'd never have had my movie. I don't mind admitting that now.'

Dear Johnny. She felt a strange rush of affection for

him but then she remembered *Hello!* and fought to control it.

'I suppose I could get away for a few days in July,' she said as casually as she could.

'So, yes to Zutty? Yes to a little holiday? Yes to some De Soto ice-cream?'

What could it hurt? thought Polly as she drove home. It wasn't as if he'd asked: 'Can I come back to you, Pol?' He'd just invited her to spend a holiday with him.

And she was surprised to find how much she was looking forward to it.

By now Luana was seeing Hector three times a week. He no longer picked her up at the office; instead he called and told her where to meet him. He had explained that he thought they ought to keep it quiet that they were seeing each other, that it was more professional if they kept it a secret for the time being.

He left for France and he would be gone for six weeks. Luana did not know how she was going to be able to bear it. She was devastated that he had not invited her to visit him in France but she supposed it had something to do with his insistence on secrecy. If only Clovis hadn't gone and said the day before he left: 'So long as Hector O'Neill doesn't go and fuck everything up by jumping on Julianne Reynard too early in the proceedin's, this fillum's got a pretty good chance of being a hit.'

Carla de Soto nodded at Mrs Flowers who was off to lunch, disappearing out of the conservatory and through the side gate.

'Polly, what is that woman's name? I always forget.'

'You've only met her once. Why should you remember? It's Flowers. Mrs Flowers.'

'Fiore. La Signora Fiore. Of course.'

'That might not be a bad name for her. Drop the Mabel Lucy rubbish. Lucia Fiore. Not bad at all.'

'Polly, what are you talking about?'

'Oh, take no notice. Come into the kitchen while I make lunch. I'm giving you pasta. Don't know how I dare. Talk about coals to Newcastle but this rocket and blue cheese sauce is just divine. You just whizz it up in the blender.'

Carla, who hovered over sauces that simmered for hours on her hob, and didn't go in for whizzing, tactfully changed the subject.

'So Gianni has invited you out there?'

'You didn't put him up to it?'

'Polly, don't be so negative. I know my son well enough to let him make his own decisions.'

'What do you think it means?'

'It could be he's just offering you a holiday like he say. Or it could be that he wants to test the water with you and he think it's good to do it in the South of France where it's warm and romantic.'

'Where he can soften me up?'

'Do you need him to soften you up, Polly? Are you so hard? I don't think so. I think you are too soft with Johnny. I warned you. I said "keep up with him", didn't I? But he got away.'

'You think I'm running after him? You don't think I should go?'

'Of course you should go. Let him pay for a nice holiday, why not? But don't be too soft with him. You must get tough, Polly. Not too tough. *Al dente*, like this pasta. It's delicious. Maybe I shall begin to whizz.'

'Has Johnny ever said anything to you . . . about me . . . about us?'

'Of course he has.'

'But you're not going to tell me what he said.'

'Of course I'm not,' said Carla, thoroughly enjoying being maddening. 'All I can tell you is I think it is worth you going down there. Beyond that, who knows? Can I have some more please with some chopped rocket leaves on the top. That's what it needs.'

What I need, thought Polly as she studied her mother-in-law sitting there in her simple elegant linen dress and her expensive shoes, is to be more like you, to decide what I want and ask for it.

A small Gentle Ghost removal van was parked outside a house in Roland Gardens where a slender brunette was supervising two men as they struggled with boxes and small pieces of furniture.

'It's the top floor,' she told them.

'It would be,' they muttered.

It took them nearly an hour to carry everything up, commenting on everything as they did so.

'You don't see many of these any more.'

'Bit poky, this place, if you don't mind my saying so. Hope you didn't pay too much for it. Why'd you ever want to sell that nice place by the sea?'

The woman ignored them. When they had gone she unpacked a few boxes then ran herself a bath and soaked for an hour. Wrapping herself in an old dressing gown she flung herself across the bed and picked up the phone.

'Surprise surprise. It's me. Edith. I decided it was time I moved back to London.'

PART THREE

As the day approached for her to leave for the South of France, Polly's anxiety level rose higher and higher on her personal Richter scale. It started when she went to Harvey Nichols to buy a new swimsuit. Despite Joan's persistent badgering, she had had the intelligence not to appear in a bikini since she was in her mid-thirties.

'For God's sake, Polly, it's not as if you've even had any children. Your stomach ought to be as flat as the proverbial pancake. Why are you so pathetic about showing it off?'

Joan, of course, had never had any children either but then she was a size 8 who occasionally resorted to shopping in children's stores in order to find something to fit her.

Polly had once been on holiday with her to Ibiza and she had been highly embarrassed, much to Joan's amusement, when Joan had promptly stripped off in front of everyone and sunbathed naked, her virtually non-existent breasts hardening to minuscule chocolate pyramids. Polly had ignored Joan's derision and refused to expose her breasts to the sun. She couldn't bear the thought of all that soft precious tissue being burned to blobs of hard leather by the time she was forty. If there had been one thing about which Johnny had always gone berserk, it was her soft skin.

Polly stood in the narrow cubicle, struggling to ease herself into a black Calvin Klein one-piece that had looked so simple and elegant when it was hanging on the rails without her 140-pound body inside it. She thought about Joan, feeling guilty that she still hadn't called her, wondering what had upset her. Whatever it was, Joan would be over it by now. Life was very simple for Joan. She woke up every day with the expectation of cheques and sex in no particular order and never understanding Polly's priorities which were food, affection, work probably in exactly that order.

Polly squeezed into the swimsuit and tried to hoist it up over her generous breasts. Nothing doing. She turned to inspect her back view and shuddered. Were those faint strips of orange peel *cellulite* running across her thighs, or was it her imagination as usual? What was the point of having good legs, long and shapely, if she always got in a panic when she saw them naked? Joan's version of the old maxim 'A man should always look at a woman's mother before marrying her' was 'A man should always look at a woman in a swimsuit before taking her to bed', and she had had a point. If a man looked at her in a skirt and high heels, Polly had more than a chance, but one look at her naked thighs – forget it! And the mirrors in Harvey Nichols were supposed to be flattering. Still, everyone was always telling her she had a perfectly good figure. Maybe it was time she started believing them.

But then there was her passport photo. Just in time, Polly had noticed that her passport was due to run out. In her panic to acquire a new one in the forty-eight hours she had left, she had rushed out and used one of the booths. Joan would have had a fit, she told herself, trying not to blink as the flash popped in her eyes. Joan had once needed a new passport before going to New York on an assignment to profile a well-known lesbian author who had made a pass at her five minutes into the interview. Polly's comment that, as she understood it, Joan was usually rather chuffed when someone made a pass at her, had not gone down well. But Joan had set up a special photographic session for her new passport photo. Hair and make-up had taken nearly two-hours. The result had made her look like a twelve-year-old Natalie Wood. Polly had not understood what all the fuss was about. Surely Joan was not planning to look good for an immigration official at JFK? Who else saw your passport photo? Only you.

But when she received her new passport complete with the photo taken ten years after the photo in her old one, Polly understood. It was the very fact that you did see it and were faced with the evidence of the extent to which your face had changed, no matter how much you might have ignored it. Polly sat looking at the two passports lying open on her desk in front of her. It wasn't as if she had any wrinkles but her whole face had dropped ten years. In the old passport a puppetmaster appeared to be holding up her face with invisible strings and in the new one, he'd let go.

This was the face she was going to present to Johnny in the South of France.

Predictably, as Polly was in the midst of her last-minute packing on the morning of her flight, Mrs Flowers called up the stairs to ask if she might 'have a word'.

'I'm afraid you'll have to come up here, Mrs Flowers,' Polly called down, trying to mask her mounting hysteria. 'I'm running late. I haven't finished packing and the cab'll be here in twenty minutes. Put the answering machine on in the office and come on up.'

'Shall I bring you a cup of coffee?'

'No! I haven't got time.' Blast the woman. Polly knew she was sounding unnecessarily harsh but Mrs Flowers had a knack of always picking the wrong moment. Yet in so many ways she was invaluable, to the extent that Polly had absolutely no qualms about leaving her in charge of the office for ten days.

Mrs Flowers shuffled into Polly's bedroom clutching a carrier bag and immediately began trying to help her pack, picking up piles of clothes and depositing them neatly into Polly's suitcase. Polly promptly removed them. She had her own system for packing dating back to the days when Matron had instructed her how to pack her trunk at boarding-school. Hard things like shoes, books, handbags at the bottom with socks and underwear stuffed into the holes. Then a layer of lightweight garments like nightdresses, T-shirts, shorts in piles and finally, spread out on top so they wouldn't crease, skirts, jackets, trousers, dresses. Polly's problem ever since had been that her suitcases were about a quarter of the size of her cavernous school trunk and she always ran out of space.

'Sit down, Mrs Flowers, over there if you will,' she said firmly. 'Now, what's the matter?'

'Well, it's a bit hard to know where to start and I know I should have mentioned it before but what with one thing and another . . .'

'You're writing a book, is that it?' Polly didn't have time to wait for her to get to the point.

'You do know all about it? I've always wondered.'

'As it happens, I've only recently found out. To be honest, I did sort of feel rather put out. I think you should have mentioned you were a writer when you first came to work for me. It's nothing to be ashamed of, after all,' said Polly, stuffing Marmite and Johnson's Baby Oil, and all the other items she feared being deprived of by the French, into the gaps between her shoes.

'I'm dreadfully sorry. I meant to tell you right at the beginning then I kept putting it off. I thought you might ask me to leave and I do so love working for you.'

Stop gushing and let me get on with my packing. Polly was getting frantic. 'I don't mind a bit but why are you telling me now?'

'Well, I've been working on this longer book. Very different. I was hoping, I was wondering . . .'

Too late Polly remembered Grania's warning: 'It's simply awful. She hasn't got a clue.' She turned round to see Mrs Flowers produce a large and cumbersome manuscript from a carrier bag.

'Is that your book?' asked Polly stupidly, feeling well and truly trapped.

'It's just I thought you might have some time to read it while you were down there, well some of it anyway. I'd just love to know what you think of it.'

Polly could not believe it. The nerve of the woman. She was going away for a rest, to have a break from work. Why on earth would she want to lug some great manuscript with her? Yet time was running out and it was a question of reasoning with Mrs Flowers and missing the plane or taking the book from her.

'Give it to me, Mrs Flowers. I'll see what I can do. Now seriously, I must get on. Perhaps you could get back to the office?'

Mrs Flowers stayed until she had witnessed Polly

putting the precious script in her suitcase then she left, apologising profusely for the inconvenience she had caused.

As soon as she heard the conservatory door bang Polly whipped the manuscript out of her case and shoved it under her bed. Enough was enough.

As her Air France flight to Nice took off Polly read the papers and saw a piece about Aroma Ross's novel which mentioned that the supermodel would be 'helped' by journalist Zoë Nichols. Polly had negotiated as good a deal as she could for Zoë, making sure she got a piece of the publisher's income on everything except film rights, which the publishers didn't control. Zoë had begun work so they could have something to show at the Frankfurt Book Fair in October. She and Polly had spent a couple of rather drunken evenings together when Zoë had attempted to brush up Polly's French conversation in readiness for her trip to the Côte d'Azur. At the end of the second evening Polly had confided to Zoë how much she was looking forward to spending time with Johnny, and Zoë had hugged her and said she hoped everything would turn out well but whatever happened Polly should be sure and have a proper holiday. Polly couldn't help thinking of the tirade she would have received from Joan about accepting Johnny's invitation.

Polly picked at her tray of airline food – a piece of

rolled-up ham, a cornichon, a triangle of Camembert, a plastic glass of Evian and a little bottle of chilled red wine – and looked out of the window at the clouds puffing by. She began to daydream. Johnny would be brown. He always went black if he so much as looked at the sun and now his close-cropped hair was almost totally white, a tan gave him a particularly roguish look like that of a sea captain. She'd missed his nervous energy. She'd even missed his endless questions: 'What are you doing, Pol?' every five minutes. At least it meant he cared what she was doing, was interested. If only he'd been a little more interested in her agency and a little less obsessed with his pretentious social life. Still, he had asked her down for a holiday. It was a gesture and she was prepared to accept it. Could it mean that he wanted to come back to her? Did she want him back?

Suddenly she could hardly contain her excitement at the thought of seeing him again. She handed her half-empty tray to a passing stewardess and rummaged in her bag for her Walkman. Listening to a tape would distract her for the rest of the flight.

The captain announced they would be landing at Nice in ten minutes. Almost before she knew it Polly was on the ground and lugging her baggage off the carousel. She wheeled her trolley into Arrivals in a daze and when a swarthy-looking bare-chested man with skin the colour of bitter chocolate and a back to front baseball cap over his crew cut tried to wrest it from her, she screamed out loud.

'God's sake, Pol, get a grip!'

'Johnny! Why are you here?'

'Polly, I'll speak very slowly. Read my lips. You've arrived at Nice. You're at the airport. I've come to meet you. Is that all right?'

'Johnny, it's wonderful. I just didn't expect you.'

'But I said I'd come and meet you.'

'Yes, I know, but I thought you'd send a minion, not come yourself.'

'So how is he?'

'Who?'

'Zutty. How is he? Does he miss me?'

No 'How are you, Pol? Have you missed me, Pol? I've been looking forward to seeing you, Pol. You're looking great, Pol.'

'Zutty's fine. He misses you dreadfully and I have a very smelly bone buried somewhere in my luggage that he insisted I bring out to you.'

'Very funny. Polly, just give me that trolley and follow me out to the car. Perhaps you'd better sit in the trolley too if you're feeling so feeble and I'll push you along with the bags.'

She followed him, watching his arse move in his tight jeans, the taut muscles in his suntanned back, his broad shoulders. She wanted to run after him and hug him to her from behind but she didn't dare. It was ridiculous. She didn't know how she stood with him. It was almost as if she was dating her own husband for the first time.

Johnny had hired a battered Renault and he drove like a maniac on the wrong side of the road while Polly closed her eyes and sent up silent prayers.

'See, Pol, sensational weather, blue skies, da da da *da*, nothing but blue skies from now on. Perfect place to film. The light's great. We're on schedule. Maybe even a day under. Henri's a terrific director, knows exactly what he wants. We didn't really get going until the second week. The crew needed time to get to know each other and of course Henri's never worked with any of them before. Nor have I, come to think of it. We've got a sensational first assistant. We're using all these Froggy extras to save costs and Spider, that's the first, he can speak fluent Frog. You should see him shift them from place to place, get them in position, get them fed, don't know how he does it. He's more aggressive than the Frogs themselves. Hector's terrific. Came out the week before last. We're shooting all his stuff in one go, of course. He costs a bloody fortune. Budget would go through the roof if we had him here all the time. He's here for another three weeks. The first week he was here we shot the sequence where Julianne – who's playing the girl cop – has her first date with him. You remember the script, Pol?'

'I remember the book, Johnny.'

'Yeah, 'course. It's when Caspar sends the girl – '

'There's no one called Caspar in the book,' protested Polly.

'No, no, Pol, Caspar Cartier is the guy who plays Frank, the cop. He's shit hot. French Canadian. The Froggy money men love him. This is his first international picture. It's going to make him a huge star. So, we've got Caspar – so he's playing the cop who suspects the womaniser, Mr Wrong, played by Hector, might be the serial killer he's looking for and he follows him to the South of France and puts Julianne – who's playing a woman cop Frank/Caspar's falling in love with but he hasn't told her yet – he sets Julianne to seduce Mr Wrong and bait him, OK? With me so far? So we shot this fabulous sequence where Hector takes Julianne out on a date and Caspar follows them and you see him really doing his nut when at the end of the evening Hector kisses Julianne and she really enjoys it – because of course she falls for him too – and Caspar's sitting in his car across the street and he can't do a damn thing about it. But the best bit, Pol, are you listening? The best bit is that we filmed all the car sequences where Hector's driving Julianne to dinner in the same places they used with Cary Grant and Grace Kelly in *To Catch a Thief*...'

'Wasn't that back projection?' Polly tried not to think about Princess Grace going over the cliff in her car as Johnny veered over to the wrong side of the road again.

'Well, you know what I mean. We've got Hector taking out all these rich American women and seducing them...'

'Real ones?' Polly was horrified.

'No, Pol, for Christ's sake, this is a movie, remember? Actresses playing rich American women, the ones he seduces and then kills.'

Polly leaned forward in anticipation for they had arrived at the Hôtel du Cap.

'Great hotel, Pol. Bill Cosby's staying here. This is the boulevard JFK and he stayed here with Jackie. Great place to stay for the Cannes Film Festival, much more chic than the Carlton. They've had no end of names here: Hemingway, George Bernard Shaw, Somerset Maugham, Chaplin, Dougie Fairbanks, Rita Hayworth, Orson – in the old days, of course. Scott Fitzgerald based that book of his here...'

'*Tender is the Night*,' murmured Polly.

'That's it. Then you get people like De Niro, Madonna, Stallone, Schwarzenegger, Tom Cruise. All been here. Place to be, Pol.'

He glanced at her to see if she was impressed. Polly smiled. Same old Johnny. Knocked out by the famous names attached to the place and completely oblivious to the magic surrounding the elegant cream-painted marble mansion with its pale blue shutters, built nearly a hundred and fifty years ago and set in acres of beautiful gardens overlooking the Golfe Juan.

As Polly walked up the sweeping stone steps, nervously trying to straighten the crumpled linen blazer and trousers she had travelled in, she couldn't help feeling a bit like a movie star herself. The cool of the marble lobby – with its floor of black diamonds on white and the staircase curving up round the little wooden elevator – was bliss. Polly sank into one of the large white sofas and looked out at the palm trees and the wide avenue that led from the hotel to the sea and the famous Eden Roc restaurant and beach club.

'Come one, Pol. Check in before we go out.'

'Go out?' Polly had been looking forward to going up to the room and taking a shower and changing.

'Yeah, I'm taking you to a little place in Juan les Pins for dinner.'

'But what about my luggage? Can't I at least . . . ?'

'Oh, don't fret, Pol. I'll have them send it up to the room.'

Polly made the snap decision that it was better to go along with Johnny to begin with. The fact that he had even thought about dinner with her, let alone planned it, was a good sign. As she checked in, she asked wistfully: 'Perhaps we could have a drink on the terrace before going out?'

'Are you crazy, Pol? They charge about fifteen quid for a fucking Campari and soda out there.'

'Well, why are you staying in this place if you can't afford it?'

'Because I'm not paying for it, am I? The Frogs who are putting up half the finance, they're coughing up for me, Henri, Julianne and Caspar to stay here.'

'What about Hector?'

Johnny scowled for the first time.

'Hector insisted on hiring a bloody villa all to himself. It's up the road on the boulevard du Cap. Fucking stars! Got me by the short and curlies. Can't live with them, can't live without them. I got this picture set up because of Hector being attached to it so I have to live with the consequences. But I ask you, what's wrong with the Hôtel du Cap? Hector, old son, I said, if it's good enough for Tom Cruise, surely it's good enough for you. You should have seen the look he gave me. Anyway, the bastard's got two days off so he's out of my hair for the time being.'

As they drove to Juan, Polly wondered if he was going to talk about the film business for the entire evening but, as she was soon to be reminded, one of the things that had made her fall in love with Johnny in the first place was his ability to constantly surprise her.

He took her to the kind of place she adored: an unpredictable little bistro in a narrow street on the waterfront where they could sit outside on the cobbled street with a gingham tablecloth and a candle between them. Polly was no stranger to the South of France. Prudence Atwell had insisted that Polly's father allow them to escape from the Norfolk winds for at least a month every year and they had invariably come to the Côte d'Azur. They had rented villas, usually those owned by friends, and in the evenings they had often eaten out at places like this.

Johnny ordered a kir for Polly and a Scotch for himself.

'Pol, I really am pleased you came out. Oh, now, look, you've gone and started blubbing. God, yours must be the world's most overworked tear ducts. Probably start charging you overtime. Oh, don't mind me, I'm thinking like a bloody producer all the time. Here, give me your paw . . .'

He reached for her hand across the table and held it in his, patting it consolingly. Polly giggled and her tears turned into splutters. He'd always called them her paws. He'd always treated her rather like a dog. Sometimes she wondered if she was interchangeable with Zutty in his mind but she couldn't deny that she liked it. Men, she reflected, were often more affectionate with dogs than with women.

'Spit it out,' Johnny ordered, 'tell me all about it: are you tired and emotional or is there something actually wrong? Are you OK? Agency doing all right?'

Polly was astounded. Had Johnny been going to night classes to learn how to be a New Man?

'Pretty good,' she replied. 'All the regulars are performing well and I've got two or three new writers who look rather promising.'

'Lawrence got any further with his new book?'

'Oh God, I completely forgot to call him before I left. Don't know what's the matter with me. I never called Joan either.'

'Well, that's understandable. Hard-bitten old bag, don't know why you have anything to do with her. You can literally see her claws sharpening in anticipation when she claps eyes on a potential fuck. She's a disaster area, Pol, you'll see. She rang me, you know, nearly blasted my head off.'

'When?'

'After I left you. Called me all kinds of names. Said I'd never been worthy of you anyway. Is that what you thought, Pol?'

'No, of course not.'

'But you were pretty angry too, I expect. We've never really talked about it.'

He had his head turned away from her. He was pretending to look down the street to the waterfront but she knew he was watching for her reaction out of the corner of his eye. It was a fairly electric moment. Your husband walks out on you and casually remarks many months later over dinner, 'We've never really talked about it.'

'I wasn't particularly angry. Sorry to disappoint you, Johnny. I suppose I'd seen it coming. You and Juanita.'

'Me and Juanita? What about me and Juanita?'

'She had such a hold over you.'

'Oh, I thought you meant we were having an affair.'

'Well, were you?'

'Oh, don't be ridiculous. She was my business partner. We needed to spend a lot of time together. Anyway if you weren't even angry when I left, what the fuck does it matter what we were doing together?'

'I said I wasn't particularly angry, or surprised. That doesn't mean I wasn't upset. I remember asking myself if in fact you had ever really loved me. You clearly had one route mapped out for your life from the very beginning. God knows, your mother even warned me about it. "Keep up with him," she told me; "don't let him go too fast or he'll get away from you." What I don't understand is why you thought I was the one who would be the right person to be by your side.'

'Look,' said Johnny, glaring at her across the gingham, 'I was always straight with you. On our honeymoon, if you recall, I said I wanted to produce movies and I wanted you right there beside me. I didn't know you had these crazy plans to go and start your own agency.'

'I didn't have any plans at the time. It just happened and there was nothing crazy about it. My agency is now one of the best in London and – '

'Yeah, I know that, Pol. You've got a pretty good rep. You did what you wanted to do and you succeeded. It's not as if I tried to stop you. Stop making me out to be the bad guy.'

'Johnny, did it ever occur to you that while you wanted me beside you while you were struggling to get your movie off the ground, I might have also wanted you beside me while I was struggling to get my agency off the ground? Being supportive works both ways, you know.'

'Well, what the hell was I supposed to do? Rush to my office, rush to Paris for money meetings and then rush home to sit beside you while you sold some little magical realism first novel to Jonathan fucking Cape? You wanted me to be in ninety-two places at once?'

'No, Johnny. I just wanted you home more in the evening so we could have kept up with each other, talked about what we were both doing.'

'But I kept calling you and asking you to join me for dinner, I kept asking you to come and meet all my friends, the people I was working with. I wanted us to be more of a couple, I wanted people to meet you and invite us to places together. You were the one who always wanted to stay at home.'

'That's just it. I stayed at home because it was always so one-sided. I had to go out and meet your friends. It was never a question of you coming out to meet my authors or my friends.'

'Like sweet and charming Joan Brock? OK, OK, strike that, Pol, it was below the belt.'

'I wanted us to be together, Johnny. Not the whole

time, but just occasionally. Together, on our own, and the only time that happened was much too late at night, when you were too tired to do anything, if we're going to talk about below the belt. But it wasn't even as if I minded that, Johnny. If you'd just come home and got into bed with me and talked like you used to do, about us, or even just about you and your problems, I'd have listened. But when you moved out, you took away any chance of that ever happening again, however much I was prepared to try. You negated all the affection and shared experiences we had had in the past. That's when I began to question if you had ever really loved me. It's understandable. Can't you see that?'

She expected an instant defensive tirade from Johnny. It was the longest time she'd voiced her thoughts on their relationship. Usually he interrupted her, forcing his blinkered view on her, but once again he surprised her.

'You're right, Pol,' he said quietly, 'I destroyed it all. You probably won't believe me but I do think about it sometimes. I do remember what we had. But you're wrong when you say I never really loved you. I loved you. The real you. But I never took it into account that you might not want the same life as me. I needed you in those early days when I was getting started. I needed you more than you needed me. I need support. I can't function on my own. I suppose I'm not strong enough. You might have wanted my support but you didn't really need it. There's a difference. You were quite capable of doing it all on your own. If you really want to know, I think I took off because I needed you as a prop, you weren't prepared to prop me up twenty-four hours a day and I knew you never would be, so I left. My mother was right. I was moving too fast. I always have. I never wait for other people. I never thought about you as someone I could come back and lean on at home. I just always noticed that you were the party pooper who stayed at home.'

'And that isn't what you want?'

Johnny looked at her and Polly was devastated by the sadness in his brown eyes.

'The truth is, Pol, I have no idea what I want any more. I remember the Polly I married. I loved her and if you're still her, then I still love you. But it would be too much to expect you to still love me.'

Another electric moment. She could sense the tension in him as he waited for her reply.

'Johnny, there is so much about you that I do love that it is never going to be overshadowed by changes in you. We've turned out to be two very different people who pretended they didn't know the meaning of the word compromise. Maybe we were meant to split up but there's a part of you that I'll always love, no matter what. You know that.'

'Yes,' he said, getting up and coming round to stand behind her and stroke the back of her neck. 'Come on, let's go back to the hotel. You must be pretty tired.'

Somehow they had ordered their food and eaten it. At some point Johnny had ordered a bottle of *rosé* and they had drunk that too. He settled the bill, holding her against him with one arm as he did so as if he were afraid she might run away from him, and once they were in the car he drew her head down to rest in his lap as he had done when they drove back from Siena on their honeymoon. As they turned off the boulevard JFK and through the hotel gates, Johnny tugged at her hair.

'Better sit up. It's not exactly the kind of hotel where the guests arrive in the middle of a blow job.'

Polly sat up smartly and blushed as the doorman opened the car door for her. Johnny grabbed her hand and they ran up the steps into the marble hall and up the curving staircase. He didn't turn the lights on in the room or check his messages, just threw her across the bed.

'Stay!' he ordered.

'Where's my bone?' laughed Polly, burrowing into the bed. She watched as he took off his clothes and found she couldn't help clambering off the bed to pat his little bare arse, stark white against his tan. She reached around his body from behind and fondled his erection. He turned and pressed it into her linen pants, reaching down to unzip her, stroke her and slide his fingers inside her. They stood together in the moonlight, bringing each other off, tongues probing in each other's mouths, her hand around his penis moving up and down, increasing the pressure until he groaned while she squirmed and rode on his finger stroking her clitoris.

They came almost together but not quite, Johnny first, Polly a second or two later, and he pulled her back on to the bed where they lay side by side, panting softly.

It was a minute or two before she realised he was asleep. She had left her jacket in the car. Now she wriggled silently out of her linen pants, opened the buttons of her blouse and reached round to undo her bra. Tenderly she lifted Johnny's sleeping head on to her bare breasts and cradled him in her arms before she too fell asleep.

Her first thought on waking was: we're back together.

But Johnny had managed to disentangle himself without waking her, and had left for the set. A note on the pillow said simply: See you tonight.

Polly stumbled off the bed and into the bathroom to splash water on her face, blearily recognising Johnny's things scattered around the basin. She looked around the room and saw no sign of her luggage. She rang down to the front desk and asked for it to be brought up.

'Where are you, madame?' asked the hall porter, as if he didn't know. Did she detect a hint of a sneer in his voice?

'Room 502. Mr de Soto's room.'

'Ah, well, you see, madame, Mr de Soto instructed us to take the bags to Miss Atwell's room: 602 on the floor above.'

Mr de Soto and Miss Atwell. Two separate rooms.

'I'll be down to collect the key,' snapped Polly and forced herself not to bang down the receiver.

The view out over the bay from her corner room was stunning. Directly above Johnny's, the room appeared to be identical except that it didn't have a terrace and instead of striped, swathed curtains and plain white covers on the armchairs, she had pink and green chintz which she could have done without. A flower arrangement sitting in the middle of the coffee table turned out to be from the management. For one split second she had wondered if it was from Johnny.

By the time Polly had unpacked she had persuaded herself that Johnny had booked her a separate room because he had been as unsure about her reaction to him as she had been about his to her. That night she'd probably find herself repacking everything and carting it down to Johnny's room.

She went for a walk amongst the pine trees, past the tennis courts. Little white Go-Karts with EDEN ROC painted on them sped past her. Entry to Eden Roc was included in the price of the room – so it should be at 4,000 francs a night, thought Polly – and she decided to spend the day there by the pool and the terrace built into the rocks overlooking the sea. She cheerfully ordered herself a Negroni, hoping it cost at least £20, and charged it to Johnny's room. Then she settled down to get a tan. Polly was lucky. She had the kind of skin that turned brown within hours of being exposed to the sun.

She returned to her room around 5.30 and called the office. Mrs Flowers reported no problems. Luckily she didn't mention her novel. Polly soaked in a Floris bath and wondered where Johnny would take her for dinner. She dressed to kill in a black silk shift which had strategically placed pleats over the stomach. Scrabbling around in her jewellery box, she found the little black earrings he had given her on their second date, when he had made her get her ears pierced. Would he remember them? Then she swept her hair back into a loose knot in the nape of her neck and held the sides in place with tortoiseshell combs. Her face was already beginning to tan and the whites of her hazel eyes stood out, making them look larger. She applied a light coating of brown eye shadow and ran a narrow line of kohl around her eyelids to make them look smudgy. She finished with two applications of mascara, a light dusting of loose powder on her nose and a touch of Lancôme's Rose Nocturne on her lips, heavily blotted. The end result was the healthy, natural look she knew Johnny had always liked.

Finally she took her Christian Dior Dune atomiser and sprayed herself liberally. She was ready. Now what was she supposed to do? She rang Johnny's room. No reply. Well, it was only 7.30. They might not have even finished filming. She really should have waited until she had heard from him before getting ready but she wanted to be waiting for him, looking her best.

At 8.30 she was still sitting there, coming to the end of her *Vanity Fair* which usually lay around the house for a month before she had time to read it. She rang his room again. No reply. She rang the front desk and asked would they have him call her when he got in and was told he'd already come back, gone up to his room and come down again.

Of course, thought Polly, he's waiting for me downstairs at the bar. She almost ran down the stairs like a girl, imagining him waiting for her in the lobby, leaning on the banisters, looking up at her and saying something like: 'So, Pol, what took you so long?'

He was nowhere to be seen. She couldn't bring herself to go back up to her room and she didn't want to sit alone in the bar so she wandered outside down the avenue to Eden Roc.

I'll go inside and have another Negroni and charge it to his room, she thought, feeling wicked. That'll teach him to be late.

He was sitting at a table on the terrace. He had his back to her and his arm was around the person he was drinking with. No, it was more than a drink. Plates of food were on the table in front of them. Johnny was in the middle of dinner and as Polly drew closer she saw he was dining with Juanita Whyte.

Polly had been about to call out, but his name stuck in her throat. Anger, disappointment and deep, deep hurt came together in a hard lump in her throat and she felt the tears well up in her carefully made-up eyes. The kohl and the mascara began to trickle down her face. As she turned and ran out into the grounds, she heard Johnny's voice in her head as she had heard it so many times before: 'Blubbing again, Pol' and then two outstretched arms stopped her and she let herself collapse against a broad chest in a white T-shirt.

Johnny had seen her, Johnny had come after her. She waited for him to stroke her hair as he always did when he was comforting her, and when he didn't she looked up at . . .

'*Hector!*'

His face was cruel, sardonic and devastatingly handsome.

'That's right. Have we met? I stopped you because you seemed to be distressed but don't I know you from somewhere?'

Yes, only then I didn't have make-up pouring down my face, thought Polly. What a sight I must look. She remembered his soft voice whispering in her ear: 'If I ever kissed you I'd make sure I didn't miss.'

'Yes, it was at the last Conway première.'

'Oh yes,' he said although he clearly still couldn't quite place her.

'I was there with my husband, Johnny, your producer. Johnny de Soto. I'm Polly de Soto. Polly Atwell.' Oh God, why was she gabbling on like this.

'Of course. I heard you were coming out. Now, are you all right? Are you ill?'

'No, I mean, not really. I've just had a bit of a shock. I felt a little strange suddenly.'

'It's the heat. It can affect you that way. Perhaps you should come and sit down in Eden Roc for a second.'

'No!'

Hector smiled. Despite her confusion Polly was aware

that he was amused by her discomfort and that he knew what was causing it.

'Well, can I escort you back to the hotel? You are staying at the hotel, aren't you?' She nodded. 'Are you and Johnny dining there tonight?'

'No. Johnny has a dinner engagement with Juanita Whyte.'

'Ah, yes. Juanita flew out today to see how her little investment was doing.'

'Her little investment?'

'Our film. *Mr Wrong*. She's put quite a lot of Gordy Whyte's money into it, you know. Johnny was pretty smart to latch on to her.'

And if he knew she was coming out why did he ask me at the same time? Polly wondered.

'Listen,' said Hector, releasing her and placing a hand lightly in the small of her back to guide her up the avenue towards the hotel, 'why don't I run you up the road to my villa and my cook can prepare us a little something?'

'Oh, no, I couldn't possibly.' Her response was instinctive, typically English, reserved. The exact opposite of what she really wanted, and he knew it.

'Yes, you could, possibly. Now would you like to go up to your room before we leave? My car's right outside.'

And do something about that mess on your face? Polly slipped up to her room and rushed into the bathroom. It would take at least twenty minutes to re-do her make-up properly. She couldn't keep him waiting that long. She removed her make-up, splashed her tanned face with cold water and left it at that.

He was waiting for her at the bottom of the staircase

just where she had been hoping to find Johnny earlier in the evening.

'You look beautiful without make-up,' he said, taking her hand; 'you don't need it, you know, and your hair is lovely. So healthy, so glossy' – and with one quick movement he had removed the combs from her hair and undone the knot, releasing it to her shoulders. 'That's better. I love hair,' he bent to sniff hers quickly. 'I love the smell of freshly washed hair. Come on, let's go.'

He had rented a Mercedes convertible and sitting beside him as he drove slowly up the boulevard du Cap towards Antibes, Polly wondered if she would ever feel so glamorous again, riding in an open car with a movie star through the sweet pine-scented night air of the Côte d'Azur.

Hector turned off into a side road and stopped in front of a pair of tall black and gold painted iron gates which he opened by remote control, easing the Mercedes through as they slid to one side. He ushered her inside before she had a chance to look around. The front door was opened for them and a tall servant in a turban and floor-length white tunic bowed as they entered.

'Hussein, we'd like a little supper out by the pool. *Tabbouleh*, salad, some of that cold chicken, a bottle of Puligny-Montrachet and some fruit. That all right for you, Polly?' But he barely waited for her reply.

Her first impression was that she was in some kind of Egyptian palace. Cool, high-ceilinged rooms with marble floors and tall archways instead of doors. Straight in front of her was a sheet of plate-glass window and through it she could see a rectangular floodlit pool with palm trees strategically placed at each corner. Hector pressed a button in the wall and the window began to rise, silently moving upwards until they were able to step out into the night.

This isn't real, thought Polly, as she sat at a glass table at the far end of the pool and looked at the pale pink villa lit up like a fairytale palace. Overhead, as if they wanted to bring her gently down to earth, planes silently lowered themselves across the navy sky on their way to land at Nice airport, their tail lights blinking on and off in the night.

'This is quite beautiful,' said Polly, 'who . . .?'

'Arabs. Lebanese. And they threw in Hussein. He's from the Sudan by way of Tunis. He looks after me very well.'

I wonder if Johnny knows about Hussein. I wonder if he's going to create a few more budget problems. Well, thought Polly bitterly, he's got Juanita to solve them for him. She picked up a chicken leg in her fingers and bit off a sizeable chunk of flesh.

'That's right,' murmured Hector, watching her, 'get it out of your system.'

'Get what out of my system?'

'Whatever it was that made you so upset. I don't want to know what it was. I just want to distract you a little, take your mind off it so you can enjoy your holiday.'

He knows, thought Polly, he knows exactly what my problem is. Well, to hell with it.

'Is the film going well? Johnny's told me about the scenes you've been doing with the women and with Julianne. He seems very pleased.'

'Don't feel you have to make conversation,' he said almost tersely, 'just relax. Hussein will bring us some mint tea to help your digestion and then I'll run you back.'

To her surprise she found she was disappointed that he did not require anything of her. It was almost too

285

good to be true. He had a soothing effect. She felt safe with him, temporarily protected from Johnny's unreliable behaviour. And she didn't even have to sing for her supper.

In the car he said: 'Tomorrow I'll take you out in the boat I've hired. We'll go along the coast, have lunch at St Tropez; come back and swim. You'd like that, wouldn't you?'

She nodded, smiling in the darkness. She didn't even need to think about it. He was going to take care of everything.

'I'll pick you up at 10 a.m. Bring sunscreen. You can really burn out there in the wind.' And then he was gone.

She was just falling asleep when her phone rang and Johnny said: 'Pol? How've you been? I rang your room but they said you'd gone out. Sorry I was so late. I got tied up, business meeting, so . . .'

Business meeting! With Juanita! Same old Johnny.

'I was asleep . . .'

'Oh, Pol, I'm sorry. I'll let you sleep. Call you in the morning.'

'Not before 10.30,' she heard herself say. 'I want to sleep in.'

At 10.30 the following morning Hector was holding her hand as she stepped aboard his boat in the marina at Juan les Pins. The boat was a 40-foot cruiser with a cabin under the prow and a seating area behind the steering wheel. Hector steered the boat himself, going about 30 knots all the way to St Tropez. To begin with Polly stood beside him and they shouted to each other over the whap whap whap of the boat hitting the water and the spray flying up on either side. Then Polly stretched out and lay supine, looking up at the pure blue sky above her. She hadn't been to St Tropez since she was a child and she was looking forward to it. When they pulled into the little walled harbour, Hector gave the harbour master 500 francs to give them a place to dock while they lunched.

'Only thing to do,' he explained to Polly. 'Expensive business, running a boat in high season. It's another £300 to fill her up with gas.'

Polly gulped. Was this all going on Johnny's budget? It seemed a lavish expense when all they wound up eating for lunch was a slice of pizza as they wandered around. Hector didn't seem to want to engage her in much conversation and for this Polly was somewhat grateful. She was beginning to unwind after the shock of her intense conversation with Johnny, the brief moment of intimacy, and the subsequent disappointment of finding him with Juanita.

On the trip back Hector continued his strong silent act, his hawk-like face a mask hidden by his dark glasses as he stood behind the wheel. Polly found herself casting surreptitious glances at his tanned thighs below his white shorts and the concentrated patch of black hair in the middle of his chest.

When they were almost back in Juan he swung the boat to the left and dropped anchor.

'Baie des Millionaires,' he told her, 'we're going to swim in Millionaires' Bay.'

Polly laughed. She looked around her and glimpsed the roofs of elegant houses between the pines, saw a bank of wide stone steps leading up to one house, several tunnels up through the rocks, and here and there people could be seen on terraces being served with drinks. Hector unhinged a ladder from the end of the boat.

'Swim to that raft over there,' he pointed to a raft bobbing in the middle of the exclusive bay with the word PRIVATE clearly painted on the side. There was no one else around although other boats were docked in the bay and Polly could see people on deck. 'Climb on to it and wait for me. I'll be with you soon.'

Polly had heard stories about how polluted the Mediterranean was supposed to be but as far as she was concerned the water in Millionaires' Bay was a dream. She felt a sudden rush of undiluted happiness. Apart from the fact that swimming in the sea was so much more refreshing than in a pool, her holiday was developing into a bit of an adventure. Swimming in Millionaires' Bay! What would Mrs Flowers say if she could see her now? Polly giggled and climbed up on to the private millionaire's raft. She slicked back her wet hair and imagined she looked like Ursula Andress coming out of the water in *Dr No*. She looked round and saw Hector swimming towards her. He reached the raft and as he climbed up out of the sea, Polly saw that he was completely naked.

He stretched out beside her on his back and she saw his long prick hanging across his thigh. He'd obviously been sunbathing in the nude since the skin around his crotch was as dark as it was everywhere else.

Polly was wearing a strapless one-piece and it took Hector about twenty seconds to peel it slowly from her. Then he leaned over and fastened his mouth on her left nipple. He sucked gently until it became hard and moved across her to begin work on the other one, easing her legs apart as he did so. Polly's body was warm from the sun and totally relaxed. She could feel his penis stiffening slowly as it lay between her legs. He eased himself totally on top of her and she raised her knees. He lifted his head and looked down at her, putting a finger to her lips to silence her as she opened her mouth to speak to him. She sucked on his finger and he grinned suddenly, lowered his head and plunged his tongue into her mouth. Soon he was biting her, bruising her lips with his. She felt herself go completely wet and he sensed it and manoeuvred his erection to the tip of her vagina. She brought her arms around him and pulled his weight down on her, clasping his naked buttocks and bringing him inside her. He began to fuck her very hard, almost violently, but she responded, bucking her pelvis up to him.

As he came he let out a yell that echoed round the bay and as he lay on top of her they felt the raft rocking furiously beneath them.

'You do know the entire bay was watching us from their terraces,' he whispered in her ear.

'I don't care,' said Polly and she meant it.

They swam back to the boat naked, pulling their swimming things behind them. At one point they came together, treading water, and kissed and pressed against each other. She climbed up the ladder in front of him and he came up behind her, pushed her on to her front and lay on top of her.

'Have you ever been fucked in the arse?' he whispered.

'No.'

'Do you want to be?'

'No.'

'Then I won't go any further.' He covered her with a towel. 'You realise we're a lot further in than the raft.

They really can see us quite clearly now – if they're looking, that is.'

He pulled on his swimming trunks and hauled up the anchor. She stood beside him at the wheel and he put his arm around her, steering with one hand. She laid her head on his shoulder and thought that as the boat slipped into the marina under the setting sun, they must look like a corny commercial or an MTV video, standing there with their arms around each other. But she didn't care. She felt about twenty-two years old.

When they got into his car she knew he was going to take her to his house on the boulevard du Cap rather than back to the hotel. I'm putty in his hands, she thought, but to hell with it. Fuck Johnny!

As they drove up the hill, he started speaking softly to her: 'This morning, while you were still asleep, I got up very early and went to the market in old Antibes. I'm so used to getting up for my call that I wake early anyway. It's Hussein's day off. I walked down to the market. It takes about half an hour, maybe a bit less, and I bought fruit and vegetables and flowers and brought them all back for our supper tonight.'

'We're going to eat flowers?'

'No, of course not, but I've put them all over the house to greet you everywhere you go. Irises. Those huge sunflowers. You'll see. We'll eat a light supper – tomato salad with olives, some shrimps with lemon juice, some asparagus maybe. A little cheese. Nothing too heavy. We want to feel comfortable. We're going to have sex all night.'

The flowers were sensational. Polly couldn't help thinking of Johnny's clumsy efforts at his Mount Street flat. Hector prepared supper and brought it up to the bedroom on a tray. They ate sitting cross-legged on the bed, naked, with the tray between them, feeding each other. He fondled her breasts as he munched on a piece of bread and cheese until Polly couldn't stand it another minute and pushed the tray aside. Was this really the behaviour of a literary lady in her forties? Apparently yes, since she wanted him at regular intervals throughout the night.

He talked only about her: her body, her face, her hands, her legs, what she wanted, how he could please her.

In the morning he slipped away to the set without waking her and she slept until noon. She found a towelling robe in the bathroom and crept barefoot down the marble staircase to find the kitchen. As she was tiptoeing – why, she didn't know – across the hall a shadow moved in the dark passage in front of her and she screamed out loud.

It was Hussein.

'Madame wants breakfast? Tea? Coffee?' He didn't seem remotely surprised to see her.

'Yes please,' said Polly, drawing the towelling robe a little more tightly around her.

He served her croissants and hot rolls and honey and piping hot coffee on a little folding table on the terrace. Propped up against a stem vase containing a single red rose was a square white vellum envelope with her name on it.

His handwriting was large and jagged:

Can't wait to be with you again.
When you're ready, Hussein will call you a taxi to take you back to the hotel. I'm filming and may be back late otherwise I'd suggest you spend the day at my house. I'll call.

H.

P.S. Take a bath and use the oil in the glass flagon. It's rose scented, rose and honeysuckle.

Polly had a tremendous urge to snoop in his drawers, his wardrobe, his desk. How many other women had been to this house before her even though he had only been in it for a few weeks?

Hussein appeared.

'I have drawn your bath, madame.'

How did he know? Had he read the letter? She nodded, yes, she was ready.

Lying in her bath she wondered how old Hector was. Younger than she was, but by how much? Then she felt a pang of guilt and sadness as she thought how thrilled Joan would be with her.

Back at the hotel she asked for her key, feeling rather sheepish, wondering if everybody knew her bed hadn't been slept in, if the *valets d'étage* were, even as she spoke, gossiping about her with the chambermaids in the laundry room.

Two days later Hector still hadn't called her and Polly went into a full-scale panic. Johnny called and left maniacal messages for her downstairs, which she ignored. Let him sweat!

Fools rush in, she told herself. How could I have been such a fool? The sun goes straight to my head and I think I'm as desirable as Cindy Crawford. I must have been out of my skull. A bored actor feels like a quick lay and I walk straight into his arms, literally. I lie on a raft stark naked and assume he never notices the way my breasts flop to the side instead of sticking straight up. He probably cricked his neck sucking my tits.

By the second day she'd remembered something more sinister. He'd hadn't used anything. How many other women had he had over the years? She thought of the ludicrous end to her evening with Edward Holland. Why had she thought about AIDS with poor Edward when it had never entered her head to say anything to Hector – although what could she have done? Told him to swim back to the boat and get his condoms like a good dog?

She ached for him and by the third day she knew it was no good. Only four more days of her holiday left and she had to see him. She rang LSR (Long Suffering Rachel as Johnny called her, who had been promoted to production secretary on the picture) at the production office in the little hotel in Juan where the crew were packed in like sardines. Rachel was sweating it out with her laptop in 97 degrees heat with a phone that was almost permanently on the blink and a groaning fan in the absence of any air conditioning.

'Bet it's not like this in Hollywood,' she moaned to Polly, becoming less long-suffering by the minute. 'I have to use the hotel fax and they don't like it one bit. It's down in the office behind reception and they won't let me in without a fight and they never bother to let me know if I've received one. If it wasn't for the fact that I'm screwing one of the sparks and he's the best fuck I've ever had, I think I'd go mad.'

Polly was a little scandalised by Rachel's explicit revelations. She hadn't remembered her as being such a trollop but then who was she to talk?

'Poor old you,' she sympathised. 'Rachel, I was wondering, do you think it'd be all right if I went and watched some filming? Would they mind if I went on the set?'

'No, I don't expect so.' Rachel's tone implied they probably wouldn't even notice.

'Is there anything interesting coming up in the next day or so?'

'Well, tomorrow morning they're shooting down at the old market in Antibes. It's very pretty. Fruit and veg and people haggling. A real old street market. It's the scene where Julianne goes shopping there.'

'Is . . . is Hector in it?' Polly fought to hide the excitement in her voice.

'Oh, yes, sure, he follows her. It's the scene when we first know he might be thinking of doing something horrible to her, like he's done to all the other women, because he doesn't let her know he's there even though they've slept together a few times. It should be pretty spooky. Always assuming Hector shows up.'

'What do you mean?'

'Your sainted husband – sorry, Polly, but Johnny really is a bit of a wanker sometimes – has gone and taken it into his head that there's a publicity angle for the film in these robberies that have been happening down here. Millionaire Americans wandering around with loads of cash – probably because the Hôtel du Cap doesn't take credit cards – and then wondering why they get hit on the head and robbed. Johnny's on at the unit publicist to get Hector to do interviews about the similarity between *Mr Wrong* bumping off the women in the movie and the pattern of true crimes happening here. Needless to say Hector's not frightfully keen and Johnny's furious and the atmosphere on the set is a bit fraught.'

'Should I leave it, then?' asked Polly anxiously.

'Oh, Lord, no, go ahead. I'll tell Spider to expect you. The call's at eight so as to get the light but the gaffers and the grips'll be there before then so go whenever you like. They'll be there all morning.'

Polly thought it would look too obvious to ask what time Hector would be there. That night she had room service for the third night running despite a note from Johnny pushed under door inviting her to dinner. What was the point? She felt sorry for herself. This was no way to be spending a holiday, sitting in a hotel room by the phone waiting for Mr Wrong to call.

At nine the next morning she took a cab to Antibes. She soon found the crew. A group of short fat gossiping Frenchwomen, dressed in black and with toothless smiles, gave the game away. Spider was trying to get them to move back out of the way and at the same time collaring stray kids who were trying to fiddle with the camera. The grips had laid down camera tracking the length of one of the aisles of the market and the director of photography was riding the camera up and down, rehearsing. The focus puller was busy colouring in a calendar of squares on a chart taped to the side of the camera. To try and make herself part of the proceedings, Polly introduced herself to Spider and asked him what the chart meant. To her surprise Spider, a strapping lad of twenty-five wearing a sleeveless T-shirt announcing he was BORN TO BOOGIE and whose arm muscles indicated he worked out regularly, blushed.

'It doesn't include you, Mrs de Soto,' he said. 'Honest!'

'What doesn't?' Polly was mystified and somewhat thrown by the Mrs de Soto. She hadn't been called that in quite some time.

'The camera chart. It's a game they play every film they work together.'

'Who do?'

'Bill, the focus puller and Ken the clapper-loader. The colours of the chart show the colour of the script girl's knickers on that particular day. They get to see right up her skirt when they do low-angle shots and lie on the ground.'

'Ah, I see.' Polly tried hard to enter into the spirit of

things. 'And where it's blank it means she was wearing white knickers?'

' 'Fraid not. She doesn't go in for white knickers, this one. It means she wasn't wearing any!' Great big Spider blushed again.

'*Araignée! Viens là, s'il vous plaît.*'

'That's Henri, the director. He will have his little joke. *Araignée* means spider. I wouldn't mind only it's a female word in French. Better go. The first set-up's ready and I should go and call the actors. Tell you what, Mrs de Soto, if you wouldn't mind, perhaps you'd like to be in this shot? Wander up and down the market, pretend to buy a few things, you know?'

'Oh,' said Polly, pleased, 'like a native?'

'Oh, no, you'd be an English tourist. Plenty of them. Quite authentic.'

'Thanks,' muttered Polly and wandered off among the stalls.

She saw a caravan parked at the far end and beside it a TV camera. Maybe Hector was doing an interview after all. But as she grew closer she heard Johnny's voice:

'Personally, eh *franchement*, I have to say the crimes may be copycat crimes based on our movie. The filming's stirring up a lot of excitement down here and . . .'

'There's been no indication that the criminals are playboys, Mr de Soto, unless, of course, you have inside information?'

'Me? No. Oh, no. I'm just saying that it sounds like *Mr Wrong*. Maybe they heard about our movie and it gave them the idea.'

Polly about-turned. Sometimes Johnny did sound just

like Rachel had described him: a wanker. A girl clutching a clipboard collided with her.

'Whoops! Really sorry. Overslept. This bloody heat. Henri's going to be mad as hell,' the script girl said. Polly couldn't help wondering if she'd had time to put her knickers on.

'Everybody very quiet now please!' yelled Spider. 'And that goes for *vous* too,' he added to the chattering housewives, who giggled and waved at him.

'Scene 34, take 1,' called the clapper-loader and then Polly saw him, moving silently out of the shadow of an alleyway. It was exciting, almost as if she were in the movie herself, which in fact she was. She saw Spider mouthing frantically at her: don't look at Hector, look at the stalls, look at the fruit and veg, pretend to be buying something.

But Hector was walking straight towards her, looking her in the eye, happy to see her, making kissing movements with his lips. Surely they didn't want all this on film. Then she realised he had his back to the camera and they were tracking him as he moved through the crowded market. In the next set-up Julianne would look up from buying some fruit, turn to face the camera and Hector would duck out of sight. In the meantime it was just him but the audience would know exactly who he was after – and it wasn't her, Polly. She'd better get out of shot. Yet if she turned and ran it would look as if she was running away from Hector. All she could do was to keep moving forward until she crossed paths with him, and as she did so he slipped a piece of paper into her hand.

Was it on film? Polly looked about her frantically to see if anyone had noticed and the director yelled '*Cut!*'

'Who's that bloody woman who's just ruined the last

take? There's nothing in the script about anyone wobbling their head all over the place like they're in a Punch and Judy show when Hector goes by.' The continuity girl was almost spitting in irritation.

'Shhh. That's the producer's wife.'

'Ex-wife. He dumped her.'

'Who for?'

'Some say Persil.'

'Who's Persil?'

'Where have you been? It's what we call Lady Whyte. Persil washes whiter. Juanita-than-Whyte. Geddit?'

'Get away. She's a tart. Even dear old Johnny wouldn't be that stupid. This one looks quite a sweet old bat.'

Don't they realise I can hear them? Polly was flabbergasted. It wasn't enough that she was mortified for having ruined a shot, now she had to listen to this. She unwrapped Hector's note.

'Dinner? Tonight? Nine o'clock? Eden Roc? Nod if you can make it.'

She might be a sweet old bat in the eyes of the crew but it didn't stop an international movie star inviting her to dinner. She looked up at Hector who was walking back towards her for the next take and nodded like mad.

'Blimey. See what you mean. Mrs de Soto can't keep her head still. I'd better get her out of here,' she heard Spider say before she turned and ran.

As she was fighting her way through the crowd of onlookers blocking the aisles in the market she ran straight into Johnny.

'There you are, Pol. I've been leaving messages for you day and night. Where the hell have you been?'

'Enjoying my holiday. Isn't that what you expected me to do?' Polly, caught off guard, was unnecessarily curt.

'Look, what the fuck have I done? I've got a film to produce here. I can't be looking after you every second of the day. Be reasonable, Pol. You knew I'd be tied up. There's no need to get into a snit. Anyway, here's what I'll do. I'll take you out to dinner tonight. Little place up the coast. Away from these cretins on the film, driving me nuts, they are. Meet you in the lobby at 8.30? We'll have a drink down at Eden Roc, bugger the cost, and then push off. Try and be in a better mood by then. See you.'

'*Johnny!*' She yelled but he was off, waving goodbye to her without looking back. Now what was she going to do? Spin a coin?

Hector solved the problem for her by having Hussein deliver what looked like an entire rose bush with a note attached saying: 'Don't forget. Nine o'clock. Hector.'

Polly felt sufficiently confident to wear what Johnny had always called her summertime *pièce de résistance*. It was dead simple, had cost, according to Johnny who had bought it for her in a rare display of fashion sense, an arm and a leg and a hip, and it exposed most of these into the bargain. Polly had been thirty-five when he had bought it. Could she still wear a strapless bit of exorbitant nothing and get away with it? Where was it written that she couldn't? Polly asked herself and banished the two words that kept popping up in her mind like a jack-in-the-box: skin tone. She was tanned, she was smooth and she had freckles not liver spots. It was her body so she knew what was what about it. All those articles in beauty magazines were wrong.

Of course Johnny was waiting for her in the lobby.

'My God, the *pièce de résistance*. I thought you'd put it away for good. They didn't have a table any later than nine so we'd better move off sharpish. No time for a drink here first. Sorry.'

But Polly was on her way out the door and down the wide avenue to Eden Roc.

'Oh, all right, Pol. Wait for me. But we'll have to be quick.'

Hector was early. He was already at the bar and came towards her, holding his arms wide ready to embrace her.

'You look truly delicious.' His arms were around her, 'Oh, hello Johnny. Join us for a drink?'

'Other way round, but yes, why not. We can't be long though. You going anywhere interesting tonight, Hector?'

'Dinner here with the beautiful Polly. About as interesting as you can get.'

Johnny looked at her and suddenly Polly couldn't bear the expression of disappointed misery on his face. She wanted to be rid of him as soon as possible.

'I'm sorry, Johnny. I tried to call out to you in the market but you just wouldn't listen. It's your own fault. You never listen.' She was getting too personal in front of Hector.

'No drink. Thanks. Changed my mind. Gotta be somewhere.' Johnny was babbling, still staring at her.

'Hector, could we go straight in to dinner? I'm starving.'

'Nothing easier. Bye, Johnny. See you tomorrow.'

Polly didn't look at him again, didn't look at anybody until the *maître d'* had seated them at a window table overlooking the sea. She watched a raft with the words Eden Roc – Cap d'Antibes bobbing up and down, looking very lonely now it had been deserted by the sunbathers. Poor Johnny. He would be very lonely too with nothing to do all evening but it served him right. Then she glanced at Hector quickly.

'I'm sorry. He thought we were having dinner. I never said I would.'

Hector ordered her a champagne cocktail.

'You two still married?'

She nodded.

'None of my business, of course, but why haven't you divorced?'

'I don't know,' said Polly, 'I simply don't know.'

'Do you still love him?'

If I did why would I be here with you? 'Of course not.'

'Otherwise what would you be doing with me?' It was uncanny how he could read her mind. Or maybe it wasn't. 'Maybe you're trying to make him jealous. Revive his interest a little? It wouldn't be the first time I've been used this way.'

'I am not using you!'

'Calm down, Polly.'

'Sorry. What did you mean, it wouldn't be the first time?'

'I look good on a girl's arm. They feel special. I go along with it. Sometimes they don't even realise I care about them. As soon as the boyfriend or the husband starts taking an interest again, back they go.'

'But I'm not like that. I really care ...'

'Do you, Polly? Bless you. Was it a good marriage?'

'Yes.'

'In what way?'

'He was my friend. He was so different from the type

302

of man I'd envisaged winding up with, I couldn't believe it. Being with him made me feel interesting.'

'You are interesting.'

'Now, maybe, but I grew up thinking I was an ordinary English girl, a pudding from the country, nothing exotic about me that would attract someone like Johnny. And he made me laugh. Best of all, I made him laugh. I never knew I could make someone laugh before I met Johnny.'

'So what went wrong?'

'I don't know. Or maybe I do. In many ways Johnny was a little boy. Still is, probably. His enthusiasm was one of the things I loved most about him, but when it came to his work his enthusiasm became obsessive.'

'Criminal.'

'Not really. It's very common. I was very tied up in my own work and I know I wanted him to take an interest in that too. It just didn't seem to work both ways. Hector, this is ridiculous. I'm talking about myself too much. What about you? Have you been married?'

It was as if Hector hadn't heard her.

'What about children?' he asked her.

'It wasn't really discussed. Johnny didn't actually say he didn't want any but we never got around to planning one. So I stayed on the pill. Besides, he had Luana.'

'Have you ever met her mother?'

'Never. Something terrible happened there and it's a big secret. Nobody knows. Johnny won't talk about it.'

Hector leaned forward in his seat and took her hand. 'You poor girl. You mean nobody's told you?'

Polly shook her head, stunned.

'Would you like me to?'

'Do you know?'

'As a matter of fact I do. But it's a depressing story. I

don't want to put you off your food. I'll tell you over coffee. Come on, eat up.'

Polly gobbled shamelessly, not because she was particularly hungry but because she couldn't wait to get to the coffee stage and hear about Edith.

'Well?' she said when they had been served with their second cup of coffee.

'Well what? Would you like an Armagnac or something? Sorry, I should have asked before.'

'No. Oh, yes, all right. Whatever. Tell me about Edith, Hector. I can't bear to wait a minute longer.'

'Oh her. Suicidal nutcase. Severe case of post-natal depression after Luana was born. She took an overdose a few years later and Luana came home from school and found her unconscious. Poor old Johnny never realised what he'd let himself in for. Apparently she's a real looker. She and Johnny got together when she was just a kid and he thought he was in heaven, wanted to start a family, couldn't understand it when she wouldn't marry him, desperate for her. Then it turns out she's a triple-A depressive, anything could trigger off another attack. It's like living with a time bomb. Are you going to come home from a hard day's work and find your woman with her head in the oven? Then she hit him with the ultimate deadly weapon.'

'What?' Polly was devastated.

'She left him.'

'I know.'

'Well, think about it. She walks out saying I can never be good enough for you, I don't want to be a millstone round your neck, I'll go and be miserable on my own and you can be riddled with guilt about me for the rest of your life. Charming! Then you come along and make it even worse.'

'What on earth do you mean?'

'Well, of course she was sitting there in Battersea or wherever it was praying he'd call and beg her to come back to him but what does he do? He meets you and marries you. Now you've split up with him she's probably waiting for him to summon her. But what I can't understand is why Johnny's never told you. Too guilt-ridden, I expect.'

'Me too. It's extraordinary.' Polly was seething. It was so typical of Johnny to keep something as important as this a secret. Typical! 'How did you hear about it?' she asked Hector.

'Oh, Lord, I can't remember. It was just something everyone knew.'

She was about to ask for more details when the bill came. Hector produced his American Express gold card. The waiter looked embarrassed.

'I am sorry, monsieur. Eden Roc does not accept credit cards. House rule. If monsieur has cash or maybe . . .'

Hector exploded. 'This bill is for nearly £200. This is the Riviera. A guest from this hotel was robbed the other day. You've got masked gunmen holding up cars and ripping off jewels. What kind of idiot is going to go around with wads of cash in his wallet?'

'Monsieur.' The waiter didn't say sorry, nor did he offer any kind of quintessential Gallic shrug. He just waited for his money.

'I'll tell you what. You can put it on Mr de Soto's bill. He's staying here at the Hôtel du Cap.'

'Without Mr de Soto's permission, monsieur . . .'

'I'm staying here at the hotel,' said Polly hurriedly. She hated scenes in restaurants. 'If you could perhaps accept my I.O.U. until tomorrow I'll come down here with some cash. Let me sign the bill. I'm Mrs de Soto.'

The waiter disappeared to confer with his superior and came back nodding. He managed not to look in Hector's direction as Polly signed the bill.

Johnny was still in the bar as they left the restaurant. He was very drunk. He lurched up to Polly.

'He let you pay for dinner, didn't he? He's been doing that approximately once a week since he arrived. Conveniently forgets they don't take credit cards. That poor old trout who was robbed a couple of weeks ago had dinner here with Hector and had to pay up. I think he's taking his role a bit too seriously.'

Polly ignored him. All she could think about was the fact that he hadn't told her about Edith.

'Look Pol, he's waiting. Better go running after him. Don't expect the earth to move, though. If you ask me he bats for both sides and never makes a run for either of them.'

'Well, I didn't ask you so shut up.'

She about-turned and ran straight into Hector.

'Like to come for a midnight swim? I heard what Johnny said. What did I tell you about my taking a woman out getting her man all jealous. Seems to have worked with your ex.'

She expected him to take her back to his villa but to her surprise he drove to the marina and led her aboard his boat. Millionaires' Bay was even more beautiful at night with the candlelight flickering through the pines as people dined on their terraces.

He stripped off all his clothes and dived in naked.

'See you on the raft.'

It was dark in the middle of the bay. If the people on the terraces could see her it would only be a silhouette.

306

They would not be able to make out she was naked. Still, Polly undressed nervously.

The water was much colder than it had been in the afternoon they were last here. Polly swam slowly, tentatively. And suddenly Hector dived in again and sliced through the murky water towards her.

'Coming to get you . . .'

She screamed, only half in jest.

He reached her and gripped her hard, pulling her with him back to the raft. Gone was the tender lover and in his place a mean, almost brutal force was carrying her through the darkness, lifting her out of the water and throwing her down on the raft.

'Hector, please, you're hurting me . . .'

He took no notice. He fell on top of her and pinioned her to the deck, forcing her legs apart so she could feel his penis hardening against her pelvic bone. His hands came up and circled her neck.

Squeezed.

Hector O'Neill was dangerous. Polly thought she had never felt so vibrant. All the way home on the plane she virtually shook with excitement at the thought of their last night together. In the morning he had just upped and left. No undying declaration of love. No promises to call. Nothing. He could be the attentive, caring listener, leaving red roses on her breakfast tray. Or he could make savage, passionate love to her and walk out on her the next morning without a word, leaving the bruises on her neck and thighs as a souvenir. But whatever he was he had brought her back to life, and made her want more of him.

There was a message from Johnny on the answering machine as she walked into the house.

'Pol. It's me. Thanks to you I've got a bloody awful hangover. I waited for you at the hotel last night. Fuck knows where you went. I must have run up the national debt at the bar. You might at least have had the decency to come and thank me for your holiday before you left. No doubt you'll inform me as to why you avoided me like the plague for most of it when it suits you. If you really want to know I'm calling to check whether you've arrived home safely. Don't know why I bother.' There was a pause. He cleared his throat. 'But I do.'

She waited to see if there was a message from Hector but there wasn't.

Upstairs she unpacked and soaked for half an hour in the tub, reliving her morning bath on the boulevard du Cap. Back in the bedroom she groped underneath the bed for her slippers and found Mrs Flowers' manuscript instead. It was Sunday night. Mrs Flowers would be in the next morning expecting her to have read at least part of it in France. There was nothing else for Polly to do but begin it that night.

She finished it at 2.30 in the morning in a towering rage. Not with Mrs Flowers, not with herself, but with Grania Henderson.

Grania Henderson had lied to her. Mrs Flowers' book was not a saga, nor was it 'simply awful'. In fact it was very much the reverse. Polly lay and wondered why she had not seen through Grania Henderson before. Grania had made a big thing about being Polly's only Mills & Boon writer, saying she felt Polly was ashamed of her. Yet it had always been understood that Grania would earn her living from writing Mills & Boons while she worked away at her blockbuster, her massive multi-generational saga that would make her a fortune. Suddenly Polly saw what had happened. Mrs Flowers, herself a Mills & Boon writer, had come along and pipped Grania at the post. Worse, she had not written a blockbusting saga for, as Grania had probably realised too late, this kind of book was no longer fashionable. The core market would always be there for the regional sagas, the downmarket 'clogs and shawls' romances as they were known in the trade, but the elephantine epics covering family dynasties over a hundred years were rarely seen at the top of the bestseller list any more unless there was a literary quality to the writing.

Mrs Flowers had written something incredibly commercial in that it was a page turner about obsessive love, murder and betrayal which could be summed up in one line: *Rebecca* from the man's point of view. The nameless narrator of the book was a young man, a quiet unassuming writer, who marries a beautiful socially prominent television personality whose first husband, Christopher, was a bestselling novelist and Rhett Butler lookalike. The first marriage was a tempestuous one of Taylor/Burton proportions, rarely out of the tabloids. All around the narrator, as he tries to write his own delicate first novel, are Christopher's books and evidence of their success. As executor of Christopher's estate, the wife is constantly embroiled in meetings with film and television companies wanting to dramatise the books or make sycophantic documentaries about their author. She does not take her new husband's work seriously, yet after the turmoil of her first marriage she craves the narrator's shy, adoring puppy-love. At the same time she expects him to hold his own in her hard sophisticated media world, to be scintillating and glamorous and entertain every night. And always hovering in the background, the constant voyeur, is Christopher's gay literary agent who was clearly in love with him and resents the narrator as a usurper to the throne. When the narrator discovers that Christopher was murdered, he knows his own days must be numbered.

Grania Henderson was obviously downright jealous

of Mrs Flowers and had blatantly undermined the older woman's confidence by advising her not to show her manuscript to Polly. She had lied to Polly in order to sabotage Mrs Flowers' chances of success. While Grania prattled away at her stupid dinner parties Mrs Flowers had been working an eight-hour day, often longer, for Polly and then going home and allowing her imagination free rein. Mrs Flowers was a real writer. Grania Henderson was an unimaginative hack.

Mrs Flowers cried when Polly asked her if she would do Polly the honour of letting her be her agent.

'And it will be an honour, Mrs Flowers. *Christopher* will be the most exciting book I've had to sell since *Mr Wrong*.'

Polly now saw Mrs Flowers in a completely different light. Gone was the old frump and in her place was a talent to be admired and a potential moneyspinner to boot. The blue-rinsed hair and the sensible shoes were still there but Polly decided she would let whichever publisher was lucky enough to secure the book decide whether or not they wanted to revamp Mrs Flowers' image.

She realised she had barely given Hector a moment's thought until she glanced at the phone – which she had switched off the night before – and saw there had been four calls already that morning.

They weren't from Hector. They were all from Joan, the first one beginning 'You said you'd be back today so I had to call and . . ' and the last one ending in tears. What on earth was wrong with Joan?

'Mrs Flowers, could you call Mrs Brock in about an hour and ask her to meet me for lunch at Clarke's. If she wants to go somewhere else say I'm out and you

can't reach me so she'll have to go there. I mean, that is
. . . if you're still prepared to go on being my . . . ?'

'We haven't sold my book yet, Mrs de Soto. One step
at a time.'

As soon as Polly entered Clarke's she remembered it
was a restaurant Joan absolutely hated. At lunch there
was a set menu. No choice and Joan didn't like that at
all. In addition, because of booking rather late, Polly's
table was downstairs tucked away in a corner.

'Why do you always manage to get a table in
Siberia?' grumbled Joan. 'If I move my chair a fraction
of an inch I'll have one leg in the kitchen.'

'I don't think so, Joan. The kitchen's open plan in full
view at the bottom of the stairs over there.'

Polly waited for Joan to tell her she looked great –
tanned, glowing from sex with Hector. Surely Joan
would be able to tell right away what had happened.
But Joan just glared straight ahead. She didn't get up to
kiss Polly hello, she didn't even ask the usual 'Any sex,
any cheques' question to which Polly had her answer all
ready. Polly was exasperated. Why did Joan have to be
so negative? She was always complaining about something, always had a grouse to be aired, some new hate
against someone.

Polly decided to ignore Joan's mood and launch
straight in.

'Let's have some champagne. I have something to
celebrate.'

'Bit chi-chi,' sniffed Joan.

'Who cares? I've met a man. I've begun an affair at
long last. I couldn't wait to tell you.'

'Where on earth did you meet him? You've only just
come back from France. Did you meet him on the plane
or what?'

'Joan, you and I didn't talk to each other for weeks before I left. You never returned my phone calls. I could have met him before I went to France for all you know but as it happens, I met him in France.'

'He was working on the film?'

'He certainly was.'

'Polly, you didn't go and screw one of the technicians? The sun went straight to your head and you jumped into bed with the third assistant director who has now gone back to his little wifey in East Sheen?'

Polly laughed. 'Nothing like that. I'm the cat that got the cream. Can't you tell? I was seduced by none other than Hector O'Neill.'

Joan didn't say a word. Polly was a little thrown. She had expected to hear a loud whoop and to be pestered for details.

'Well, don't you want to hear all about it?'

Joan still didn't answer.

'Oh, for God's sake, Joan. You've been on at me to get myself a man, have some sex, and now I have and I've done it in style. I bumped into him outside Eden Roc and he whisked me off to this villa he was renting on the boulevard du Cap and it just sort of took off from there.' Polly was aware that she hadn't mentioned her disappointment at finding Johnny with Juanita but she didn't want to give Joan the impression that Hector had taken her up because he felt sorry for her. That simply hadn't been the case.

Had it?

'And he took me out in his boat, all the way to St Tropez for lunch and I watched the filming, in fact I was actually in one scene with him. You'll see it when the film comes out. I've never had such a wonderful time. You were absolutely right about the sex. I should have done something about that ages ago. Did me the power of good. He's a wonderful lover. Joan, what's the matter?'

Joan had stood up.

'I've just looked at this ridiculous set menu, Polly. There's not a thing on it I feel like eating.'

'Well, we'll go somewhere else. Across the road to Kensington Place. You love it there. It's so vast, they're bound to have a table.'

'Polly, would you mind awfully if we did this another day? I just don't feel like it. Mrs Flowers didn't give me a chance to say so on the phone. Just told me you'd booked a table here and rang off. Bit inconsiderate if you don't mind my saying so.'

'Look, Joan, you were the one who left messages on my answering machine suggesting lunch . . .'

'It wasn't your idea. Is that what you're trying to say? Well, if it's such a chore . . .'

'For God's sake, don't be so bloody defensive. What on earth's the matter with you? Why were you crying when you left a message? Joan!'

But Joan had fled.

Polly felt cheated. She had been looking forward to holding her own for once in a conversation with Joan about men. She simply could not understand why Joan just wasn't interested. Something was up.

Walking slowly back home, Polly remembered Zoë Nichols. There was someone who could be excited to hear about her holiday. But Zoë's answering machine informed callers that Zoë was away in New York researching a book – Aroma Ross's novel, no doubt – and wouldn't be back until the following week. Polly left a message and wondered when Hector would be back in town. She realised she didn't even know. Should she call him in France – or wait for him to call her? Of course he would be filming all day and probably so exhausted every night he fell asleep without so much as eating whatever Hussein had prepared for him. So he almost certainly wouldn't have time to call her, she told herself, by way of prior consolation in case she didn't hear from him. Why had Joan gone off in such a grump? She needed Joan to remind her that men were bastards, no understanding of how women needed things like phone calls and constant communication. For despite her caustic, bitchy surface Joan was normally a good listener and she knew when to be comforting. Polly chastised herself for having let her relationship with her other close women friends slide once the agency had begun to demand more and more of her time. There was no one she could call and gossip with about Hector, no one she could trust anyway.

In the end she called Luana out of sheer loneliness.

'Polly, you're back? How's Dad?'

Oh, God, now Luana would want to go on about Johnny.

'Driving everyone crazy. You know your father. Come to supper. I'll tell you all about it.'

'When?'

'Tomorrow night? I'd say come right over but there's absolutely nothing in the house.'

'Actually, Polly, how would you like to come here?'

'Where?'

'Here. My flat. I'll cook you something.'

'Christ, that'll be a first.'

'What do you mean?'

'Well, half the time you don't even bother to show up when I ask you over here. Have you any idea how many perfectly good meals I've thrown away because you've forgotten all about me?'

'Polly, what's the matter?'

'Nothing. Why should there be? What do you mean?'

'I've never heard you sound like this.'

'Like what?'

'Sorry for yourself. Listen, you come over here and I'll cook you a delicious meal and cheer you up about whatever it is.'

Shall I tell her, wondered Polly. What were the rules about discussing your love life with your stepdaughter?

'The thing is,' Luana giggled, 'I've got a surprise for you. I want to tell you my secret. I can't bear to keep it to myself any longer.'

Join the club, thought Polly. Aloud she said:

'Take no notice of me. Too much boring work, such an anti-climax after all that sun, sea and se — sleep in the South of France. So what have you got to tell me? Going to spill the beans about that boyfriend of yours?'

'How did you know I had a boyfriend?'

'Oh, your father and I aren't exactly blind. You dropped hints all over the place. We just didn't know who it was. You were being really cagey.'

'Well, by the end of tomorrow night you will, only I'd rather you didn't tell Dad. By the way, did you and he . . . ?'

'See you tomorrow, Luana. I'll be there about eight.'

'Could you make it 7.30? The film starts at eight.'

'We're going to the movies?'

'No, there's something on the box I want to see.'

Charming, thought Polly. Invites me to supper then spends the whole night watching television.

The minute she stepped through the door of Luana's

poky little flat in Shepherd's Bush, Polly regretted having come. There was a smell of fish hanging in the air. A rickety card table had been placed in front of the television and two places laid with chipped, mismatched china. Luana opened a bottle of rather dubious-looking plonk and Polly kicked herself for not having brought some decent wine. Yet in spite of herself she was intrigued by the identity of Luana's boyfriend, especially if it was someone Johnny shouldn't know about.

'You look sensational, Polly. I've never seen you looking so good. So brown! You must have been really attractive when you were younger.'

Polly had to laugh. Luana meant well. She had no idea of the implications of what she thought was a compliment.

'And your hair's grown too,' Luana went on. 'It really suits you longer. Makes you look younger.'

'Your father always liked it short. He was kinky about my ears, wanted to be able to see them.'

'Really?' Luana looked mildly horrified yet fascinated at the same time. 'Dad kinky? What else was he kinky about? Is he still kinky?'

'I wouldn't know,' said Polly. 'Make mine a spritzer, will you?'

It was just as Luana was struggling to lift a soggy-looking fish pie out of the oven that Polly remembered what Hector had told her about Edith.

'Why didn't you tell me your mother was a depressive?'

Luana dropped the pie. The dish cracked instantly and the runny cheesy sauce spread all over Luana's rather dirty kitchen tiles and she burst into tears.

'Why did you have to bring her into this? Who told you, anyway?'

'I understood everyone knew. I was the only one who wasn't allowed to be let in on the secret. Here, give me a cloth. I'll help you wipe this up then I'll go out and get us some hamburgers to eat in front of the box. It'll be like old times when you used to come and visit us from Cornwall. We can have them with that nice salad you've made.'

The lettuce leaves were tired and wilting and the avocado had turned grey but Luana looked pathetically grateful and flung herself into Polly's arms.

When Polly returned, Luana was curled up in one corner of the sofa, knees tucked up under her chin, chewing her knuckles – an old childhood habit. The remains of the fish pie was still splattered all over the floor and Polly cleaned it up as best she could. Luana didn't move.

'Darling Polly, you are an angel but do get a move on. The film's really good and you'll miss him. Did you get the burgers?'

No 'Thanks, Polly' or 'Leave that, I'll do it later.' Like father, like daughter.

'Here's your burger. Who will I miss? Is your boyfriend in the film?'

Luana nodded happily, her old self again.

So what Johnny suspected was true, thought Polly. Luana was sleeping with the actors.

'It's one of his old films,' Luana told her, 'I couldn't believe it when I saw it in the *Radio Times*. Look, it's beginning. Isn't he just divine? Who would have thought he would take the slightest bit of interest in me? So, how was he in France, Polly? Did you see him at all? Did he . . . did he mention me . . . did he ask about me at all?'

Polly sat, rigid, tense, forcing herself not to react. It

was an old Conway film and she found herself staring at a younger Hector as he moved through the opening credits. He looked stunningly handsome. If she watched another second of this Polly knew she would begin to cry.

'Hector O'Neill.'

'Doesn't he look a scream? Much better now I think.'

'You met him during the casting of *Mr Wrong*?'

'Yeah. Then he asked me out. He was so understanding about Mum.'

'You told him about Edith?'

Luana nodded.

'And yet you never told me.'

'You know that Dad told me not to.'

'But he said it was all right to tell Hector?'

'He doesn't know about me and Hector. You won't tell him, Polly. Promise me you won't tell him. He wouldn't get it. You know what he's like. He'd say Hector was too old for me. He'd say he was wrong for me.'

'And he'd be right?'

'What? Oh no, Polly, you can't say that. I thought you'd understand. You've always understood. I've always thought we were so close. Polly, what are you doing? Don't turn it off. I want to watch him. I think I'm in love with him.'

Polly hated what she was about to do but she couldn't stop herself.

'Luana, there's something I have to tell you. You won't like it but you're going to have to listen. Better you find out now than when it's too late and you've been hurt.'

Luana had buried her head under a cushion.

'I'm not a kid any more, Polly. I can be with whoever I like.'

'Of course you can. And you can still see Hector after you hear what I'm going to say – if you want to. You know you said earlier about how you were frightened that he might not want you any more, about how he might have met someone else out there. By that I realise you mean France. On the film. Well, Luana, that's exactly what happened. I was there. I saw him. He was with someone. He had this villa and he took her back there at night. She . . . she slept there . . . with him.'

'*It's not true!* Was it someone on the film?'

'No.'

'Then how do you know? I don't believe it.'

'I just know. I saw it. You can believe what you want but someone like that . . . he will always have a woman . . . somewhere.'

As she spoke Polly realised she was explaining Hector to herself as much as to Luana.

'But he's sent me postcards . . . look – '

Luana leapt up and scrabbled in a drawer, hurling a pile of postcards at Polly.

'Luana, maybe he will call when he gets back and you can go on seeing him but he doesn't love you and you're not the only person in his life. Just so long as you understand that.'

'You're jealous. That's what it is. Dad's dumped you and you'd like someone like Hector O'Neill yourself, wouldn't you, Polly? But you're too old. He wants someone young and firm like me. You can play the kind old stepmother looking out for me all you want but I won't believe a word of it because you know what, it's sour grapes. Jesus, Polly, you're getting on. You've got to give it a rest. OK, we had some good times when I was a kid but I'm a woman now. The last person I need to give me advice about my sex life is dear old Polly Pushover. Did you know we used to call you that? Hey, Polly, where are you going? Let's watch the end of the movie. So Hector has other women. Big deal. He's just like all the rest. I'll learn to live with it.'

But I won't, cried Polly, all the way down the stairs to the street.

If things don't change, a wag once told Polly, they'll stay as they are. This was meant to be reassuring but it didn't take into account the fact that things often changed for the worse. What Polly could never have foreseen was that they could get worse in a sauna.

She found it was the only place where she could lose herself in her agony and relax at the same time. She could not remember a time when she had felt so utterly humiliated. It wasn't that she cared what other people thought about her making a fool of herself over Hector. It wasn't as if other people even knew, unless Hussein was running round the flower market in old Antibes spreading the word that there was a situation vacant for a new sucker on the boulevard du Cap. But she, Polly, knew. She had betrayed Luana, she had betrayed Johnny even though neither of them knew it, but worst of all she had betrayed herself. She might get enraged by Joan's refusal to take the success of her literary agency seriously but what was the point of that success when she was making such a disaster of her emotional life. How could she be shrewd and clear thinking in her professional life and so completely gullible in her private one?

Why had she let her imagination race ahead of reality? Why had she started thinking of all the nights she was going to spend with Hector, all the places they would go, all the people they would meet – together? Why had she rushed blindly into the non-existent role (for her at any rate) of celebrity's girlfriend? Were all women like this? Receive a crumb and imagine they could be president of the bakery chain the next day?

One thought kept her going. Three times a week she made it to the gym at lunchtime and rewarded her vigorous efforts on the treadmill and the stairmaster with half an hour in the sauna. As she lay soaking up the heat, she found herself appealing silently to Johnny: take me back, ignore what I did, take me back. Not once did she remind herself that in fact it was Johnny who had left and she who had the option of taking him back. She would call him and beg for his forgiveness. It was all that mattered. It had become like a mantra: take me back, Johnny, take me back.

The door opened and a woman stood there, letting in the cold air, waiting for someone to follow her. Polly hated people who did that. It was so inconsiderate. They were invariably strangers with a guest pass to the club, women who didn't know the ropes. She peeked at the naked woman. She was almost skeletal with an angular body, olive skin, tiny pointed breasts like Joan's and an utterly beautiful gaunt face with huge expressive brown eyes. The body was in perfect condition, rock hard without an ounce of flab. Only the neck gave her away, and her mottled hands. The woman was probably around the same age as Polly. She was impatient, nervy. Polly could sense it. She had long dark hair and she flicked it over her shoulder constantly with an uncomfortable jerk of the neck. The kind of person who would remain wired no matter how long they tried to chill out in the sauna.

The woman was joined by her friend, a different animal altogether. Slow moving, placid, pink and white skin already blotched red by the heat, heavy thighs, pendulous breasts, thick ankles, flat feet below a tiny head, a pretty face with a turned-up nose and a mop of short platinum curly hair. The dark woman almost catapulted herself on to the top shelf and her plump friend clambered up after her. Polly was on the bottom shelf so they had to climb over her. They barely glanced at her and once they were above her she could no longer see them. But she could hear them.

They talked in that low tone just above a whisper which people imagine cannot be heard by anyone else in the room but which remains infuriatingly audible, so that Polly found herself straining to listen and gave up all attempts to relax. From what Polly could gather the two women had not seen each other in quite a while. Dark and Nervy was the out-of-town guest invited by Plump and Blondie. They spent several minutes trying to pinpoint how many years it had been since they had last seen each other – as if it mattered, thought Polly irritably – and then Plump and Blondie suddenly asked:

'So tell me, how is your depression? It's a good sign that you've decided to brave living in London again.'

'I'm never going to feel completely better,' Dark and Nervy spoke very quickly in rather a smoky voice, 'but I'm certainly on the mend. I feel so much more positive. The truth is. I had this little fling down in Cornwall last year. Just some guy who picked-me up in the village, offered to carry my shopping, walked me home. He was staying at the pub, doing research on local churches or something. He told me I was beautiful – like a gypsy, he said. Turned out we'd done all the same things in the Sixties and Seventies. One thing led to another. It gave me back my confidence.'

Like me, thought Polly, with Hector. The bastard.

'The reason I was excited was because I was able to take it for what it was, just a bit of fun.'

Not like me, thought Polly, sweating below.

'And it made me realise what I really wanted. Or rather who I wanted.'

'Johnny,' said Plump and Blondie.

Yes, just like me. Polly turned over.

'Exactly. I've never stopped loving him.'

'Are you quite sure about that, Edith?'

Polly's heart lurched.

'What do you mean?' snapped Edith.

'Well, I always wondered if you really did love him or if you were just in love with the idea of being in love with him. Why did you leave him?'

'Because I loved him so much, I had to let him go. It's like that American general said about that massacre in Vietnam: it was necessary to destroy the village in order to save it, or words to that effect. That's how I felt about our marriage. It was better to leave it than destroy it. In many ways it was the perfect marriage until I became really ill after Luana was born.'

'But you weren't even married. There you go again. I only hope you haven't passed on your daft idealism to your daughter. Is she pleased to have you back in London?'

'I haven't seen her yet. She's coming over at the weekend. I mean, I haven't even called her yet but that's what I've planned.'

'Doesn't it occur to you that she just might have a life of her own?'

'Oh, she does. She's a casting director. She cast Johnny's film.'

'And I suppose you assume Johnny's going to be there for you just like that. You have to face the truth, Edith. Besides, didn't he get married?'

'Yes, and he left her.'

Polly couldn't ignore the note of triumph in Edith's voice.

'He's free as a bird and I've already rung him. He's definitely coming round at the weekend. I'll get Luana over and it'll be just as if I've never left London. Come on, I can't stand it in here a second longer.'

Polly pulled a towel over her face as they climbed over her and walked out of the sauna. She left what she hoped would be enough time for them to get dressed and leave the club before she slipped out to the locker room.

She had arranged for Zoë Nichols to meet her downstairs in the restaurant for lunch. As she made her way to the reception area, trembling all over, she saw they were still there. Edith was in the process of joining the club. Seeing her fully dressed, Polly wondered how on earth she could ever have imagined that Edith was this shy, fragile mouselike creature shivering down in Cornwall. Before her stood a horribly familiar beast: a man's woman, a predator, brittle but lethal and 100 per cent worldly wise. And her clothes! She must have been on a shopping spree since she arrived in London. Surely you couldn't get what looked like Issey Miyake – a designer Polly wouldn't have a clue how to wear and only recognised thanks to Joan's merciless education –

326

in Cornwall. Where did Edith get the money? Was Johnny paying her extra-marital alimony?

'No smoking in the club, please, madam.'

'Oh fuck you!' But Edith was laughing as she blew smoke in the girl's face. She was unpredictable and exciting and suddenly Polly wondered what Johnny had ever seen in the woman he had actually married.

Zoë, coming in, stood aside to let Edith past.

'Who's that?' Zoë was very impressed. 'She could give Aroma Ross a run for her money. Or Lauren Hutton at any rate.'

'Don't ask,' said Polly miserably and dragged Zoë in to lunch.

They ordered vegetable lasagne and salad and Polly couldn't help remembering the one time she had brought Joan here. Joan had taken one look at the menu and gone across the road to pick up a hamburger, returning to eat it at the health club. Thank God Joan hadn't seen Edith. Polly could just imagine Joan being utterly fascinated by her and the instant lecture that would inevitably follow on how if only Polly could be like that, Johnny would never have left. It was a relief to have Zoë to turn to for comfort and reassurance but as it turned out Zoë had another agenda.

For a start she was high on New York and wanted to talk about Aroma Ross now she was getting further into the book.

'I met with this black model agent and I asked her if she thought anyone would ever give Aroma one of those lucrative cosmetic contracts and she said, "No way! Aroma's scandal, always will be. They want Family Hour." And as I watched her, Polly, I'm telling you that agent was dead right. Aroma's supposed to be engaged but if a man takes her fancy they'd better watch out.

She whispers in someone's ear and she expects them to set it up with whichever guy she's got her eye on. And she's so capricious. One night her manager was taking her out to dinner with a party of ten and she couldn't decide which restaurant she wanted to go to so she made him book these huge tables at half a dozen restaurants. Then when she walked in she just sort of looked around and decided she didn't want to eat there and moved on to the next, leaving a wake of bewildered *maître ds*. She's crazy but she can be absolutely enchanting at the same time.'

Zoë continued in this vein right through to coffee, pausing only to chomp on her lasagne, before she noticed she did not have Polly's attention.

'Polly, what's the matter? Oh my Lord, you've been in France and I haven't asked you how it went and you think I'm a self-obsessed bitch. Well, you're wrong. Now I want to hear what *you* think of my adventures with Aroma Ross.'

Polly didn't smile.

'Joke, Polly. What is it? What's happened?'

Polly told her about France and the dinner with Johnny and the nights with Hector and coming back and discovering he had been involved with Luana. She told her about her rage and humiliation and the comfort she had derived from knowing that maybe she still had a chance of getting back together with Johnny. And then she explained that the wildly exotic creature Zoë had admired on her way into the club had in fact been Luana's mother, newly arrived back in London to reclaim both Luana and Johnny.

'Which leaves you where exactly?' asked Zoë.

'I just don't know. I didn't return Johnny's calls in France. I was there at his invitation. He left a pretty shitty message on my machine when I got home, I haven't dared ring him since. For all I know he can't wait to see Edith at the weekend. I can't even call Luana since we had that bust-up over Hector.'

'You didn't tell her . . .'

'No, but I told her Hector had been seeing another woman in France. I just didn't say it was me. I couldn't let him go on deceiving her as well. She was so upset she threw a complete wobbly, started telling me I was over the hill, that I didn't understand, that I was jealous because I was too old and Hector would never have an affair with me. It was pretty hurtful but I don't hold it against her. Still, I can't just carry on with her as if nothing's happened. I don't trust myself, what I might say to her without thinking.'

Zoë ordered two glasses of wine.

'We'll need these if we're going to talk this through. Just suppose you do manage to get Johnny back, what would be the point? You're on a roll with your career. The agency's doing fine. From what you've always said he's competitive rather than supportive as far as your careers are concerned . . .'

'Well, yes, he was,' said Polly, 'but I think that's changed now. He's had to face the fact that I've made it work and if I hadn't commissioned Lawrence to write *Mr Wrong* as a book, Johnny would never have had his film.'

'But why would you want to give up your hard-won independence? Why not retain control of your life now you've finally got it? Men are such control freaks they always want to interfere. I was watching that kid of an editor who's in charge of my book, Artie Allen-Jones. I was sitting in his office and a call came through from a literary agent. Even though I only heard Artie's side of the conversation, I've become pretty good at deciphering what goes on. He said, "Thanks for returning my call", and then he launched into how one of his female colleagues had just come back from New York and was jumping up and down about this potential bestseller she'd heard about over there, and when the time came to submit it to Hollywood House could the agent please be sure to send it to Artie, not the woman editor. I mean, of all the cheek! Those little boys always want all the kudos for everything and it never stops, I'm telling you, Polly. It's all show. If you ask me, you should just lie low and let Edith try and creep back into his life because if he wants a trophy female like that then he's welcome to her and he's not what you want. Just ride it out and see what happens, although personally I think you'd be better off staying on your own. At least you know where you are and you can have a bit of peace and quiet.'

She's bitter, thought Polly. I never realised it before. She's had these bad experiences with men, she's told me about them, and she's opted out of the race. But is that what I want too? On the one hand I have Joan urging me to jump into bed with every available man and now here's Zoë telling me life's better without a partner.

It came to Polly gradually over the next few days that she was not going to give up on Johnny. As she moved through the house and came upon his things still stashed away in cupboards and drawers, she refused to accept that it was over, Edith or no Edith.

What irked her about Zoë's suggestion that she opt for a solo existence was that just as Joan dismissed Polly's career in favour of her love life, so Zoë dismissed Polly's emotional needs in favour of her work. OK, so she was Zoë's agent but Polly was sure that wasn't what was behind Zoë's push for independence at all costs.

What they don't realise, Polly thought crossly, as she drew up a list of editors to whom she would send Mrs Flowers' book, what they don't seem to understand is that having made a success out of my career, I want to make a success out of my marriage. They see me as a woman on my own like them. But I'm not. I'm still married to Johnny and to be his wife in name only is to be a failure. It's as if my time on my own has been a little fling I've had on the side, my version of an extra-marital affair. Now it's time I settled down to the business of fighting for my marriage and making a profit out of it. All I have to do is corner the market and see off the competition.

That night she removed her make-up sitting at her dressing table with its hand-painted triptych mirror. Three different reflections looked back. In the right-hand panel Joan's disgruntled face glared at her. In the left-hand panel Zoë gave her an encouraging smile.

In the middle panel the New Polly returned her confident gaze.

Then the reflections changed and suddenly there in the right-hand panel Polly saw Juanita's immaculately made-up face and in the left-hand panel there was Edith, cigarette dangling out of the side of her mouth.

In the middle Polly Pushover was back, trapped between them.

PART FOUR

He was a bit young to be having a mid-life crisis but as the pre-launch publicity for *Mr Wrong* mounted and Hector O'Neill was confronted daily with pictures of his handsome face in all the tabloids, he found himself suffering a severe and hitherto unexperienced crisis of confidence. This wasn't about not being able to act beyond the role of Conway. Hector knew his performance in *Mr Wrong* was very good, and that with the help of Henri, the director, his character had emerged as a complex one, a charming and sophisticated psychopath who beguiled the audience one minute and petrified them the next so that they remained in a state of constant ambivalence.

The trouble was, so did Hector. But this was not about Hector the actor. This was about Hector the man.

Throughout the Conway years, when it came to relationships with women, Hector had been Conway both on and off screen. He had never questioned why women were attracted to him. He took it for granted that it was a combination of his lethal looks and his fame as Conway. Nothing more was required.

Now, having acted a more complex character, he had been forced to admit that that was what he had been doing: acting with women all his life. He, Hector O'Neill, was a million miles removed from the fascinating creature up there on the screen in *Mr Wrong*. Not that he wanted to go around murdering women. Far from it. But the experience had dislodged him somehow, made him more introspective, something up till then he had avoided. He took to spending less time going out at night and more time staying in, wandering round his newly acquired penthouse apartment in Bishop's Park with its stupendous view of the Thames. He was even trying to learn to cook, although this was a bit of a throwback to the old Hector since he had an ulterior motive. He had heard someone say that men who cooked for women were irresistible to them. He had received a vicious little note through the mail from Joan Brock – how had she discovered his new address? – informing him that she had wangled a lucrative commission from a publisher she didn't name to write a biography of him. Since she didn't anticipate his cooperation in this project he could expect the dirt to be dug up and dished. When he diced spring onions that evening and tossed them into his wok, he imagined he was chopping up the spindly bones in Joan's pin-like legs.

Without being fully aware of what he was doing or why he was doing it, he set in motion a process of reinventing himself. It wasn't the first time. Hector O'Neill was an invention. The lonely boy who grew up in a trailer and watched his drunk of a father return from the steelworks was still there somewhere, buried underneath layers of surburban Surrey and superficial cinematic hype, but it would take Hector a long time to find him if he ever bothered to look. Now he was propelled towards a course of self-education which would take him even further away from the stench of the steelworks.

Over the years he had kept a series of little notebooks in which he recorded the tastes and likes of his various conquests. These records served as useful seduction aids when it came to buying presents or selecting restaurants that would impress. Now he found himself immersed in the names of books, clothes labels, artists, wines, delicacies, perfumes which had in the past meant precious little to him beyond an instruction to a sales assistant or a secretary in the Conway production office.

'I'd like a copy of something called *The Innocent* by Ian McEwan.'

'Send a box of marrons glacés to Marie Christiansen at this address.'

'I want a CD of an opera called *Tosca*. Gift wrapped, please.'

The notes were copious. Sarah dresses at Joseph, size 12. Lucy likes Maud Frizon shoes, size 6. Angela likes Jazz. Someone called Ben Webster. Also Coleman Hawkins. Judy likes plants, followed by a string of unpronounceable Latin names.

Once back in London, using his notebook as a guide, Hector worked his way through the items, going out and buying the books, the wine, the food, the music – everything but the clothes and the perfume – for himself. It was no longer enough for him just to know the names. He had begun to feel he was missing out on something. There was a wealth of experience he wasn't getting first hand.

It didn't work. He didn't understand or enjoy half the books. He thought the opera sounded like caterwauling. He had only come half-way to building profiles of his conquests and he was still light years away from nailing down his own.

It wasn't until he came to his notes on Polly de Soto that the penny began to drop. It wasn't so much what he had written – 'likes flowers, especially roses; baths, essential oils (lavender, geranium, melissa from Neals Yard), food, is the agent for authors called Lucy Richards, Rebecca Price' – it was more the fact that Polly was somehow different from the usual women who were attracted to him. For a start she was older, more mature, had her own business. But there was something else. She reminded him of someone. She was big and tall, attractive rather than glamorous. She was warm, she was genuine, she had seemed grateful for his attention rather than taking it for granted, she had listened to him and she had seemed comforted by him and – here was the surprise – *he* had found *her* presence oddly comforting.

He missed her.

There was only one other person who had had that effect on him, someone he had never forgotten, someone he still missed: Gracie Delaney.

Hector had called Polly upon his return from France and she had not called him back. Time and again he had come up against her formidable assistant, Mrs Flowers. Mrs Flowers, he could tell, was enormously excited to be talking to the great Hector O'Neill himself but when it came to putting him through to Polly she turned into the most stubborn mule he had ever encountered, launching into a never-ending stream of excuses and fabrications as to why Mrs de Soto was not available.

Hector wanted to see Polly. He wanted to impress her. To this end, although he did not really admit it, he was trying to reinvent himself as someone she might want to know off screen and out of bed. What he couldn't really decide was whether he wanted to see Polly for herself or because she was the first woman who wouldn't take his calls.

Polly could have set him straight in one short, sharp sentence. She was not about to waste any more time on someone who two-timed her with her own step-daughter, someone who obviously thought he was a real clever dick leading both of them up the garden path.

Polly had been relieved when the phone had rung rather late at night and she had answered it with some trepidation, hoping it would be Johnny, dreading it would be Hector and rejoicing to find it was Luana nervously asking to be forgiven.

'I don't know what came over me, Polly. All those things I said. I didn't mean a word, I swear. I think you're stunning for your age. I think I've been a complete idiot about Hector O'Neill. He just wanted a quick fuck and I gave it to him thinking he wanted me for myself, that we were beginning a real relationship. In my dreams!'

Tell me about it! thought Polly wryly. She longed to console Luana by telling her that she too had fallen for the same blarney but in the end she opted to retain what little dignity she had left.

'Make what you can out of it,' she advised Luana, 'amaze your friends, tell them you had an affair with a movie star, tell them you finished it but it was great while it lasted, accept it for what it was.'

'What it was was the latest in a long line of romantic disasters.' Polly could tell Luana was close to tears. 'Why does every single man I meet treat me like shit, Polly?'

Because you've been treated like shit by your mother and now you treat yourself like shit without realising it, thought Polly, knowing that while she was dredging up oversimplified platitudes there was an element of truth there somewhere.

'Just try to be patient. Better these lousy men treat you like shit at the outset before you get too involved. Look on the bright side. It's almost as if you're always drawn to the type of man who'll turn out to be wrong for you in the end. You'll know when the right man comes along. You'll recognise him. Seen your father lately?'

She slipped it in innocently at the end, but she was unprepared for the shock of Luana's reply.

'Sure. Dad and I are getting together quite a lot these days because of Mum. That's one of the reasons I called you, Polly. Has Dad told you about Mum coming back to London?'

No, of course he hasn't. Your father has barely spoken to me since I virtually ignored him in the South of France. Once again Polly edited what she said out loud to Luana.

'He hasn't, actually. How do you feel about that, Luana? Do you see a lot of her?'

'I'm gobsmacked, Polly, I really am. If you'd said to me even six months ago that my mother was coming back to London I'd have freaked but now that she's here I'm thrilled. I can't get over how much she's changed. She's so positive, so determined. She looks great. We go shopping together, we go to the movies, all the things you and I used to do. She doesn't treat me like a kid anymore. It's like she's my older sister. I'm trying to get her and Dad together as much as possible. It's so great when it's just the three of us. I can pretend I have a family.'

What about me? wailed Polly silently. I made a family for you in my home with your father. Doesn't that count for anything?

At least it took her mind off Hector. For the next few days Polly raged with jealousy. Her conversations with Johnny since their return from France had been abrupt and to the point – 'I need to come by the house and pick up a raincoat I know I've left in the downstairs closet, I won't disturb you'; 'Lawrence Bedford is due a final payment when *Mr Wrong* opens, anything you can do to speed up the cheque, Johnny, I'd appreciate it' – with any further conversation floundering as if they were two people who had once been friends, who hadn't seen each other for a long time, who had nothing left in common and who no longer knew what to say to each other. It was terrifying. She and Johnny had become near strangers to each other just when she wanted to bridge the gap between them. Now Edith was back in the frame Polly suddenly lost her nerve. She remembered what Zoë had said: sit tight and let it all work its course. Let Johnny discover for himself that he was through with Edith once and for all.

But what if he discovered just the opposite?

In any case Zoë was in a bit of an irrational state herself. She was having a difficult time with Hollywood House, who had suddenly decided that she should not do any publicity whatsoever for Aroma Ross's novel.

Since it was a ghost-written project, this would have been perfectly acceptable except that when the project had first been announced the press release sent out by Hollywood House had stated quite categorically that Aroma Ross would be 'helped' in the writing of the book by Zoë Nichols. At the request of the Hollywood House publicity director, Zoë had even given an interview to one of the tabloids about how she would be writing the book with Aroma. Now suddenly she was not allowed to talk to them. Zoë had no problem with her name not appearing on the dust jacket or the title page. What she did want was to be credited with having conceived the characters and the plot of the book. This she felt was only fair. Aroma had been positively paranoid that the book should not be remotely autobiographical, which meant that Zoë had had to come up with a totally fictitious story. Where Aroma had proved enormously helpful was in opening as many doors as she could to enable Zoë to research the world of modelling. Zoë had interviewed model agents, other models, photographers, fashion editors, attended fashion shoots, been given front-row seats at the Paris collections – all of which helped to authenticate the background to her story. But it remained *her* story.

It was during one of her telephonic tirades against Artie Allen-Jones that Zoë dropped a piece of information into her lap that really shook Polly.

'And another thing. I've been meaning to talk to you about an idea I had about doing a biography of Hector O'Neill. From what you've been saying he's about to move into a whole different league once *Mr Wrong* comes out. The word is he's going to be dynamite. Well, I began mumbling about it to that little prick Artie Allen-Jones when I last had lunch with him and do you know what? He's only gone and taken my idea and commissioned a biography from Joan Brock. Joan Brock! That old slag! I'm so furious, I could . . .'

Polly let her ramble on. She was so shaken that Joan had gone ahead and got herself a commission without asking Polly to represent her that she forgot to tell Zoë that in fact Joan had had the same idea about a book on Hector before filming had even begun. She also conveniently erased how angry she had been that Joan had automatically assumed Polly would be her agent.

So who had Joan asked to be her agent? What had Joan been up to? Polly hadn't heard a word from her since that abortive lunch at Clarke's. For some reason which Polly simply could not understand, Joan had not returned a single one of Polly's calls.

Throughout everything Polly was grateful for the calming influence of Mrs Flowers, who went about her work in such an unassuming way that Polly sometimes had difficulty remembering that here was the person who would become her next bestselling client. Sometimes she watched Mrs Flowers out of the corner of her eye, marvelling at her energy. She wondered how old Mrs Flowers really was and what kind of passion she had experienced in the past that had enabled her to write the steamier scenes in *Christopher*. Maybe that was the answer, wondered Polly, indulge in unbridled lust until a certain age and then give it all up and plunge your energy into something else. It would certainly make for a calmer life. But hadn't that been exactly the life she'd adopted pre-Hector, the life for which Joan had had nothing but contempt but which Zoë had advocated? Why do I seem to be the only person without a view? Polly asked herself.

'Mrs Flowers, do you have any thoughts as to where

343

you'd like *Christopher* to go? You must have built up certain impressions about the various editors I deal with. Any preferences?'

'Oh, Mrs de Soto, I leave that entirely to you. You're the expert.'

Polly hated it when people said, 'You're the expert.' It usually meant they thought they knew better but didn't want to get involved, but if you made a mess of it they'd be the first to criticise you. She had forgotten this rather priggish side of Mrs Flowers.

'Well, do you want them to know who you are? Should I say this is a wonderful novel by my assistant who has been writing Mills & Boons up to now?'

Mrs Flowers looked aghast. 'Do you have to say I'm your assistant? Not that I'm ashamed or anything, it's just . . .'

'That's what I mean. You have to get involved in some way. Of course, I won't say you're my assistant but are we going to use your real name? Mabel Lucy Flowers? Everyone knows you as Mrs Flowers. They might guess. It's not such a terrible thing. People think you're wonderful, Mrs Flowers, they really do. And are we going to send a photograph?'

'I just want it to be published by someone who really loves the book,' was all Mrs Flowers would say.

In the end *Christopher* went to just three carefully chosen editors and Polly made sure one of them was Sally Mackenzie, the young female editor who worked alongside Artie Allen-Jones at Hollywood House who Zoë said was being upstaged by Artie. Mrs Flowers brightened visibly when Polly mentioned her name. It transpired they had talked often on the telephone when Sally had rung up to request Polly's books.

'But why didn't you tell me?'

'I did in the beginning but nine times out of ten when it comes to Hollywood House you always seem to have a note that Mr Allen-Jones has asked for it. It's as if no one else exists there.'

She's right, thought Polly, I'm as much to blame as anyone. I should make more of an effort to get to know the up and coming editors. I'm getting lazy in my old age.

The *Christopher* sale worked like clockwork. Sally Mackenzie loved the book from page one, bid more than the other two editors, and, most important, got on famously with Mrs Flowers when they met for lunch.

Then it all fell apart.

Sally Mackenzie called Polly early on a Monday morning before Mrs Flowers had arrived.

'She's not here yet,' Polly told her. 'Shall I get her to call you?'

'No, it's you I want to talk to. I don't know how to tell you this and if I don't know how to tell you, you can imagine the difficulty I'm going to have in telling Mabel Lucy.'

Polly stifled a giggle. It was going to be very hard to get used to hearing Mrs Flowers referred to as Mabel Lucy.

'Telling Mabel Lucy what?'

'I'm leaving Hollywood House. I've been offered the job of editoral director at Odeon Books. It'd be my chance to shape my own list . . .'

'And get away from Artie,' Polly finished for her. Odeon had only been going about five years but already they had made a good reputation for themselves as publishers of upmarket and middle-brow fiction and non-fiction. They were about to launch their own paperback line.

'Mabel Lucy Flowers would be so perfect for Odeon. I just don't know how I'm going to leave *Christopher* behind but I do have to take this job. I may not be offered such a great opportunity for ages if I wait.'

'You know that Odeon were the underbidder on *Christopher*.'

'What are you saying, Polly?'

'I'm saying that I can always ask Mrs Flowers, I mean Mabel Lucy, what she wants to do. It could just be that she'd like to move publishers with you if you can persuade Odeon to up their offer to match Hollywood's.'

Mrs Flowers didn't bat an eye.

'Of course I want to go with Sally if she'll have me. No question.'

Artie Allen-Jones, who by this time had read the book, had other ideas. He persuaded Hollywood to up the advance payment by £5,000 to £40,000. He began calling Mrs Flowers three times a day, flattering her, cajoling her, telling her she was a star. He faxed Polly a revised marketing plan with a budget of £50,000. He biked over stunning visuals for a very commercial cover design. Polly began to realise that with so much money thrown at it the book was destined to go straight to Number 1. She owed it to her client to recommend she stay with Hollywood. There was no way Odeon could begin to compete in these stakes. But as she soon discovered, Polly did not know her client.

'Now I've got this far I'm going to go on writing for a long time,' said Mrs Flowers, maddeningly calm as ever. 'I've only just begun. The trouble with this Allen-Jones chappie is that he can't really tell the difference between me and that supermodel Aroma Ross. To him we're all authors whose books will sell and he can take all the credit. We're not individuals. We're just names he can chalk up in his spring catalogue. I want to go with Sally and be treated properly. I don't care if it is for less money. That young man needs to be taught a lesson.'

That young man promptly announced he was going to sue for breach of contract, but once again Mrs Flowers had the last word.

'I think he might have a bit of a problem.'

'I hope you're right.' Polly was beginning to feel a little nervous.

'You see I haven't been very efficient this week, Mrs de Soto. I've been so distracted with all this business, all the contracts we've had from the publishers for the authors' signatures, I've forgotten to do anything about them. They're all just sitting here in a heap.'

'Don't worry about that now. I never even noticed, Mrs Flowers.'

'You don't get it, do you, Mrs de Soto? One of those contracts is mine with Hollywood House. I haven't even signed it. Young Mr Allen-Jones hasn't got a leg to stand on! Perhaps you could give Sally a ring and ask her to get a contract round here as soon as she gets her feet under her desk at Odeon. By that time I'll have put a little ink in my pen.'

It was a problem solved but at the same time Polly felt even more dejected. It seemed not only was she doomed to the life of a single woman whether she wanted it or not but her professional abilities were also deserting her.

Still, life went on. If there was one person who was in the same boat as Polly it was Luana so, fighting her apprehension about hearing more glowing stories about

Edith, Polly invited her stepdaughter to accompany her to the opening of a new restaurant in Chelsea.

'Why have they asked you?' asked Luana, tactful as ever.

'One of my authors, a foodie writer, has put some money into it. He's asked me. He's a bit pompous, sports a bow tie now and then, but it's not as if we'll be stuck with him and at least we'll get some food and drink.'

'Sounds wild. OK, you've twisted my arm.'

Polly picked Luana up the following evening. Luana obviously thought she was in for a very boring time since she had dressed very conservatively in a simple short-sleeved beige dress. The hem was at least six inches above the knee but it didn't alter the classic image. Polly thought she looked beautiful. On the way she filled Luana in on her client, Winthrop Hamilton.

'He's half American, I think. His mother's from one of those old Eastern seaboard New England families, he summers in the Hamptons and all that. He's not short of a bob or two is our Winthrop. Known as Win, by the way. Owns a town house in St Leonard's Terrace and a country manor in Wiltshire. He's only about thirty-five but he seems much older somehow. He's doing rather well as a food and wine writer. There's a new gourmet magazine starting up and they've offered him a column.'

Polly knew she was prattling on so that Luana couldn't get a word in edgeways about Edith and Johnny but as they turned into the King's Road Luana began to talk about Edith.

'She made me wear this dress when I told her where I was going. You never know who you might meet, she kept saying. You won't get riff-raff at an event like this. I couldn't believe it was Mum talking. You'd never think she was once this batty hippie with an alternative lifestyle. She's got this new thing where she refers to everything in decades – 'That's so Seventies,' she'll say. This from someone who still listens to her Neil Young albums. Her fashion sense is weird. She's discovered deconstruction with a vengeance but if you think about it that's a bit Seventies. Yet she wants me to be so uncool with my clothes.'

'Did you tell her you were coming out with me this evening?'

'I didn't, actually.' Luana looked shifty.

'Does she ask about me?' Polly couldn't resist it.

'She thinks she knows all about you. Dismisses you as the archetypal career woman. So Eighties!'

They arrived at the restaurant which was crammed with hoorays and their dates stuffing themselves, most of them already rather red in the face. Polly hadn't met any of Win's friends before, hadn't expected this kind of braying crowd. But it was too late. They were here now.

Win was standing by himself in a corner and the minute Polly saw him she knew this wasn't his scene either. If she'd only stopped to think about it she might have guessed he'd be embarrassed by this kind of crowd. He wasn't exactly shy but he was quite reserved, quite private. Polly realised she knew absolutely nothing about his life beyond the sketched profile she'd given Luana.

'Who is that dreamboat?' asked Luana beside her.

Polly followed her gaze and saw she was staring straight at Win. And suddenly Polly noticed Win's looks for the first time. He wasn't Polly's type – for some reason blond men did nothing for her – but she had to admit he was a bit of an Adonis. Well over six feet, with almost silvery fair hair, a straight nose and a strong jaw, he looked rather like a blond preppy Elvis.

Polly couldn't believe it. She introduced Luana and didn't see her again for over an hour. When she wanted to leave and went to find her, Luana was still talking to Win. Polly stood beside her, not wanting to interrupt. When Luana finally noticed her, she grasped Polly's arm.

'Are you off? Don't worry about me. Win's taking me out to dinner away from all this racket.'

'Will you j-j-join us, Pp-polly?' Win asked politely. Polly had forgotten to tell Luana about the stammer. She caught the look of panic on Luana's face and took the hint.

'I have to get back. Thanks, Win. It looks as if this place is going to be a big hit.'

Luana kissed her on the cheek and handed her an envelope.

'Dad asked me to give this to you. I nearly forgot. Thank you for bringing me tonight, Polly. Thank you, thank you, thank you.' She leaned closer to Polly's ear. 'You knew, didn't you,' Luana whispered, 'you knew he'd be perfect for me and you never said a word.'

Polly had known nothing of the sort. She had always assumed Win was gay, which proved how wrong she could be. As Joan was always pointing out: 'You are such a goose, Polly. You always think the ones who aren't gay are, and the ones who are aren't.'

In the car she opened the envelope Luana had given her. Inside was an invitation to the première of *Mr Wrong* and on it Johnny had scrawled: 'You will come, won't you, Pol? See you then.'

Polly nearly blasted the horn in exultation. Johnny wanted her by his side on his big night.

I t was one of the worst evenings of Polly's life.
The day before, Zoë came round and took her in hand.

'What are you going to wear?'

'Oh, I expect I'll get out my . . .'

'You'll get out something you've worn a million times before, something you feel comfortable in, as you always put it, you'll give it a bit of a dust down and say it'll have to do. No, Polly, that's not good enough. You want to make a sensational impression on Johnny, on everybody who's going to be there. What we're going to do is we're going to make an appointment for you to go to the hairdresser's tomorrow afternoon. Meanwhile you're going to take the rest of the day off and we're going to hit the shops. One of the perks of writing Aroma's novel is that my profile has been heightened about an inch or two in the fashion world and before they realised how insignificant I really was some of those pushy designer PR women heard Aroma's name and promptly offered me a discount at one or two stores. Now's the time for me to make use of it.'

As she rang for a minicab the next evening Polly decided she had never felt so glamorous. Her hair was up for the first time in her life, piled on top of her head in an exotic chignon all the better for Johnny to be reminded of her ears with their tiny lobes that he had always admired so much. Her midnight blue silk trouser suit was from Armani and its brilliant cut was flattering and emphasised the fact that she was tall and striking with long legs.

She strode confidently into the Odeon Leicester Square imagining she must know how it felt to be a model on a catwalk. The press were milling around outside with cameras at the ready. Polly's euphoria was slightly dented when they gave her a quick look and moved right on past her. She consoled herself with the thought that at least her appearance had been sufficiently stunning for them to look and see if she might be a somebody even if she was instantly dismissed as a nobody.

The foyer was buzzing. A hand clasped her elbow and she looked round to find Spider, the first assistant on *Mr Wrong*, looking quite ridiculous in what was clearly a borrowed dinner jacket much too small for him, a bright blue shirt with ruffles all down the front and a blue velvet bow tie.

'Nice to see you Mrs de Soto. How've you been keeping?'

'I've been keeping absolutely fine, thank you, Spider.' How much did Spider know about me and Hector? was Polly's first thought. 'How about you?'

'Getting married, as it goes. You remember Pauline?'

Polly found herself face to face with the script girl on *Mr Wrong*, the one whose knickers had kept everyone guessing.

'She's wearing 'em,' Spider whispered with a broad wink. 'They're blue tonight to match my shirt.'

'And your eyes,' said Polly and had the satisfaction of seeing great big Spider blush. 'Now congratulations, you two. Speaking of marriage, I'd better find my old man.'

She noticed Spider and Pauline hesitate for a second. They might call her Mrs de Soto but they couldn't quite reconcile themselves to the fact that she was still Johnny's wife.

'His big night tonight,' said Spider; 'he's over there.'

Johnny was more nervous than she'd ever seen him. He was also being very Johnny. He was still wearing his long black overcoat over his dinner jacket and his baseball cap. Not only that – and Polly had to look twice to make sure her eyes weren't deceiving her – he had Zutty on a lead.

Johnny was working the foyer, pumping hands like a politician, going 'Hi, how are you, great you could make it' to absolutely everyone. He got as far as 'Hi, how are you?' before he realised it was Polly.

'Pol, great, isn't this terrific? Like my new monkey suit? Bought it specially for the occasion. Dead snazzy, what do you think?'

No 'You're looking great, Pol.' Nothing changed.

'Look, here's Pol, Zutty.' Zutty was completely ignoring her. 'He's really pleased to see you. He insisted on coming. I told him you were going to be here. I thought maybe you could sort of look after him for me. He really adores you, you know that. Perhaps you could go on ahead, take him upstairs. I've got a special seat for you, Pol. Front row of the balcony.'

This is Johnny, Polly told herself. This is the man I married. He's never going to change. If I want him back

I'm going to have to live with this. She continued with this positive, rational line of thought as she tried to make her way as elegantly as possible up the staircase with Zutty frantically yapping at her ankles.

When she arrived at the entrance to the circle, Zutty pulled furiously on his lead so she was forced to run down the steps to the front row. The centre section had place names on the seats reserved for Johnny's party.

'Good evening, Polly. You're here.'

Polly could not believe it. Sitting right there bang in the middle of the front row with a place between them were Juanita and Edith. It was Juanita who had spoken to her.

Edith was looking wild and mysterious wrapped up in a velvet opera cloak with a hood.

'No, stop, you're there. One away from me,' Juanita said. Looking down, Polly saw her name on her seat. The place next to her had been reserved for Henri the director. She looked for the place name on her other side and found that Juanita had managed to knock it on to the floor. It had to be Johnny. Obviously, he would have to have Juanita as his co-producer on his other side.

Wrong.

Johnny came bounding down the steps a few minutes later followed by Carla, Luana and Win. He picked up Zutty and handed him to Polly.

'You'll have to hold him up otherwise he won't be able to see.'

Polly found herself sitting in all her finery with Zutty on her lap while Johnny brushed past her and threw himself into the seat between Juanita and Edith. But if Polly was filled with disappointment at this arrangement, Carla was outraged.

'Johnny, I sit next to you.'

'No, Mamma, I've put you between Edith and Luana so you can – '

'Johnny. I sit here.'

Carla stood in front of Edith until Edith shrugged and moved to the next seat. Luana and Win took the seats next to Edith. In spite of her fury at being upstaged Polly couldn't help smiling at the way Luana was literally bubbling over with happiness. Win waved to Polly. Luana gave her a secret thumbs-up sign and made an 'I'm in heaven' look. And then Carla stood up and moved past Johnny to kiss Polly on both cheeks.

'I didn't see you. I'm so sorry. How are you? Why haven't you been to see me? Come to lunch next week.'

Carla's small act of warmth defused Polly's rising anger. She thought she saw Johnny sneak a guilty look at her, or was it her imagination? Nobody, she noticed, introduced her to Edith. She prayed it was impossible that Edith would recognise her as the naked woman lying below her in the sauna.

As the lights went down Polly made to move into the empty seat next to Juanita, offloading Zutty in the process, but Juanita pressed her back.

'Here he comes.'

There was a rustle of anticipation throughout the entire cinema. Downstairs the audience had risen and were looking up at the balcony. How *could* she have forgotten? He was only the star of the film.

Hector was born to wear black tie. His sleek frame looked as at home in it as Johnny's stocky build seem ill at ease. Hector's evening clothes fitted him perfectly: made to measure, obviously. He was tanned and his black hair was short and swept back away from his temples with just one stray lock falling over his forehead.

Old-fashioned words like suave and debonair lodged themselves in Polly's brain. He sauntered down the steps of the balcony, waving to the crowd, and slipped into the empty seat beside Polly. He rose to kiss Juanita, shake Johnny's hand and slap him on the back. As he turned back to Polly the film started.

It was an experience for which she could not possibly have prepared herself, no matter how hard she might have tried – to sit there and watch the man on the screen looking so breathtakingly handsome, to know that every woman in the audience was secretly (and in some cases not so secretly) wanting to sleep with him, to know that she had slept with him and that he was sitting so close that if she moved a fraction of an inch she would touch him. Her composure lasted until the scene in the old market at Antibes and suddenly she saw herself on screen and Hector moving towards her. They passed and she remembered the note he had given her and it all came flooding back. Her throat constricted, her shoulders heaved and try as she might, her eyes filled with tears.

She felt a hand take hers and squeeze. In her head she heard Johnny say: 'Blubbing, Pol. Brilliant! Film must be really good. But why are you crying at this bit? It's the beginning of all the excitement. Suppose I'd better lend you my best silk handkerchief – come on, give me your paw.'

She waited for the wad of filthy screwed-up Kleenex and when it didn't appear she remembered. She wasn't sitting next to Johnny. She was sitting next to Hector. It was his hand she was holding.

She snatched her hand away and felt Hector flinch beside her.

From the first few frames it had been clear the film

was going to be good but by the time the final credits rolled, what was also clear was that it would be a huge success. It was suspenseful, and entertaining. Hector and Julianne were dynamite together as were, to an appropriately lesser extent, Julianne and Caspar who played the cop boyfriend who arrested Hector in the end and claimed Julianne as his own. Johnny had a hit on his hands and Polly was proud of him. She was also surprised at how cool he had been about it up to now. There must have been screenings. He must have known what he had.

Downstairs in the foyer it was bedlam. The press were descending in droves on Hector, Julianne, Caspar and Henri. Polly heard a loud Irish voice proclaiming: 'So Froggy had it in him after all. Didn't think he could direct his way out of a tub of cottage cheese.'

'Clovis, leave it alone,' Polly heard Luana's embarrassed voice.

'Hello stranger.'

Lawrence Bedford was beside her and Polly felt riddled with guilt. In her excitement – pointless, as it turned out – at the thought of accompanying Johnny to the première, she had forgotten to find out what would be happening with Lawrence. He should have been sitting up there with everyone in the front row of the circle. In fact he had far more right to be there than she did. How could she have been such a neglectful agent?

'Come on, Polly, don't look so horrified to see me. Take my arm. I'll escort you to the post-première party. I thought the film was absolutely brilliant even if I did write it myself. What about you?'

'I agree. Just think what it's going to do for sales of the book. I shouldn't be surprised if you don't sell another quarter of a million copies. Now tell me, how's the new book coming along?'

She barely listened to Lawrence as they made their way through Soho to dell'Ugo where Johnny had booked two floors for dinner and dancing. It was typical! She had set out for the evening as the glamorous wife of the successful movie producer and wound up back where she started: playing the sympathetic agent supporting her client.

Yet if she were honest she was using Lawrence just as much as he was using her. Without him she would have been lost. She needed an escort. At the party she introduced him to Luana and Win.

'Winthrop's a food writer,' she explained quickly. Clients often became jealous of each other, vying for her attention: 'very successful.' It was Lawrence's night but she didn't want Win to feel put down. Hector, who had been swallowed up by the press, made his entrance and Luana moved closer to Win. She wouldn't look at Hector. Polly wondered what Win must be making of her performance. But at least Luana had Win. Polly knew that clinging to Lawrence wasn't going to fool anyone.

She survived the dinner thanks to Carla, who needed a certain amount of attention – or pretended she did. Johnny flitted about the room, wallowing in all the adulation. Polly was pleased. Edith had rushed to sit next to him but now she found herself neglected. When the dancing began she crossed the room and man-oeuvred her way into Johnny's arms. Carla clucked disapprovingly.

Suddenly she turned to Polly.

'In France? What happen? I never ask but I want to know.'

'I was foolish. He gave me a chance but I made a mess of it. Please don't ask me for the details.' Polly knew it was pointless to be anything but straight with Carla.

'I told you to keep up with him. Look at you, here you are. There he is. And look who he's with. You know who that is, don't you? Now, if Johnny gives you another chance, take it and hold on to it. Wait here, Polly.'

Carla got up. Polly watched in fascination as the tiny woman, a good head shorter than anyone else on the floor even in her little high-heeled shoes, made her way over to Johnny and Edith. She took Johnny's arm, pulled him gently away from Edith and made a big show of being apologetic, was Edith quite sure she didn't mind? Then she waltzed off with her son, leaving Edith standing there.

Carla monopolised Johnny for four whole dances and suddenly Polly saw what she was doing. She was engineering her son closer and closer to the table until finally they were almost on top of Polly, at which point Carla literally handed Johnny to Polly.

Polly had forgotten what an utterly hopeless dancer Johnny was. He didn't dance, he walked, and not necessarily in time to the music. Keep up with him, Carla had said. Well, Polly was trying in more senses than one.

'Great party, Johnny.'

'Great party, great movie, great evening. Everything's great.'

'Including you.'

'You said it, Pol.'

'Your mother's having a wonderful time.'

'With Mamma it's a question of so far so good. She won't be truly happy till I've won an Oscar.'

'I never realised she was so ambitious for you. She's quite an impressive woman. In different circumstances she'd probably have been a pretty successful career woman herself.'

Johnny stopped dead in the middle of the dance floor.

'Mamma's not a career woman.'

'I didn't say she was. I said she could have been.'

'No she couldn't.'

'Why not?'

'She's my mamma.'

'Meaning you don't like women having successful careers.'

'Of course I do. Look at Juanita.'

What about me? screamed Polly inside but kept smiling.

'You must be pleased Edith's here.'

'How do you know Edith's here?'

'You might well ask since no one's bothered to introduce us.'

Johnny looked very nervous.

'Anyway she looks very well, Johnny.'

'Why wouldn't she look well?'

'I heard she'd been ill.'

'Who told you that?' He was very defensive now.

'Luana. Tell me, how do you like Win?' Polly longed to quiz him more about Edith but if it was going to alienate him, there wasn't much point.

'I don't. Looks a bit of a wally to me. You introduced them, didn't you?'

'Is it something specific or just the fact that he's screwing your little peachy girl?'

'He isn't. That's what's bothering me.'

'What do you mean?'

'He isn't going to bed with her. Says he respects her. Sounds like an old-fashioned matinée hero who's only allowed one knee on the bed. Forget about respecting her. I've never heard such crap. He just doesn't fancy her.'

'Well, would you like him if he did – and I'm sure he does.'

'No.'

Polly gave up. She should never have mentioned Edith. Then, unpredictably as ever, Johnny suddenly pulled her closer.

'I left a message on your machine for you when you got home from France. You never rang me back.'

'We've spoken plenty of times since then.'

'Yes, but only about Luana or work. Did you have a good holiday?'

'Of course I did. I should have thanked you. I know I should.'

'What made it so good?'

'The hotel. Being able to relax.'

'What else? You didn't seem to have much time for me after that first evening. I'll lay it on the line, Pol. I was a bit pissed off with you for not wanting to see much of me. It felt a bit like you were using me, tell you the truth.'

'You were busy. You had a film to produce. I didn't want to get in the way.'

'That's all it was? No hidden agenda?'

'No hidden agenda.'

'I'm quite pleased to hear that, you know, Pol.' He was holding her very close now. 'I'm going to have to network a bit. It's my party and all that, but we could sort of have a dance later on and . . .'

'Mind if I step in and take this opportunity to renew an old friendship?'

Hector was looming over Johnny's shoulder, gently but firmly moving him aside and drawing Polly to him. Polly couldn't bear to look directly at Johnny. She could sense him, standing there, fists clenched, smaller than Hector, stocky, pugnacious, angry. Tell him no, Johnny. Say you want me to yourself. Send him packing. Fight for me. Do something.

'How can I refuse my star anything? I'm surprised he didn't write you into his contract, Pol. Take her away, Hector. Good to see you, Pol. Thanks for looking after Zutty.'

'I have my uses,' said Polly bitterly, and was rewarded with one of Johnny's blackest looks.

'I shouldn't have done that, should I?' said Hector. 'Do you want to go after him?'

'I'd rather run after his flaming dog.'

'You're looking so beautiful tonight.'

Right words. Wrong man.

'Polly, I've never had to do this before but I want an explanation from you.'

She looked up at him as he moved her expertly round the dance floor. He was an effortless dancer and after Johnny's clodhopping she relaxed in spite of herself. He was so undeniably handsome. People were watching them. She knew he was making her look good.

'What kind of explanation?'

'Why didn't you return my calls after I returned from France?'

'Why didn't you tell me about Luana?'

She had nothing to lose and it made her bold. Hector tensed. He didn't answer her for several minutes.

'I can see I'm the one who owes you an explanation.

I'd like to give it to you but I can't do it while we're shuffling round a dance floor surrounded by all these people. Can I see you some other time?'

Polly was about to say thanks but no thanks when she saw Johnny looking at her. He was dancing with Edith. Without taking his eyes off Polly, he buried his lips in Edith's neck. Polly didn't stop to think. Before he looked away she moved her hands up to stroke the back of Hector's neck.

'Of course you can. Call me tomorrow and we'll make a date.'

Luana sat at her desk and tried not to think about the kind of mood Clovis would be in when she arrived for work. Clovis had taken the week off after the première and during that week as *Mr Wrong* opened to sensational business, Hector had given several interviews to the press. Luana's personal view of Hector was that he was a piece of dog turd but she couldn't ignore the fact that he had stated several times in print that she, and she alone, was responsible for the idea of casting him as Mr Wrong.

Clovis was going to be furious. Hadn't she always said that one of the most important things Luana had to remember about a casting director's job was that it was always, repeat always, the director's idea. Of course Clovis was the first to accept compliments about the casting. Now Hector had blown her whistle. She was going to go ballistic.

As if that were not enough, Luana had, in the week Clovis had been away, already been offered three jobs, two to work for rival casting directors with the promise of much more responsibility and a third to cast a film on her own. Ordinarily she would have been flattered and excited, but this week all she could think about was how soon would Win propose? They had spent the weekend in the country. Not at his place in Wiltshire, he still hadn't taken her there despite her constant begging. Apparently some kind of renovations were being carried out, the place was filled with dust, it just wasn't a good idea. He had taken her to some friends who had a weekend place in Suffolk. They were a couple in their forties, childless, old friends of Win's. The wife, Peggy, had confided in Luana during the washing up in the kitchen.

'Perhaps I shouldn't tell you this but we're both quite excited about you and Win. It's the first time he's brought a girl to stay and he's been coming here for years. The truth is, he's always been incredibly secretive about his private life. George and I decided he was probably once very badly hurt and has decided to be very careful.'

Luana had started hearing wedding bells before they'd even finished loading the dishwasher. And she too, she realised, had been careful. She hadn't introduced Win to all her friends as she usually did, rushing him round to meet everyone as the new man in her life. That would come. She sensed that he wanted to take things one step at a time. She banished the irritating voice that kept saying: if you introduce him to your girlfriends the first thing they're going to ask is what's he like in bed? And you're going to have to say you don't know. They wouldn't understand about him respecting her.

So how could she think about going for a new job when this time next month she might be planning her wedding?

Clovis arrived in a real grump but it didn't have anything to do with Hector's interviews. The minute she entered Reception she delved into her bag and brought out a bottle of syrup of figs. Clovis suffered from chronic constipation and did not see the need to keep quiet about it. Luana was kept constantly informed as to the state of Clovis' bowels. Clovis downed half the bottle.

'I seem to have run out of the stuff at home. Now, what've I got on today? Give me me call book, I'd better get on the phone.'

'Did you have a nice holiday, Clovis?'

'Oh, don't be makin' small talk while me stomach's like the Rock of Gibraltar. What's this? Lunch with Joan Brock. Who the fock's Joan Brock?'

'Well, I can help you there,' said Luana, 'she's an old friend of Polly's. I met her quite a few times when I was living with Polly and Dad. She always came to the house when Dad was away because he couldn't stand her.'

'And why was that?'

'I never really discovered. Dad always said her breath smelt.'

Clovis laughed. 'Sounds like yer father. Poor bitch probably suffered from constipation like meself. Why am I having lunch with her?'

'She's writing this biography of Hector and she wants to interview you about him.'

'Maybe she'll want to talk to you too.' It was a throwaway remark as Clovis disappeared into her office but Luana didn't miss the implication.

'You're due to meet her at Chez Gerard in Charlotte Street at one o'clock,' Luana called as Clovis slammed the door.

'Why me?' asked Clovis rather ungraciously as Joan Brock took her place opposite Clovis in the banquette. 'I'll have a Dubonnet and lemonade. Don't look like that, Miss Brock. We don't drink Guinness all the time.'

Joan had been unable to stop herself wincing at the request for Dubonnet and lemonade. How naff could this woman get?

'Do call me Joan. I'll have a Kir Royale.'

'Ooh, very chi-chi, Joan.' Clovis emphasised the Joan. 'Polly's an old friend of yours, I hear.'

'We were at school together. Juanita was there too, under another name.'

'You mean she was incognito?'

'No, no, no. She was called Sandra something. She's changed her name since then.'

'She's not the only one.'

'What do you mean?'

'Oh, we'll get to that. So what was Polly like at school?'

'Much like she is now.'

'And how's that?'

'Oh, you know, sweet, of course. I adore Polly. But she's a bit of an innocent when it comes to men, sex, that sort of thing. Can't really hold her own.'

'Really?' Clovis knocked back her Dubonnet and lemonade. 'Didn't look that way to me at the post-première party the other night. She was dancing with Johnny and then Hector came along and cut in and waltzed off with her. She had her pick of the two of them. Hector was with her for the rest of the evening.'

Clovis had the satisfaction of seeing she had taken the wind right out of Joan's sails.

'Now, Hector. Why you?' Joan was back on course.

'You cast *Mr Wrong*. You must know him pretty well. Did you cast the Conway films?'

'I did not, as you'd have known if you'd done your homework. If you really want to know I first met Hector before he was even cast as Conway.'

'How was that? Who did cast him as Conway?'

'I forget but you can easily check. When I met him I was working as a casting director for an advertising agency. I had a young assistant, sort of like the job Luana has now but with more responsibility. This kid actually went out looking for people, scouting in the streets. She was pretty good. We were looking for a hunk for this commercial. She found him. Hector. John Hector Maguire I think he was called then. He was up a ladder.'

'He was where?'

'Up a ladder. He was a brickie. She made him come down and brought him in and the client went for him just like that. It was after the commercial came out that someone thought of him for Conway.'

'And this girl who discovered him, has she become some top flight casting director with her own business? Where is she now?'

'She was American. I hired her because she had a good Irish name. Gracie Delaney. Red hair. She went back to Philadelphia to get married. Poor kid, she was sweet on Hector.'

'They had a thing together?'

'I don't really know. All I remember is that she came in really cut up one morning because he'd spent the night blurting out all his deep dark secrets to her, confided in her like, and she said she'd felt so sorry for him she'd wound up spending the night with him. But she wasn't stupid. She knew he was trouble. She knew he'd probably done it on purpose to get her to succumb. She didn't allow it to stop her going back and getting married.'

'What were his deep dark secrets?'

'She never said. I didn't ask.'

'Are you still in touch with her, Clovis?'

Clovis looked at the little rat-like woman on the other side of the table, positively salivating at the thought of getting at those 'deep dark secrets'.

'I am. I get a Christmas card from her every year.'

'Does it give her address?'

'It does. I'll give you a bell with it tomorrow. Now, let's order ourselves a real drink and I'll tell you all about the scumbags in the British film industry.'

Polly wasn't entirely sure about Hector's suggestion that he try out his new cooking skills on her but in the end she couldn't resist a peek at his new apartment. She was disappointed by it.

He had obviously done what so many people do. He had gone out to expensive stores and chosen large cold masculine pieces of furniture with no apparent thought as to how or where they would fit into his home. Someone had obviously told him grey was *the* colour. A vast grey leather sofa stood plonked in front of the plate-glass window. A 10-foot slate-coloured table monopolised the dining room, making it look like an operating theatre. The chairs dotted along it were much too small and spindly by comparison. His kitchen was cavernous and steely. He took pride in the fact that he hadn't hired a decorator and had put the place together himself but as far as Polly could see, if anyone needed a decorator it was Hector. He had absolutely no taste. With his wardrobe it was a different story. He was a natural clothes horse and designers flocked to have him wear their suits, sportswear, whatever. He just had to put it on in the right size and forget about it. He had clearly imagined he could apply the same approach to his home.

On top of everything he was a lousy cook. Polly couldn't help thinking that she'd had a better meal when Johnny had cut open cellophane wrapping and upended the contents into bowls. Hector attempted a cheese soufflé which failed to rise, before which he served some seriously poisonous pâté. Polly suspected it was meant to be chicken liver but it tasted – and certainly looked – more like putty. Finally he produced one of the stodgiest chocolate cakes Polly had ever encountered. Hector was looking utterly crestfallen.

'Leave it. It's hopeless. I'm hopeless. I do everything the cookbook tells me to and this is what happens.'

'Don't be so hard on yourself,' said Polly. 'Very few people are natural cooks and I've never been able to make an acceptable soufflé. Why do you bother cooking anyway? You love restaurants, don't you?'

'I read somewhere that women like men who cook for them.'

Polly choked to stop herself from laughing out loud.

'Anybody likes someone who cooks well for them. I don't think your cooking is going to get you anywhere.'

'I know that,' he snapped.

'To be a good cook you need to love food. Food, not restaurants. And I think you have to be caring about other people, to want to please them.'

'I want to please women.'

'Tell me about it, but you must want to please men as well. So did you cook for Luana?'

'Polly, I met Luana and took her out a few times long before I met you in Antibes.'

'But you never even mentioned her.'

'There was nothing much to mention.'

'She doesn't see it like that. She was pretty upset when you didn't call when you came back from France.'

'I didn't even call *from* France. I just sent a few postcards. It was no big deal.'

'Hector, I just can't believe this. You seem to have no consideration for other people's feelings. Is there anybody you actually care enough about to try and avoid hurting them? What about your mother?'

'She's dead.'

'I'm sorry. Were you close to her?'

He didn't answer.

'Hector?'

'What's the score between you and Johnny?'

'Score? There's no score.'

'You're not back with him?'

'Why do you ask?'

'I'm curious, that's all. I could never figure out your marriage. I've been thinking about it. I can't understand why you jumped into bed with me in France.'

'You were there.'

'Oh great. I was conveniently to hand. Don't you remember what I told you about women who go out with me because they like to be seen with me? Because I'm famous. So they can make their man jealous. You hear about trophy wives. I'm the trophy date. Is that what I was for you?'

Polly didn't know what to say. She had used him. There was no denying it. She had seen Johnny with Juanita, jumped to an instant stupid conclusion and rushed straight into Hector's arms.

'Not exactly. I mean, I didn't go out and flaunt you, Hector. We had one dinner in public. Apart from that we were on our own. But yes, if you really want to know, when I first saw you outside Eden Roc I had just seen Johnny engaged in what I thought was amorous contact with Juanita and it destroyed me. I confess I had built up in my mind the notion that Johnny had asked me down to the South of France as the beginning of a reconciliation. In fact we'd even had a wonderful dinner together. Seeing him with Juanita threw me right off track. You caught me on the rebound. You were fantastic in bed. You made me feel wonderful. You listened to me. Johnny never listens.'

'Yet you fell in love with him.'

'Yes, I did. I fell desperately in love with him. What we always forget is that you don't fall in love on paper. If a woman is asked what is her type of man, she's going to say something like "Tall, dark, he must have a sense of humour, he must be kind and considerate, he must listen to me, he must be a New Man" – whatever that is – "someone who lives close by and has a regular income and is reliable", and then they go and fall in love with a short man who treats them like shit and is probably a visiting American, to boot. A woman knows who her Mr Right is on paper but when she meets him she's usually bored to tears. It's Mr Wrong she falls in love with. Don't you always fall for Miss Wrong?'

'No.'

'Well, of course you're Superman. I forgot. I suppose you only fall in love with Superwoman.'

'No, I mean I don't think I've ever fallen in love.'

'Not ever?'

Hector shook his head. He looked miserable.

'Hector, that's so sad. Why is it, do you think?'

'I've never thought about it. Maybe it's because I do all the listening and no one ever listens to me.'

'Now you're really feeling sorry for yourself.' Polly

got up and went and sat beside him on the dreadful hulk of a sofa. 'Maybe you just don't open up to them enough. You have to let people in, let them get close to you.'

'I listen to women because I know they like it and it makes it easier to get them into bed.'

Polly flinched.

'Charming! At least you're honest and God knows, it worked with me.'

'But look where it's got me. I've been out with all these women, I've been to bed with them but I've never had a proper relationship. I wouldn't know where to begin.'

Polly was feeling rather confused. She had drunk enough for Hector's undeniable physical charms to have begun to have an effect on her. She had meant it when she told him he was fantastic in bed. He was the last man she had had sex with. She could recall what it was like with him more vividly than she could remember sex with Johnny. Poor Hector. He was so magnetically attractive that it really was a question of if he was there to be had, any woman would take him. Polly understood why he felt used. His effect on women made them behave like men, made them think only of sex without bothering to get to know him first – or indeed afterwards. His sudden vulnerability was also very attractive.

His hand was lying on the sofa between them. She took it and stroked the palm with her thumb.

'You'll find someone. I just don't think you've been looking.'

He keeled over to rest his head in her lap and she cradled him in her arms, bending down over him to bury her face in his hair. Then he had turned his face to hers and they were kissing. He moved so that he was kneeling on the sofa above her, clasping her head in his hands and she could see the shape of his erection through his jeans. She unzipped him, fondled him, let him push her down into the depths of the sofa. He pushed her skirt up to her waist and stabbed at her stomach with his penis. She raised her buttocks and eased her way swiftly out of her underwear, then shifted herself so that he could enter her.

He came almost as soon as he was inside her and she rocked him on top of her until his breathing subsided. To her surprise instead of climbing off her he began to kiss her, sucking gently on her mouth, stroking her tongue with his own, over and over until she was melting. He was still inside her. She felt him grow hard again and moved her pelvis slightly, up and down, up and down, until he matched her rhythm then overtook her. This time they came together and he shouted out loud.

Polly smiled into his shoulder. It had been fantastic in France but this was different. He had let himself go. He had surrendered to her.

Still sprawled on the sofa, he watched her as she stood up and straightened her skirt. She held out her hand and when he took it she pulled him to his feet.

'I'm going to go home. We might spoil it if I stay. Do you understand?'

He walked her out to the lift, rode down with her, holding her tight against him and looking into her eyes. When they hit the ground floor he let her go so suddenly that she nearly fell over. He stayed in the corner of the lift as she left and pressed the button to ascend before she had even reached the front door. She turned to see his long legs disappearing upwards.

It was just like it had been with Gracie Delaney, thought Hector. In France he had listened to Polly and she had succumbed to him. Tonight he had used his other trick. He had poured out his heart to her and once again she had surrendered.

Yet he hadn't meant to. He hadn't been aware of what he was doing. He had reached out to her naturally, instinctively and, he realised, he wanted to again. You'll find someone, she had told him, and she had been right.

'What is so amazing is that you just don't need sex when you're really in love,' Luana informed Polly and Carla.

It was a glorious May day, the type of day when everyone assumes summer has arrived early and throws off their clothes to bask in the sunshine only to come down with a cold a few days later.

Carla had invited Polly and Luana to lunch on what she called her terrace. In fact it was a tiny square of paved roof leading off her kitchen, big enough for several tubs filled with the herbs Carla grew for her cooking, a little round wrought-iron table and two chairs. Luana had to perch on an upturned orange box.

She was a very different Luana these days, Polly observed. Gone were the skimpy black dresses, the bandage-like skirts that had barely reached her crotch, the black leather jacket, the giant crucifix, the DMs, the stilettos, the leggings, the tank tops that exposed her navel. In their place Luana now wore crisp white cotton shirts buttoned up to the neck and dress-for-success grey or taupe classic straight-leg trouser suits. Her long black tangled hair was harnessed in a sleek pony tail hanging down her back. She was even wearing a rope of pearls.

On top of everything she had been pontificating about love ever since she arrived. Normally Polly would have felt inclined to hit her but the warm weather made Polly feel so relaxed that she let Luana witter on uninterrupted. Carla, refusing all offers of help, was in the kitchen chopping and dicing and stirring sauces, and, Polly hoped, had the good fortune to be out of earshot.

'I just don't understand why none of you told me what it was like to be in love like this. Win and I are coming together on a spiritual plane every time we meet.'

'How often do you see him?' asked Polly, bored out of her skull, 'on this spiritual plane, I mean.'

'Three or four times a week.'

'Does he snore?'

'Polly, you know we don't do it. I don't spend the night with him. That's why our love is so special. It's not cheapened in any way.'

'You mean you don't have to worry if he snores or not?'

'You're just not trying to understand. He's the first man in my life who has respected me. I have discussed all my previous affairs with him, I haven't kept anything from him. He believes we should be able to communicate on a purely platonic level before we even think about sex. He says there is so much more to me than my body. He thinks I have a really creative mind and that I haven't even begun to use it.'

'Oh, by the way,' Polly interrupted, 'those jobs you were offered, how did you get on?'

'Win thought I shouldn't rush into anything just yet.'

'I thought you were supposed to have this creative mind. Does Win think you're fulfilling your creativity by taking phone messages for Clovis?'

'Polly, why can't you just listen? I'm being creative in other ways – for Win.'

'How?'

'I'm writing his new book with him.'

'He never told me that. He's writing a book on medieval Italian food from the first century AD. It's full of recipes from Cuminatum in Ostrea et Concilla and Lus in Dentice Asso Olus Molle or, if you prefer, oysters and mixed shellfish in cumin sauce and roasted sea bream with celery purée. I gave some of them to your grandmother. God forbid, she's probably knocking them up in the kitchen as we speak. How has he got you involved?'

'Yes, I know, Polly, I'm typing it for him.'

'I see. Now that's what I call being very creative. I thought his manuscript was becoming easier to read. No wonder he doesn't want you running off to cast movies of your own.'

Carla emerged from the kitchen and climbed the four steps up to the roof terrace, struggling with a large tray over which she could barely see. She had made a mushroom risotto accompanied by a spinach salad, and she had heard every word Luana said.

'When I marry my Mauro I am supposed to be a virgin. I am a good Catholic girl. But on my wedding day I am not a virgin. I make love with my Mauro many many times before. We go into the countryside on a hot day like this and we make love on the ground, on the earth.' Carla raised her face to the sun and basked for a few moments, her eyes closed. Polly guessed she was remembering those days of early passion. The heat made Polly think of sex on the raft with Hector in the Baie des Millionaires. Carla continued: 'When we fucked – what's the matter, Luana? You think your generation invented fucking? – when we fucked before we were married, I thought my Mauro was the most exciting man in the world. I thought my life with him would be an adventure. But I was wrong. He was just a boy when we made love like that. When he became my husband and he grew into a man he became boring. Successful, yes, but boring. His sense of adventure left him. You know what happened? I think he passed it to Johnny. So what I am saying is who cares if you make love before or after you marry. You just have to make sure your man is not going to change when he does marry, that he keep his sense of adventure. Does Win have this sense of adventure?'

No, he's a pompous stuffed shirt, thought Polly, even if he is one of my clients.

'He's my hero in my adventure,' said Luana, and Polly thought she was going to throw up. To think Johnny had once worried about his little peachy girl having a reputation as a nymphomaniac.

'Polly doesn't have to worry.' Carla ladled risotto into large wide bowls, 'Johnny will always have adventures. He is too much. You need to have a rest from him sometimes.'

Polly had to admire the old lady. It was a diplomatic way of referring to the fact that her son had left Polly, not the other way around. She knew what Carla was getting at. When were Polly and Johnny going to get back together? But Polly was not going to be drawn into that discussion.

Carla leaned back in her chair.

'It's good to have you both with me. Here we are,

three generations exchanging views about our men. I am feeling very modern, very Nineties as they say.'

Luana spoiled it as Polly had known she would.

'That's not quite right, Nanna. Polly's not my mother.'

It was very telling, Polly thought, that Carla had asked her and not Edith to the lunch.

'So how is your mother? Edith, who never calls me, never comes to see me like Polly does.'

'Well, you never liked her and she knows that,' protested Luana. 'Why didn't you like her?'

'It's hard to like someone when they don't know who they are. She did not know how lucky she was with Johnny, with you,' said Carla, 'but I wish her well. She is your mother. That's why I ask: how is she?'

'Oh, you don't need to worry about her. She's having a ball. She's out every day, she's going on spending sprees. She's buying all these things.'

'What things?' Polly and Carla demanded, almost in the same voice.

'Clothes. Then there's this new house Dad's bought for her, she's buying lots of furniture for that.'

'Who told you Johnny's bought her a new house?'

'She did. And he's paying for all those clothes. He has these charge accounts for her at Harvey Nichols and everywhere and that little apartment in Roland Gardens is getting chock-a-block with shopping bags. Don't worry about Mum, she's in heaven.'

Polly looked Carla straight in the eye. So much for your plans for me and Johnny getting back together, she thought. It's just as well I've got Hector to keep me warm.

As if to crown it all, Luana announced:

'Win thinks she's a truly elegant woman. He's crazy about her and she thinks he's 100 per cent right for me.'

'Then of course he must be,' said Carla; 'no question. Now, eat your risotto before it gets cold.'

'Don't eat too much,' said Polly drily, 'or else you won't be able to get into your virginal white wedding dress.'

'Oh, I've got tons of time,' said Luana, totally missing the irony. 'He hasn't even asked me to marry him yet.'

Polly had begun to read scripts for Hector. He was inundated with them following the success of *Mr Wrong* and Polly noticed he never looked at them but left them lying around his apartment. He was rather shamefaced when she tackled him about it.

'I just can't stand reading the bloody things. I never got the hang of it. I just leave it to my agent to recommend something but lately there have been so many he's just been sending them on. I'd better have a word with him.'

It wasn't until a script arrived heralded by a frantic message from Hector's agent on the answering machine that Polly began to understand the problem.

'Hec, are you there? OK, you're not. Listen, I'm sending over a script this afternoon and I've fixed a meeting tomorrow with the director. Hec, this man is a major player in Hollywood. We're bypassing casting directors on this one. This is your big chance. You're up for the part of the brother. Call me when you've read it.'

'What does he mean, this is my big chance? That's what he always says. Doesn't he realise I've made it?'

Polly said nothing. The director was a huge name. Surely Hector would take the part seriously.

Polly took the script from him and read it in just over an hour. Then she talked him through the part as well as the overall story. She read a few scenes with him. He met with the director. He didn't get the part but as he and Polly had agreed before the meeting, he wasn't right for it. His agent had been blinded by the thought of his client working with such a big name.

From then on Polly read Hector's scripts for him and gave him advice. She was still lying in his bed on Saturday morning finishing a script when he went out to get the papers.

'Bring me a *Telegraph* and an *Independent*,' she yelled after him. She heard his front door bang and settled down to finish the script. After a while she grew restless. She looked around at the austere sleek lines of Hector's bedroom, the ubiquitous grey, wall-to-wall cupboards, the total absence of Hector's possessions negating the stamp of an individual personality. How could she possibly work here even if it was just reading a script in bed? It was a beautiful summer's morning and she could have gone out on to the terrace overlooking the Thames but Hector's apartment was on the ninth floor and Polly was neurotic about heights. She thought with affection of the perpetual chaos spread across her trestle tables in her conservatory, leading safely out to the garden. Everyone always asked her how on earth she knew where anything was. The answer to that was simple. She knew exactly where everything was because she could see it all laid out before her.

While she put everything on display Hector hid it all

away, and not just his possessions either. Their affair was a private one. Once when she took him to a signing session for one of her authors in a bookshop, Polly witnessed the effect he had on the public. His sudden appearance had rendered them first self-conscious, trying not to look at him, then, when someone had approached him, the rest had followed in a wild stampede to gather round him. Polly had found herself shut out to the extent that no one even realised she was with Hector. They had been seeing each other for nearly two months now but from that day she had avoided going out with him in public, which was just as well for it meant that neither Johnny nor Luana knew about their relationship.

At home alone with him it was hard to reconcile the insecure man who was becoming increasingly dependent on her with the public Hector idolised by his adoring fans. He may be lithe, he may move with animal grace, thought Polly, his bearing may be aristocratic even, but it's all part of his outer casing. The Hector I am beginning to know is little more than a clockwork toy who's been wound up and pointed in the right direction for fifteen years and now his mechanism is getting cranky and he doesn't know what to do.

Hector threw the newspaper at her from the bedroom door and it landed on her stomach. She heard the bathroom door slam and the sound of the shower running. Hector never showered until after they had made love and he always made love to her in the morning when they spent the night together. Something must be wrong.

She unfolded the paper and cursed him. He'd brought her the *Mail*. Then she saw why. Down in the right-hand corner of the front page was a grainy picture of an old man, dishevelled with a long beard, slumped against a wall and clutching a bottle in a brown bag. Even though the picture was blurred it was possible to see the abject misery on the man's face. But it wasn't the picture that caught Polly's eye. It was the headline above it:

CONWAY'S FATHER A DOWN AND OUT DRUNK

Shaking, she read the text below.

Movie idol Hector O'Neill's father is a down and out drunk who does not even know where his son is. A tramp who haunts the slum areas of the Pennsylvania town where O'Neill allegedly grew up (although he claims to have hailed from Boston) has been identified by journalist Joan Brock, biographer of Hector O'Neill, as Jimmy Maguire, O'Neill's father.

Arthur Allen-Jones, Publishing Director at Hollywood House who are bringing out the biography of O'Neill, said Joan Brock had confirmed she had tracked down O'Neill's father.

'She was very excited about her discovery,' said Allen-Jones. 'She had a lead which took her to a small defunct mining town in Pennsylvania where she met this man called Jimmy Maguire whom a woman friend of Hector O'Neill's from his early days in London identified as being his father. Maguire didn't recognise his son when shown a photograph of the actor. He told Joan Brock he had gone to fight in Vietnam and when he returned he found his wife and son had fled. He never saw them again.

'The cheap bitch!' shouted Hector. He had a towel wrapped around his waist.

'Who?'

'Joan bloody Brock! Where did she get hold of this stuff? No one knows my father is called Jimmy Maguire. Nobody back home knows I've changed my name. I was a kid when I came over here. My mother's dead. Tony's parents are dead. No one knows who I am•or where I came from.'

'Someone must have known,' Polly chatted on while trying to come to terms with the fact that from what Hector was saying, this miserable creature in the picture really was his father. 'They mention a woman from your early days in London who identified your father.'

'Gracie. Has to be. But Gracie could never be a bitch. It was that other prune mouth, that shitty little bundle of bones Joan Brock who turned on me. She must have wormed it out of Gracie somehow.'

'This man really is your father?'

'Everyone has one, Polly. Yours was a lord of the manor and mine's a drunken bum. You want to make something of it?'

'You know I didn't mean it like that. It's just you've never spoken about your father. You said your mother was dead and I suppose I assumed your father was too.'

'For all I knew he was.'

'How did you lose touch with him like that?'

'Read the piece. He went off to Vietnam.'

'But he came back. Where were you?'

'My mother ran off with someone else while he was away. An Englishman. That's how I wound up in England.'

'But didn't your father contact you when he got back from Vietnam?'

'He didn't know where we were. My mother never let him know. She even let me believe he'd been killed over there.'

387

'And this is the first time you've found out that he might still be alive?'

'More or less.'

'More or less. What does that mean?'

'It means I don't want to talk about it. It means I was born in a place I wanted to forget about. I loved my father, Polly. I know that now. I still have this one picture of him in my mind. He's coming home from the steelworks, he's coming over the hill with his buddies and he's got his lunchbox under his arm and he's laughing and bullshitting with them and he's happy. It was the only world he knew before Vietnam. My mother was the bitch. She left him and then she left me. But she was right. She had to survive. My father was a loser. Underneath I guess I'm still my father's son. But my mother made sure I became as much like her as possible. Keep an eye out for the main chance and grab hold of it.'

'But deep down you think you're probably like your father. Do you remember anything about him at all, apart from this picture you have of him?'

'He never spoke to women. He was scared of women.'

'But he liked them?'

'I never asked.'

Scared of women. Scared of getting close to them. That sounded like the Hector she was beginning to get to know.

He had picked up the phone and was dialling, punching the numbers angrily.

'Joan? You're a fucking bitch, you know that? Yeah, of course I've seen it, why else do you think I'm calling you? What? I don't care who told them. So what if it was Artie whatsisface. It was a shitty thing for him to do,

388

I agree. Shitty for me not for you. He knows what he's doing. By planting this in the press way ahead of publication, he knows damn well it's going to make your book sell like crazy.'

When did he get to know Joan? thought Polly listening. When she interviewed him for that profile, of course, but why had Joan never talked about that?

'Yes, excuse me, you are a bitch. You know why? Because you had to go and put all that crap about my father in your book in the first place. How else would Artie have found out? That was a real petty way to get back at me, not that you had any reason. What did I ever do to you? What? It was over, Joan. Three days! Christ! It was never anything serious. Like I said, we're both adults. It wasn't a question of me not wanting to be with you any more. A few nights together isn't being together. Wise up. Get a life.'

He put down the phone and Polly understood why Joan hadn't been returning her calls. Before Polly there had been Luana. And before Luana – or maybe even since – there had been Joan. Well, for once she seemed to have got the better of Joan in the man department. And why not, for heaven's sake? Suddenly Polly was seething. All these years Joan had been putting her down for not trying hard enough, making her feel she was badly groomed and too big when in fact she'd done just fine for herself. What's more she'd worn far better than Joan as the years had gone by. Johnny had always maintained Joan was jealous of her and for the first time Polly was inclined to believe him.

'By the way, this script's crap.' Polly threw it across the bed and got up to get dressed. 'You tell Joan to get a life, Hector. Don't think it's about time you got one of your own?'

For some time Polly had been feeling guilty about the fact that since her affair with Hector had blossomed she had been neglecting her authors. She had taken to reading film scripts rather than books in the evening and Mrs Flowers had begun to make rather a show of placing a pile of manuscripts in front of her each morning and asking:

'You haven't forgotten about these, have you, Mrs de Soto?'

When she first started her own agency Polly had fully intended only to take on those authors she liked, but she soon realised this was being naive. Yet she was constantly amazed at the way her least favourite authors managed to know exactly when she was below par and chose that time to call her *en masse*. There was one particular first-time woman author of a middlebrow novel which, of course, she thought of as literary, who whined daily down the line into Polly's ear.

'Poll-eee, I just don't think my readers will like this cover. It's too downmarket. It's not what they're expecting. They'll be disappointed.'

Polly was mystified as to how anyone who had not yet been published could actually have any readers.

Another arrogant young male writer seduced his publicist in a hotel room in Manchester in the middle of his author tour but by the time they'd reached Edinburgh he'd gone off her. The publicist, having already telephoned her fiancé in London to break off her engagement, was now left high and dry and in floods of tears and refused to continue the tour. The publishers insisted that Polly sort her author out.

'What exactly do you want me to do?' Polly asked the hysterical editor in London. 'Go up there and tuck them both up in bed?'

'He should never have slept with our publicist in the first place. So unprofessional.'

'It's a bit late to say that now,' countered Polly reasonably. 'Besides, haven't you got it the wrong way round? What was she doing jumping into bed with him if she had a fiancé waiting for her in London?'

'But she won't work with him any more and we might lose him to another house,' wailed the editor.

'Then lose your publicist and keep your author.'

Zoë Nichols was a breath of fresh air, calling as she did with updates of her sightings of Aroma Ross.

'I was sitting there the other day in her hotel suite and she suddenly whips up her tank top and shoves her stomach in my face and she goes: "D'you like it?" Polly, I swear, I didn't know what to do. She's got the world's flattest most beautiful stomach. Why did she need my approval? Then I noticed this little diamond tucked in her tummy button and all I could think of was, "Ow, that must have hurt!" '

From time to time Polly had asked herself whether it was a good idea to have become so friendly with one of her clients. Then she would see Zoë for lunch or supper and have such a good time, and come away feeling so uplifted by Zoë's constant praise for her efforts, that she always banished her qualms. The only area where they skirted around each other, never actually coming to blows but never really saying what they felt in order to avoid just that, was the subject of men and relationships. Polly had confided in Zoë about Hector and waited for Zoë's endorsement of the affair. After all, Zoë had not been very encouraging about Polly's chances of getting back with Johnny. But Zoë seemed to see danger in any relationship with a man. She intimated that she had been blown up in too many emotional minefields and that now she valued her serenity at any cost, even if it meant a life devoid of excitement. However much Polly tried to persuade her that that was exactly how she, Polly, had felt after Johnny had left, and that things changed in time, Zoë would not be moved.

One client whose personal relationship did become a little too close for comfort was Winthrop Hamilton. Because he was so important in Luana's life Polly treated him with kid gloves and dreaded the day when any trouble might arise. Inevitably it did.

Winthrop had had a disastrous time with his last publishers. The work in question, a cookbook divided into four seasonal sections, had had a highly inexperienced copy-editor who had managed to place spring menus in the winter section and summer menus in the spring section throughout the book. Worse, she had mislaid several captions for the photographer and had been too terrified to own up to Winthrop and ask him to replace them. Instead she had looked at each photograph and taken a wild, sometimes highly imaginative guess at what it might be. Thus Winthrop's famous chocolate mousse found itself described as a pheasant terrine. Polly thought she had solved the problem by moving him to another publisher for his new book on medieval Italian food.

She hadn't. But through no fault of the publisher.

His editor rang in a panic.

'Polly, he's delivered the book. It's truly divine as far as it goes but we can't find the basic recipe section anywhere.'

'The what?'

'In each recipe Winthrop instructs us to "use the basic fresh pasta dough as described on page whatever in the section at the end of the book" or the basic dressing on page this or the basic bread recipe on page that. He keeps referring to them all the way through but he's gone and left them out. The book doesn't have a centre. Without this missing section it simply doesn't work.'

'And I suppose it was due at the printer yesterday. Have you tried asking Win for it?' Polly tried to be patient.

'Of course we have. It's not as simple as that. He's gone away to stay with some friends in Suffolk and they don't have a phone.'

'Well do you have an address?'

'Yes but by the time we write to him . . . we need the text today.'

'Give me the address. I'll drive there this afternoon and doorstep him till he hands it to me or comes back to London to find it.'

It was a sun-drenched August day. Perfect for a drive to the country. Polly called Luana.

'Suffolk? I thought he'd gone to Wiltshire. Oh I know, he's gone to see that sweet couple we went to stay with.'

'Without you?' Polly was guarded but curious.

'I'm frantic. I couldn't get away. Anyway he never

takes me to Wiltshire. It's his bolthole. I'm assuming I'll get to see it when we're . . . anyway. I suppose he changed his mind at the last minute. He only went today. I expect he'll ring me tonight and tell me where he is.'

'I can't wait that long,' said Polly and explained why. 'Can you let me into his Chelsea house so I can have a peek there before driving all the way to Suffolk.'

'Oh, I couldn't. He'd hate anyone going through his things. He's very particular like that. I'm not allowed to touch anything. Besides, I don't have a key.'

Polly thought it very odd that Winthrop seemed to shut Luana out of so much of his life but since Luana didn't seem particularly worried, Polly didn't comment.

The drive to East Anglia gave her time to think. What to do about Hector? Her anger about his affair with Joan had enabled her to view him in a more detached light. As she drove – much too fast – through the flat countryside towards Newmarket she embarked upon a mental checklist for and against him. He was breathtakingly handsome and sophisticated on the outside but, as she was discovering, a rather childlike character underneath. He had no real taste. It had dawned on Polly rather belatedly that the beautiful house that had so impressed her on the boulevard du Cap had not been Hector's. He had rented it and the stunning interior decoration that came with it. As a companion he had no real depth, his conversation was becoming rather one note and there were times, increasingly, when he bored her. For example, he never made her laugh. True, he was terrific in bed but he had never heard of the concept of fidelity. He had been an attentive listener in the past and that had indeed been flattering but, as she had become aware, that was part of his overall seduction plan. Now he was opening up to her, the tables had turned and she listened to him but the more she listened the less interested she became. Poor Hector. It seemed the one thing he had been intelligent enough to understand was that he was the perfect trophy lover. He looked good but it was best to leave it at that.

Yet somehow he was good for her. He had given her confidence to the extent that she was the one now pulling the strings in the relationship. She could walk away from it at any time, and as she realised that she also realised that she was not remotely in love with him.

On arriving at the village where Win was staying Polly checked the address. It was nowhere near where Luana said they had gone for the weekend. The house turned out to be a rose-washed timber cottage set at right angles to the road. Polly parked up a lane beside it next to a barn and walked around the house to the little porch.

The man who answered the door was in his early twenties and very neatly dressed in a pale green Lacoste shirt and white jeans. He was medium height and of very slender build with thin arms and legs. His hair was short at the back and parted in the middle with two curled locks caressing his temples. His skin was smooth like a baby's and lightly pink from the sun. He peeped – rather than peered – at Polly through round granny spectacles.

'Can I help you?'

He was American.

'Gracious,' said Polly, a little thrown, 'have I come to the right place? I'm looking for someone called Winthrop Hamilton.'

The young man's face lit up.

'Right place. You missed him. He left about an hour ago. He had a bit of a crisis on. He delivered his book to his publishers and he suddenly remembered he hadn't given them some of the text. He's gone back to London for the night to sort it out.'

'Great. I've come all the way to Suffolk to ask him to do just that. Well, at least it'll all be sorted out. Could I just use your phone to call his publishers and put their mind at rest? I'm Polly de Soto, his agent, by the way. Oh, of course, you don't have a phone here, do you?'

The preppy young man looked surprised.

'Sure. There's a phone. Why wouldn't there be? I'm Jed Wharton. Good to meet you. Win's talked about you. Come on through and make your call.'

It was a typical ultra-English country cottage with an inglenook fireplace and beams. The ceilings were too low in places for Jed to stand up. Large floral chintzes covered the sofas either side of the fireplace and the long velvet curtains were gathered up by tassled cord tiebacks. The roses in a circular glass bowl were beautifully arranged.

'Sit here, and there's the phone. Coffee? A drink? I've just made some lemonade.'

Polly nodded 'yes please' while she dialled. As she spoke to Win's editor she studied the photographs in silver frames either side of the rose bowl. They were both of Win with Jed on a beach. In one Win had his arm slung round Jed's shoulders.

'Win apparently left word that you weren't on the phone,' Polly told Jed when he returned with a pitcher of lemonade.

'Can't imagine why he would do that unless it was just to work-related people so he wouldn't be bothered.'

Polly was about to say that he hadn't even told his girlfriend but something stopped her.

'Are you and Win related?' She picked up one of the photographs. 'His mother's American, isn't she?'

'We met in America,' said Jed, 'but we're not related.'

'This is a sweet little cottage. Do you own it or have you rented it for the summer?'

Jed was like a bewildered marionette, raising his arms and letting them fall and shaking his head at the same time.

'I don't get it. Where did you get the idea that this is my place? It's Win's. He's rented it.'

'What on earth for?' Polly was so surprised she forgot to be polite. 'He has a house in London and a place in the country in Wiltshire.'

'So we can be together.'

'Are you working with him on a new project? Something I should know about? Maybe I could help.'

'The only thing you should know, and I'm sorry to drop it in your lap like this since I guess it might come as a shock, is that Win and I are lovers.'

When Polly didn't say anything he went on.

'It's so typical of Win to keep me a secret. As I'm sure you know, he's one of these people who keep their life totally compartmentalised. Lots of people do, but if you're part of that life it can be pretty hurtful. I've known him since I was at Yale. We met in the Hamptons when he was summering with his mom. I was there with my parents. We went off to Fire Island together and after that we met in New York. Frequently. I know nothing about his life in England but from your shocked reaction it looks as if he hasn't even come out. When I told him I was going to come to England for the summer he straight away rented this cottage and installed me here. I don't even get to come to London.'

'He's seeing my stepdaughter in London.'

'How cute. He dates girls, especially when his mother's around. He has these fantasies about getting married but he never goes through with it. How do you think it makes me feel?'

Polly had had enough. She wanted to get out of this

snug little hidey-hole and away from Win's secret life and this polite young man who looked as if he might burst into tears at any second.

'I can imagine how it makes you feel and I'm sorry. If Win hadn't forgotten to include those pages in his book we would probably never have met. Maybe it was meant to happen. Will you say something to him about my coming here?'

'You know I think I will. I've had enough of being shunted into the background.'

'You do that, Jed, because I'm going to tell my stepdaughter. I have to. Who knows, maybe you'll have Win all to yourself from now on in a totally decompartmentalised world.'

'Yes, but will I like it?'

Polly laughed. She rather liked this young man. He'd obviously had to put up with a lot and he still had a glimmer of a sense of humour, which was more than she could say about Win.

But how was she going to tell Luana?

Luana took it very badly indeed and only rallied slightly when Johnny offered to take her to Paris for the French première of *Mr Wrong* to cheer her up. Polly thought fondly how kind Johnny could be sometimes. She imagined him in Paris embarrassing Luana by insisting on speaking his execrable French. Johnny had to be the only Italian who spoke French with the worst possible English accent. He began every sentence with the word 'Alors' on which he never failed to sound the 's'.

But it wasn't his French that let him down. Luana called Polly as soon as she got back.

'I had the worst time,' she wailed down the line, 'the worst! Dad was just awful.'

'But why?'

'First off he was in a foul mood because Hector pulled out of the trip and the French were really pissed at him and took it out on Dad.'

Polly opened her mouth to spring to Hector's defence and explain that the news about his father had sent him into a terrible depression and remembered just in time that Luana didn't know she was seeing Hector.

'Yes, I can imagine that must have been a bit awkward. Then what happened?'

'Well, it wasn't so much what happened, it was more that this little jaunt was supposed to be about cheering me up and Dad did nothing but talk about himself. I tried to talk about how I was feeling but he just doesn't listen. It's like he took me over there so he could tell me about his problems.'

'What are his problems?' Poor Luana. At least Hector listened, if for all the wrong reasons.

'The Big Question is what's he going to do next. How is he going to follow *Mr Wrong*? Apparently Juanita doesn't have a clue about scripts and keeps getting excited about these real pieces of shit. Dad's words. And she won't agree to hiring a script editor so he's having to plough through all this stuff himself. Do you know what, Polly? I don't think Dad knows a good script when he sees one either. Do you remember *The Wolf One*?'

'He told me you were crazy about that idea.'

'Oh, please! No, the truth is Dad needs someone like you. He kept going on and on about you, asking me how often I saw you, how did I think you were, did I know if you were seeing anyone? I mean I adore you, Polly, but I did get a bit sick of listening to him go on about you. It was weird. Maybe he wants you back.'

'As a wife or a script reader?' laughed Polly. Because if it was the latter she already had a job.

Polly was secretly relieved when Hector announced he was making a trip to Pennsylvania to see his father. Familiarity was breeding far too much contempt. Sex with Hector gave her an extraordinary energy and sense of well-being but beyond that he was beginning to drive her insane.

Yet she was touched by his excitement at being reunited with his father.

'There was always something missing from my success all the way down the line and that was that I didn't have anyone to share it with. I didn't have my mother and father to be proud of what I'd done. Now I have you but you can understand, can't you, what it's going to be like to sit down with my dad and tell him everything. I can barely remember that place. I'm prepared for it to be a real dump even though they closed the steelworks, but I'm going to do right by my dad now I know he's alive.'

'Have you let anyone know you're coming? It's going to be something of a shock for him to see you after all these years.'

'I've called Gracie. Gracie Delaney, you know, my friend who went back to Philadelphia. She's been looking out for him, going over there whenever she can.'

'But why?' Polly didn't get it.

'Search me. Guess some people are like that.' But Hector wouldn't look her in the eye. 'All I need to know, Polly, is that you'll be waiting for me when I get back.'

'Where else am I going to be? Zoë's book's about to be published. And Mrs Flowers'. I'm not going anywhere.'

'You just don't get it, do you? Are you doing it deliberately? I'm trying to tell you that I love you and I

400

want you to be here for me when I get back. I know you're really busy at the moment otherwise I'd ask you to come with me. I'm scared shitless at the thought of going back, don't you see? I ought to be going home like a conquering hero, the hometown boy who made good. Instead all anyone's going to be thinking is how come he never looked after his dad? I don't even sound American any more. It's as if I never existed there.'

He looked terrible. Polly knew he had been agonising over his father ever since Artie Allen-Jones' leak to the press of the contents of Joan's book but he had refused to talk to her about it. Now he was telling her – probably the first time he had told anyone – that he loved her. He needed her. Maybe that was what it was all about: mutual needing. Filling a gap in the other person's life. Maybe she was expecting too much of him. Maybe it was her fault, not his, that she had been growing bored with him. He was younger than she was. She always forgot that. Perhaps now she knew how insecure he was inside she could work at building his confidence. Maybe it was her fault that he seemed one-dimensional. She just hadn't been trying hard enough with him. She had met him as a glamorous movie star, reacted to him on the rebound as a sensational lover, been disappointed that his glamour was only skin deep and now, at a traumatic time in his life when he was trying to show her the man underneath, her response was to be irritated. She was being unfair. It wasn't even as if there was anyone else offering her a better deal.

She drove him out to the airport, stood proudly to one side as he signed a mass of autographs and then clung to him in the First-Class lounge.

'Of course I'll be here when you get back. Call me as soon as you can and let me know what's happening.'

401

He went through the gate and turned back to wave at her but all she could see was the figure audiences all over the world saw on screen. Someone so handsome it was hard to imagine he could be real.

He didn't call.

For the first few days Polly didn't worry. She hadn't even asked him for a number, so sure had she been that he would call her. When a week had gone by and she still had no word she called his agent, who was the only person who knew of their relationship.

'Yeah, I spoke to him. He's fine. Worked out exactly as we planned.'

'What do you mean?' asked Polly.

'When this whole thing broke about his father, I got him together with his publicist and we said Hec, you have to go out there, be reunited with the man. He didn't want to at all, said, "What's the point? My father doesn't even know me" and all that crap, but when I explained to him what a good publicity story it would make, how we'd get the press there and turn the whole thing to his advantage, get his father all cleaned up, show Hec with his arm around him, buying him a new house, all that stuff, he loved it. Hec's no fool. He knows that Brock woman's raking up all kinds of dirt about him and if he can show her stories to be crap before the book's even come out then he's ahead of her game. She can say anything about him and he'll be right there proving her wrong. That Allen-Jones character played right into our hands.'

Polly read the stories in the papers the following week. It was exactly as the publicist had predicted. There was Hector with his arm round his father who had indeed been shaved and fitted out with suitable clothing. The older man looked bewildered, Polly noted, as well he might. There was even a snapshot of father and son taken when Hector was barely five years old with the steelworks looming in the background.

Hector talked of his shame in lying about his background by pretending that he came from Boston. He expounded on his theory that everyone had to face up to who they really were at some time in their life and his time had come. Columns of syrupy prose turned Polly's stomach as she remembered that she had actually felt sorry for Hector.

What most astounded Polly was the revelation that he had been reunited not only with his father but also with his childhood sweetheart, Gracie Delaney. Gracie, now a lonely divorcee, had apparently been overjoyed when Hector had come home and had welcomed him with open arms. The couple were said to be talking seriously about their future.

Another publicity stunt, wondered Polly, or should someone warn this woman to stay away from Hector? No, let her learn from experience. We all need a Mr Wrong – if only to show us who is Mr Right.

Polly was dreaming about tape recorders when she was awakened at two in the morning by the sound of her front doorbell blasting persistently through the house.

She had been at Zoë's publication party, or rather Aroma Ross's. Zoë had needed her support. She was having a hard time controlling her temper with the book's publishers, who had released some cock and bull story to the press about Aroma having dictated the novel on to tapes which had then been transcribed by Zoë into the book.

'Yes, Aroma had a little tape recorder. Yes, she did say she would be recording stuff for me on transatlantic flights and who knows, maybe she did, but I have never received a single tape from her. Aroma's so out of it half the time she probably believes she really has done it all herself via tapes. What irritates me is that the publishers can't keep their story straight. One minute they announce I'm writing it with Aroma, the next minute there's no mention of me whatsoever, I feel really tempted to start stirring it up by . . .'

Polly had calmed her down and led her away from the party. She had seen this coming. Zoë wouldn't regret it in the long run once the royalties started rolling in. The publishers had, after all, done a great job marketing the book. She had had enormous fun doing the research and writing it. She bore no grudge against Aroma and her agent, whom she had liked. It was the publishers' lack of attention to the ghostly details that had understandably enraged her. Either she was a ghost or she wasn't. The pre-publication press had been snide and nasty and it looked like poor Zoë was in for plenty of flak without any credit.

Besides, Polly felt bound by guilt to be especially mindful of Zoë's needs. Hadn't Zoë warned her that men were not worth the trouble they caused? And hadn't she been proved right by Hector's defection? From now on Polly resolved to listen to Zoë and take all men with a fistful of salt.

A rain of pebbles clattered against her window.

Johnny was standing in the street with his long black coat over his pyjamas, his baseball cap on his head back to front as usual, and Zutty in his arms. Half asleep, Polly opened the window and instantly regretted it.

'Polly, let me in. Please.'

'Fuck it, Johnny. I am not having Zutty at this hour. Go home and call me in the morning.'

She slammed the window shut. No sooner was she back under the covers than the pebbles started again. Then the doorbell. Then more pebbles. She could hear Johnny through the closed window, shouting away in the street.

'Christ's sake, Polly. It's an emergency. You have to let me in. It's Joan. She's had an accident.'

She gave him a stiff whisky and tried to prise Zutty from his arms without success.

'Johnny, you can't drink and hold Zutty. Hand him over and I'll give him something to eat.'

'He's all I've got,' she heard him mumble. Who left whom? went through her mind but she kept it to herself.

'So what's happened to Joan? You wake me up in the middle of the night. It'd better be good.'

'She's dead, Pol. She was on the motorway driving back from doing an interview somewhere and they think she must have run out of petrol. They found her car with an empty tank by the side of the road. Silly cow must have been trying to flag down a passing car in the middle of the road by the looks of things. She got hit. Strawberry jam all over the M6.'

'Johnny!' Polly was horrified.

'Sorry, Pol. I wasn't her number one fan but I shouldn't be so flippant. Was she still your best friend?'

'I don't really know,' said Polly, too shocked for tears.

'You haven't even asked how I know. The police couldn't find a next of kin. She didn't have an address book on her, just one of those personal organisers and they didn't know how to work it so they came up with the idea of calling some chap called Artie Allen-Jones because they'd seen his name in the papers quoting her about Hector's father. So anyway he goes and tells them no, you don't want to talk to me, you want to talk to the agent, Polly de Soto. So they get your office number and there's just a machine and then they check out Enquiries and would you believe there's only one other De Soto in the book besides me and his initial is E so they call the poor bugger first and wake him up, then they try me, "J", and I say yes, I'm Polly de Soto's husband – well, I am, Pol, don't look at me like that –

and they ask me if I knew a Miss Joan Brock and I suss what's happened right away by the "knew" and ask if I can be the one to break the news to you. I didn't think you'd like the police turning up on your doorstep.'

'Thank you, Johnny.'

'There's a bit more to it than you think.'

'Bit more to what?'

'Someone has to identify the body.'

'*No*! I couldn't, not if she's all, like you said . . .'

'Would you like me to do it?'

'Johnny, could you? Would they let you?'

'I think they would.'

'Could you bear it? It's probably a gruesome task.'

'It is.'

'You mean you've had to do it before?'

'In a way.'

'Who with?'

'Edith.'

'Edith's *dead*! Christ, Johnny, why didn't you ever tell me? Why didn't Luana tell me?'

'Take it easy. She's not dead. It was all a mistake that happened years ago. The police in Cornwall rang me. Don't bloody know why. I'm not her husband but she had me down as her next of kin. They said she'd taken an overdose but, typical Edith, apparently she'd got herself all dolled up in one of her long white nighties and taken herself out to die some kind of idiotic pagan ritual death lying on the grass on the top of the cliffs. So, of course someone saw her and she was taken to hospital. They thought she was going to pop her clogs and called me. I hurtled all the way down there and it was like something out of *Casualty*. They come running straight at me as soon as I walk through the door, tell me my wife has died, how they did all they could for her, etc. etc. and would I please identify her for them. I'm marched into this cordoned-off cubicle and there's this total stranger lying on a gurney all mangled to pieces. But her face is intact and it's not Edith's. They made a right cock-up.'

'But Edith did take an overdose?'

'She did.'

'Was she depressed?'

'How should I know?'

'Don't be so defensive, Johnny. What I mean was, did she have a history of depression?'

Now was his chance to tell her about Edith.

'Polly, Edith was stark raving bonkers. I never told you before because, frankly, I didn't think it was any of your business. I thought I ought to be the one to deal with her, I could take care of everything. I was playing what Luana calls my all-embracing Italian father role to the hilt, trying to be a father to Edith as well as to her. I didn't want anyone else getting in on the act. Besides, I thought you'd think I was heartless for leaving her. Except I didn't leave her. That was the whole problem. *She* left and somehow I just couldn't bring myself to go and get her back. I knew someone ought to look after her. I thought I could handle it by flitting down there every now and again and, yes, lying to you about it. But I was wrong, I realise that now. I knew Luana shouldn't spend too much time with her, that it was wrong for her to see Edith how she was. That's why I let her come and live with us. And then you had to go and be successful and I kept thinking that's made it even worse for Edith. She never could do anything, couldn't keep a job down. Poor Edith! Out on the cliffs in her nightie. You were always a T-shirt-to-bed girl. Still are, I see. Edith wore these long diaphanous things with bits of lace all over

408

the shop. She put flowers in her hair to go to bed, for Christ's sake, said she could commune with nature while she slept. Fine for her but I was always waking up with a bloody dandelion in my ear or a cornflower in my mouth.'

Polly let him ramble on. It all came pouring out and she pretended she was hearing it for the first time.

'She looked pretty glamorous to me at the première. Have you been seeing a lot of her since she moved back to London?'

'As little as possible. Now it looks as if I'm going to have to do something serious about her.'

'What do you mean?'

'She's gone completely over the edge. It's all the more frightening because when you see her she appears perfectly normal but she's not. She's going – there's no other word for it – insane. She's got these crazy delusions. She thinks she's very rich, fabulously rich. She's under the illusion that I'm giving her money, loads of it. She goes into shops and buys clothes that cost a fortune. We're talking thousands of pounds' worth. She tells people I've bought her a new house and she's running round London shopping for that. Her cheques are bouncing all over the place and because she keeps on citing my name, I've had a visit from the police. She's going to be declared bankrupt. That's a given. I'm not responsible for her financially but what can I do? I can't let her starve. Her parents are dead. She won't go and see a doctor, any kind of doctor. The awful thing is that she thinks she's totally cured and she's not. She's dangerously ill. Several people have told me she's going to have to be committed but if she is, who's going to commit her?'

He looked so forlorn sitting there on the sofa in his

pyjamas. He was so untogether, so un-looked-after. Yet here he was taking responsibility for identifying Joan and coping with the demented Edith. He might never listen but no one could accuse Johnny of being unkind. She felt a rush of affection for him and sat down beside him, wrapping her arm around his shoulder, trying to give him a comforting hug. To her amazement, he turned his face into her chest and began to sob.

'Blubbing again, Johnny?' she whispered softly.

'I'm not blubbing,' he insisted, sniffing and snorting into her neck.

'No, of course you're not,' she smiled into the darkness above his head.

'I came round here to comfort you about Joan and here you are mopping me up.' He raised his head and looked up at her. Their lips were almost touching. She lowered her head. He opened his mouth.

She had never forgotten Johnny's kisses. Long melting kisses that went on for ever until everything else was obliterated from her mind.

'I have to go,' he murmured. 'Wish I didn't.'

She risked the question she'd always wanted to ask. 'Did you love Edith, Johnny?'

He put his baseball cap back on his head, buttoned up his overcoat, told Zutty to 'Stay here and look after Pol', then he laid his head briefly on Polly's shoulder.

'Not like I love you, Pol, but yes, once, I must have done.'

He was out of the door before it hit her.

He'd said, 'Not like I love you.'

Very present tense.

Polly had witnessed authors come unstuck when their book was published. The sheer anti-climax of it all was often enough to pitch them into the depths of gloom. For weeks there would be the publishers' hype and anticipation of sales, the publicity, the celebration party and then suddenly the book was out there in the shops and after all the fuss the author had to go home and begin the agonising wait to see what happened to it. And these were the authors who were fêted by their publishers and the press. Some authors just sat at home.

Mrs Flowers' publication went to her head. Literally. She rushed out to the hairdresser's on the day of her publication dinner and returned with a disgusting blue rinse which looked like a cotton wool special effects halo on top of her head.

The dinner given by Odeon Books at Christopher's restaurant in Covent Garden for the publication of *Christopher* the novel was a rather grand affair with several rival, self-important literary editors showing off to each other and being rather patronising to the author. As a result Mrs Flowers grew nervous and drank so much that Polly had to slip her away before the end of the dinner.

In addition the press opted to focus on the story of a staid older woman writing about sex.

But *Christopher* sold out of its first printing in less than a week, and kept going. Mrs Flowers booked herself a cruise.

At any other time Polly would have been overjoyed but everything was clouded by Joan's death. To Polly's amazement she learned that Joan had left her her house. When she went there for the first time since Joan's death and sat on her high brass bed – Joan had had to use library steps to climb into it – and stared at her walk-in closet, Polly wept. The doors were open and Joan's immaculate size 8 suits and dresses hung in a row like toy soldiers. Underneath stood a line of tiny high-heeled shoes with toes pointing inwards almost as if Joan were still standing in them.

Overflowing ashtrays covered every surface, severely out of kilter with the stultifying neatness everywhere else. Polly could smell the smoke, could hear Joan's husky voice demanding fiercely: 'Well? Any sex? Any cheques?'

On Joan's desk beside her Apple Mac, downstairs in her office, Polly found a typescript. A fax was attached to it.

> Dear Joan,
> Can we call it a day? I'm off to France
> to begin filming in a month or so. It
> was fun but it was really only a fling.
> Let's be adults and put it behind us as a
> terrific memory.
>
> Hector

Not even 'love, Hector.'

The book – as far as it went – was vicious. Polly had assumed it would be a hatchet job but she was not prepared for the sheer vitriol that had dripped from Joan's long red nails as she tapped away at the keys of her computer.

The real revelation was from Gracie Delaney, the alleged childhood sweetheart, whom Hector had not met until he was grown up and living in London. The most damaging section was where Gracie recalled how she had been asked by Hector to go and find his father, how she had written to Hector begging him to do something about the washed-up Vietnam vet, and how Hector had ignored her pleas.

Polly wondered what the real story was about the reunion between Hector and Gracie. There was one scenario in her head that would not go away. Hector, knowing that Gracie must have told Joan everything, had gone all out to charm his way back into her life so that they could present a united front to the world when the book came out and deny everything Joan had written.

The book was unfinished. Even if it were completed by someone else and published it could only hurt poor Gracie Delaney, whoever she was. And try as she might, Polly found she didn't really want to hurt Hector with it either. She was an adult. She had walked into her affair with Hector with her eyes wide open and she could not deny that she had derived a fair amount of enjoyment from it.

Polly took the typescript down to the end of Joan's tiny patch of garden and made a little bonfire out of it. On top of everything else, she was more than happy to cause problems for Artie Allen-Jones, who would now find himself with a big hole in his spring publishing programme.

Joan's funeral was a nightmare.

No one turned up except Polly and the faithful Victor, the crime reporter from Nottingham who had been in love with Joan for twenty years. Not a single editor for whom Joan had written countless pieces had shown his or her face; her parents were long since dead and she had been both an only child and childless. Not even her ex-husband had made the effort to come. Somehow, standing in the gloomy chapel, Polly became convinced that Joan knew no one had turned up to say goodbye to her. Polly simply could not bear the pathos of it. Poor Joan. She had never given up, waking up every day with the expectation of cheques and sex in no particular order and never understanding Polly's priorities which were food, affection, work, probably in exactly that order.

As Joan's coffin was lowered into her grave there was a sudden scrabbling in the earth and a ball of red and white fur charged towards the hole.

'Zutty! Come here, for God's sake.'

Johnny had arrived. Late, but at least he'd come and his baseball cap was the right way round for once as a mark of respect.

Not that he'd ever had much respect for Joan, as he hastened to point out.

'It's you I've come for, Pol. Thought you might need a bit of support. Couldn't stand the woman myself but I know she meant something to you. Lord knows why.'

'Johnny, get Zutty out of there before they go and bury him too. You do realise it's all over, don't you? Bit pointless to come at all.'

Polly knew she was sounding shrewish. She couldn't help it. Joan was gone. There would be no more competitive lunches. There would be no one to keep her up to the mark, no one to chivvy her into finding a man and smartening up her act.

'Take it easy, Pol.' Johnny put his arm around her shoulders.

'I'm sorry, Johnny. I'm going to miss her so much. I know you think she was a cow and in many ways you were right but for some reason I needed her approval. She mattered to me. She was spiky and difficult and I suppose she wasn't as smart as she thought she was but she had what they call edge. I don't care if she was a bitch. Give me a bitch any day rather than some mousy little twit who's going to bore me to tears.'

Johnny was looking at her with interest.

'That's a bit strong for you, Pol. I thought you were the caring, sharing type.'

'Well, I've wised up. It's good to trust people in your life but you shouldn't rely on them. The only person you can rely on is yourself. Yet in a way I could always rely on Joan. One thing about her, she was constant. She never changed.'

'How did you get here?'

'In that great big black car. Joan left money for her funeral. The awful thing was that she left enough money to cater for at least fifty people coming to it and look how many turned up.'

'Who's that funny-looking bloke walking away?'

'That's Victor. Joan claimed he loved her and I never believed her but I do now. I've never seen a man cry like that.'

'I'll give you a lift back home. You can't sit all by yourself in that Bentley or would you like Zutty to keep you company? He really . . .'

'Yes, I know, he really adores me even though he

415

ignores me half the time. No, you can drive me home, Johnny.'

'What's happened about Edith?' Polly asked tentatively as they approached the Shepherd's Bush roundabout.

'She's in hospital, you know, a clinic. The police called me in the middle of the night at the end of last week. First Joan, then Edith.'

'Edith had an accident too?'

'Not exactly. They found her wandering up the Old Brompton Road at two in the morning in her nightdress. She was so out of it we were able to get her straight into hospital and then I got a doctor to see her and get her admitted to this place. I don't know what'll happen from here. No, it's Luana I'm worried about now.'

'Still pining for Win?'

'Not in the slightest. She's met someone new.'

'And?'

'She's madly, passionately, totally in love with him.'

'Of course she is. Why should anything change? Have you met him?'

'No, but I know all about him. He's in advertising. He's extremely successful. He's a good-looking guy even by my standards as to who's good enough for my little peachy girl.'

'But?'

'He's married. Very married, whatever she thinks. It has to end in tears.'

'With Luana it always has to end in tears. I'm sorry to say this, Johnny, but I think that's what she gets off on.'

'What does she get off on?'

'Being a victim. I don't think she's ever had a married man before. It had to happen.'

'Well, Jesus Christ, what will she move on to next?'

'Axe murderers.'

'Now I think you're going to have to ask me in for a drink to help me get over the shock.'

Polly couldn't get the front door open. Johnny took her keys from her and tried again but he couldn't get it to budge.

'Fucking hell!' he said suddenly. His fingers were covered in wet paint. 'Polly, you might have told me you'd had the door painted. It's blown shut with wet paint on it. No wonder it's stuck. Don't tell me, it's . . .'

'Arnold Pinner!' they shouted together.

'Got your back-door key, Pol?'

She shook her head.

'Don't worry, I have.'

'I thought I took your keys off you.'

'The front door keys, yes.'

Without thinking she took him up to the little sitting room on the first floor. He wandered about while she poured him a drink, making irritating comments about what she'd done to the room. Finally he sat down.

'So were you a bit cut up when Hector went off to Pennsylvania?'

'Why would I be cut up?'

'Because you had a thing with him.'

Polly sat down too. Rather suddenly.

'How did you know?'

'I know you. I know what happens to your skin and your eyes when you've had good sex. It started in France, didn't it?'

Polly nodded, not looking at him. 'Didn't you mind?'

'It was none of my business who you slept with. I was the one who left in the first place. I couldn't very well dictate who you had sex with after that.' He thumped the cushions between them. 'But why on earth would you choose Hector O'Neill? The man is such a total bore.'

'I know.'

'You know? Well, what made you have anything to do with him?'

'You didn't want me. He was there.'

'Just like that? And who says I didn't want you? Don't you realise I've regretted leaving you since the day I left? Or rather the night I left. Didn't it occur to you that I might have made a terrible mistake?'

This was typical Johnny. Trying to make her feel guilty for his mistakes.

'So there was never anything between you and Juanita?'

'There was – and still is – a great deal between me and Juanita. It's called a business partnership. Although I'm considering walking out on her in the middle of the night too, she's so useless when it comes to recognising a good script.'

'And you, of course, are an expert.' Polly couldn't resist it.

'No, but you probably are. Why don't you come in with us, Pol? Make it a sideline to your agency, scout for properties for us, read scripts. After all, that's what you were doing when I first met you.'

'I've moved on a little since then.' Was that all he wanted from her? Someone to read scripts for him?

'I know that, Pol. You've moved on a lot. In fact, I don't know where you get the energy, frankly. The thought of producing another movie fills me with dread. I'm an old man now, Pol. I need someone to look after me.'

'Do you?'

'I do. I absolutely do. Why are you sitting so far away from me? Come on, give us a kiss.'

Zutty interrupted them, demanding to be fed.

'I suppose you want something too?' Polly asked

Johnny. He sat up and begged, imitating Zutty, and she hit him on the head with a cushion. He bobbed about behind her in the kitchen as she cooked, driving her mad.

'What's that? Don't put too much salt in. Got to think of my sodium intake. Can I have some of this pâté? Are you going to make a salad? What's for dessert?'

He gobbled, had seconds and eyed her until she gave him what was left of it.

'That was great, Pol. Now I'm going to watch the news.' She loaded the dishwasher and went upstairs to find him in her bed with the TV blaring. She picked up a manuscript and climbed in beside him. It was as if he'd never left.

Until she found the manuscript taken out of her hands and placed on the floor beside the bed.

'I've missed you so much, Pol,' he told her as he made love to her. 'You were meant to beg me to come back the day after I left except you became such a hard-bitten old career woman I suppose you never gave me another thought. Don't you realise that I've been waiting for some kind of signal from you.'

'What kind of signal?' Polly's voice was muffled as Johnny pressed her face into his chest.

'The kind of signal you're giving me now.' He released her for a second and then clasped her face in both hands and kissed her endlessly until she wriggled out of her underwear and jerked the remote at the television to turn it off. Since he seemed reluctant to let go of her even for an instant, Polly unzipped Johnny's jeans for him and pushed them down over his buttocks. She could feel the moist tip of his erect penis protruding from his Y fronts. His tongue was still stroking the inside of her mouth, building up a steady rhythm with her own. They lay locked together. Every now and then Polly would begin to open her legs but he held her at bay, tantalising her until she could stand it no longer and in one urgent movement she flung a leg over him and drew him into her.

Afterwards he fell asleep beside her, Zutty curled up in a ball between them, his bushy tail covering his nose like a fox, and she lay awake in a state of panic. Johnny had come almost immediately, which meant that unlike her he probably hadn't had sex with anyone for a long time, but even so he had given her a taste of the Johnny she used to know.

Trust Johnny to place the onus on her to ask him to come back. He might have left in the first place but of course it was still up to her to climb down. He might joke about having made a mistake in leaving her but he'd rather die than admit it for real. Well, she could play that game too. She'd make sure she was up in the morning before him and hard at work, incommunicado in the conservatory, if he came looking for her. Let him sweat for a while.

Besides, did she really want him back? He would be as infuriating as ever, probably even more so. If she agreed to read scripts for him and help him in any professional capacity whatsoever she knew perfectly well he would take unspeakable advantage of her. Her life would no longer be her own until he had another project to produce. Even if he wasn't around during the day he would be calling her all the time to find out what she was doing, demanding this, suggesting that. If she didn't love the conservatory so much, she would offer to give Johnny back his house and go and live in Joan's. But she knew it would destroy her to live in Joan's house with all its memories of her. She supposed she could offer it to Johnny. No, she couldn't. But what about Luana? She needed a decent place to live. And if Johnny did come back he wouldn't need it anyway. But if he came back it would be with all the baggage that went with him. Was it worth it?

She got her answer when she awoke and found he had crept out of bed in the middle of the night and slipped away once more while she slept so he wouldn't have to discuss it.

She was devastated.

Arnold Pinner rang the front doorbell at eight o'clock the next morning while Polly was sipping coffee in the kitchen and pressing ice-cold oranges from the fridge to her eyes to reduce the puffiness from two hours' crying.

She went to the door and then remembered it wouldn't open. As she bent down to speak to Arnold through the letterbox, there was a crunching sound and the door was winched open. Arnold stood there looking very pleased with himself.

'Mr de Soto asked me to come and sort you out. That should do you, missus.'

Behind him stood Johnny surrounded by a mass of luggage. He had Zutty in his arms. He handed him to Polly.

'Zutty insisted that he couldn't live without you. He's been on at me for ages about it. I finally couldn't take it any longer so here we are. Oh, Christ, Pol, not blubbing again!'